Blue Fire

A novel by Joel Canfield

"Canfield successfully weaves together an Ayn Rand subplot, CIA-backed LSD poisoning, and gay conversion therapy into a heartfelt thriller that will leave readers eager for more."

- Publishers' Weekly

Feel the Burn of Blue Fire

A missing comic book genius. An all-powerful hallucinogenic.

Max Bowman is haunted by both of them – and he just might lose his mind as a result.

When Max takes on the mission to find the long-lost creator of cult superhero Blue Fire, he ends up getting dosed with a chemical that upends his sanity just when he needs it most. Now he's got to contend with zombies on the Upper East Side, a cult run by a clueless pawn, a hipster rapist who knows her way around a sword, and a secret CIA spook program left over from the Cold War—all while trying to keep his mind from crashing and burning for good.

Blue Fire's mantra in the old comic books was, "For good to be purged of evil…Blue Fire must endure." But now it's Max Bowman who must endure – and he's as far from a superhero as you can get.

Copyright 2016 © joined at the hip inc.

Edited and abetted by Lisa Canfield

www.copycoachlisa.com

Cover illustration by A.J. Canfield

www.ajcanfield.com

This is a work of fiction. Names, characters, businesses, places, events and incidents are either the products of the author's imagination or used in a fictitious manner. Any resemblance to actual persons, living or dead, or actual events is purely coincidental, with the exception of Shawn Shepheard.

Find out more about *Blue Fire* and other Max Bowman books at www.facebook.com/MaxBowmanBooks

Table of Contents

Mighty Mel 3

The See-Saw 15

Eydie 26

Betty and Veronica 41

MK-Ultra 60

Crazy Jelly 69

Messages 83

Freemansburg 102

Becky Parks 117

Rape 130

The Interview 142

The Nurse 156

Little Latin Lupe Lu 177

Zombie Apocalypse 187

Intervention 205

Augustine Bravino 223

Dr. Reginald 238

SaveMaxBowman.com 260

Keenan 277

Comic Con 295

Blue Fires 312

The Clinic 322

Rosenbaum 335

Inferno 349

The Edge 366

Last Call 379

For my two crazy blondes and Ethan, David and AJ.

"Our society is run by insane people for insane objectives. I think we're being run by maniacs for maniacal ends and I think I'm liable to be put away as insane for expressing that. That's what's insane about it."

- John Lennon

"Give me a child and I'll shape him into anything."

- B. F. Skinner

Mighty Mel

"You're him. You're the guy!"

I thought I would be the one saying those words, but no, none other than "Mighty Mel" Chesler was aiming a quavering bony finger at me as he flashed an excited grin that showcased some disconcertingly gleaming white teeth. I hadn't been this creeped out since the last time I had sex with my ex-wife, which I mentally refer to as The Time She Moved. But at the same time, I was completely blown away.

Comic book legend Mighty Mel was excited to meet *me*.

Melvin Chesler, better known to millions of comic fans as "Mighty Mel," had been a legend in the comic book business, one of the many moneygrubbing publishers who paid writers and artists peanuts while he made millions. From the nineteen-forties on, whatever trend was hot -- crime, horror, Westerns, funny animals, romance and, of course, superheroes -- he quickly jumped on every potential cash cow and then milked it until its teats ran dry. Like any good cold-blooded businessman, Mighty Mel valued money, not creativity, unless, of course, that creativity could make him money. And if you were an artist or writer who provided that kind of profitable imagination?

Well, then he'd find a way to squeeze you until you bled to death.

Of course, I had no idea about any of that when I was a kid reading his comics. Even though the artists and writers were what attracted the change in my pocket, you don't know when you're nine years old that the wrong guy almost always ends up with the biggest bank account.

Even when a creative type did make a killing, it was usually under fraudulent circumstances. Take Bob Kane, the "creator" of Batman, who managed to lock himself into a lucrative lifetime contract with DC comics. In reality, he could barely draw and a guy named Bill Finger actually came up with most of the great ideas; Kane just happened to be as big a swindler as the publishers. Meanwhile, the two guys who invented Superman, Jerry Siegel and Joe Shuster, were as far from businessmen as you can imagine. Both ended up unemployable and living in poverty until the lawyers finally got them some measly payback in the late 1970s, when both men were on their last legs.

All I knew was comics saved my life. Growing up as the final child of two indifferent parents meant I had to find solace elsewhere -- so, until I finally got laid, comic books served as my personal Fortress of Solitude. Then I grew up and left all that behind, until a few years ago when I reconnected with my childhood passion, through book compilations of my favorite stories as well as candid histories of the shit that really went on back then.

And that's how I came to find out that Mighty Mel, the guy who presented himself to his readership as the funnest fella in the world, had been in reality an epic asshole.

Still, my childhood awe was in overdrive. I couldn't believe he had personally called me in on a job, but there he was, sitting across from me behind an ancient battered desk that looked like it weighed more than a Dodge pick-up loaded up with fertilizer.

Giving him the onceover now, I had to say Mel wasn't looking so mighty these days. First of all, he had to be close to entering his second century of existence on this planet Earth, leaving his tight translucent skin a never-ending festival of liver spots and wrinkles. Secondly, he looked like he weighed about thirty pounds soaking wet. He was as close to being a skeleton as you could get without actually being a skeleton.

Worse still, Mighty Mel was not working out of a spacious Park Avenue office with five or six beautiful twenty-three-year-old assistants at his beck and call, as I would have thought a man of his age, stature and money would have been. No, here he was sitting in a small cruddy office roughly the size of my second bathroom, the one with just a toilet, located upstairs from a trendy vegan restaurant in the Village. That meant the scent of tempeh filled the room and intermingled with the microscopic particles of grime flaking off walls that hadn't been cleaned or painted since Carter was president.

All of which left me nauseous, but still intrigued.

"You're the guy!" he repeated and then he cackled like there was dust caught in his throat.

I nodded and put on my best happy horseshit smile while I sighed internally. It had come to this. I was bigger than Mighty Mel.

In my new unwanted role as an almost-celebrity, I had learned the dirty little secret that every public figure encounters -- it gets boring as shit to have people pretend you're special. And I was only Max Bowman, I couldn't even imagine how Tom Cruise got through the day without tearing off his own head. I guess that's where the Scientology came in handy.

"You're the guy what took down that whole meshuggah Dark Sky. And the big guy with the rifle and the weird guy with half a face."

"Well, it just kind of turned out that way…"

"And the number one, the guy with the rifle's father, the one with the bum leg pullin' all the strings…"

"Uncle Andy."

"Uncle Andy?"

"Just my nickname for him. Real name's Andrew Wright."

He nodded slowly and solemnly.

"Andrew Wright. I hope that cock-a-roach got put away for a long time."

"He just retired, sir. Nothing could be proven. He wasn't directly involved in the Dark Sky operation. On paper, anyway."

"The big fish. They always get away. Well, anyway, they always had to in the comic books, am I right? What, you want Lex Luthor to get life? Who's the Superman going to fight? His maid? The good villains, they always gotta come back and make more noise, don't you agree? Am I wrong?"

"Believe me, sir, I'm aware you know your business. I have to tell you, I can't believe I'm meeting with Mighty Mel himself."

Whatever life was still in the bag of bones sitting in front of me got sent up his internal elevator to his eyes and actually managed to light them up with excitement.

"You know me?"

"Mighty Mel Chesler, of course I do. I read your comic books in the sixties."

His arm went horizontal as his bony finger extended out at me again.

"You were a fan!"

"To be honest, sir, I mostly read Marvels and DCs. Whatever was left of my allowance, you got."

More cackling. Cackling that wracked his entire bony body.

"I'll take it! I'll take it!" He banged on the desk.

"You *did* take it," I answered pointedly.

He saw the look in my eye and to his credit, he didn't mind it. He clearly was comfortable with his own greed.

"That was my business model, you know, do what's popular, put 'em out cheap and give 'em a flashy cover. I didn't have the Superman, I didn't have the Spider-Man, it was just me, Gold Key and Charlton picking up the crumbs, young man."

Young man. I was 59.

"You had *Blue Fire*, sir."

His face rapidly turned serious, even solemn at the mention of that name. I had hit a nerve -- or something else.

"And THAT is exactly why you are here. You liked that book?"

I almost laughed at the question. "Who didn't? Mikov completely changed the game."

"Mikov and *me*," replied Mel with more than a hint of anger and resentment.

Ben Mikov was the J.D. Salinger of the comic book world, a once-in-a-lifetime wonder boy who turned everything upside down with a singular work and then disappeared down some rabbit hole of his own making. Blue Fire was his wondrous achievement, a superhero with a weird and rigid life philosophy that he applied to his crime-fighting exploits during his one year of existence. But after those twelve monthly issues?

Nothing.

Because after that, Mikov supposedly left the comics business and no one could even attempt to duplicate his peculiar take on the superhero genre. Mighty Mel got Mikov's inker to plot and draw one more issue by himself, but it had no chance of working -- it was as if Michelangelo wasn't available to finish the Sistine Chapel so the Pope got some housepainter in his neighborhood to take a crack at it. Fifty years later, it was still regarded as one of the biggest fiascos ever put on the newsstands

Still, Mikov stuck in Mighty Mel's craw. It was common knowledge that Mighty Mel could *never* get over the fact that no one gave *him* credit on *Blue Fire*, even though he was listed in every issue as the co-creator of the character. But those who had worked for Mighty Mel Comics at the time knew what the real and extremely limited extent of Mel's actual contribution to the comic book had been. And it was this:

Mikov had wanted the character to be named Purple Fire. Mel changed the color to Blue.

"Blue Fire was as much mine as Mikov's. People don't accept that. To them, he was this great amazing pie-in-the-sky genius and I was some obnoxious gonif stealing credit. You're hearing this straight from me -- it was a team effort. If I could draw a fucking straight line, I wouldn't have even needed Mikov. Got it?"

Got it.

That hateful little speech had just confirmed that everything I had read about Mighty Mel was true, that he was, in fact, a stingy miserable credit-stealing old fart. The child in me had expected more, but this was the reality and the reality was really fucking repellant.

Time to grow up and move things along.

"So, Mel, what are we up to here? What do you need me for?"

He smiled slyly and pulled a small key out of his shirt pocket. With it, he unlocked the bottom drawer on the right side of the desk and pulled it open. He then reached in and carefully pulled out a vintage comic encased in a plastic bag. With shaking hands, he gingerly opened the plastic bag, then handed the comic to me as if it were a bottle of ten-thousand-dollar wine. Which it was, as far as I was concerned, once I realized what he was handing over to me.

It was the first issue of *Blue Fire* from 1967. Rarer than a likeable cat.

I gently opened it. Holy fucking shit. There were only a few hundred of these ever released. At the time, Mel was having a beef with his printers over unpaid bills and they refused to finish the run on what would go on to be one of the most famous books in comic history. I could feel the old man's orgasmic glare on me as I stared at the splash page in disbelief. Story name, *The Coming of Blue Fire*. Credits, Co-created and written by "Mighty Mel" Chesler, Art by "Bombastic Ben" Mikov, Inking by "Awesome Al Bearing."

"Nobody has this issue," I murmured.

"Those fucking printers, I was gonna pay the fuckers, but no, they go and shut down the presses on this masterpiece. Broke my heart. And they wouldn't even give me back the fucking ART!"

"Why didn't you just pay the fuckers?" I asked reasonably enough.

"FUCK THEM!" he almost screamed, "almost" because he didn't have enough of a voice left to reach that level. His face was red and his hands were gripping the front of the desk so hard I thought his fingers might snap off.

This was a guy who held a grudge.

Feeling a little woozy, I handed him back the comic. Being responsible for its safety made me too tense. If for some reason it spontaneously combusted in my hand, I was pretty sure his heart or some other vital organ would do likewise.

Mighty Mel calmed down and carefully replaced the comic in the plastic bag and then put it back in the drawer, which he locked again. When he was done, he looked me in the eye with that same solemn look he had assumed when I had first said the words, "Blue Fire."

"You need to find Mikov."

"Mikov? *Why*?" I said with much more intensity than I had planned.

Mikov had meant as much to me as Stan "The Man" Lee, Jack "King" Kirby, or "Swinging" Steve Ditko. He was a comic book God and I wasn't worthy to be a piece of lint in his pocket. Sure, I wanted to meet him. But the fact was comic book fanatics had been searching for this guy for almost a half a century and had always come up empty-handed. So far, in my new career as a professional private investigator, everything had been a snap. This? This was *Mission: Impossible.* And again, I was no Tom Cruise.

Mighty Mel leaned over the desk as if he was going to tell me the biggest secret in the world and he didn't want to chance anybody downstairs ordering a Tofurky sandwich to hear.

"What year was *Blue Fire*, kid?"

"1967."

"What year is it now?"

"2016."

"So next year…"

"It'll be fifty years."

He nodded as if I made the head of the class.

"They want to make a movie."

"They?"

"Some big people with a lot of money. They want to get into the superhero movie business and make all those millions for themselves. They want to buy the *Blue Fire* IP, reprint all the comics in a deluxe edition and make a goddam IMEX 3D blockbuster."

I let the IMEX thing go.

"But *Blue Fire* is so…"

"…fucking weird, yeah, but they don't care. They just know it's a cult classic and a hot property. You know and I know that movie audiences are gonna look at this thing and throw up in their popcorn. And you know what, kid, I like that you understand these things, it makes things easy, I don't have to fucking explain shit like I do with everybody else. Anyway, there's a lot of money in this for me. A. Lot. But I don't get any of it…if you don't find Mikov."

"But they don't need him."

"No, you're right. But they do need his *signature.*"

Another thing I understood.

The real creators of the comic books, the artists and the writers who thought up all the costumed legends, had finally made some progress in the courts in recent years. Studios were paying creators off -- and, if those creators were dead, their widows and kids -- to avoid any legal claims down the line. Settle in advance: that was the new mantra, because there was too much money at stake.

Now apparently it would be Mikov's turn to cash in, if he was still alive. He was in the catbird seat. If he didn't sign a settlement on the dotted line, nobody was going to make a *Blue Fire* movie.

"What a fucking farce," Mighty Mel whined. "We paid these jerk-offs for their work the first time around. Now they come crying at the door, 'Waahhh, give us money, give us money, we're geniuses!' You know what, young man?"

Again, I was 59.

"Here's fucking what. If this shit was really fair, we wouldn't just pay them for the four or five great ideas they might have had. We'd also take into account all the money these losers with pencils cost us with their other five million shitty ideas! They'd end up owing *us* money, am I right? Don't you agree?"

I bobbed and weaved with a shrug and tried to get back to business. "Look, do you have anything for me to go on? From what I've read, this guy's been gone for around fifty years, so this won't be easy. And he might be dead. Which would make getting his signature a little difficult."

"I got nothing."

"You must have a social security number. You paid him."

"All those files were destroyed years ago."

"So you expect me to find him…how?"

"That's for you to figure out. That's why I called *you*. Because right now…you're the guy."

We were back to that.

"And because of that, I'm not cheap these days," I answered back, knowing who I was dealing with. "And I need to make sure I get paid."

I hated to be blunt, but he didn't, so why not?

"This needs to happen," he said with determination. "I want to be alive to see this happen. I want to see my name on the big screen and I want my kids, my grandkids and my great-grandkids to see it…at least the ones who still talk to me." He took a business card from a little holder on the desk and held it out to me.

"My email is on the card. Send me your bank account information and the amount you require. The money will be in there the next day. The *whole* amount."

I remembered what happened with the last guy who was too anxious to overpay me and shuddered.

"Look, a fifty percent deposit is fine…"

"No, goddammit, I don't want you fifty-percent trying. You give me one thousand percent of an effort, and I give you everything upfront." He paused. "As long as there aren't too many figures."

"There'll be five. In the mid-range of that five."

He stood up more quickly than I would have thought him capable and held out his hand. His speed indicated I could have gotten a lot more and he wanted to make sure to lock me in at this price.

"You get me. You get this business. You *are* the guy. The perfect guy."

I shook his outstretched hand. Mighty Mel asked me if I wanted to go get a drink with him. Shit, he actually did like me. Of course, people usually did until they realized I only played so much ball.

"No thanks, Mel. Sorry, but I gotta get back."

"So where you live?"

"Roosevelt Island."

"Yeah? Never been there. Well, at least you got the East River between you and the zombies."

I blinked. "How's that?"

"On the Upper East Side, you didn't hear about this shit? Zombies, that's the word on the streets. I heard cabbies won't even go up there anymore after dark."

I didn't have any idea of how to respond to that. At the very least, if there was even the hint of a zombie invasion, the *Post* would have had it on the front cover and blamed it on Barack Obama. So color me skeptical.

While I was mulling over the idea of the Living Dead roaming down Third Avenue devouring all the baristas in the multitude of Starbucks up that way, Mel asked again if I was sure I didn't want to go get a drink.

"Sorry," I said, "Maybe next time. I got somebody back at my place waiting for me."

He smiled knowingly and winked.

"Give her one for me."

I wasn't lying. I did have somebody to get home to.

Too bad she wasn't human.

The See-Saw

"*Now* what?"

The way Howard said those two words didn't bode well for our conversation.

Not being all that anxious to get back to my apartment, I decided to forego the pleasures of the F Train and instead walk the two-and-a-half miles to the tram station and take that almost-good-enough-for-Disneyland ride back home to Roosevelt Island. And while taking that walk, I decided to get things rolling on this new case by calling my best pal at the CIA, good ol' Howard Klein, the guy who had almost delivered my head on a platter to everybody trying to kill me during the Dark Sky drama.

But Howard's bad attitude took me by surprise, causing me to make the rookie mistake of stopping on the sidewalk in front of a subway exit. Fortunately, I noticed the unruly mob rising up from the depths and quickly sidestepped it, almost crashing through an upscale clothing storefront in the process. You have to move fast in that situation. When a pack of growling, surly commuters is coming up the stairs and you fail to get out of the way, you'll spend the rest of the week scrubbing shoe dirt off your forehead.

"What's with the tone?" I asked.

I leaned against the store window as Howard unleashed his verbal hounds on me.

"Well, let's see, first of all, you only call me when you need some information. Second of all, you're no longer working on cases we hire you for, so you're asking me to use official government resources to help you make bank. And third of all, it needs to stop."

"Well, here's my side of the story. Remember last year — *when you almost got me killed?*"

"Oh yeah, I dimly recall you were too dumb to quit a suicide mission and didn't care that I would be part of the collateral damage. You put me in an untenable position, asshole. And that's the first time I've used 'untenable' in a sentence in about thirty years."

"It pays to increase your word power."

"Still getting the *Readers Digest*, I see. Well, today, laughter isn't gonna be the best medicine. Look, Max, I can't do this shit anymore. Remember that whore wife of that asshole stock broker you asked me to check out? Well, it turns out she's the cousin of a supervisor over in Clandestine Service, who raised holy hell over somebody using CIA databases to find out if she was screwing everybody on the Upper West Side."

I started walking again to try and get warm. It was late February and the winter chill was all around me -- but the real deep freeze was coming at me through the phone.

"Well, she *was* screwing everybody on the Upper West Side, as it turned out."

"Point taken, but here's another one for you to take and shove up your ass. I've repaid my debt to you several thousand times over. You've made a small fortune over your Dark Sky escapades, right? Well, little baby sparrow, it's time to jump out of the nest and fly on your own -- or break your neck hitting the ground. You're not my brother and I'm not your keeper. Go private detect on your own, I'm not going to be the guy who buys you a Jaguar."

Howard knew I had about as much interest in buying a Jaguar, or any sports car for that matter, as the Dalai Lama. But he was way too pissed off to think straight. He had been waiting for me to call so he could pounce. At the moment, I would have been better off letting the subway riders use me for a doormat than try to argue with him.

Still, I needed his help and I needed to figure out how to make that happen. That kind of cognitive labor was difficult for me when the temperature was below freezing. Luckily, I was walking past Bloomingdale's, so I ducked inside and made my way to the women's lingerie department because it was…well, the women's lingerie department. Mannequins in sexy underwear were the biggest thrill available to me these days.

It was true I had asked a lot from Howard in the past few months. I worked his guilt as hard as I could, because I was suddenly getting hired by all the one-percenters, lots of incredibly rich New York douchebags who brought me in for a lot of pedestrian jobs, just because I was suddenly a status symbol. They got to tell everybody they knew that they had hired *the* Max Bowman, *the* guy who had brought down an entire shadow paramilitary organization.

From my viewpoint, I was just a fucking mess. My insides were jangly and my brain was reeling from some serious PTSD; too many nights, I woke up from vivid nightmares featuring rifles, tomahawks and a whole lot of blood. The only way I could calm down was to watch infomercials until dawn.

And being allowed entry to the inner sanctums of the wealthy and powerful didn't soothe my jitters. Instead it did the opposite -- it amped up my paranoia and rattled my nerves until they turned to Jell-O. I felt like I had to deliver to these three-thousand-dollar suits or be exposed as the two-bit phony I thought I was.

I didn't feel like a genius case-breaker or an unstoppable tough guy. I felt like Max Bowman, a guy just stumbling through life on a day-by-day basis. And even though I was currently the Flavor of the Month in certain circles, even though I had actually accumulated a whole year's rent in my bank account through my new lucrative status, even though professionally I was on top for the first time in my life, personally everything was a complete ball of shit.

So I had to hang my hat on my new career for any ray of hope, it was the only thing going right in my life. And that meant I needed Howard. The trouble was I had wasted all of his guilt and good will on cases I probably could have handled myself. Now, I had to talk him into one more assist, because I needed every resource available to find Mikov. So I had to think fast.

My first move? Play humble.

"Howard, I've got a Nissan Rogue, I'm not a Jaguar guy, you know that…"

"Look, I don't give a shit what you drive, I just know I'm not going to subsidize your fucking life anymore. I mean, Jesus, while I'm still working over forty hours a week and then, at the end of the day, all I have to come home to is that thing I still have to consider my wife, you're shacked up with your sexy little singer, making a bundle on pathetic adultery cases, just because you got lucky on that fucking Dark Sky case."

I got lucky. Huh. My then-girlfriend got a tomahawk to the head. I got my leg broken in three places. I had to kill a man for the first time in my life. And I still kept the lights on at night because of the imaginary threats that lingered in the dark. But I bit my lip about all that because it wasn't going to do any good. He gave me the clue I had needed to make this work.

This was all about sex. He thought my penis was being well-tended, while his was forlorn and overgrown with weeds.

"I don't have a sexy little singer any more, Howard. I got nothing. I'm fucked. And these jobs you've been helping me out on are all I got going for me."

I let out what sounded like an involuntary and painful sigh. It came out more real than I expected and that frightened me a little.

"Oh. Jeez, I didn't know." A pause. "I thought you really cared about her."

Now that I had punctured his self-righteous balloon, it was time to step on the gas.

"I did care about her. But that's that. Look, Howard, I need one more fucking favor, just one more, then I'll leave you out of my shit for good. I swear on my mother's grave."

"Last I heard she's not dead."

"She is to me. Just like I'm dead to my kids. Proud family tradition."

Another good move by me -- remind him that I didn't have anybody else. I was so clever I felt like crying. But I had finally found my way to the women's lingerie department and that cheered me up some. I began eyeing some very red bras as a saleswoman eyed me. I winked at her. That made her move on.

Meanwhile, after a few seconds, it was Howard's turn to let out a painful sigh. That meant the beast was defeated. I could make this work.

"What's this shitfest about?" he said in his wonderfully whiney way.

"Ben Mikov. He's been missing for almost fifty years."

"Who is this guy?"

"A comic book artist."

Howard laughed.

"Oh Jesus, a comic book case? You must be in hog heaven! You still read those things, don't you?"

"Just the old ones."

"This guy do any of your favorites? Little Lulu or Richie Rich?"

"I don't read *those* old ones, Howard."

"How about Baby Huey? Remember that one? What deviant freak thought of Baby Fucking Huey, a giant duck in a diaper walking around getting shit on his ass feathers?"

"Howard…"

"What's this guy's name again?"

"Ben Mikov, and he didn't do funny animals. He drew a superhero. One. Blue Fire."

There was a pause.

"Blue Fire?"

My turn to pause. He put more than a little spin on the ball with the way he said that.

"Yeah, it was a cult comic from the sixties. He did the thing for a year, then he disappeared."

"Huh."

"Why the 'Huh?"

I was now by the panties, randomly picking through the more exotic varieties hanging from the pegs on a display wall. Out of the corner of my eye, I noticed that the saleswoman had surreptitiously circled around to see what I was up to. She was probably thinking I had pulled a pair out and was about to yank down my pants and rub them all over my crotch. Come to think of it, that might feel pretty good.

"Just kind of weird," Howard finally said. "We got a call to check out something called Blue Fire the other week."

"What was it?"

"Who knows. A couple days later, they called and told us to forget about it."

"They must have told you something about it if you had to investigate it."

"Doesn't matter. Before we could do much of anything, somebody higher up shut the whole thing down." He was picking up my suspicion. "It was probably nothing," he added in as light a manner as he could manage.

"You're not sounding like it was nothing."

My gut was blaring an internal car alarm into my head and it was giving me a headache. Why would the CIA care about a fifty-year-old cult comic? How the hell would those dots connect? This had to be my stress talking. Despite what I had been through with Dark Sky, I couldn't let myself turn into a conspiracy freak. The truth had to be that Blue Fire was something else they were worried about, maybe it was the name of a terrorist group or rogue nuclear weapon or just the code word for Putin's farts. Who the hell knew. Coincidence, that's all. Calm down, Max. Go home and drink a few quarts of Jack Daniels.

"Well, I don't know what the hell it was because we never got a chance to find out. So drop it. You want help, give me this guy's name again and anything else you know about him."

"Ben Mikov, M-I-K-O-V. I'm assuming the full name is Benjamin. He worked for Mighty Mel Comics, run by Mel Chesler, C-H-E-S-L-E-R. Who's still alive and 900 years old, but had nothing to offer. He's the guy trying to find him."

He repeated the names as he wrote them down. He was being careful. Which again made me think he knew more than he was telling me, which again made me tell myself to take a deepie and let it all go.

"Okay," he said after he was done making his notes. "I'll do this one thing, Max. Last call, though, got it?"

"Thanks, Howard. I got it."

"So things didn't work out with the singer?"

"It's complicated. Maybe the ball's still in play."

"Well, good luck with it. You know women."

"No, I don't and that's part of the problem. I think I'm finally getting my education and it's late in my senior year."

"Fuck, I flunked out in Junior High. Listen, man, call me when you have time and we'll catch up. And I'll let you know when I dig anything up."

"Appreciate it. And let me know if you hear anything about zombies invading the Upper East Side."

"What?"

I hung up, turned towards the exit and found myself face-to-face with a burly-looking Bloomingdale's security guy.

"Can we help you with something?" he asked in a not very helpful way.

"I just came in out of the cold to make a phone call is all," I answered. "Tell the saleswoman I didn't leave any fluids on the floor."

He couldn't hold the stone face after I said that. He cracked up and then he gave me a second look.

"Hey -- you're the guy!"

I nodded. I was the guy.

As I got into the tram on this beautiful blue-sky winter day, I noticed a text had come in while I had been on the phone with Howard. It was from my entertainment lawyer, Todd Rabash. Yeah, I had an entertainment lawyer. The head of a big New York publishing house had seen me on *The Today Show* and thought I should be a book. Now, she was offering me a six-figure advance even though I told her I was a lousy writer with an even lousier memory.

Still, she was persistent, so I remembered that one of the rich douchebags who had hired me was a top entertainment lawyer. I called him and he reacted like a three year-old who was just given a bright blue balloon; he was so giddy he was almost clapping his hands with joy. He'd get me the best deal and I wouldn't have to do any work, he'd make the publishers hire me the best ghostwriter and the whole project would be a snap. Then he'd sell the thing to a big studio and make me a few more million. He said more words in five minutes than I said in five months.

Exhausted by his energy, I gave him the go-ahead a few days ago. Now, his text said to call him ASAP and it made me feel exhausted all over again. I knew I should be thankful to be a book, but I also knew it wouldn't give much of a boost to my overall happiness quotient. That's because I had learned at least one important secret of life. I knew the more money I made, the more opportunities that came my way, the more I was fucked, because if there was anything life had taught me, it was this:

God always evens the score.

The worst trick you could pull on the playground when I was a kid was when you'd be way up high in the air on your side of the see-saw and the kid sitting on the other side would jump off, leaving you to slam down on the concrete so hard, your ass hurt for days. That's what Whoever was in charge did to me on a regular basis: If one side of things goes way up to the sky, you can bet the other side is going to plummet to the earth in two seconds flat.

So I got pleasure where I could take it. It was why I made the walk to the tram instead of taking the underground train. I loved the view from the tram, the spectacular aerial views of the city, the East River and my island that the ride offered from on high. Best of all, you rode right alongside the Queensboro Bridge and you could admire the amazing architecture from the closest possible vantage point. They didn't build shit like that these days, with all that incredible detail and stonework on display. That took time. And who had time anymore?

The tram began to descend on the other side, down to Roosevelt Island, and as it did, I felt my heart sink a little. I had to return home and home was where I didn't want to be. I could just go jump in the East River, I supposed, but that water was too disgusting even for suicide.

I entered the lobby of my building, thought about checking the mail and decided it was too early, it wouldn't be there yet. The elevator was already on the ground floor, so the doors lurched open when I hit the "Up" button. In I went, along with two others who had walked in after me. The insides of the elevator smelled as strange as they normally did -- generally, a mixture of the stench of take-out food, residents who didn't practice good hygiene and whatever cancer-causing chemicals the custodial staff used to clean the floor, along with just the vague hint of urine that most of New York City was blessed with. The two people who were along for the ride were an Asian woman in her eighties who was about three feet tall and a big black kid who was over six. The kid got off at four and the old lady got off at ten. That left me to go to thirteen on my own.

Once there, I walked down the long empty hallway and, near its end, I paused by the neighbor's door, as I almost always did, to remember the one guy in there who got murdered by who knows and the other guy who was killed by yours truly. Did the charming young couple who lived there now know about all the blood that was spilled inside? I wasn't going to tell them. Happily, they had managed to survive living next to me for almost six months now. Good for them. I was sure we would have a better relationship if I could even begin to understand what fucking language they spoke.

I moved on to my door and took out my key from my pocket in the quietest way imaginable. But it didn't matter. She knew I was there. I had no doubts that she had been sitting there all day at the top of the stairs that led down inside my apartment, waiting for me to come home. Because this was the only female in the world who couldn't live without me.

Naturally she had a sewed-up vagina.

Eydie

I opened the door and the fucking dog came barreling out of the apartment, flying up off the ground as if jet-propelled.

She seemingly hovered in mid-air at the top of her leap and literally looked me in the eye to make sure it was me and that I had actually came back home before she allowed herself to fall back to Earth. But only for a moment, because she, as she always did, went on to repeat this move fifty or sixty more times, whining and crying nonstop until I finally managed to herd her back into the apartment.

Then it was a matter of getting back down the stairs without one of us breaking our necks – because I knew she would be jumping on me all the way to the bottom, while constantly letting out loud yelps that registered somewhere on the dial between joy and distress.

I am aware that most dogs are happy to have their owners return. But most dogs are not this fucking dog. There was only one person in the world she cared about. There was only one person who could make her feel safe and loved and happy about living. There was only one person she wanted to have in the room with her at all times.

That lucky person was me.

Do we ever know what's going to start a shit storm in our lives? Sure, sometimes. But in this case, I never saw it coming and I was very disappointed in myself that I didn't. This four-legged fucker currently jumping up at my face was supposed to be a blessing. She was supposed to represent the crowning achievement of newfound happiness snatched from the jaws of misery and despair, not the first disastrous step in an endless foot march towards overpowering exhaustion and chronic depression.

Last Fall, I had finally asked Jules to formally move in with me, the first time since my marriage had expired fifteen years earlier that I had allowed a woman to get that close to me. After all we had been through, namely both of us almost getting killed, I lowered my emotional shields and opened my heart to this very unnatural blonde who unbelievably had an even fouler mouth than my own - because this time I was a big enough idiot to trust it would be different.

True, Jules was as emotional as they come, but her intense moods would counterbalance my normally walled-off heart – we would bring out the best in each other. And that's how it initially seemed to go, with the added bonus of amazing sex. She could do this thing with her vagina that I didn't know was possible.

Just as importantly, we both suddenly had career paths packed with promise for the first time in years. I was just starting to score the big money while she was sure her singing career was about to reignite, now that the surgery had brought back her voice and made it better than it was in the first place. Neither of us expected this kind of upturn in our fortunes and we were a bit goofy about everything as a result.

So she gave up her place in Harlem and brought her stuff over to my place. She kept her day job at the Midtown legal firm for the time being while she prepared to resume her performing career. She took voice lessons to regain her technique and continued to diet to slim down as much as possible. When body and voice seemed ready, she would try again to make it in the New York cabaret scene and maybe I would even be making enough to support her while she did. I had no doubts about her talent, only about her ability to crack the steel-plated nut that was the Manhattan niterie scene. However, she had filled in a couple nights here and there at a few cabarets and received rapturous applause at every gig.

What could go wrong?

Well, of course, everything -- but, for once, I kept my general cynicism at bay. Happiness was a new commodity to me, I hadn't really experienced a lot of it in my life and I didn't know enough to distrust it when it came. So, when she suggested for the eight millionth time that we should get a dog, I shrugged and said "Why not?" Two stupider words have never been uttered by a man, even by one who had just gotten laid, and that was a very low bar to set.

I had been avoiding the procurement of a pooch up until then because my own personal dog story was so horrible, people I told it to didn't know whether to laugh or cry.

It went down like this.

On my sixteenth birthday, I was a newly-licensed driver and I wanted to go over to a friend's house, so my parents let me use their car. I slowly backed it out of the garage and onto the driveway, when *ba-boom*. It felt like I drove over some kind of bump. But there were no bumps in our smooth, suburban driveway.

Then I thought I heard a little whimper.

I rushed out of the car and then I saw what that *ba-boom* had been all about. it. Frieda, our family dachshund, was laying horizontally between the back tire and the front tire of the car. I hurried over to see whether she was okay and, of course, she wasn't. There was literally a dent in the dog's very long stomach and she wasn't moving at all.

I stood there, shell-shocked. Had this really just happened? Why, yes, it had and a happy birthday to me. But no worries, my family was there to give me the emotional support I needed, right?

Here's how *that* went down.

First, my older brother, who was home from the service and visiting, came out of the house and said, "Way to go, Max!" Then, my mother stuck her head out the front door and told me in a very matter-of-fact voice that I'd better take the dog to the vet.

What?

And yet, I listened. I didn't know what else to do and at least someone was giving me a suggestion, even though it was dumbest suggestion in the world, coming from a woman who didn't seem to have any tears for the dog or for me.

So, all by myself, because everybody else had gone back in the house, I put the dog on a piece of cardboard that my dad had lying on the garage floor in case the car leaked oil and I carefully placed that cardboard stretcher in the trunk. Then I drove to the vet, crying hysterically the whole way. When I brought her, still on the cardboard, into the vet's office and put her down on the counter, the vet looked down at her, then up at me and asked, "What do you want me to do with it?"

It.

After that incident, the thought of getting another dog never really appealed to me. But that last time Jules asked me, I felt good, she felt good, the world felt good, so sure, why not? Get a dog. Share the love with a furry friend. Get over it, Max.

It was just another sign that somebody should lock me up and swallow the key.

Suddenly, I heard Kanye West rapping. His song *Power* was currently my ringtone, so I hurried into my home office past the still-jumping dog, fished my iPhone out of my pocket, sat down and took the call. Meanwhile, the dog did what she always did, which was to stay within zero to four inches of where ever I was.

"Good afternoon, Todd, how's tricks?" I said into the phone. Because, yes, the caller was Todd Rabash, entertainment attorney extraordinaire, who had hit the speed dial on me again.

"Tricks?" questioned the harsh New York voice on the other side. And then Todd laughed like a son of a bitch. He was one of those guys who was tickled to death with whatever I said, whether it was funny or not. "Well, I've had clients call me a magician, so yeah, I guess I *do* do tricks!"

"So make all my troubles disappear."

"Hey, if I was that good, you don't think I'd do that for myself?" He laughed it up again, this time at himself. "The shit I go through! It's crazy! Crazy, bud!"

Crazy, bud.

"Man, just glad it's Friday. Hey! Listen! So I talked to the book chick and the lawyer on that side and here's where we are…."

And that's when my brain went away. Located somewhere in his next non-stop barrage of sentences that would never make any goddamn sense to me were the terms "back end," "hardback versus trade," "foreign rights," "China," "second use rights," and "dildo." I wasn't sure how that last one fit in, but I think that's what he was calling the book "chick."

"Sounds good," I said noncommittally.

"Do you even know what the fuck I said?"

He wasn't dumb, I had to say that for him.

"Todd, I appreciate you keeping me informed, but just go ahead, close the deal and get me the money. I don't need to read the fine print."

"Get you the money? What, you in a rush for it?"

"Kind of. I'm aiming to build a rocket to the moon and take it there."

More laughing.

"You crazy son of a bitch, I'm getting you a deal like nobody gets and you could give a shit! You're like the last honest man, you know that? Jesus, you know what your story is worth? Well, I do and I'm going to get you every last cent! You deserve it, you're a goddamn American hero and don't forget it!"

"I don't like things to drag out, Todd. That just invites the gremlins in to yank out the wires and turn off the lights. That money's going to be my retirement fund and I'd rather nothing go wrong with this. So don't work so hard, I don't need every last cent, just something approaching it."

"Look, with what I'm going to make you, you can take a rocket all the way to FUCKING MARS! I mean, this is just the start, Max, just the beginning! Once this is done, then we're talking movie rights. Dark Sky -- the MOVIE! How does that feel?"

"I'll wait for it to stream on Netflix."

"MANIAC! You're a MANIAC! Shit, I got another call coming in, I gotta take this -- BUT STAY TUNED!"

And then he hung up. Todd was okay, but I didn't need to know how the sausage was made. Just grill it and put the fucking thing on a Kaiser roll and let it go at that. Maybe with some mustard.

Since I was still sitting at my desk, I checked my email on my PC and deleted the spam that was trying to sell me a walk-in bathtub. Give me a couple more years, boys, then we'll talk. Then I moseyed over to Facebook, which Jules had finally forced me to join a few weeks ago so I could "like" her performance "events" that she sent me "invites" to. I already had twelve "friends," so I felt good about my "social media presence." Just for kicks, I typed "Ben Mikov" in the Facebook search box to see what would come up.

And lo and behold, I found a Facebook group devoted to the guy's *Blue Fire* comic books.

Wow. Was this for real? People actually talked about old comic books on this thing? For the first time, I was interested in social media. You had to ask the group for permission to join, so I put in my bid -- just as the fucking dog started jumping up on me again. I knew what she wanted. It was time for me to shit and piss her.

How did I end up with a dog who should by all rights be in an animal asylum for troubled mutts? Well, it's because we've all become such good people. By that I mean you're not allowed to just go to the pet store anymore and pick out a perfectly good puppy right off the rack. No, good people didn't do that. Instead, good people go to "rescue" pets at an animal shelter -- at least that's what Jules told me. Okay, why not take one of man's best friends off death row and give it a new leash on life? Why not be a good person? Made sense, I supposed.

So, one Saturday afternoon last October, Jules and I hit the Humane Society shelter in the city, just on the other side of the river. As we rode the tram into the city holding hands (like I said, I was going goofy), Jules said to me over and over with absolute certainty, "We'll know the dog we're supposed to get when we see it. We'll know it."

Truer words were never spoken.

An animal shelter is, of course, the saddest lock-up you can imagine. Some of the beasts behind bars were doomed, you just knew it. There were a few dogs the size of a small barn who seemed psychotically violent, lunging at the door to the cage when we walked by -- and I was pretty sure they were going nowhere. Nobody wanted to take home Cujo's angrier brother. Then there were the animals that just seemed to have the life already drained out of them -- they laid in heaps on the floor, resigned to not being wanted by anyone. I could cry if I let myself, but I never did.

I glanced over at Jules to see how she was reacting to our tour of the facility, figuring she was going to start bawling hysterically at any given moment, but she had turned on her tunnel vision full blast. She was looking for the one precious pooch we would save and only that precious pooch, instantly filtering out all the others from her consciousness. That's how she kept it together.

After a few minutes, a funny feeling crept up on me. Like I was being watched. I looked around, but nobody on the shelter staff was really paying any attention to us. Still, I couldn't rid myself of the notion that eyes were staring intently at me and monitoring my every move. I began looking around furtively to see what I was missing.

"What's wrong?" Jules asked me.

"I don't know," I answered. She didn't always understand my extrasensory moments and I didn't talk about them until I had them confirmed.

It didn't take long.

Because a second or two after she had asked me what the problem was, I turned and saw, sitting on the floor in a nearby pen, the saddest pair of eyes that had ever stared right into my goddamn soul.

The eyes belonged to a shivering underfed bone-thin mutt of a terrier who wouldn't stop giving me the deep stare. If I walked to the right, she kept looking at me. If walked to the left, she kept looking at me. I even did a little two-step, going this way and that, to test her -- and she never took her eyes off me.

Jules, who had been looking elsewhere, finally turned and saw what was in play. And she ran up to the very edge of the pen, stared at the little dog with delight, gave a whoop of joy and screamed, "SHE – IS – SO – FUCKING CUTE!"

I couldn't deny it.

Even though the dog was clearly not in the greatest shape, this was a beautiful little animal. The little index card on the pen said "Terrier Mix" and stated her name as "Alex." She was about a year old. The card also stated that she weighed nineteen pounds and had been brought in from the street five days before. I gave the dog a closer look. Her color was mainly blonde with some white around the face and the closer I looked at her, the more I could see she was not pure terrier. She looked like she might have some beagle in her, maybe even some golden retriever and God knows what else. Whatever was in her gene cocktail, it came together to create a gorgeous creature with soft eyes, soft eyes that would not let up on me. Jules grabbed my arm in amazement.

"Ohmigod, she LOVES you. That dog FUCKING LOVES you."

Maybe. But to me, it felt more like the gaze of a stalker. The kind of stalker that would motivate me to move in the middle of the night so she could never find me again. That's when I remembered "Alex" was the name of the Glenn Close character from *Fatal Attraction* -- the one that stalked Michael Douglas and finally had to be shot in a bathtub to stop her from stabbing everybody to death.

A Humane Society volunteer heard Jules' yelling and swooped in behind us. It was like being on a used car lot and having the salesperson immediately move in for the kill after hearing you comment that the '95 Taurus in front of you didn't have *that* many miles on it.

"We've only had her a coupla days and already had a *lot* of people askin' about her," the volunteer said as nonchalantly as possible.

We turned to her and she introduced herself as Dale. I figured her for around fifty. Dale had the dye job of Lucille Ball, the voice register of Popeye and the face of Andrea Martin. She was wearing a simple but faded jumpsuit, probably one that had animal urine washed out of it about five million times, and, for some reason, I could see Dale smoking a cigar and pulling it off.

"Did you hear that, Max?" Jules turned to me with a desperate glare. "Other people want this dog -- but, Jesus, she belongs to us, you can tell! She loves you, she'll love me and she's beautiful and we have to have her!" She breathlessly spun around back to Dale. "Can we have her?"

Bears, shit, woods.

"Well, if you're really interested…"

"HOLY SHIT, ARE YOU FUCKING KIDDING?" shouted Jules and suddenly people were staring at us.

Dale laughed, because this was going to be easy. Saps like us didn't show up every day.

"Then let's get you guys acquainted -- just go wait in that room over there…" she pointed to a small glass-encased room with four folding chairs in it, "and I'll bring in the little cutie."

We entered the get-acquainted room and waited. While I waited, Jules hyperventilated with excitement.

"Did you see how that dog stares at me?" I said uneasily.

"Max, it's just a little dog and you don't have to worry. This will be MY dog, I'll take total care of her, you will hardly have to do a fucking THING! Especially since she already LOVES YOUR ASS!"

I nodded. I was already in a non-negotiable situation.

Dale brought in the panicked creature, who was squirming to get away. Alex may have been obsessed with me, but she was also scared to death of everything outside the confines of her pen. "This poor girl," she said, "she won't eat, she's lost two pounds since we got her."

"Ohhhhh, that's a lot when you only weigh that much," said Jules. "OHHHHH but she's so FUCKING SWEET!"

Dale set the shaking mutt down in front of us. The dog promptly looked around in terror and pissed all over the floor, so Dale jumped up and ran to get some paper towels, leaving me, Jules and the pup alone for our meet and greet. Alex started staring at me again and tentatively walked towards me. Against my better judgment, I held out my hand and she actually started to smell it.

"But I don't want to call her 'Alex,'" Jules whispered as if somebody had the room bugged. "They just give them some random name when they bring them in, it doesn't matter. So I want to call her 'Eydie,' for Eydie Gorme. Okay?"

I shrugged. Jules grabbed my arm and kissed me on the cheek. I was earning some relationship points anyway. But then came a quick change of energy. Jules turned back to the dog and reached out to her, so Alex could smell her hand like she had smelled mine. But the dog had other ideas.

The fucking sweet dog growled and snapped at Jules' hand.

"What the fuck…?" Jules jumped back, just as Dale came back in with a helper to wipe up the piss.

"The dog doesn't like me!" Jules said sharply to Dale.

"Have you ever adopted a rescue animal before?"

"No," Jules and I said in unison. My "No" had a bit more behind it.

"Well, see, here's the thing. Usually, the poor things have been mistreated in some way by the original owner. And this one probably had a rough time on the streets. It can take some time for them to really socialize, they have a hard time trusting."

"Oh," Jules said with a decidedly downbeat tone.

"The good news is if they get in a loving home, they become great pets -- if you're willing to work with 'em."

"So we can really make her feel okay?"

"Look, if she has a loving home, she'll come around," Dale said reassuringly. "And judging by the two of you, I think she hit the *jackpot*."

Jules smiled and nodded. Done deal.

The dog had already had her shots and her puppy-making machinery shut down, so we were okay to take her home. But first we bought a leash, a food dish, a water dish, a collar, a dog carrier, some toys, dog food, dog treats, dog bones, and some other shit that all added up to over three hundred smackers. Oh yeah, and Dale also convinced us to contribute another fifty to the shelter. Like I said, she knew how to sell.

The first real sign of how deep the shit was that I would soon be sinking in with this dog was when we got home and I went to the bathroom. When I dared to put a door between us, the dog went ballistic. She howled. She ran all over the apartment, jumping on and off the furniture, terrified and mad and inconsolable. Frankly, it made it hard to focus on getting the piss out.

"MAX!" yelled Jules. "GET THE FUCK OUT OF THERE, THE DOG IS GOING CRAZY!"

Excuse me for taking a leak.

I did what I could, hurrying so fast I got a few drips on my jeans, and quickly opened the door, just in time to see the dog come skidding around the hallway corner. When she recovered her equilibrium, she continued running down the hallway at full speed and finished up with a leap into my gut with all her might. I didn't know nineteen pounds could hurt that bad. I went into the bedroom and sat down on the bed to catch my breath. The dog jumped up on the bed and then on top of my head.

She would never be Jules' dog. No matter how much Jules tried to bond with her, my new best friend did not ever want to be out of my sight. She would follow me from room to room, no matter if I was just getting glass of water out of the kitchen or getting a shirt out of the closet. I just had to look down at the floor and she would be standing there by my foot, gazing up at me with expectant eyes, wondering what amazing thing I might do next.

Then there was the matter of sleep. I told Jules before we even went to the shelter that I would never let a dog sleep in our bed. I didn't need a smelly dog ass in my face at three in the morning. That first night, at three in the morning, guess whose smelly dog ass was in my face?

Then, the next day, we discovered that I was the only one who could walk her. If Jules tried on her own, the dog would cry and cry and cry. Jules would end up dragging the crying dog down the sidewalk and enduring the judgmental stares of bystanders who thought she was torturing the poor animal.

Yes, Jules' dog would never become Jules' dog. She was my dog. And she was a lunatic. And right now she was jumping up and down on me again like her water dish had been filled with coffee. I couldn't put her bathroom break off any longer.

I took her down in the back elevator, which let us out in the back courtyard that was lined on each side by the complex of apartment buildings. There was grass and several large trees, now leafless due to winter, but the real attraction for the fucking dog was the wild game that was plentiful and always in view.

The thing about Roosevelt Island is it's overrun with squirrels, or, as I like to call them, tree-dwelling rats. And these squirrels are *fat* -- because all the islanders think it's the cutest thing ever to feed them every chance they get. That makes the squirrels slow and that, in turn, made the fucking dog think she actually had a chance to catch one. So, when she spotted one, she would abruptly go after it with all her might and nearly separate my arm, the one holding her leash, from the rest of my body.

There was nothing about today that was going to be any different.

After she dumped a load of steaming crap on the frozen ground, she saw a squirrel munching on something at a nearby tree and went for it with all her might. As I lurched forward after the dog, I heard Kanye rapping in my pocket again.

"No one man should have all that power…"

As the dog jumped up the tree after the squirrel, the nine millionth one in a row she didn't catch, I pulled the phone out of my coat and answered it, after first checking the screen to see who it was. Howard.

"Already?" I said as I answered the phone.

"The news is not good, my friend," replied Howard. "I got nothing."

"Nothing? On Mikov? You gotta have something. Just give me the basics, where he's from, where else he worked, was he married, did he have kids…"

"You're not hearing me. I mean literally nothing. Mikov must have been a pseudonym or something."

I stood there dumbfounded and watched an obese squirrel run six inches behind the fucking dog, who was completely oblivious.

"Or somebody scrubbed the file," I finally said.

"C'mon…"

"Howard, something's not right. Are you sure this doesn't have anything to do with that Blue Fire investigation you were…"

He quickly cut me off. "Don't start, Max, don't turn this into *Three Days of the Condor…*"

"I won't, I hated that movie. But I'm telling you something's not right here."

Howard breathed in and out in a deep and profound way.

"All I know is, you're on your own, ace," he said. He hung up.

The dog was looking up at me with concern. Did I mention she had psychic powers too? Yeah, it was true.

She always knew when I was fucked.

Betty and Veronica

I had them all.

A couple of years ago, a graphic novel house reprinted all twelve issues of *Blue Fire* in a large softcover compilation and, when I saw it on Amazon, I ordered it immediately -- hell, I thought I'd never read those stories again and I was amazed somebody cared enough to put them back on the market. That's how naïve I was about the continuing obsession of all the comic-reading baby boomers like me. They didn't want to let go of their childhood habit any more than I did.

My return to comics as an adult, however, had been a recent one, starting about five years before, before I met Jules. It was a period of time when I was drinking too much Jack Daniels while I stayed up all night immersing myself in collections of old comic books that I had ravenously read as a kid.

Back then, I had no idea I had dived right into the middle of a historic comic book era -- the so-called "Silver Age" that began in the late fifties and ended in the late sixties to early seventies, depending on who you were talking to and which comic you were talking about. What I did witness with my excited adolescent eyes was the form morphing right in front of them on a monthly basis. The superhero stories grew more cosmic and universe-spanning even as they also became more personal and psychologically grueling.

In the middle of all that came *Blue Fire* and its own brand of glorious strangeness.

Brian Gerger was a twelve-year-old boy who came from a small steel town in Pennsylvania, back when there were steel towns in Pennsylvania, and one day the kid discovered a magic box sitting under three layers of dust on a shelf in an odd antiques store. It was never explained why a preteen boy would be in an antiques store by himself, but that was how comics worked -- they cut to the chase, even when the chase made no sense. Anyway, the box glowed when Gerger touched it and the weird and wizened store owner told him excitedly that he was THE ONE.

It was kind of like when people told me I was the guy.

Anyway, Gerger opened the box and inside was a glowing blue gas that shot out and immediately penetrated the kid's mouth, nose and ears, as an ancient (and, of course, blue) spirit appeared before him and introduced himself as the LawGiver, whose harsh face looked like a cross between Clint Eastwood's and a panther's.

The LawGiver told the kid that he had been chosen to receive the power of Blue Fire, a purifying force that would literally incinerate evil in the world. And with that, Gerger, like Billy Batson before him, immediately transformed into a grown-ass adult with a skintight blue body suit and mask that glowed with blue power. The LawGiver then explained that whenever evil threatened, Gerger would become Blue Fire -- and he would have the power to shoot blue flames from his fingertips, blue flames that were not hot to the touch, but still would, in fact, sear the psyches of evildoers that threatened society.

There was one big catch to this whole thing, and this was where it all got really weird.

Gerger the boy *had to keep himself morally pure* or Blue Fire wouldn't be able to shoot those blue flames out of his blue fingertips. There was definitely something unsettling about a boy entering adolescence who had to adhere to this strict policy, which is why kids my age were fascinated with this thing. If Gerger cheated on a math test in school, if he lied to his Mom about cleaning his room, then Blue Fire's flames fizzled.

Those transgressions were understandable. But -- if Blue Fire got too interested in a *girl* -- he also got dinged by the LawGiver. WTF ??? I had to wonder if the kid tried to jerk off, would blue flames envelop his fist and cremate his penis? Naturally, I knew that situation wouldn't be addressed under the then-puritanical Comics Code Authority, the regulatory agency set up in haste when moronic "sociologists" started accusing Batman and Robin of having man-on-boy action, but the subtext was inescapable.

As was Mikov's genius. His dark and creepy shading, his bizarrely-shaped panels, his tense and sweaty faces all gave *Blue Fire* a strange and compelling intensity that made you come back every month for more. Until there was suddenly nothing left to come back for, because Mikov pulled the plug and disappeared. And now somebody wanted to make it look like he never existed.

I still remembered the incantation that young Gerger had to chant in order to transform into his powerful adult alter ego.

Blue Fire must be pure…

Blue Fire must be sure…

For Good to be purged of Evil…

Blue Fire must endure!

It wasn't T.S. Eliot, but hey.

I stayed up late, drinking Jack and listening to Sinatra, rereading the entirety of the *Blue Fire* saga, especially his epic battles against his arch-enemy, the evil Dr. K, who was the ultimate mind-fucker. The only way to really stop Blue Fire was to scramble his brain so he wouldn't be sure what was right and what was wrong. That was what Dr. K excelled at.

"You look a little confused!" Dr. K screamed at Blue Fire in one issue, the one where Dr. K used hypno-rays to make Blue Fire think he himself was a danger to the world. "Well, I'm going to end your confusion - *forever!*"

Dr. K did no such thing, of course, and he also escaped before Blue Fire could incinerate him. For some reason, he was the only villain that Blue Fire never quite conquered. He was also the creepiest, because he wasn't about physically defeating the hero -- he was all about trying to turn his brain to mush.

It was two a.m. when I finished issue 12, the final horrible one completed by a second-stringer after Mikov had bolted, when the fucking dog, who was sleeping between my legs, began doing her strange hiccup sound, the sound that meant she was having one of her frequent nightmares. I shook her awake because I hated to see anybody deal with bad dreams. I had enough of my own.

I got up to take my final piss of the night -- well, the final one for about three or four hours anyway -- when something caught my eye on the TV. It was the sign I was looking for.

The TV was on a news channel. I had turned the sound down so I could focus on the comics, but now I saw on the screen a picture of a man I knew fairly well. Senator Abe Marks, the New York Senator, the guy who had started up the government hearings against Dark Sky and brought me to Washington to testify, was missing, according to the on-screen graphic. I cranked up the volume.

Senator Marks had actually been MIA for over a month and nobody, including his family, had any idea of where he had gone to. The New York governor was going to have to appoint an interim replacement for him in the meantime.

Marks was the real deal, a Senator with some actual integrity and I liked him enormously. He had managed to stop Dark Sky's government contract from being renewed but wasn't able to prosecute the management. Did that same management come right back and prosecute Senator Marks -- in a trial in the shadows, a trial where the sentence was never in question?

If they *had* made Senator Abe Marks vanish from the planet, that would mean Uncle Andy and his spooky cronies hadn't given up after last year's bloody takedown. It would mean they were still out there and up to no good. And that would mean they could still reach into the CIA whenever they wanted to do whatever they wanted to do -- to me or anybody else.

And that all brought me back to Howard and how some vague request about investigating Blue Fire landed on his desk just before Mighty Mel called me in to look for Mikov. That was weird. That was too weird. And if Uncle Andy had his fingers in any of this, I wanted no part of it.

I had enough problems.

Monday morning, after shitting and pissing the dog, I ventured back into the big, bad city to officially turn down the job. I had never sent that email with my bank account info to Mighty Mel and I never returned his call that came in over the weekend to remind me to do it. I wasn't being ornery, I was being self-protective. If the CIA was involved, I didn't want to use any kind of electronic communication regarding Ben Mikov that could be traced, because that hadn't worked out so well for me last year.

No, I was going back to Mighty Mel's office and give him my "no" in person.

This time, to get there fast, I took the F train, got off at 14th Street, and headed a couple of blocks south to the aging building which held

Chesler's office. It was warmer today, one of the first days that you could sense spring actually might show up next month like it was supposed to.

During the short walk, I checked my iPhone out of habit because I was now as dumb as the rest of humanity, and saw I had a notification on my Facebook app. I opened it up and saw that the administrator of the Ben Mikov group, a guy named Bruce Canun, had granted my request to join. I scrolled down the page and was stunned by the trivial bullshit the members were arguing about -- every single little detail was picked over again and again. I came in the middle of a heated discussion about the intent of a particular word balloon on page 5 of issue 7. Did the italicized words indicate sarcasm -- or enthusiasm? *Who the hell cared????*

But obsessives can be useful, so just for kicks, I stopped and typed the following post:

> *Looking for Ben Mikov. Is he alive or dead? Important.*

There were about 450 members in the group and, if they were all this hardcore about Mikov, some of them would have already done some amateur detective work of their own to track down his whereabouts. Even though I was turning down the case, I was still curious. Maybe I could at least throw Mighty Mel a lead as a consolation prize.

I closed the app and entered the building. As I walked up the stairs in back of the vegan restaurant, gagging on the smell of broiled tofu, I knew my decision to bail on the case wouldn't make Mighty Mel happy. But I was not in the business of making Mighty Mel happy, I was in the business of staying alive. I knocked on his door.

"Come in," answered a young and bright female voice.

Well.

I opened the door to find a young and bright woman, in her early twenties, dusting the large framed print of *Blue Fire* hanging on the wall. She was wearing a modest but fashionable dark green dress and a pair of heels that were as sensible as heels could be and still be heels. She radiated a certain energy of being clean-scrubbed that triumphed over any hint of sexuality, despite the fact that most would judge her to be very attractive. To me, she was the kind of "good girl" you might find heading up the Honor Society in high school. She seemed pleasant and pretty, you could find no reason not to like her, but there wasn't much to hang on to beyond that.

I eyed the empty chair behind the desk.

"I was looking for Mel."

She eyed me.

"OMG, you're Max!"

She ran over and actually hugged me. I hadn't had a female body close to me in a few weeks, but I managed to keep my equipment in check.

"And you are…" I asked as she broke off the quick embrace.

"I'm Candy, Mel's my uncle. Well, my grand uncle. He really only comes in here a couple days a week, otherwise I handle things for him. Let's sit down! I'm soooo excited you came down while I was here!"

She went and took Uncle Mel's seat. I sat down on the chair I had occupied the day before.

"Is there much to handle anymore?" I asked. "Mighty Mel's pretty much out of business, isn't he?"

"Oh, reprint rights, some internet stuff. Otherwise, just the biggest project of Mel's life -- the mooooovie!"

Yes, she said it like that, almost singing the last word. The excitement of youth in full bloom. And here I was about to pour a barrel of cold water over her lovely little head. She kept on a little as I gathered up the courage to douse her with my version of reality.

"I'm the one who told Mel to hire you. He doesn't watch the news or anything, so I showed him the video of you on *The Today Show*. Matt Lauer was very impressed with you!"

"He smelled good," I offered.

"And then I showed him you testifying on Capitol Hill with Senator Marks? You were so great there."

She caught my brief grimace.

"Ohhh, I saw the senator went missing, that is soooo sad. Do you know what happened to him?"

I shook my head.

"Well, Uncle Mel watched everything and agreed -- he said you were definitely the guy to get! So we were going to transfer the money for your fee to your account, but we never got the info from you…?"

"Look, I can't take Mel's money. I can't take his money because I can't take this case."

Her forehead suddenly had furrows. "I don't understand…"

I frowned, and then said more than I was going to. For some reason, I wanted her to know the score. Maybe so she didn't think I was a complete shit.

"Look, Mikov's a genius, which is why I was excited about this. But you know I have CIA contacts…"

"I know!" she said, her perky tone quickly returning. "That's part of why we thought you'd be great for this."

"Well, after an initial check with the Agency, the hard truth is…there are no records of Ben Mikov out there. No records at all."

More furrows.

"How could that be?"

"You tell me and we'll both know. Do you have any information at all? Your uncle didn't seem to."

"Ben Mikov left on very bad terms with Uncle Mel."

"So you have no contact information from even back then?"

"My uncle says Mikov would just stop by to pick up his pay every week, which he got in cash, and to get his story ideas approved. Mikov never gave him a phone number or an address. He insisted on keeping everything under wraps. He was a…a very odd dude from what my uncle says."

"So I hear. I know Mikov was into some weird philosophical shit that he wrote into the comic -- really hardcore Ayn Rand kind of stuff."

"Who?"

"Ayn Rand? The writer who believed kindness and charity should be shot at sunrise?"

"Ay-an? What kind of a name is that?"

Okay, so maybe Candy was dumb as candy. I thought by now everybody had heard of Ayn Rand, still the darling of the conservative movement despite the fact that she had been dead for thirty-odd years. I had first encountered her work when I wasted a summer as a teenager struggling through the one thousand pages or so of her epic novel, *Atlas Shrugged*. And I only made it to the end because I couldn't believe what I was reading. Its basic theme was "Fuck everybody and get out of my way."

"Doesn't matter, Candy. What does matter is I don't know where to start to find Mikov and I don't think I should. I'm very sorry."

"Is that all? I think you're being silly."

A Silly Billy. That was me.

"Well, it's not exactly all. I kind of have to get my life in order…"

"Are you married?"

"No."

"Do you have a lady friend?"

"I have a dog."

She laughed. It was a nice laugh, I had to admit.

"Well, Mr. Max Bowman, I'm not letting you get away with this. I'm going to buy you lunch," she said with a firm tone. "And we're going to talk about you being silly."

"You win," I said, without really knowing why. She was far too wholesome to give me unwholesome thoughts. "As long as we're not eating at the place downstairs."

"They make the *best* quinoa kale salad."

"As long as we're not eating at the place downstairs," I repeated.

She shook her head with a rueful smile as if I was a really bad boy. I guess I had graduated from Silly Billy.

There was a Greek place a few blocks away from Mighty Mel's office that Candy said served a decent lunch and I was all for that. As we were walking over, her cell rang and she indicated with her expression that she had to take the call but didn't want to.

"Hello…yeah, nothing. I'm taking Max Bowman to lunch." She looked at me carefully. "No, he just showed up. He doesn't want to do it. I'll explain later."

Another pause. Whoever was on the other end wasn't happy.

"I don't know what you want me to do…the Greek place. No, I don't want you to. No, *especially* if you're…"

The call was over, as far as the other person was concerned. Candy frowned and put the phone back in her purse.

"We're going to have company."

She didn't explain further and I didn't push it.

The place ended up looking pretty good, one of the few Manhattan lunch places left that wasn't either outrageously expensive or scarily cheap. We got a table near the back, the kind with two chairs on one side and a two person cushioned bench attached to the wall on the other. I sat on the one chair and gave her the cushion.

The waiter, a twenty-something scrawny guy with something on his chin that he had grown himself but shouldn't have bothered with, immediately hovered and asked if we wanted drinks. Candy just wanted water. I ordered a Coke Zero but I was informed they only had Diet Pepsi, which I wasn't a fan of. But I agreed, I needed caffeine one way or the other. Then another shorter busboy who didn't speak English brought some pita bread and a spread to put on it and it was pretty good. The two of us made some meaningless happy talk, until she turned at the sound of the door opening -- it had one of those bells on the top that jingled when it moved. When she saw who it was, she again was not pleased.

The company had arrived.

It was another young woman, close to Candy's age but very different in appearance. This one was a little shorter, had a little more meat on her and was wearing a hoodie, black leggings and a knit hat. She also had long jet black hair, sharp piercing eyes and seemed more than a little loopy.

I stood up as she walked over. Candy introduced her as Janine. I shook her hand as she took stock of me.

"You look skinnier than on TV."

"I lost some weight since then."

"Looks good on you, Max Bowman."

She nodded with approval and winked at me. Okay.

Just then my Diet Pepsi arrived, but I would have to wait for my caffeine fix because Candy asked me to leave her and Janine alone for a moment. Things felt awkward, so I went ahead and walked back to the men's room, where I took a little piss that wasn't necessary but would serve me down the line.

Since I wasn't sure how long they needed to hash things out, I went into the stall and sat down on a closed toilet lid, where I checked the Facebook app on my phone again. I already had ten replies to my query about Mikov, because, of course, these aging comic book geeks had nothing better to do. As I scrolled through the posts, I didn't see much that was useful. Unverified sightings in this place or that, other rumors and whispers, nothing that led anywhere…but, what the hell, it had only been a half-hour or so, I'd let it ride.

I walked back out into the main dining room. If they weren't done with whatever they were doing, fuck 'em. The two girls were next to each other on the cushioned bench against the wall, about two inches apart physically, but about fifteen million light years mentally.

I sat back down, this time across from Janine because that chair was closest to me -- but also because I wanted to see just what her weirdness was all about. It could just be me, but I was pretty sure she was on something and on something that was rather potent.

"Everything good?" I asked the two lovely ladies.

Candy nodded eagerly like a Girl Scout, while Janine smirked lasciviously like Vampirella at me. I was more than a little alarmed. She was young enough to be my kid, but, then again, she wasn't my kid. That kind of situation hurts a guy's brain.

"So -- who are you, Janine?" I asked, only to have Candy quickly jump in with an explanation.

"Janine's my cousin, Max, she's Mel's grandniece too. We've been sort of running things together, actually."

"Or not running things," snarled Janine. "What the hell is there to run? The only thing anybody cares about is Blue Fire and you just pulled the rug out from under us on that one, Mr. Super Dick."

"Wha-a-a-at?" exclaimed Candy in horror.

"'Dick' is another word for detective," I kindly explained.

"Really?" deadpanned Janine. "I was talking about your penis." She then picked up the menu and buried her nose in it.

"Janine!" exclaimed Candy, mock-swatting her with her menu.

What was it with these two? Then, as I took a big swig of my Diet Pepsi and looked back and forth from one to the other, it hit me.

Holy shit, I was having lunch with Betty and Veronica.

Betty and Veronica were the girls from the old Archie comics, the two sexy babes who were always hanging all over the dweeby high school guy with the bizarre red thatched hair for reasons nobody could understand. Betty was the sweet All-American blonde and Veronica was the dark-haired pampered princess with an attitude. Every boy could determine what kind of woman he would end up running after by whether he favored Betty or Veronica. They presented a pretty clear-cut choice: Betty would cook and clean for you and be frigid in bed, Veronica would shit on your rug, eat your heart for lunch and scream like a banshee when she came. Needless to say, I was a Veronica man, which made Janine all the more dangerous to me.

"Well, thanks for the compliment," I said to the menu in front of Janine's, aka Veronica's, face. "But I don't think I live up to the billing."

"Why, you got problems down there?" the menu replied.

"Nothing like that. Like Matt Harvey, I'm great on a few days' rest."

"Matt Harvey?" asked Candy, aka Betty, obliviously.

The menu came down so Veronica could give her cousin the full force of her sarcasm.

"Mets' pitcher. Remember the *World Series* last year, Candy? Game 5? The game the fucking Mets had in the bag before they FUCKED IT ALL UP?"

She knew baseball? Huh.

"So I don't get it," I said to both of them to change the subject from my cock and the Mets. "Why does Mel have two of you working for him if there's nothing going on with the business?"

"Because our parents made him give us incomes," answered Veronica, returning to the menu with a bored expression. "I don't know if you got the memo, but jobs don't pay people anymore, especially when you're our age. I've written for four different websites here in town, either for free or lunch money."

"She's a good writer," nodded Betty vigorously.

"Me and eight million other English majors in Williamsburg. I wasn't getting anywhere, my parents didn't want me to become the world's oldest intern, so…Mighty Mel to the rescue." She let out a blast of disgusted air.

"He really wants this to be a family business," nodded Betty with her usual perkiness.

"Yeah," agreed Veronica. "Thank Christ there aren't any boys in our generation or they'd be eating with you and we'd be rolling burritos at Chipotle."

"But don't tell him we told you we're related to him. He likes to people to think he hired us because we're smart go-getters."

"Instead of slackers spinning our wheels."

My neck was getting tired from moving back and forth between them. Veronica finally slammed down the menu on the table with an air of finality, then looked me in the eye with even more attitude than before.

"So why aren't you doing this for us? Can't you see our futures are at stake here? Why the FUCK won't you find Mikov?"

Betty gasped at the language and Veronica shut her down with a glare.

"It's nothing personal," I offered.

Veronica leaned forward on her elbows and gave me a wicked, wicked smile.

"Let's make it personal, Super Dick."

I leaned back from the impact.

"Look, girls…"

"We're women, Max, millennial women closing in on thirty and without a game plan," shot back Veronica. "And we need some help here, chief. Mighty Mel doesn't have fuck all properties besides Blue Fire."

"Well…there's Ruffer the Flying Dog…" I recalled, less-than-fondly. A stupid flying dog. That's what passed for an idea in Mighty Mel's shop.

"Yes, Max, and there's our other dynamite characters, like Captain Bones, The Fantastic Ferret and the Human Razor. And they all *suck*. Studios are making a fortune with superheroes right now and we're on the outside looking in."

"It's kinda sad," said Betty as she looked glumly down at the table as if she lost her favorite barrette. I took another big swig of Diet Pepsi and examined the fire extinguisher on the wall.

"Look," I finally said, aiming my remarks at Veronica, "I already told your cousin, there's something weird about Mikov. Something that maybe reaches into the CIA, if you can imagine that. I can't afford to get mixed up with that shit again, I have less of a game plan that you do."

Veronica wasn't having it. "C'mon, Max, you're a Super Dick. You took down a whole multi-billion-dollar army military whatchamacallit. Look at you, you studly man, what can't you do?"

I was having a hard time accepting what was going on, but I finally had to accept the fact that somehow…*I actually had a groupie.* There she was, sitting right across the table from me, aiming sex in my direction, big heaping piles of sex, sex so vivid I felt like I could see the damn sex.

Suddenly, I was tingling and it felt like my skin was on fire.

"I got a hunch," I said to Veronica. "*You* were the one who told your cousin about me and *she's* the one who told Mel to hire me."

Veronica smiled and smiled and smiled, while Betty looked away. I don't think she approved of whatever was happening.

"But it doesn't matter," I went on. "I can't do this. Sorry."

"You got kids?" asked Veronica with urgency. Behind her, the wall started to melt.

"Um…"

Wait, *the wall was melting?*

"…yeah. I got two daughters, around your ages, probably a little older. They don't talk to me."

"Perfect!" said Veronica. "Fuck them, you got us now! Pretend we're your kids! We hate our parents anyway – but you, you're aces with us! Be our daddy and help us!"

She stretched out her hand and put it on top of mine. I let it stay, because I was distracted by the glowing multi-colored particles in the air that were suddenly popping up all around my head.

"You see all that?" I asked.

"See all what?" said Betty.

Then I looked at Veronica's hand. It was literally melting into mine. Our mutual flesh was bubbling as if it was in a skillet on a high flame on a stove. I shook my head a little because now it felt like my entire soul had moved up to the top of my skull. I was nervous, tense, almost panicked and feeling trapped, like maybe jackbooted thugs from the government might bust in here and take me to Guantanamo at any moment. How that thought flew into my head out of nowhere, I had no idea, but I looked around, checking out the rest of the tables.

"So, Mr. Super Dick, how about it? Is Daddy going to help his girls or what?"

"Janine, stahhhhhhhp," whined Betty. "He's uncomfortable, look at him!"

"I…I think I have to leave," I said. I felt sweaty.

"You *don't* look good, Max," said Veronica with something approaching concern, although it seemed like something else entirely. Were her teeth green and razor sharp? "Maybe you should come back and lie down at my place…"

Betty shot her yet another dirty look. "He can come back to the office…"

My panic was building, because now I knew what Veronica was trying to do. I could feel it. She was trying to pull my soul out of my skull. Her spirit was clawing at mine with vicious intent, trying to wear it down and suck it dry.

With some difficulty, I got up and watched the room briefly flip upside down.

"Max!" exclaimed Betty. "Sit down!" She glared at Veronica.

"Dude, listen to Candy," agreed Veronica. "You've lost it. Let us take care of you…"

I quickly backed away from the table, then finally turned and bolted out the restaurant door. Outside, the colors were exploding in the sky, colors I had never seen there before, colors I never knew even existed. I started walking, as fast as I could, because I knew I couldn't use the subway, I knew if I took whatever was going on with me underground, it wouldn't go well.

As I hurried away, I heard Betty and Veronica yelling after me from the restaurant entrance, maybe even chasing after me, I didn't know and I wasn't going to find out, because I wasn't going to turn back to look. I was focused on forward motion and ahead I saw the last couple of seconds of a "WALK" light flashing at the intersection in front of me rapidly counting down. That was my chance. I ran across the street, in front of a few long lines of frustrated traffic, just as the traffic light changed. A couple of cabs went after me with their horns when they got the green and the noise flew into my head and bounced around in there for a few seconds.

I hit the sidewalk and kept on moving as fast as my legs would let me. I had to again make the long walk to the tram and hope whatever was going on would pass and my head would clear.

And I definitely had to stay out of the Bloomingdale's lingerie section.

MK-Ultra

The pigeons looked more like buzzards in the afternoon sky and black steam seemed to be rising up from the sidewalks in front of me. Clouds had moved in front of the sun, delivering a level of darkness and cold that was dealing a death blow to my already mangled mood.

But this was too much to be just a mood. Sure, I hadn't been getting much sleep with the dog and with Jules being gone. Sure, I had some stress and depression as a result. But I had been through worse -- and during the lowest of those low times, I don't remember my hands ever leaving technicolor streaks in the air in the air like they were now.

SHIT. SHIT FUCK!

I banged my shin into a fire hydrant while I was staring at those hand streaks. Christ almighty, that hurt. I continued to scream some creative obscenities and people backed away from me like I was a homeless guy holding a broken bottle.

What the hell.

If this wasn't just a mood, if it wasn't just exhaustion or depression or fluoridated water or too much bacon, only one thing made sense. My Diet Pepsi at the Greek place had been tampered with. With what? To what end? I didn't know, I had never done anything worse than a little weed back in the day, because otherwise the CIA never would have hired me, even though *they* never stopped at a little weed. Or at anything at all, for that matter.

Which made me remember MK-Ultra. Which made me think the Agency had to be involved with what was happening to me somehow. But why? Again, no answers. Yeah, I had embarrassed them last year, but so what. Was it about Mikov? What the hell did they care about him? And how did I again become the fall guy for something that had nothing to do with me? And where was Senator Marks?

My shin still smarted. I was hungry and wanted a hot dog.

I stopped again and stared at the top of a subway exit, which was displaying a movie poster featuring a couple of cute Hollywood stars suffering from a severe case of Photoshop. There was a flying car and a large man with a gun and an explosion going off behind their smiling faces. Looked like another winner.

I staggered a little. My stomach suddenly wasn't hungry for food, it was more anxious to evacuate its contents. But I didn't want to vomit on Sixth Avenue, aka the Avenue of the Americas, which nobody called it except the maps. I really didn't. I looked up at the skyscrapers, where baboons seemed to be crashing through the windows and flying across to the adjacent high-rises. Maybe they weren't baboons. Maybe I was a baboon. Was that King Kong on the Chrysler Building? He was supposed to be on the Empire State. Monkeys were unreliable.

Keep it together, Max. Keep it together.

The Diet Pepsi had been spiked with something very serious. MK-Ultra. Who was carrying out the orders? Were Betty and Veronica the culprits? They could have done it while I was in the bathroom, after all they were the ones who had asked me to leave. But why the hell would they? Maybe it was someone in the kitchen. The CIA could have had somebody in the kitchen. But how the hell would the Agency know I was going to eat lunch there?

Jesus, I didn't even like Diet Pepsi that much.

I moved in the direction of the subway exit and my timing was once again impeccable -- a mob was coming up the stairs and right at me, but I was too out of it to get out of the way in time. They batted me around so hard I felt like I was flying around inside a pinball machine with a million flippers knocking me in different directions. I endured the gauntlet like a passive prisoner who didn't care what happened to him. Somebody yelled at me that I was a fucking idiot. And go fuck yourself as well, good sir!

Then, just like that, I came out through the other side of the crowd. And my stomach had calmed down. I went back from nausea to hunger.

I saw there was a hot dog cart up ahead. I pulled out my wallet. Maybe something in my stomach would help counteract whatever was in my blood. I walked up and started talking to the guy in the cart, who was Middle Eastern or Central American or Eastern European, one of those places where it didn't matter if you shaved or not because it still looked like you hadn't. Was that racist? Was my white privilege showing? I just wanted a hot dog, I had to focus on that, not geo-political observations.

But the guy in the cart wasn't answering me, he didn't seem to understand what I was saying. What else would I be saying to a guy in a hot dog cart except I wanted a hot dog? What the hell was the matter with him?

Then I realized my throat was dry and I was whispering, so I went all out to let him know what I needed.

"I WANT A HOT DOG. A FUCKING HOT DOG."

He stared at me like I was crazy but who gave a shit if I got the hot dog.

"RIGHT FUCKING NOW!" I added helpfully as I threw a twenty at his face.

He made me a hot dog really, really fast and I got some mustard on it. But as I walked away I thought about what if the CIA owned that hot dog cart and they put some more shit in the mustard. I threw the hot dog in the trash as somebody else looked at me like I was crazy, somebody else who was completely ignoring the baboons and acting like I was the problem, and I remembered I didn't get any change back from the guy in the hot dog cart. Should I go back?

I stopped. The vomit impulse returned with a vengeance and I leaned against a pole. Down at the bottom of the pole, I could see a dog had recently peed there. It was probably a big dog because it was a lot of pee. My fucking dog would spend hours sniffing that big a load of pee. The fucking dog. I straightened up. In a few more hours, she would have to eat and I would have to shit and piss her again. So I had to make it to the tram. If I could get home, I could lay down, get my bearings and then take care of the fucking dog.

I took a few steps forward. I could get back on track. I could get past this.

Unless there was no getting past it. My head was fucked up, but it was also still overthinking as usual, because everything I knew about MK-Ultra kept playing through my mind. Allen Dulles and all the CIA mind-fucking in the fifties. It had all supposedly been stopped -- but what if it was still going on?

The colors swirling around my head seemed to be turning into bugs of some sort, the kind of sparkly bugs you might find in an ancient Disney cartoon if Mickey Mouse had collapsed in a heap in a muddy ditch and died there, then, a few days later, rats were gnawing on his rodent flesh which I guess would make them cannibals. That's about when Disney bugs would start buzzing around his rotting corpse, bugs that would match up with the classic colorful family-friendly Disney animation with which Uncle Walt had gifted us all. Anyway, that's what the bugs around my head looked like. Disturbing, but Jiminy Cricket cute.

Did Disney really hate Jews?

The CIA. Allen Dulles. It was all out there on the public record, but everybody acted like this shit never happened.

I changed course. I didn't think I could make it to the tram. I was only a few blocks from another place where I might get help or I might get killed. Fifty-fifty, as the doctor told Lou Gehrig when the Pride of the Yankees asked about his chances of surviving his own disease.

Was that Senator Marks that just passed by? I turned and yelled at the guy's back. The guy turned and he looked like a thirty-year-old stockbroker. I told him he wasn't a senator and kept walking.

MK-Ultra started in 1953. The "MK" indicated that the project was under the supervision of the CIA's Technical Services Staff, while the "Ultra" was left over from World War II -- it was what the most heavily-classified toppest-secretest paperwork was tagged with. And the World War II connection was appropriate because the Agency started this operation with the help of Hitler's best and brightest evil scientists, who were very available after the war ended. It all started at some of the Agency's secret European "interrogation facilities," where the Nazi doctors played with prisoners' brains at our behest, after which we relocated the sinister scientists (along with their families, because we were a caring people) back here to America in an effort entitled Operation Paperclip, where the aims of MK-Ultra were formalized and put into motion. The primary tool? LSD, Dr. Albert Hofmann's new and magical breakthrough drug.

The impetus for Allen Dulles, the creepy head of the Agency for most of the nineteen-fifties, was concern that the Soviets were winning the mindfucking race. With the Cold War scaring the hell out of the entire government, he had no problem securing tens of millions of dollars that didn't need to be accounted for and sinking them into the MK-Ultra program, a program so secret nobody found out much about it for two decades and then only by accident. The

Agency had ordered all the files destroyed during the height of Watergate paranoia -- but, bureaucracy being bureaucracy, they had misfiled twenty thousand documents that finally became public a year or so later.

Running MK-Ultra was Dr. Sidney Gottlieb, a stutterer with a club foot from the Bronx. Dr. Gottlieb had a lifelong passion for folk dancing as well as finding new ways to completely crush the human psyche, and he devoted most of his professional life to those twin pursuits. Talk about compartmentalizing.

As these things go, there ended up being barely any limits on MK-Ultra's perverted pursuits. One of the first actions the U.S. took was to spike the food in the French village of Pont-Saint-Esprit with an LSD derivative, just, presumably, to see what happened. Well, what happened was five people died and dozens more went insane and ended up in an asylum, most of them by their own request. There was one unlucky Pierre who shouted, "I'm a plane" and jumped out of a window.

Back in America, the CIA boys in white coats experimented on inmates (mostly black) and set up brothels in San Francisco where the Johns were dosed with LSD without their knowledge. Most bizarrely of all, Gottlieb established a "drug recovery" center in Lexington, Kentucky that actually offered free heroin to junkies needing a fix -- all they had to do was agree to take part in MK-Ultra's LSD test trials.

Of course, these same junkies ended up leaving with not only their addiction intact, but also with their minds turned inside out. And, of course, you can't give away heroin without word getting out, so addicts ended up swarming the place looking for their free fixes. Celebrities also were victims of the not-really-rehab facility, because whenever they were caught in a drug bust, they were routinely sent there for "treatment." Sonny Rollins, Chet Baker, Ray Charles,

William Burroughs, Peter Lorre, and Sammy Davis, Jr. were just a few of the famous names that passed through its doors.

And the ongoing MK-Ultra horror show wasn't just inflicted on in-the-dark civilians. CIA personnel -- *and members of Dulles' own family* -- were given secret doses of the drug as well. His own son, whose anger at his father knew no bounds, ended up committed for a decade because of his harsh treatment.

Then there was the sad case of Dr. Frank Olson. That one always made me shake my head.

Why was the CIA so intent on mind control? It had two end games. One, it wanted to find ways to bend potential informers' minds so they'd tell the Agency what they wanted to know without a struggle. Two, the Agency wanted to create their own Manchurian Candidates, subjects whose brains they could drain and rebuild from scratch, and then reuse as programmable agents who would follow instructions without any qualms. All of this resulted in more than a few vegetables being strewn along the roadside -- vegetables that used to be thinking, feeling human beings.

There were even some who said that Lee Harvey Oswald and Sirhan Sirhan were both victims of MK-Ultra, brain-fucked by the CIA to do its bidding and play the fall guys in the assassinations of John F. and Robert Kennedy. Of course, you can read conspiracy theories on the internet until even Oliver Stone will tell you to shut your cakehole. Doesn't mean they're wrong or right. It just means these kinds of lunatic plots were *possible* considering everything else the government had gotten away with *that was already in the public record.*

I reached the alley I was looking for and I stopped to lean against a dumpster. The rats scurrying out from under it were also in technicolor. The smell wasn't helping my stomach. I weakly pulled out my phone and went to the other side of the alley, where I hit the name I needed to talk to.

"Hello?" Howard said.

"I just paid twenty dollars for a FUCKING HOT DOG and then I THREW IT THE FUCK AWAY."

I was breathing hard.

"Max?"

"Just tell me, man-to-man. You guys are running the hot dog cart, right? How many of the carts are working for the Agency?"

"What the hell is wrong with you?"

"WHAT DID YOU PUT IN MY DIET PEPSI?"

He had no answer. What could he say? HE KNEW WHAT HE DID.

"Look, man, I don't know what's happening with you, but…"

"And what happened to Senator Marks, Howard? Was it the same thing that happened to Dr. Frank Olson?" I asked belligerently.

"Frank Olson? That name sounds familiar."

"Of course, it does – THE CIA KILLED HIM."

"Wait, now I remember. Didn't he kill himself?"

"YOU TELL ME, HOWARD. A primary scientist in the MK-Ultra effort in the 1950's, he was the only one who apparently had a CRISIS OF CONSCIENCE. He was going to LEAVE the LSD program, Howard, LEAVE IT, and they gave him LSD WITHOUT TELLING HIM and he goes into a spiral of shame and depression, he gets paranoid and has a nervous breakdown and then he FALLS -- YEAH, RIGHT, "FALLS" -- out of a 13th story window on NOVEMBER 28th, 1953. We're SURE he fell, aren't we, Howard, 'cause the CIA Agent in the room with him at the time SAID he fell!"

"Calm down, calm down, the family sued and couldn't prove anything."

"SHOCKER! You know and I know that we killed him and now we want to kill ME!"

"Where are you? Max, let me make a call and get you some help. I don't know what's going on, but…"

"DON'T TRACE THIS CALL." I hung up and turned the phone's power off.

The enormity of what I was up against overwhelmed me. I started sobbing and sobbing. Everything was crashing down on my head.

"Max? Why the fuck are you here?"

That sounded like her. I knew this was the place where she came down during the day to have a smoke, when the office was getting to her and the beige walls felt like they were closing in on her, that's why I came here. But I didn't tell her that. Instead, I kept my back to her. I couldn't look at her.

She grabbed my shoulder and pulled me around to face her.

"Jesus, Max! You look like holy fuck on a stick!!"

I fell into her arms and we both almost hit the pavement.

Crazy Jelly

Jules held onto me and managed to keep us both upright. Good thing I was skinnier these days. Still, everything was swirling, the world was flipping around, colors were exploding and, again, I felt like vomiting.

"Max, what the fuck? You got the goofy eyes, what's wrong with you? Why are you even here?"

"Betty and Veronica slipped acid into my Diet Pepsi."

"WHAT?"

"I really…don't know…how to explain it any better." I looked down at my black Converse sneakers, which were looking back up at me. "And Senator Marks is gone."

Jules looked around furtively.

"Shit, what the hell can I do with you?" she said, more to herself than me. "I can't take you back up to the office. I can't take you back to Pete's place."

"Pete?"

"I gotta try to get you back home, your place is still in one fucking piece, isn't it?"

"Yeah, but I'm really hungry, but I couldn't trust the hot dog cart guy."

"Max, how the fuck long have you lived in this city? You can't trust ANY hot dog cart guy, they'd jack off in the relish if they could get away with it!"

She pulled me down the alley back to the street. I tried to keep up, but I was suddenly exhausted. Part of me was letting go because someone was helping me, and that, in turn, turned my legs into rubber.

"Max, you gotta help me with the walking, can you just put one fucking foot in front of the other? Do you need to go to the hospital?"

"I need lie down."

"You need lie down. How does this shit happen to me?" she muttered, and kept holding me up while she hailed a cab. But it wasn't a cab that pulled over, it was some random sedan.

"NO!" she screamed at the twenty-something guy after he rolled down his window. "YOU'RE GONNA CHARGE ME EIGHTY BUCKS TO GO TWO BLOCKS, EAT ME, ASSHOLE!"

The sedan quickly pulled out and a cab instantly took its place. She yanked me towards it, opened the back door and shoved me in. She then ran to the other side of the cab and jumped in next to me.

"Second and 59th," she said to the driver. "Roosevelt Island Tram Station."

I stared at the little TV screen on the back of the front seat, mesmerized by the Jimmy Kimmel clips that were playing on it as the cab took off. Drew Barrymore was dumping chocolate milk on Guillermo's head. I laughed. Well, it was funny.

"Now," she said, "what the FUCK is going on?"

"MK-Ultra," I said. "The CIA hired people to fuck up my head."

"Why'd they bother? Didn't they know you manage to do that on your own every single goddam day?"

It felt good to sit down. I almost felt safe. I shook my head, hoping it would clear now. It didn't. Jules was looking at me with a potent mixture of overpowering concern and searing anger.

"Are you sure you're okay? I can get you to an emergency room."

"Just need to get home. I'm good."

It was a mistake to say I was good, because she suddenly felt empowered to switch over to litigator mode.

"This is fucking rich. You expect me to babysit *your* bad drug trip -- but you just dump me by the side of the road during mine!"

"You left," I muttered.

"Is Eydie okay?"

"Eydie?" I asked.

"THE DOG. IS – SHE -- OKAY?"

Oh yeah. Her name was Eydie. I had stopped calling her that. Now she was just the fucking dog.

"I shit and pissed her before I left…she's fine."

She turned away from me, so I looked at her more closely as she dug into her purse. She was wearing her little professional office worker outfit, something boring, but still showing her legs. She had kept the weight off, she looked good, her latest blonde dye job was better than usual and if it wasn't for the Disney bugs flying around in the cab, I could have jumped her right then and there. Finally, she found her phone in her purse and called her boss. When she got him, she made up some shit about a family emergency.

I closed my eyes and tried to remember how long it had been since I had actually seen Jules. Two months? Well, it was now late February and the end for us had come back around Christmastime, the time when all couples on the edge traditionally fall off and break into a million pieces.

Again, it started with the fucking dog.

Her fantasy of having a loving and affectionate pet wasn't working out, mostly because the pet in question hated her guts. Then again, the fucking dog hated everybody but me. Which meant she guarded me zealously. Meaning if I was sitting in my office working at the computer and Jules came down the hallway to talk to me, the fucking dog would jump out of her little floor bed, growl like a bear in heat and charge Jules like she was going to rip out her throat.

Made it a little tense around the apartment.

But Jules tried. She would say the dog would get used to her, this was just temporary. A trainer advised Jules to work with the dog, give her treats, put her dinner in the bowl for her. But the dog wouldn't eat unless I was in the kitchen with her. The dog wouldn't go downstairs to shit and piss unless I took her. The dog wouldn't do *anything* unless I was involved. And when I started to get busy with cases and had to go into the city to meet with clients, the dog would howl and cry and shake and run around the apartment jumping on and off all the furniture and drive Jules nuts, if she happened to be home.

Even all that might have worked itself out if Jules hadn't decided to juggle the dynamite lurking in her head.

She was convinced she needed to lose twenty pounds before she genuinely made a stab at launching a new cabaret act. So first we both did a "cleanse," some crazy-ass monster diet to get rid of toxins and simultaneously cause a huge weight loss. I went along with it because…well, let's just say attendance was mandatory. Besides, I was turning into a huge blobby man and didn't fancy ordering bigger pants.

The month-long march to starvation culminated in the final week where we consumed no meat, no dairy, no sugar, no grains and no alcohol. It was a race to the bottom as to which of us would become the most miserable. Me, I ended up looking awesome, but she only shook off a couple of pounds. She was frustrated, furious and desperate, and what she did next was just plain disastrous.

She fucked with her meds.

Over the years, it had taken a while for her to arrive at the perfect cocktail of pills that would keep her bipolar mood swings at an acceptable level. That had all happened before I met her, so I had never seen Jules' demons truly unleashed. But there was a price to pay for keeping her level-headed and that price was paid in pounds; one of the antidepressants she took on a daily basis made it difficult for her to lose weight and she wasn't having that shit anymore.

So she did some online research and discovered there was a whole new wave of meds that eliminated the whole weight problem. She could stop taking the old one and start taking the new one, she would get skinny and life would be wonderful. She talked to a psychiatrist about it and got the green light. As a matter of fact, they both decided maybe she didn't need to be so medicated anymore, she had gone so long and kept it together so well, with the exception of swearing like a sailor at every given opportunity -- but you would have had to staple her lips shut to curtail that quirk.

Me, I didn't know anything about all this crap, so it all sounded good to me.

She made the switch in early November and at first, nothing seemed different. But then, a week or two later, came the night when I knew everything was about to spin out of control. We were in the living room watching HGTV, I had the fucking dog on one side of me and Jules on the other, and one of those pharmaceutical ads selling pills to stave off moderate to severe death came on during the break. As the announcer went through the litany of all the horrible things this particular random medication could do to you over soothing string music, Jules said softly, "You know when they talk about drugs causing you to have suicidal thoughts?"

I said absently, "Yeah?"

Her eyes remained glued to the TV.

"For the first time, I know what that means."

A cold shiver went through me.

The cab came to a halt and I opened my eyes to see where we were -- and I saw the tram station outside my window. Jules paid for the ride, ran around to my side and pulled me out. I was able to use my legs again. As I stood there on the curb, regaining my equilibrium, she looked into my eyes.

"You still look looney tunes. You gonna be okay to go on the tram?"

I nodded. I didn't see the problem. She pulled me towards the elevator and said, "I'm not even going to try to get you up the fucking stairs."

We rode the elevator to the top of the tram station and headed for the turnstiles that stood between us and the waiting area for the tram car. She swiped her Metro Card twice at the turnstile, once for her, once for me after she had passed through, and we both stood around with a bunch of other random people waiting for the next car. Luckily, there weren't too many others waiting and it wouldn't be a full car. Maybe half a load.

I could see the tram coming towards us, it was gleaming in the winter sun. I looked around. Things seemed maybe normal. I was doing okay. I was doing okay. I was doing okay. Jules was on her phone again. She was telling somebody I needed a babysitter. I didn't ask who. Because suddenly my attention went elsewhere.

I spotted a guy to the side of the waiting area who looked like a CIA agent I worked with, a guy I had always hated, one of those by-the-book pricks who always assumed you were screwing up. He seemed to be giving me the onceover -- and suddenly, I knew, I knew I knew I knew, without even one microscopic doubt to make me question myself, that he was there to capture me. And because he was there to capture me, he wasn't alone. I knew the protocols.

I played it cool until the tram arrived. When the doors slid open, Jules led me on and pulled me towards the back. She looked into my eyes again and I could tell she wasn't happy with what she saw.

"Now listen, Max, you're going to stay fucking calm. You're going to trust me. Or I'll rip your dick off and shove it up your ass, I swear."

She saw me looking at the CIA prick I hated, who was now standing on the other side of the tram cabin.

"Who are you looking at?"

"Nobody," I lied. And I turned away to make sure she believed me.

But, oh, looky.

Looky, looky, looky!

There was *another* guy who looked just like him on the other side of the tram car.

And, oh shit, looky, looky, looky!

Behind him, in the far corner, there was yet *another* lookalike.

Then I remembered. That CIA prick, the guy I hated, had actually died of bladder cancer a couple of years ago. Which could only mean…HOLEEE SHIT.

The three of them were all clones. Prick clones.

I shook my head to clear the green acrylic cobwebs that had built up inside my skull, then I turned to Jules and whispered, "We're in danger," as the tram, suspended from its two support cables, lurched forward and headed out over the eastern edge of Manhattan.

IT WAS TOO LATE TO GET OUT.

"Max," she said quietly, but forcefully. "Your brain is filled with *crazy jelly* right now. Do you understand? *Crazy jelly.* You don't listen to crazy jelly, you don't pay attention to crazy jelly, you understand it's crazy and it's jelly. So, please, do NOT depend on the crazy jelly. You depend on me, you trust me, you *listen* to me or we're going to have a big fucking problem, get me? Your own cock in your own ass. It *will* happen."

Okay, okay, I could keep it on the down low. I knew how to play it like Rico Suave. But, at the same time, hey buddy, I was going to watch those three prick clones like an eagle-eyed hawk. The minute they made a move, I'd make a move. And that move would be epic.

I kept waiting and waiting and waiting as the tram went up and up and up. We were approaching peak height, the point where we were almost off the island of Manhattan and traveling past the huge glass apartment building at 59th and First, the building where you were so close to the side that you could look through the windows and count the number of apples in a fruit bowl on a table if you wanted. Usually, I just searched for someone running around naked, but not today. Hells, no.

Today was about watching the prick clones.

Shitballs! One of them was moving his hand in a weird way. It *had* to be a secret signal. But to who? To whom, I mean?

The plot thickened along with my tongue.

Then I saw that the tram operator was *also* looking over at the prick clone who made the hand signal. Wait, did the tram operator nod, in a way that made it seem like he was not nodding? Like he was waiting to get that signal?

But what did the signal signify? What was about to happen?

I looked outside and saw the tram car was about to move over the East River.

The hand signal could only mean one thing.

The traitorous tram operator was going to stop the car and throw me out, plunging me into the treacherous bacteria-packed waters below.

Sure, there would be a lot of witnesses, but the CIA would threaten them into keeping their mouths shut. They had ways, we all knew that. MK-Ultra. Dr. Frank Olson. The dead Kennedys. The political guys, not the band.

I didn't have much time. I had to make my move. I eyed Jules. She eyed me right back.

"Okaaaaaay?" she whispered.

I nodded. "I love you," I said. I figured I should tell her, this might be the last chance I had.

She looked at me uncertainly for another moment, then muttered, "Crazy jelly," and turned away with a sneer. Well, I tried. Besides, she was no longer looking at me and wouldn't have time to stop me.

Game time.

"BLAHHHHHHRRRRRRRGHHHH" I yelled and rushed the original prick clone, who was by the right side of the tram car. I figured if I could overpower him and get him in front of me, my one hand on his throat, the other holding his arm behind his back, then the other two clones would back off.

Somehow, I pulled it off. Element of surprise and insane screaming.

"MAX!" Jules shrieked.

The tram operator looked at her, then looked at me holding the clone. He grabbed his radio-phone thing that hung from the side of the vertical control box because his plans were foiled and he had to notify his contact at Langley.

She waved desperately at the rest of the passengers, who had no idea what was going on (if they did, *they would understand*) and addressed them as if we were all at a school assembly. "Somebody gave him some acid -- he doesn't know what he's doing! He's really not going to hurt anybody!"

Nobody knew what to do. Just me.

I waited, holding on to the prick clone, waiting to see how the others were going to play it. The tram operator was talking rapidly into the radio-phone while the other two prick clones just seemed to be trying to avoid detection. Fat chance, fellas. Good luck getting away *when you two look exactly like the schmuck I'm holding.*

But shit.

Maybe the prick clones were only here to distract me from the *real enemy agents*? Agents who looked nothing like the prick clones, agents who, instead, resembled tall Asian college students?

Because that's who was coming at me from the side! The two not-college-students who were now trying to pull me off the prick clone I had already subdued!

"GET BACK," Jules screamed at them, "You're just going to make this WORSE!"

She didn't know what was really going on. Enemy assassins don't listen to shit like that.

I broke away from the Asians and threw myself against the other side of the car, which rattled the glass door and caused the whole cabin to sway back and forth. Then two more CIA agents, cleverly disguised as German tourists, pretended they wanted to calm me down EVEN WHILE THEY GRABBED MY ARMS SO THEY COULD THROW ME INTO THE RIVER.

"MAAAAAAX!" Jules screamed.

I broke away from the Germans and threw myself back towards the other side of the tram.

"Nein!" they yelled.

WHAAAAAAAAM, I went against the side of the tram.

My impact caused the car to sway even more crazily and I could see, through the windows on the south side, a guy on a bicycle over on the Queensboro bridge who had stopped and was staring at us in disbelief.

WAS HE CIA TOO?

I raised my arms threateningly at the bicycle guy, like I was going to turn into the Wolfman, and then I growled like him -- "*GRRRRRRROWWWRRR!!!*" -- while somebody near me threw up and some kid screamed for his mommy and suddenly, everybody was recording my actions with their phones.

Yes! Phone video! The CIA couldn't stop those videos from getting out on the internet! FACEBOOK WOULD SAVE ME! The CIA had to back down, otherwise how could they explain the three prick clones or the Asian students or the German tourists? Answer? THEY COULDN'T.

That's when Jules grabbed me and shoved me up against the back of the tram and pushed me down on the bench, where everybody who had been sitting there quickly cleared out to make room for Maxie. I stayed down, because everything was suddenly cool, because social media was going to expose the truth. Jules faced the rest of the car and held her hand up to keep everybody away, and everybody seemed to agree that she had a good idea going there. That girl was aces in my book.

The tram was descending now and I could see a group of uniformed RI Public Safety Officers waiting for me at the bottom. I knew they wouldn't believe me. So I'd keep my mouth shut. The clones would get them soon enough. Served them right.

As Jules helped me off the tram, after everybody else had gotten off as quickly as their feet could carry them, the cops were there in the waiting area, waiting for me. The lead cop looked me over, then said with a big smile…

"Hey! You're the guy!"

Jules was good, real fucking good, because she was able to convince the cops that I was working on a case when somebody tried to stop me by dosing me with LSD or whatever the kids called it nowadays. It helped that they recognized me. The officers accompanied me and Jules back to my apartment to make sure I wasn't going to make any more trouble and also made Jules promise she would stay until I came down from whatever it was that I was on.

We got back to my place and I found out that Jules still had her key, because she unlocked the door before I could fish mine out. The cops told her to let them know if I needed any more help, but she told them I just needed to sleep it off.

Then she opened the apartment door and the fucking dog came after her.

She screamed, but then the fucking dog saw it was me and started leaping up to my nose, letting out her yelps of intermingled agony and joy. I was sweating hard as I half-stumbled down the stairs, the fucking dog jumping and jumping and jumping on me. I made it to the bathroom and closed the door on the dog, who kept yelping and jumping at the door as I relieved myself.

I looked at the bathroom clock. It was around 4 p.m. I knew from friends this shit could last up to twelve hours and it had only been in me for about three or four. I stripped and put on the bathrobe hanging on the hook on the back of the door, then I came out and headed right for the bedroom.

"Hello?" Jules called after me in a not-so-nice way as the dog barked and growled at her -- causing Jules to turn and yell "SHADDUP!" at her.

I laid down and closed my eyes. Jules came in and shut the door behind her, keeping it between her and the demon beast from hell, then tried to get the covers over me. Just as quickly, I pulled them off. I was already steaming hot and sweating like a pig.

"What time does Eydie eat?" she asked.

"Around 5:30," I said hoarsely. "Then I take her down again to shit and piss. Usually just piss at that time."

"Okay, I'll stay for that. If you seem to be okay, I'll leave. So you might be asleep when I do. But this shit should wear off by then, right?"

I nodded.

A big, big pause.

"Hey, asshole," she asked tenderly.

I nodded again.

"Remember when you said you loved me?" she asked.

Another nod from me.

"Did you mean it?"

I didn't nod. Instead, I asked, "Who's Pete?"

"He's Cuban." Her tone darkened.

I laughed. "He's Cuban Pete?" I asked. "He's the king of the rumba beat?"

"I KNOW THE SONG!" she yelled. And then, at a lower volume, "I'm opening with his combo this weekend and we *have* to rehearse tonight. I'm only staying with him because I needed a place to live, in case you didn't fucking hear."

"Speaking of fucking…"

"We're NOT."

More yelps outside in the hallway from the dog.

"Poor Eydie…" she sighed.

"How can you love that dog?" I muttered. "She wants you to die."

"She's so cute…I'm going to go play with her."

I heard her open the door, I heard the fucking dog growl and snarl, I heard Jules scream and I heard the fucking dog chase her around the apartment. And through it all, I kept my eyes closed because I didn't have the strength to open them.

I hadn't told her that I loved her this time. Why? Because I was too worried about Pete. Actually, it was because, as usual, I was too worried about myself, I thought, as I felt myself slip into a half-coma and what was left of my brain flew away to a distant planet.

Messages

Blue Fire wouldn't leave me alone.

I had dreams and nightmares all night, beautiful technicolor horror shows with one recurring theme: The superhero Blue Fire, taunting me, constantly goading me on, daring me to come get him.

Relief came when the morning sun poured in through my bedroom window, waking me up, up and away from my internal hallucinations. And even though my head was pounding and my body felt greasy from the thick layer of dried perspiration that coated it, I felt like whatever I had ingested had finished its evil mission. I was okay.

I was still in my bathrobe and nothing else, on top of the covers. I was chilly. I opened my eyes and waited for them to focus.

The fucking dog was asleep by my side, but if I moved an inch, she'd be all over me in a flash. I wanted to delay that too-familiar, too-enthusiastic morning greeting. So I carefully moved my eyes to the side, as far as I could without actually turning my head and giving away to the pooch that I was awake. I spied that the bedroom door was open and that, down at the end of the hallway outside the door, about twenty-five or thirty feet away from me, somebody was sitting in a chair, watching me.

Was this a good person or a bad person? I could only see shadows at this angle.

I didn't want to make any sudden moves, but I had a full bladder that was urgently requesting evacuation and an aching brain screaming for Advil. I decided to get it over with and find out who was guarding me and for what reason. I turned my head to the side ever so slowly.

Of course, as soon as I made that head turn, the dog jumped on my chest hard and suddenly her big wet tongue was licking my face. Oh shit.

I quickly covered my head with my arms, because I knew what was next. The fucking dog was going to jump up and down on my face and I had to protect my eyes if I didn't want them punctured by her claws. I had already written off my nipples, one of which always routinely ached from a paw scratch.

"Max?" came a tentative call from down the hall. I got to my feet weakly, pushing the fucking dog to the side, and staggered to the door of the bathroom, where I stopped and turned to see who my warden was.

"Max? You okay, dude?"

PMA got to his feet.

I hadn't seen PMA since the end of last summer. He stuck around for a while after the Dark Sky episode and nursed me and my broken leg and Jules and her broken head back to health; then he had to go start his first year at George Washington University back in the D.C. He missed Jules' descent into madness by a few weeks, so he had no idea what had happened after his departure.

It was an instant relief to have PMA back. This was somebody I could trust without hesitation and, as a bonus, he wasn't bipolar. He looked healthy. He had put on a little muscle, like maybe he was doing more working out at the gym and less amateur Kung Fu kicking to instructional videos hosted by his idol, former UFC fighter and current motivational speaker, Andre Gibraltar.

Gibraltar was PMA's guru, the guy who had inspired PMA's nickname. "PMA" was a Gibraltar-created acronym that stood for "Power, Mind, Action," the thought process PMA used to get him through difficult spots. He was all about the self-help – but now I would need him to help *me*.

"Why are you here?" I asked.

"Jules called and asked me to come. What happened? I hear you had a bad trip." He sort of chuckled at the idea of me on acid.

Very funny.

"I gotta piss," I managed to croak out. As I slipped into the bathroom, I heard the fucking dog growl and charge him. Served him right. Only I was allowed to have an inappropriate sense of humor.

A couple minutes later, after I had put on my sweats and went down to shit and piss the dog in what was left of the winter snow, I got more details from PMA. He was the person Jules had called from the tram station. She asked him to come babysit me, he flew in from D.C. as quickly as he could make it happen, and she stayed with me until he got in at about nine last night. That was pretty late, so she probably skipped rehearsal with Cuban Pete. Maybe she did still care.

PMA came in the living room with a cup of coffee he had brewed for himself with Jules' coffeemaker, which she had left behind with a ton of her other crap. I was sitting in the living room, holding on tight to the dog's leash to keep her from devouring him.

"What's with the dog?" he asked.

"Satan obviously," I replied as I sipped a bottle of Coke Zero I grabbed from my stash in the fridge. The dog growled, right on cue.

"That thing's dangerous."

"Yeah, sometimes little kids will reach over to pet her before I can stop them. Nobody's lost any fingers yet, but I don't know if that trend will hold."

The Advil was starting to work, I was awake and doing okay, so it was time to reconnect. I turned on my phone, which had been powered off since yesterday, back when I was sure the CIA was about to take me to a secret prison. The first thing I wanted to do with the phone, however, was to use the delivery app to order a couple of sandwiches, because I hadn't eaten since I threw away the hot dog yesterday. I watched impatiently as the little Apple icon lit up for an eternity during the reboot.

"So you stayed up all night watching me?" I asked PMA while I waited for the phone.

"Yeah, from what Jules told me, I thought I should. You yelled a couple of times in your sleep."

"If that's the worst I did, you got the easy shift. Jules had to…"

"Yeah, I saw what happened on the tram."

"You *saw?*"

Then I remembered. Many people with phones shooting video of me trying to subdue all those clones.

"It's all over social media and shit."

Oh, Christ, this would not be good for business. I put my head back against the wall. Fuck, fuck, fuck.

"Why did somebody slip you drugs?" a baffled PMA asked. "Did this have to do with a case?"

"I have no clue," I answered. "It was either a girl being a little too cute or something more sinister. You missing class?"

"It's okay, Max. As long as I get back tomorrow morning. If you're okay, that is."

"How's your mom?"

"Still hates me, still hates you."

"How's your love life?"

"I'm seeing somebody, sort of."

"You're always seeing somebody, sort of."

He looked around, afraid to ask the next question. But he finally got to it.

"How about you and Jules?"

I frowned. He got the idea.

"Max, you and me, we text all the time, and you never told me any of this happened?"

"Sometimes I don't feel like talking."

"How about now?"

I shrugged. No getting out of it, I supposed. So I told him the whole story, starting with the dog and getting to the part where Jules switched out her meds. I told him about how, when she changed pills *and* lowered her dosage, she slowly got crazier and crazier, yelling at me over nothing, or crying in bed for three hours over nothing, or getting insanely giddy over nothing. Her huge bottomless well of emotions had been released, which, on the upside, meant amazing fireworks for her in the bedroom. She kept telling me she saw colors; me, I didn't need to see anything, I heard her yelling to God and Christ so loudly that I was surprised They didn't show up to tell her to cool it.

But that was the only upside. The downside was considerably more powerful. When you can't control the happy and sad, you can't control much of anything else. When you also have the dog you rescued attacking you whenever you turn a corner, well, that just adds fuel to an-already raging mental wildfire.

At work, her boss was tired of riding on her emotional rollercoaster. At home, so was I. It was sucking up too much of my energy, which made it hard for me to get work done. That in turn put me on edge; I knew I had a window to make some serious money and I knew I didn't want to be left with nothing before it slammed shut.

So we slid down a death spiral that didn't seem to have any bottom in sight. It wasn't exactly Paradise Lost, but it was at least Paradise Misplaced. I wanted to reverse course. I knew how we could turn the page to Paradise Regained. That way was simple, obvious and twofold.

First, she had to get back on her old meds.

Second, we had to return the fucking dog.

I thought I had a winning case when I went to present it before Judge Jules. What I forgot was she was running a kangaroo court.

"You WANT me to be a fat failure, don't you?? A BIG FAT FUCKING FAILURE!!!" was her response to my first bright idea. Her response to the second was equally emphatic.

"YOU'RE A HEARTLESS FUCKING MONSTER WHO WOULD PROBABLY MURDER A BABY WHO CRIED TOO MUCH AND EAT IT! BABY-EATER! YOU'RE A GODDAM BABY-EATER!"

And with that, she snatched away my last vestiges of hope. So I snapped.

After denying ever eating babies, I said I couldn't babysit -- yes, that's when I used the "b" word -- a psycho who wouldn't even *try* to get better. I said the dog would hate her forever and people took insane rescue dogs back to the pound all the time. Then she said a few more things and I said a few more things, none of which should ever be repeated by anyone anywhere. I will say that I kept up my end of the crazy. I don't get mad often, but when I do, flesh gets seared off bone, neighborhoods get leveled to the ground and the earth shakes on its axis.

The kicker? All this happened on Christmas Eve. Ho ho ho.

She packed a bag and disappeared into the night. I didn't know where she went, because she blocked my number on her phone. Evidently she landed on her feet, because she continued to text me several times a day to tell me that if I took the dog back to the pound, I would be dead to her forever and I would never see her tits again. Worst of all, she defriended me on Facebook. As a last resort, I finally tried cornering her at work, but she had security throw me out.

So it was over, just like that. As with ISIS, negotiation was out of the question and if I was found in her territory, I might wind up getting beheaded on camera.

"It's wrong. It's just wrong" said PMA after he listened to my tale of woe. "I should talk to her. You two belong together."

"Kid, forget about it. She's got to work through this, she knows it and that's why she's keeping her distance. As long as Pete keeps his distance too…"

"Who?"

"He's Cuban. Cuban Pete. King of the rumba beat. Look, don't get involved in my problems. It's great you came up to look after me, but go back tomorrow and get back to your own life, I'll cover your airfare and give you a ride to La Guardia."

My phone suddenly started buzzing like a son of a bitch. Everything that was waiting for me out there in cyberspace hit all at once -- a whole swarm of messages and voicemails.

"Jesus, I got a lot of calls…"

"Well…the videos…"

"Find one for me to look at, will you?" I asked with an air of resignation.

He hit a few buttons on his phone and carefully handed it to me as I held down the snarling dog. Soon I was looking at the riot I had caused on the tram. People screaming, Jules trying to help me, the car swaying, the operator talking nonstop on the radio about a crazy man who was going to kill everyone and me yelling about MK-Ultra, hot dogs and Dr. Frank Olson while I assaulted innocent people.

"There's about ten different ones like this online," PMA continued. "Oh, and I had to unplug the phone in your office. You were getting a lot of media calls."

Oh good God. I wasn't going to go back and talk to Matt Lauer about *this* embarrassment.

I handed PMA back his phone -- just as mine started rapping, *No one man should have all that power.* I quickly asked the kid to go to the bodega downstairs and get us a couple egg sandwiches, I needed something in my stomach and it looked like I would only be using my phone for talking for a while. He left and I reluctantly answered the call.

"Hello, Todd," I said glumly. My head was starting to hurt again, because entertainment lawyers caused too much pain.

"I've been trying to get ahold of you for hours, Jesus, bud, you okay?" Todd almost seemed sincere about caring, but I easily detected the "almost."

"Yeah, Todd. I'm fine." I braced for myself for my punishment.

"Well, that's awesome…but listen, bud, *you can't do shit like that.*" There it was. I had endangered his percentage of my book deal and this was no laughing matter

"Todd, it wasn't my idea of a good time. Somebody slipped something in my Diet Pepsi."

"Well, Jesus bud, when that happens, you go lie down in the park or something, but you don't try to kill everybody on a goddamn tram! Do you know how many videos of you completely losing your shit are all over the internet? I tried to do some damage control yesterday, bud, and you know what? I couldn't even get the publisher's people on the phone!"

"Maybe they were busy. Maybe somebody put something in their Diet Pepsis."

"Max, I don't care what happened, but just lie low, bud. Just lie low. I'll try to save this thing."

I hung up. My window of prosperity was indeed in danger of slamming shut, which meant me going back to my threadbare existence. I felt weak and thought about going back to bed. But suddenly, Kanye was rapping at me again. I answered the new call.

"Hey, man. You okay?"

"Yeah, Howard. I'm fine." I winced in advance. Would there be more yelling?

"You sure?" he asked. No yelling? That made me more nervous. "I saw the videos of you on the tram. You weren't kidding yesterday, you really were on something."

"Yeah, some kind of LSD type of thing, I don't know. I was having lunch with two girls about the job I told you about yesterday. Next thing I knew, the walls were melting."

I paused. And then I tried again. "Got any ideas about why that might have happened?"

"How you got drugged? No, why would I? I only know what I told you, which isn't much." Pause. "Did you find out anything more about Mikov?"

"No. You find out anything more about Senator Marks?"

"That's the FBI's department."

A Mexican standoff. Howard wanted to know what I knew, I wanted to know what Howard knew. On my side, though, I had no cards to show. Howard, I wasn't so sure.

"Look, man, are you sure you don't need any help? Like I said, I can send somebody over…"

"No, Howard, I'm good."

Pause.

"So you're going on with the Mikov case?"

"I turned them down yesterday."

"Great. I think that's a *very* good idea." The relief was oozing through the phone and that was the tell. Now I was positive he knew something and he didn't want me to get killed by it, just like the last time around. He was actually looking out for me, but, as usual, withholding information wasn't the way to do it. "If anything changes, if you need something, call me, okay?"

"I always do."

"Yeah," he said with a laugh, "I know."

I hung up.

Before I had a chance to process Howard's call, fucking Kanye was rapping about power again. *The clock's tickin', I just count the hours.* And how. This time, the call was from a number I didn't have in my contacts. I thought about not answering, but then something told me I should.

"Hello?" I said warily.

"I am sooooo sorry," she said quietly and forlornly. It was Candy, aka Betty. I was glad I took the call, because it was one of two people I definitely wanted to talk to.

"Just tell me what happened, Candy. I'm all ears."

"Okay, well, Janine…?" The other person I wanted to talk to. "She was already on something when she came in the restaurant…"

"Surprise me more…"

"…yeah, and, well, she thought it would be funny to get you…"

"…fucked up."

"Yeah. Mr. Chesler is SOOOO mad at us, he saw all the videos of you and asked what happened and he's going to fiiiiiiiire us if you don't go look for Mr. Mikov!"

"Really. Even with you guys doing such a great job." Yes, I was being sarcastic.

"Please, reconsider, Mr. Bowman, please take the job, we'll wire the money into your account today."

"I'm thinking about it."

Pause.

"YOU ARE? Oh, that's the LEAST I can ask for after what we put you through!"

"You got that right." Then I visualized the rapid downward trajectory of the window of my prosperity and quickly finished my thinking. "You know what? I'm going to email Mel my bank information. Tell him to send the money. I can't guarantee anything, but I'll try my best. Okay?"

"Oooo-KAY! Thank YOU, Mr. Max Bowman!"

"You're welcome. And tell your cousin to go take a leap into the East River."

I hung up. And immediately felt like Peter Parker when his spider-sense indicated danger.

If I knew this job was trouble and I still went ahead and took it, then what the hell was wrong with me? I still had some money in the bank, it's not like I was on the verge of going broke again, but I still felt that way. It was like I was grabbing for a big fat piece of cheese sitting in the middle of a monster mousetrap with a lethal razor-edged hammer. Why did I reverse course so fast? Why couldn't I calm myself down? Was whatever the hell drug that was in me still talking?

The fucking dog looked up at me, because she sensed my confusion. She sniffed out moods like she sniffed out squirrels. I petted her back and thought about going back to bed again, but then…

Bing!

A noise from my phone I hadn't heard before.

I looked at the screen and saw that somebody had sent me a private message on the Facebook message app. Who the hell would message me on Facebook? I barely knew anybody on there.

I opened up the message and saw who it was from.

It was that Canun guy, Bruce Canun, the administrator from the Ben Mikov Facebook group. I remembered Canun had "friended" me the other day after I had joined. He was my lucky thirteenth Facebook pal and he had some interesting information for me.

> *Saw your message about Mikov. One guy who might know something is Al Bearing, inked Mikov's stuff on Blue Fire and drew that one issue after Mikov left.*

Huh. I wrote back.

> *Yeah, I know who he is. The bad Superman artist. He's still alive?*

I waited. Then…

> *85 years old, in great shape saw him at last Comic Con. Lives in New England somewhere. Did phone interview with him for my comics blog few months ago.*

Huh.

> *You got his number? This is a big deal or I wouldn't be asking.*

A couple seconds later, he gave it to me, along with one final note.

> *Don't know how helpful he'll be. I tried to get some things out of him, but didn't get much. But he's the guy who worked closest with Mikov back then.*

Just then, PMA returned from the bodega with the sandwiches. I held the fucking dog down so she couldn't go after him.

"You ready to eat?"

"Yeah," I said, "and then I have to call a bad artist."

I locked the fucking dog up in the bedroom, and, over the sandwiches, brought PMA up to date on the case, because I felt like I needed a sounding board. Besides, it wasn't hard to tell him everything because I knew nothing. But PMA didn't care, he was just happy to be a part of whatever I was doing.

"This is awesome, Max. Last time around, you treated me like I was ten years old. Now, it's like we're partners."

"Yeah, but you're a very silent partner, in that I keep all the money, so don't get too excited. I just want your thoughts."

"Well, first of all, I think you're being paranoid. The one girl just drugged you to get you back to her place because she wanted your hot body, as every woman does." Yes, he was being sarcastic. "I mean, even I was hot for you after watching the tram videos, the way you took on all those guys all by yourself. I got excited personally."

"I'm sorry I asked."

"Seriously, I don't get why you think there's any more to it."

"Maybe there's not."

I took a few more bites. Food was helping.

"So then there's Mikov," the kid went on. You know, I actually read your book of *Blue Fire* comics last summer. That was pretty hardcore. Never saw a superhero who fought crime by burning anybody who did anything wrong to bits."

"Well, he didn't actually kill them technically, the Comics Code back then wouldn't allow that. Remember, the villains were put into that ghost jail, whatever it was, the place the LawGiver set up."

"Whatever. But here's the thing you should focus on when it comes to finding Mikov. You remember my dad's an artist…?"

"Matter of opinion. He paints fruit on naked women."

"Agreed, but he once said something that kind of stuck with me – he said every artist leaves some part of himself in his work."

"You think Mikov put some clues in his comics?"

"Sure, he wrote and drew them himself, how could there not be something autobiographical?"

"For instance…?"

"Like maybe where the kid lives in the comic books, the kid who turns into Blue Fire. It's some crappy little steel town, right?"

"Yeah, in Pennsylvania. But the name of it is Freeman, as in "free man," get it? The name's obviously part of his philosophical Ayn Rand bullshit."

"But, on the other hand, maybe it refers to someplace real. At the very least, he's probably from a crappy little steel town, right?"

I chewed on the sandwich. "He drew it pretty realistically, like he knew that kind of town well. Could be worth thinking about."

"And there was that doctor…the guy who was always messing with him?"

"Dr. K."

Dr. K was the comic book's main arch-villain, a nefarious "doctor of the mind" who always tried to confuse Blue Fire about right and wrong -- which would of course shut down his powers, as Blue Fire had to possess moral clarity in every given situation. It was yet another homage to Ayn Rand's black-and-white world view.

"Yeah," said the kid. "Dr. K."

"What about him?"

"Don't you think it was kind of weird that he wasn't a normal kind of super villain? That he was an insane psychologist? Maybe that meant something?"

"You mean I should go try to find a nasty doctor whose last name starts with a 'K'? That could take a while."

"It's just an idea."

PMA stood up a little too quickly for the dog's liking. She tried to lunge, but I held her back, so she was limited to just a passing snarl.

"So," PMA asked, glaring at the fucking dog, "You are taking that thing back, right?"

"Back where?"

"To the shelter. You're getting rid of it, right?"

I chewed some more.

"Yeah," I answered.

After I ate, I had a little nap and when I got up, I went into the office. I plugged the landline back in and the phone screen said I had 127 voicemails. I wasn't going to deal with those at the moment. Instead I dialed the number of Al Bearing, the guy who might have something to say about Mikov.

"Al Bearing," said the old but still vibrant voice on the other end. He sounded a little like an aging teamster.

"Mr. Bearing, I was referred to you by a Bruce Canun, he said he interviewed you for a blog post a while ago."

"Oh, another comic fan?" he said with suspicion. "You really want to talk to the bad Superman artist?"

Ouch. I didn't know these old comic vets were so self-aware.

From dabbling in the Facebook groups, I was finding out just how opinionated and, okay, just plain rude most comic fans my age could be. But Al was right, to my generation, he was known as "the bad Superman artist." In the late fifties and throughout the sixties, DC published many, many, many comic books featuring Superman. There was, of course, *Superman*, but there was also *Action Comics*, *Superman's Girlfriend Lois Lane*, *Superman's Pal, Jimmy Olsen*, the annual 80-page *Superman Giant* issues, and *World's Finest Comics*, which featured Superman AND Batman teaming up in contrived stories where the Caped Crusader had to be shown as being not completely useless next to a guy who could literally do anything. And yeah, there was also Superboy ("the adventures of Superman when he was a boy!") who appeared in *Superboy* and *Adventure Comics*, because why not, kids would pay for it.

In other words, there were a lot of Superman stories that had to get out the door -- and not enough top-quality artists around to draw them all. And that's where Al came in. He always did the Superman story in the back of one of the books and it was always borderline horrendous. Heads wouldn't be quite right, anatomical details would be out of proportion and people having a conversation would appear to be looking at a wall or pieces of furniture rather than each other. You could call him incompetent -- and apparently, a lot of old bitter comic readers did these days, right to his face. DC finally dumped him in the mid-sixties when Marvel was really starting to breathe down their neck, and Al landed in the cellar of the business, which was, of course, Mighty Mel's comic line.

But that's where Al ended up shining, for a while, because it turned out he was a pretty good *inker*. When comic illustrators like Mikov would turn in their penciled panels, an inker's job was to ink over their pencils and prepare the artwork to be colored and printed. Al ended up being better on details than the big picture -- he actually improved on other people's work. So when Mikov showed up with his genius artwork, Mighty Mel put Al on *Blue Fire* as inker. It was a combo that worked great until Mikov bolted. That's when Mel made a fatal mistake. He thought, since Al knew Mikov's work better than anyone, he should be the guy to take over the strip -- which resulted in that one lone horrible final issue where Blue Fire's flames of justice looked more like somebody vomiting blueberry whipped cream.

But I didn't bring up the vomited whipped cream analogy to Al. Instead, I lavishly praised his inking job on Blue Fire. He had heard all that before too, but he wasn't resistant to hearing it again. It was better than hearing about how his Lois Lane looked a lot like Milton Berle.

After I was done praising him to the skies, he softly said, "Thanks, kid." Kid? These *alter kockers* were sure making me feel young. He went on. "It was an honor to work on that book, it really was. It was an honor to work with Mikov. I think only Steranko made as big an impact on comics with so little output, you know?"

"Well, Mikov is who I'm calling about, I'm looking for him on behalf of Mighty Mel."

"What, does Mikov owe Mel money? That'd be the only reason that old bastard would be looking for anybody. What a worthless piece of shit."

"Well, money's in the equation. Can you keep a secret?"

"Sure."

"Somebody wants to make a *Blue Fire* movie. A big expensive one. And they need Mikov to sign off."

I heard a sigh.

"You know how many times people have asked me what became of Mikov? Me, I could be face down in a ditch somewhere, nobody would give a shit, but this guy..."

"You gotta admit, it's a big mystery."

"Mystery. What are you, some kind of detective?"

"Some kind. I'm only asking because you spent the most time with him."

"Yeah, and it still wasn't much. He kept to himself. Weird guy. You know all this already."

"I haven't heard it from somebody who knew him like you."

"Look, nobody really knew him, he was a closed book. He would come over to my studio to go over panels, he wouldn't let me come to his. But he wanted me to do things exactly as he wanted them done, and, boy howdy, I'd hear about it if I didn't follow the leader on something. You must have gone through public records, right? You find anything?"

"Not a thing. Did he use a pseudonym?"

"I don't know who the hell would use 'Mikov' as a pseudonym. Hell, my real name's Bramowitz. So he's not dead?"

"Have no clue."

"Well, again, don't have much to tell you. We didn't talk about much outside the work, y'know? Certainly nothing personal."

"Well, the kid in *Blue Fire* – he was from a small Pennsylvania steel town. Was Mikov from that kind of place?"

"Could be. I remember one winter when it started getting cold, he started talking about the canal that ran through the small town where he grew up, how it froze over in the winter and he'd go ice skating on it. It was like I got hit by lightning, him talking about something like that. That is literally the only personal thing I can remember him saying to me back then and I remember it *because* it was the only personal thing."

"In the comic, the name of the town was Freeman."

"Yeah, but Mikov prob'ly made that up. It's a comic book, y'know."

"Just looking for anything that could get me started."

"I hear ya."

"Anything else you can remember?"

"I'll think about it, nobody's asked me for detective clues before, this is exciting. Hey, where are you calling from?"

"New York City."

"I'll be down for that Jersey Comic Con in a couple of weeks, we can get together then if you want and see if we can come up with something. I sure would like to know what happened to that guy."

"I'll keep that in mind, I thank you for your time, Mr. Bearing."

"Aw, what the fuck else do I have to do?"

I hung up and turned to PMA.

"You and me? We're going to have a race."

"A race?"

"Yeah. To see which one of us can be first to find a Pennsylvania steel town with a canal."

Freemansburg

Once again, I was going to be David Muhlfelder.

I still had the fake ID and credit card that Howard had gifted me with last year, as well as the magical CIA smartphone with the encryption software so I could make sure nobody would track my calls. I decided to put all of those back in action for the time being to protect myself, now that I was going back on the road. I didn't want anybody knowing where I was going or what I was doing. Maybe the paranoia was still spilling over from the drug, but I wasn't keen on taking chances.

It was Wednesday morning and I woke up feeling all right, the best since I got dosed by Veronica. Last night, PMA had won the race and found the town that seemed to fit all the criteria that Mikov put out there. But then again, PMA had a distinct advantage when it came to internet searches, he was a digital native and I grew up with an AM radio and a black and white TV. Back then, we all listened to the same music and watched the same shows because we had no choice. How else could you explain *Mr. Ed* running for six seasons?

Anyway, turned out PMA had the right idea -- Mikov's town of Freeman in the *Blue Fire* comics did have some basis in reality. There was a town named Freemansburg on the south side of Bethlehem, Pennsylvania, where Bethlehem Steel ruled supreme for decades until it got crushed with the rest of American manufacturing. And the little borough did, in fact, have a canal, the Lehigh Canal, which ran parallel with the Lehigh River. If Mikov was drawing on his own childhood, Freemansburg was the best candidate for a hometown.

Since I was driving PMA to the airport, I thought I might as well keep driving and check out Freemansburg afterwards -- Mighty Mel's mighty deposit had landed in my bank account, so why not get started? However, as PMA and I drove the short ten minutes or so it took to get to La Guardia from the island, I could tell he was not happy about me going on with the case without him.

"If I didn't have to take that damn exam…"

"Kid, this whole trip might be a waste of time. Mikov's gotta be at least ten years older than me, who knows if anybody remembers him even if this does turn out to be his hometown? So be a good boy and go to class."

Pause.

"Can I come back this weekend and stay with you? I want to see what's going on." A beat. "And there's something else."

I looked at him. He didn't want to tell me. I looked at him again.

"Andre Gibraltar's having a special event. I've been handpicked to attend."

I looked at him a third time.

"Handpicked?" I said with the proper degree of sardonic awe. "His hand actually picked you?"

"That's what the email said. I mean, he knows about me from the whole Dark Sky thing, knows I'm on his mailing list, and he…he wants me to be a part of a new elite group."

"New elite group??? Wow. You've been holding out on me, kid." I took the off ramp to the terminal.

"Okay, Max, bust my balls all you want, but his program really helped me focus and get through a lot of stuff. You could use a little help from him, in my opinion."

"You think I'm that bad off?"

"Max, no offense, but you have some issues."

I laughed. "You're welcome here any time, kid, you know that. So write back to Andre and tell him you're in. Hey, ask if I can come along for shits and giggles."

I was kidding, but he wasn't.

"I'm gonna do just that. Maybe you'll learn something," the kid said. He was in earnest mode. You didn't argue with PMA in earnest mode.

I pulled up to the curb of the terminal. He grabbed his overnight bag and got out of the car.

"Let me know when you're coming in," I called after him. "The Max Bowman car service will be at your beck and call."

"Thanks, Max. And maybe get rid of that thing while I'm gone." He pointed to the back seat and turned to head into the terminal. Yeah, the fucking dog was sleeping back there on the blanket I put across the seat to catch the twenty pounds of fur she was bound to shed on the drive. Why did I bring her? Because it was going to be a long day, at least a couple hours each way with traffic, and I didn't think I should leave her alone that long or she'd spontaneously combust.

"Just you and me now," I said to the dog as I pulled away. "Just you and me." I thought a moment. "Maybe it's time we started a conversation. Because I have to figure out what to do with you. If I get rid of you, Jules will never speak to me again. If I keep you, she'll never come back to the apartment again. So…what the hell do I do?"

She stared at me with her strange combination of obsessive love and extreme agitation over what was going to happen next in her life. And still, I had to admit, she was the cutest damn dog in the world.

"Maybe we need to bond. Maybe I need to try with you."

She continued staring.

"I'll even start using your name. Okay, Eydie?"

She made some kind of strange dog yawn and rolled over. Our talk was finished.

Jan, the sexy robotic voice of my GPS, took me across the George Washington Bridge and down to the I-78, which took me into the back side of Bethlehem, where the steel factories used to be. A big slice of them had been replaced by a glittery casino a few years ago, which, I suppose, summed up America at the moment. If we weren't going to make anything anymore, we might as well put everything we had left on red and let it ride.

From the casino, Jan smoothly maneuvered me, as only Jan could, down to Main Street in Freemansburg, which I had set as my destination, figuring that was where the center of the town's activity would be. Unfortunately, I didn't see much activity to be had. Main Street was just an old two lane road that ran parallel to the canal with a bunch of old clapboard houses lining the cracked sidewalks on either side. There was a church that was apparently Spanish-speaking if the sign out front was any indication, and that was about it for anything interesting. I was immediately glad I had stopped at a fast-food place for a burger on the way, because it sure didn't look like there was any place to eat here.

I got to the end of Main, where it curved and turned into a bridge that went over the canal and the river and maybe to a better grade of town. But I turned off before that happened - and into a big gravel parking lot next to an ancient bar that looked like it might have predated the canal. I checked the car clock and saw it was about two in the afternoon.

I parked the car, got out and buttoned my coat – it was maybe in the mid-forties, warmer than it had been, but still not Miami in May. As I shut the car door behind me, Eydie howled like she had an embolism and jumped up at the window, giving me her haunted stare. I wished I really was the cold-hearted son of a bitch people thought I was.

I got her out and pissed and shit her in a clump of grass next to the parking lot, then, as I dumped her poop bag in a dumpster near the back, I took a good look at the bar - not that there was anything good to look at. The entire exterior was disgustingly filthy, like it hadn't been cleaned…maybe ever? I couldn't tell if there were any lights on inside or even if the place was still in business. There was a sign outside promising free Wi-Fi, however, so that was a good omen that it was still a going concern in the 21st century.

What the hell, might as well give it a go.

The dog and I went up to the door, and I turned the knob. It was unlocked, so I went on in. The door, just like the Greek place in the Village, had that little bell attached that rang to let people know you were coming in. But I didn't see any people around to hear it.

My eyes adjusted to the darkness and I quickly saw that the filth factor wasn't much improved from the outside. There was a big square of a bar in the main room, which had its back up against the wall, where the cash register and all the bottles and glasses were kept. Some tables and chairs lined the other wall. I sniffed the air and quickly regretted it -- there was stink piled on stink in this place and it was best to switch over to mouth-breathing mode to survive.

"Hello?" I asked.

Suddenly, a burly guy with the face of a bulldog and short salt-and-pepper hair, maybe a few years older than me, wearing a dingy-white t-shirt and work pants with a dirt-splattered apron on top of the whole appealing ensemble, walked in behind me and switched on the lights. Eydie, of course, immediately growled and lunged at him, but the guy just laughed at her as I pulled her back.

"I used to have a Doberman named Rex. That little pussy dog ain't gonna make me lose no sleep." He went behind the bar like he owned the place and I had the feeling he did.

"Okay if I have the dog in here?" I asked. "Just drove down from New York and she gets a little nervous in the car."

"Yeah, sure," he shrugged. "Can I get you something?"

"Jack, on the rocks."

"Kinda early for the hard stuff, huh?"

"Must be, since you didn't have the lights on."

"People don't start crawling in here until supper time. New York, huh? You visiting somebody?"

He threw some ice in a drink glass and poured in a generous dose of Jack. He figured me for somebody who was going to have a few more, so he wanted to get on my good side.

"Not sure yet. Trying to track down somebody who was from here. Guy named Mikov, Ben Mikov, ever hear of him?"

He shook his head as he put the glass down in front of me.

"Never heard of no Mikovs. A lot of fucking weird names around here, but not that one."

"You been here long?"

"All my life. My dad ran this place. First business in Freemansburg before him."

I took a sip and looked around. "So you should know."

"Well, don't know all that much about the whole town, just about the folks who come in here. Most live up on the hill, in the newer neighborhoods around where the school is, and I'm not too tight with them, 'cept the ones I went to school with."

I finished the drink. He was right about me, because I immediately ordered another one. A professional knows his audience.

"Any old-timers who live around here? The person I'm looking for would be in his seventies now, so I need to talk to people who go way back like you."

He poured me another Jack. "We got no shortage of old-timers, but not all of 'em are actually from around here. Although God knows why else they'd end up here. I got some thoughts, but…well, you got a minute? I can go in the house and ask the wife and put some names of a few lifers on a list for you."

"I'd appreciate that."

He poured me my second drink and left. I toasted the dog and took care of it.

After leaving a hefty tip, more than the price of the Jacks, I left with a list of six elder residents. The bartender and his wife gave me the potentials – people who had grown up here and were still around. Most were on or around Main Street, old steelworker families that had worked long enough to own their homes and make their pensions, even though Bethlehem Steel had closed down their last furnace around twenty years ago.

So the dog and I walked around the neighborhood and knocked on the appropriate doors. People either didn't answer or weren't helpful. The dog snarling like Old Yeller after he got rabies didn't help. As I walked back the way we came, I only had one name left on the bartender's list. We turned right at the corner before the bar and walked up the hill that was Market Street, a steep bastard that curved up and around so that I actually ended up looking down on the bar. At least I couldn't smell it from up here. The house address was 48, on the right side and up some steps, and the place looked old enough to be haunted. I popped a Mentos in my mouth to hide the Jack afterglow and pulled Eydie up towards the front door.

"Be nice," I said to her. "You almost blew out the last guy's pacemaker."

I pressed on the doorbell, but heard nothing. It always irritated me if I couldn't tell if a doorbell was working or not, because that meant I had to knock to make sure, and that made me seem like an impatient asshole if the doorbell had already made some noise inside. But I knocked anyway. Besides, I *was* becoming an impatient asshole, roaming around what was left of this rotting town.

"COMING!" yelled a pissy old lady voice.

The bartender had specifically warned me about Mrs. Michaels. She had moved back to Freemansburg about eight years ago, after her husband had died. She had left here all sweetness and light when she was in her twenties, now she was surly and didn't leave the house much -- and when she did, everyone she encountered secretly wished she hadn't. She was said to be unpleasant and abrupt. Those weren't the exact words the bartender used, his were a lot more colorful and wouldn't be appreciated by the National Organization for Women.

She opened the door and Eydie started barking and lunging for her.

"Shush!" she said with such murderous precision that the fucking dog actually stopped barking. I needed to take this woman home with me.

Mrs. Michaels was in her seventies, wearing a surprisingly stylish housecoat and matching slippers. As I was expecting the Wicked Witch of the West, I had to admit she didn't look bad for her age. Her face was relatively unlined and she had amazing, long white hair that flowed down her back. She wasn't exactly sexy, but there was definitely more to her than a bad disposition.

"What do you want?" she demanded.

"I'm trying to track down someone who lived in this town a long time ago."

She looked at me a moment. People always want to size you up.

"It's too cold and I don't see you paying my gas bill, so come in. Leave the damn dog out."

"She won't like that. She's a rescue dog. She has abandonment issues."

She looked at the dog, she looked at me and she turned to go inside, muttering, "Don't we all…" I was hoping that meant we could both come in, so I pulled the dog into the house with me, shutting the door behind us.

The interior was not what I expected. Mrs. Michaels' living room looked like something out of a *Mad Men* episode, showing off the kind of well-preserved mid-century modern furniture 21st century decorators paid big bucks for. All very cool and clean -- she definitely wasn't the hoarder type. She also wasn't the warmest person in the world. She didn't invite me to sit down on one of her perfect designer chairs, nor did she say anything else designed to put me at ease. Instead, she just stood there, waiting for me to get whatever it was over with.

I was very glad I had lubricated myself with some Jack before this little get-together.

"Well, like I said, I'm looking for someone I think is from this town? His last name is Mikov."

She stared at me without saying a word.

"Ben Mikov," I continued.

"What makes you think I would know him?" she suddenly fired back.

The dog was pulling at me. Eydie wanted out. Dogs know shit.

"Nothing in particular. The bartender down on Main Street…"

"Billy Dallitz? He hardly knows me. That punk used to steal from his father right and left, would just go into the cash register and…"

"Okay, maybe let a guy talk?" My minor counter-attack shut her up. "Look, I just asked the bartender for the names of some older people around here, people who might have known Ben Mikov or his family from when they lived here. You were on the list, he didn't assume you knew anybody, okay?"

Ordinarily, I would have been out the door by now because this woman was way too much work. But my gut was telling me this was where I needed to be. She had reacted too strongly to the name and I needed to see what her next move was in whatever game we were playing.

"So I'm 'older?'" she said sharply.

"If it's any consolation, I'm closing in on your demographic."

She looked at the floor for a moment, then she sat down. She kept staring at the floor, like there was a mouse down there dancing the mashed potato.

"Why are you looking for this man?"

"Because he has the potential to make a lot of money."

That made her look up. "Did he win the Publisher's House Sweepstakes or something?"

"No, Mrs. Michaels. Ben Mikov used to draw comics, in particular a superhero by the name of Blue Fire. Now some people want to make a movie out of this character and they need him to sign off on it. And they'll pay him a lot for that signature."

She looked back down at the floor. I stayed standing, since she had yet to invite me to sit down.

"You know him, don't you?"

She stood up again without difficulty, she was pretty strong for her age. Then she cocked her head, basically inviting me to follow her as she approached a closed door off the living room. Eydie and I followed as she opened the door and led us in.

My fucking mouth dropped to the floor.

What had been a dining room was now an art gallery – featuring framed original works that were obviously done by Mikov. They were nightmarish paintings, paintings that seemed to be fueled by extreme mental anguish, paintings by someone who had to get his punishing visions out of his head and onto a canvas. There were brains opening up to reveal ghoulish monsters, men screaming and fleeing nebulous, terrifying apparitions, and…a huge wall-length painting of Blue Fire.

But not the Blue Fire from the comics. This was an older Blue Fire, a superhero on his knees reaching up to the skies for…what? Redemption? Forgiveness? Just an answer or two? I couldn't tell, but I couldn't stop staring at it.

Mikov had done this. Mikov had done more. And only I knew about it.

Meanwhile, Mrs. Michaels couldn't stop staring at me. She saw how deeply I was affected by what I was seeing.

"You know his work. You're not just some hired lost-and-found department."

I shook my head slowly. "I was a big fan when I was a kid." I turned back to her. "How do you know him?"

"I'm his sister, Debra."

I looked at her and then I saw the family resemblance. There was only one decent photo of Mikov, a picture taken without his consent at the Mighty Mel offices during a moment when he was hovering in the background looking over a finished copy of Blue Fire. He was either warned or sensed the picture was being taken, because he looked up just as the pic was snapped, the camera capturing a disturbed and surprised expression. He and his sister shared the same nose -- a pointed, Spartan kind of nose that couldn't help but make itself known.

"Do you know where your brother is?"

"Yes," she said softly, "Yes, I do."

She started moving and Eydie growled, straining at the leash to make a lunge at her. I held her back as Debra, not giving the dog a second glance, walked over to a small table on which sat a small urn.

Oh.

"His ashes," I guessed.

"He committed suicide a few years ago. He was in a lot of pain."

"He was sick?"

She looked at me sadly. "Just in the head."

Eydie had calmed down and now was napping on the floor next to the perfect midcentury chair that Debra allowed me to sit on. She offered tea and I readily agreed. Now she wanted me to stay and talk. Maybe it brought her brother back a little for her, maybe she thought he had been forgotten forever. She probably wasn't on Facebook reading all the posts about how brilliant he was. We sat on a pair of matching chrome and leather chairs in the living room.

"So…your original name is Mikov, not Michaels?"

"No, I was born with the name Michaels. So was Ben. When our great-grandparents came over from the old country, they Americanized it. When Ben heard that had happened, he hated it and changed his name back to the original as soon as he was old enough. I could give a crap."

"And you never took your late husband's name?"

"I took my old name back after he died. We never had children, so why not? Are you finished with your questions now?"

I was starting to wear out my tentative welcome.

"Well, I just wanted to say that there are a lot of comic fans out there who would love to talk to you about your brother. It might keep his work alive."

"I have no idea if people remember or care about my brother, Mr. Bowman. And to tell you the truth, it would be too painful for me to participate in any of that kind of nonsense. It still hurts everyday what happened to Ben."

"What *did* happen to Ben? Why was he such a mystery man?"

"He was just a very private individual."

"Well, there's a difference between being private and being desperate to avoid any exposure whatsoever."

She looked away. I had pushed her too far.

"Did he leave a family behind? Wife, kids?"

She shook her head, still not looking at me.

"So, I'm assuming you're the next of kin? Are there any other siblings?"

"Just me."

She turned back to me. There was something ferocious in her eyes.

"Well, Debra, then it's your lucky day. You sign off on the movie…and you get the giant check."

She shook her head. "I don't want it."

"Why? Your brother's work…"

She interrupted me. "My brother's work will be raped and mutilated. You know what the movie people will do to it. And you probably know how protective my brother was of his art. He wouldn't allow anyone to change anything without his consent. Well, now he's not here to consent to anything and I'm not going to speak for him. I have enough from my late husband to live on and…that's enough."

"Yes, but…"

She interrupted. "I also ask that you not disclose my name or location to anyone else," she went on. I want my privacy. I shouldn't have told you anything. I was just shocked anybody had tracked me down after all this time."

"Debra, I'll be honest with you. Mel Chesler hired me and…"

"Mel Chesler's still alive?"

"Yes, ma'am, he…"

"My brother's ashes in that urn and that miserable insect is still alive?"

Her temperature was rapidly rising.

"I could make a call. Maybe he never woke up this morning."

"My brother hated that bastard. HATED him. He should burn in hell. I think I really need you to go, Mr. Bowman, revisiting all this just upsets me."

I knew this visit was over five minutes ago, but I sipped my tea, stalling for time. There was still a lot I wondered about, things I wanted to know for myself, not for Mel, like what Mikov had been doing all the years after he stopped drawing comics, why he was in such pain, and why had none of his other work ever gotten released.

From the artwork she had on the wall, he had obviously continued to create – so why was everything kept so secret?

"Mr. Bowman?" she asked as she stood up. "Did you hear me? I need you to go." She paused and softened. "I'm truly sorry…"

I could see she was sorry. She had no anger towards me, but the rest of the world wasn't getting off the hook. I stood up and pulled on Eydie's leash to wake her up from her nap on the floor.

"I get it," I said, "We all have our histories that we don't particularly care to relive."

She gave me a closer look. "Your eyes are sensitive. You could have been an artist."

"You making a pass at me?"

She actually laughed. "Maybe in another life."

"Can I ask one more question?"

She shrugged and nodded at the same time. I wasn't sure I should ask this, but I had to throw it out there to see what happened.

"What's the connection to the CIA?"

The anger returned in a flash. I had taken a stab in the dark and I had hit a motherlode of pain.

"Who are you?" she demanded.

"I'm just trying to…"

"Get the hell out."

"Look, I don't…"

"GET THE HELL OUT."

I got the hell out.

Becky Parks

Driving home, the drug came back at me.

First I felt agitated. Then I started sweating. Then I saw the colors. It was a different experience than before, because I knew what it was and it wasn't as strong -- so this time, I managed to keep a lid on the madness. I figured some of the drug must have lingered in my system, and the flashback didn't last very long. I just focused on the road and kept going. Hopefully, I wouldn't have many more of these spells.

Maybe it was just the reintroduction of CIA weirdness that had jolted the drug's remnants into action. Again, I had to ask myself -- and I did, over and over again -- what the hell connection did Ben and the CIA have? Why was it so difficult to find any information about the man? If he was some kind of spook, he was the most talented spook imaginable. His sister clearly knew *something*, but just as clearly, she wasn't going to tell me.

I stopped back at the bar on the way out to ask Billy the Bartender a few more questions. Did he remember Debra's brother, Ben? He thought a moment. "Oh yeah, there was a brother."

Was?

The bartender didn't know much, except the kid was shipped out when he was around thirteen to live somewhere else. Never saw him back in Freemansburg again.

Why does a kid leave home at thirteen and never return? Who knew? Not this guy. As for Debra, as the bartender had already told me, she got married in her twenties, left town and didn't come back even to visit until she moved back as an old woman. What happened to the parents? The dad had worked at Bethlehem Steel, got laid off and found work elsewhere, out of town. They had bolted not too long after their daughter and also had never returned.

Freemansburg told me a lot, and told me nothing at the same time.

And now the drug was actually still making me feel crazy, so I quit thinking, tried to ignore the swirling colors and turned up the satellite radio. I had it on the sixties station and they were playing *Hats Off to Larry*. This was the song that Del Shannon put out after the success of his *Runaway* single and he should have been ashamed of himself, not least of all because no song should ever have the name "Larry" in its title. I switched over to the Sinatra station, which was playing Frank's version of *Don't Sleep in the Subway*. Somedays, you can't win or hear a decent tune. I decided to join the living and hit the button for the hip-hop station, where somebody was rapping about strippers and where they kept their money. Progress was an illusion.

The colors faded and I made it back to the island in one piece. I got home after dark and fed the dog, who was plenty hungry. Then I finished off a frozen pizza I had started the other night and went into the office. Eydie came in right after me, of course, and plopped herself down in her little bed on the floor. I sat down, put away my David Muhlfelder fake identity kit, took my iPhone out of the desk drawer and booted it up. Then I steeled myself for that night's unpleasant task -- reviewing the over one hundred voicemails that had been left on the landline after the tram incident.

As I went through the voicemails, I discovered that almost all of them were media outlets wanting to interview me about the viral tram video, wanting to know why I decided to lose my mind at two hundred fifty feet above the East River. The only exceptions were two calls from potential clients who had seen the tram video and were now going to look elsewhere for detective help, fuck you very much. Those couple of brush-offs made me feel I had to take action fast to save what reputation I had. Luckily, as I deleted one voicemail after another, I had my first useful thought of the day.

I called Todd on the iPhone. I knew it was after work hours, but I also knew he never quit working.

"Max?" He sounded very unToddlike, low energy. "I tried to call you today, you didn't pick up, bud. You're staying away from the wacky sauce, right?"

"Yeah, I was working on a case today," I answered.

"Look, I'm getting more worried about the book deal, nobody will take my call and I…"

I interrupted. "Listen, you must know a publicist or two in your line, right?"

"I know 'em and I've fucked 'em, baby!" His energy was back in a flash and I regretted it in a flash.

"Good for you, Todd, listen, what do you think about hooking me up with one of them? I've gotten all these calls from reporters, but I was thinking if I did just *one* media interview, one that had a lot of juice, I could explain I got drugged and that's why I acted out. People could see I'm fine and…"

"Jesus, Max, that's it, bud, that's genius! I bet that would save the book deal too!" Suddenly, he was angry. "Why the *fuck* did I not think of this?"

There was a pause. I think he was actually attempting some soul-searching. The effort was short-lived.

"Listen," he came back at me, "first thing tomorrow I'll put you in touch with the best publicist in New York, her name's Becky Parks, she's amazing, she'll know just how to handle this."

"Great, give her this number."

"You'll have to pay her, you know."

"I'm aware, Todd."

"Live long and prosper, dude!"

He hung up and I got rid of the rest of the landline voicemails. Then I checked out the remaining iPhone messages -- the ones that weren't from Todd. They were all from Jules.

Maybe she was ready to forgive and forget. Or maybe just the latter and not the former.

I called her and lead with, "Hi."

"Fuck you, you ballsack on legs, I can't talk, I'm rehearsing!" she shot back.

"Okay…so why did you answer the phone?"

"Because I at least wanted to make sure you were okay. I was afraid you might have another psychotic episode and maybe think Eydie was a fucking roast turkey and eat her."

"So you do care."

"Yeah, about the dog. You didn't give me the nicest fucking send-off the other day, you know."

"Did you notice I was out of my mind?"

"That's when people tell the truth, Max. When they're out of their minds. I have to go rehearse."

"Wait…let's get together and talk…"

I was interrupted by music coming from her end, a small jazz combo in the background counting off and starting up a song. A song I thought I recognized. "Wait, what song is that?"

"Max, hop off my tits, I'm not going to run down the act for you, we're opening Saturday night. *I have to go.*"

But she wasn't hanging up, which was her usual move. So maybe I had an opening. I listened to the music a little longer while I figured out what to do with that opening. Then, to my horror, I figured out what tune was being played.

'That can't be…"

"Max, don't start…"

Oh no. Oh no. It wasn't…

"…*Little Latin Lupe Lu???*"

"I have to go!" She was flustered. Little Latin Lupe Lu was a minor hit for the Righteous Brothers back in the early 60's. My oldest brother had the 45 single and I detested the tune from the get-go. Now I knew why she wasn't hanging up. This was a cry for help -- a desperate plea for the taste police to crash the scene of this crime and bust some heads.

"You are going to sing *that* shit song? Is this the Cuban's idea? It can't be, no self-respecting Cuban would ever play that shit song!"

She whispered, "Max, stop."

I couldn't make fun of *Little Latin Lupe Lu?* This wasn't like her. In the old days, if we ever saw anyone daring to sing *Little Latin Lupe Lu,* we wouldn't have stopped making fun of the person until the apocalypse came. And even after that, depending on circumstances.

But she still was on the line. She still wanted to talk. I was beginning to think she wanted back with me as much as I wanted back with her.

"Okay, Jules, I'm stopping. I'm assuming you're in a musical hostage situation. But, look, I…I gotta thank you for looking after me the other day. You probably saved my life. Or at least kept me out of the bughouse."

"Fine, thanks for the thank you, now *I have to go back and rehearse…*"

"Jules…come on. You want to talk. Otherwise, you would've hung up five minutes ago."

She was quiet a moment. Unfortunately, I still had *Little Latin Lupe Lu* for hold music.

"Max, I can't do this, not until we open," she finally said quietly. "This is my chance, you know how important this is to me and I can't fuck this up."

"Well…I don't want to fuck us up."

"I've got a delicate balance going, Maxie. I think I finally got my med mix right."

"Now it's my turn. Look…"

I heard angry band members murmuring in the background, giving her shit.

"I…I gotta fucking go," she said with a voice that was cracking with sadness and this time, she hung up.

But, for the first time, I saw some light at the end of the tunnel. Unless that was just daylight coming in through the cracks in my brain.

The next morning, Thursday morning, after I shit and pissed the dog, I took a shit myself -- with the dog watching as usual. I supposed it was fair, I got to watch her take a dump, so she got to watch me. I just never expected to be part of that kind of arrangement.

I put on a nice shirt, a white one that buttoned and everything, and my best black jeans, because I needed to go back into the city yet again. Becky Parks had called me bright and early and suggested I come in to talk, she had an opening at 11. I figured I'd go in to see her, then come back and work more on the Mikov case. Becky's office was up near Gracie Mansion, where the mayor bunked down, so I'd have to take the F to Lexington, then transfer to the 4 or 5 train and take it to 86th.

I was going to the Upper East Side, where the zombies were.

Her offices were in a small commercial building right on 86th near First, a couple floors above a florist. I pushed open the glass doors that had "Becky Parks Communications" emblazoned on them and walked up to the reception desk. The girl behind the desk was cute because she had to be.

"Can I help you?"

"Max Bowman and I can't believe I ended up here."

"What's wrong with here?"

"I'm not the publicity-seeking type. I'm more the stay-at-home-and-hide kind of guy."

She smiled and didn't seem like a zombie at all. "Are you here to see Becky?"

I looked around and saw hers was the only office, besides a small conference room, so I asked back, "Who else is there?"

She laughed and then looked behind her as if she was afraid somebody would see her laugh. That somebody would of course be Becky, who was, in fact, coming out of her office with a big beaming fake bullshit smile. Becky was early forties, long teased blonde hair, wearing an expensive pantsuit. She had beady little eyes that seemed desperate to give the illusion of a wonderful personality and, overall, she very much resembled the spokeswoman who used to lie about oil and natural gas on those informative commercials funded by the fossil fuel industry.

"Max Bowman, come on in," she said and waved me into her office.

I walked in and she closed the door behind me. The walls were filled with autographed pictures of stars -- Howie Mandel, Patrick Duffy,

Tipper Gore and a few others who weren't near the A-list but had drifted in and out of the zeitgeist over the years -- giving the room the overall feel of an upscale dry cleaners' office. She sat down behind her desk and asked me if I'd like something to drink. I asked if she had Coke Zero on hand and she wondered if a Diet Coke would be okay. It would be. She buzzed Denise, that was the cute receptionist's name, and asked her to get me the soda.

"Sit down," she said and I did. "Todd tells me you need a little help."

"Definitely. I'm assuming you already know who I am…"

"The Dark Sky thing, very impressive."

"And I'm assuming you saw what happened the other day…"

"The tram incident." Her face grew somber and bullshit sympathetic. "Yes."

"Well, that's what I need a little help with. I've gotten about a billion calls from the media and my thought was to set up just one interview…"

"Just one." She nodded.

"…but one that would reach a lot of people."

She started making notes with a beautiful shiny pen on a new yellow legal pad.

"Have you done any media interviews before?"

"I had a sit down with Matt Lauer last year. He has even less hair in person."

She looked at me blankly, slowly realized I was joking and then pretended to laugh.

"I also testified in front of Congress last year, if you saw that extravaganza. Thanks to Senator Marks, wherever he is."

"Oh yes," her voice lowered with bullshit concern. "That is such a sad situation, I hope they find him. I hear the governor's appointing a replacement today." She made a couple notes while she shifted mental gears, finally looking up at me and taking a moment to ask the difficult question. "Can I ask what happened on the tram? Between me and you, this…doesn't have to go anywhere else."

"I don't have anything to hide, Becky. What happened was I had lunch with a couple of young women about a case I'm working with. One of them dropped some kind of drug, something like LSD I'm guessing, in my drink when I went to the bathroom. My head wasn't in the best place and I got paranoid and crazy. When I got on the tram to go back home, I thought people were going to attack me, so I attacked them first."

She made some more furious notes. "Why did the woman spike your drink?" she asked as she wrote.

"I think she wanted to take advantage of me."

She looked up and laughed.

"I'm not joking."

She stopped laughing.

"Trust me, I didn't believe it either at first. But apparently I have a groupie."

"Okay, you might not want to mention that part. Do you have any proof you were under the influence of this drug when you were on the tram? Did you go to a doctor or anyone and get a diagnosis?"

"No, but a good friend was with me. She knows what I'm usually like and she could vouch that something was wrong with me."

"And there are no other incidents like this on the record."

"No, and none off the record either."

She smiled at me, like that made her happy.

"Wow, so you really got taken by surprise. Now…is anyone pressing charges against you because of what happened? Assault maybe?"

"Not to my knowledge. I didn't really hurt anyone, just shook 'em up a little."

She scribbled on the tablet again. "Well, I'll check with the NYPD to make sure, I have connections there."

"Somebody like you has connections everywhere, right?"

She shrugged with an "I'm special but I don't talk about it" kind of expression.

"Max, I like your plan and I'm thinking you need an interview with a very credible person. Someone on a CNN, perhaps, you don't want to turn left at MSNBC or right at Fox, we want right down the middle and primetime if we can get it. Not that it matters, the interview clip will get around on social media, we'll make sure about that, people are intrigued by you."

Denise came in with my Diet Coke -- a glass with ice, nice -- and then exited.

"So you handle that too? The social media stuff?"

"Of course, Mr. Bowman! But we need to act fast, while the video is still top-of-mind. When did the incident happen?"

"Monday."

"We're already a little late for a response, but this was a heavily viral clip, we should be okay. Are you available the in next few days? Ideally, I'd like to make this happen tomorrow."

"I'm here."

"Great. Now, what I'll want you to do is rehearse the story of what happened to you. Talk it out when you're at home puttering around…"

"I don't really putter, but I'll figure it out."

"…and when you think you have it down, you call me and you repeat it to me. I'll point out any trouble spots."

"Well, it is what it is…"

"Yes, but there are ways to make what it is better than what it is."

I tried to wrap my head around that.

"You'll want to wear something nice for the interview…still casual, but…well, better than what you have on now, for example."

So much for my nice white buttoned shirt.

"But, again, I think the single interview is perfect for your situation. They'll say it's an exclusive and make it look like they engineered the interview, not you, so they look good and you won't look like you're trying too hard. You just need to show you're perfectly all right. We'll review the impact of the interview after you do it and we can discuss anything else that might need to be done then."

"Well…this is all I intend to do."

She gave me that smile again, the happy bullshit one. "Well, we'll see. There's a lot we can do with you, Max Bowman!"

Put my name on a blimp? Put my face on the side of a bus? Put somebody in a Max Bowman costume in Times Square and have them take pictures with tourists? The mind boggled, but I wanted to get home and back to work. So I gently worked my way out of her office and she asked me to leave all my contact info with Denise the receptionist. As soon as I left her office, she picked up the phone to start working on my behalf.

As I was spelling out my email address to Denise, I asked her the big question.

"See any zombies lately?"

Denise froze. "That's not funny."

"You mean there's something to it?"

She nodded emphatically to herself as she continued typing on her desktop. "You bet there is. My friend was almost attacked the other night. She got away. Luckily, these are the slow kind of zombies."

"Are you messing with me?"

"Do I look like I'm messing with you?" She didn't. "I try to get out of here every afternoon before it gets dark, I mean, I cannot wait for Daylight Savings Time. They only come out at night, you know."

"Like a zombie should. So why isn't there anything about this on the news?"

"Because they don't want a panic! The mayor only lives a few blocks away, you know, they've beefed up Gracie Mansion with extra security."

"You know this for a fact."

"Becky's pretty plugged in." Denise shot a glance at Becky's office, where Becky was sitting behind her desk, continuing her phone conversation and simultaneously looking at us, wondering what we were talking about with our very low voices. Denise looked frightened for her life and turned back to me with a colder and more professional demeanor.

"I've got all your information, Mr. Bowman," she quickly said in a higher, louder voice. "Thanks very much."

I straightened up and gave Becky one last look and she gave me one last bullshit smile and a wave. I waved back. I didn't know much about Becky Parks, but it certainly seemed like it was much better to be her client than her employee. As I was in the elevator going down, I realized Becky hadn't talked money, but I supposed it was like going to an expensive restaurant and seeing that the menu didn't list any prices for the dishes.

If you had to ask, you shouldn't be in there.

Rape

Bing.

Thursday afternoon. When I got back home from Becky Parks' Bullshit Emporium, I did some more research. I couldn't turn up any death records for a Benjamin or Ben Michaels that would have matched up with Ben Mikov's profile - or any news reports of a suicide for either name. I had to have some proof of Mikov's death for Mighty Mel, but I was still hitting dead end after dead end.

Bing.

Now, I was out walking the dog past what was left of the lighthouse at the north end of the island. The rubble was still roped off, while the various authorities argued about whether to rebuild the historical landmark or demolish it. This was the place where I usually let Eydie run a little, in the trees where the killers had stalked me last year. Even though the sign said she was supposed to be on a leash at all times, I knew there were times when a dog had to be a dog, and there was nothing the mutt loved better than running from tree to tree trying to eat squirrels.

Bing.

But now my iPhone was making a noise. I unhooked Eydie's leash so she could run through the park ahead of me and hunt her prey. Freed for the moment of dealing with her, I pulled out the phone and saw that I had another Facebook message from Bruce Canun, Ben Mikov authority.

Did you find anything?

I didn't know anything about this guy and I didn't want to tell him anything. So I played vague.

> *Nothing leading anywhere*

I watched Eydie run down a squirrel, I watched the squirrel run up the tree, I watched Eydie jump up the side of the tree after the squirrel with unbridled joy in her eyes. She really thought she could climb trees, just like I really thought I could figure out this case.

Bing.

I looked at the phone again.

> *Attached is something that has made the rounds over the years. We all think it looks like Mikov's, but obv we can't post on Facebook. Very NSFW.*

I downloaded the file he had sent along with the message.

Holy shit.

He wasn't kidding about the NSFW warning. I was looking at a crudely-scanned piece of artwork from some kind of publication that was decades-old -- maybe an underground comic from the 70's.

The piece of art was a very explicit gay comic.

Penises were flying everywhere into all sorts of openings. And, yes, it was clearly Mikov's work. I stared at it in disbelief for what felt like hours, amazed that this had been dropped in my virtual lap. The only thing that snapped me out of it was the sound of barking.

Savage barking.

I looked up. Eydie was closing in on a small shih tzu being walked by its owner on the other side of the park. Holy shit.

I ran as fast as I could, which wasn't fast at all.

Eydie ran up close to the terrified dog's face and barked, snarled and growled two inches from its nose, while the owner screamed.

And even though this had happened a hundred times before with Eydie, even though she never actually bit or attacked another dog beyond the growling and barking, even though I knew she was a complete coward in her heart of hearts and she just tried to scare off things she was threatened by, even though I knew all that, terror once again filled my heart and sweat poured from my forehead.

Huffing and puffing, I actually dove towards Eydie, grabbed her and rolled on the ground, holding her close to me.

I came to a stop, lying flat on the ground on my back, holding fast to the fucking dog who, for once, was looking at me like I was the crazy one. The shih tzu's owner, a middle-aged woman who was ready to ream me out before I tackled my own dog, now stared open-eyed at me.

I looked up at her with what I thought was a reassuring smile. "She doesn't actually bite anybody," I said, still panting from all the effort. "She's a rescue."

She immediately walked on with her dog at a slow gallop.

I struggled to get to my feet, holding tightly to Eydie's leash. I was shaking and I had grass and dirty snow all over my coat.

I was losing my mind.

I had calmed down again by the time I got back to the apartment, where I downloaded the file Bruce had sent me and printed out the pages. There were about ten in all.

Mikov. Gay porn comics. I hadn't seen that coming.

What plot there was involved a mad therapist named Dr. Kanuskey giving electroshock treatments to a guy to make him stop being gay.

The guy would scream in agony -- but while he shrieked, he fantasized extensively and in great detail about having sex with many different men. Great, great detail. The detail was in fact astonishing. So much detail. There were many acts illustrated in breathtaking strokes -- and sucks and thrusts, for that matter. I wasn't into man-play, but I couldn't see how any of this could be arousing, because Mikov's visions were so dark and disturbing.

And, in this case, really messy.

The title of the story was *Gay No More Again* and it was actually pretty funny in its own very twisted way, if you could look past the penises to the jokes.

And to another big clue.

Dr. Kanuskey. Another insane evil therapist. Like Blue Fire's arch-enemy, Dr. K. And, gee, what letter did Kanuskey start with?

Once again, PMA had been on to something.

I went to work on my online search sites. Luckily for me, Kanuskey wasn't a very common name -- as matter of fact, I could only locate a handful in the entire United States. And the most promising lead of the group was definitely Dr. Frederick Kanuskey, a psychologist who practiced in Astoria, right across the river from me on the Queens side, during the 1950's and 1960's. The problem was he had passed away in the early 80's. So he wasn't available to tell me anything.

But I found a nurse who was.

After some more searching, I discovered Sandra Bennett's name in an ancient medical directory that had been scanned and posted online. She was listed as being Kanuskey's primary assistant at his office at the time, so I did a little more digging around and discovered she was still alive and still in Astoria, in a nursing home in the northern section of the neighborhood.

I felt like I was getting somewhere.

Just then, my doorbell rang. Eydie barked and ran up the stairs as she always did to greet visitors. I closed the browser and headed up to the door. There was a face waiting behind it that I very much didn't want to see.

"Hiya, Super Dick."

"Whatever you're selling today, I ain't buying," I said to Veronica, aka Janine, the woman who had completely fucked up my head. She was wearing loose sweatpants and a baggy sweatshirt under her winter coat, so she didn't appear to be selling anything this time around. I stood between her and the dog, who was jumping and snarling. One little sidestep and Veronica would be running down the hallway for dear life -- and I would make that move depending on what she said next.

"Look, can I come in?" she said flatly. "I came over here because what I gave you was serious, I just found out how serious and we should really talk."

"We can talk here in the doorway," I said.

"C'mon, Max, you afraid of a girl?"

"You, yes."

She lowered her face and raised her eyes to create a waif-like impression. I sighed, picked up the dog and let her in, then I followed her down the stairs.

"Make a left," I said when she reached the bottom of the stairs. "Then another left." That took us into the living room, where she sat down on the couch. I put Eydie in the office and closed the door, then I returned to the living room, where I remained standing. I didn't know how to play this yet.

"You know, I kind of feel threatened by you, standing there like that," she said, looking up at me.

"Gee, I feel bad about that," I said. "I also feel bad that everyone in the world thinks I'm a lunatic."

"Look, I'm sorry, Candy's pissed off at me, Mel's pissed off at me. I don't know what to do. That shit fucked me up too, I had just taken it before I slipped it to you, I didn't know it was bad shit, it just hit the street. I've been wigging out too, y'know?"

"Who'd you get it from?"

"A guy who knows a guy." She frowned and looked out the window at the Queensboro Bridge. "You got a nice view here."

"Yeah, I got a view."

She kept looking out the window, then she turned to me and I saw tears in her eyes.

Oh, hell.

"Look, I screwed up, I really thought you were a cool guy, I've read all about you…I thought we could have some fun. But I always screw everything up. Mel doesn't even want me in the office anymore."

She took a tissue out of her battered blue leather hipster bag and blew her nose. I finally sat down in a chair at the far end of the couch, away from her. I wanted to keep my distance and not send out any signals.

"So why are you here?" I asked in as kindly a manner as possible.

"I don't know, man. I just…wanted to make amends somehow, and I'm not good at that shit."

"How'd you get my address?"

"It was on the bank account info you sent Mel. I got Candy to give it to me."

"You're as old as my daughters. Even a couple years younger. I don't know what you were expecting."

"Just…forgiveness, maybe. And maybe you could put in a word with Mel for me." She gave me a hopeful look as she wiped her eyes.

"This is only the second time I've met you. I don't know if I'm the guy to give you a ringing endorsement."

I put my head back. Something was coming on again. It was the stress. Veronica brought stress back into my life and that seemed to trigger whatever drugs were left in my bloodstream.

"You're getting another flashback, right? The colors, the tingling…"

"I'm okay."

"Let me get you something to drink…that shit makes your throat dry."

She had that right, so I didn't protest when she got up and hurried to the kitchen. But I did protect myself. "Just bring me a bottle of Coke Zero from the fridge," I yelled after her. "And let *me* open it."

"You don't trust me?" she yelled back as I heard her opening the fridge.

"Not for a second."

"C'mon, Max. I left my knives at home."

"You have knives?"

"Yeah, and swords. I'm a killer, Max."

For some reason, I didn't think she was kidding.

"Where are the bottles?" she finally asked.

"What, are you blind? There's four or five of them right there on the bottom shelf."

"Oh yeah…"

She came walking back in, proudly holding the bottle in front of her – and then she twisted off the cap with a flourish, so I could see it had been unviolated.

"Now do you trust me?"

"No," I answered, "but I do trust the bottle."

I took the cap off the rest of the way and took a big swig. She looked at me happily and quietly clapped her hands together.

"Yay! I gave Max a beverage!"

"You'll get a medal later." I took another long drink and tried to shake off the colors. "First, if you want to make amends, answer a couple of questions for me."

"Shoot."

"Who wants to make this *Blue Fire* movie? Do you know?"

"All I know is they've never made a movie before, but they have a lot of money. They put a million in escrow for a deposit on the rights from Mel."

"Rich amateurs. You got a name?"

"Nope."

"Okay, then let's go back to the guy who knows a guy and gave you the bad shit. Tell me a little more about him."

"Not much to tell. He's just a street dealer."

"He know anything about me?"

"No. Wow, are you paranoid or what?"

"I've got a few things to be paranoid about, trust me. So you can't tell me anything else about this guy."

"Alls I can do is go back and talk to the guy who knows the guy. Other than that…"

I closed my eyes and leaned my head back again. Inside the office, I heard Eydie start whining and yelping. I wondered what took her so long.

"Look," I said, eyes still closed, "You should go. I gotta feed the dog and do some work."

"So soon?"

I opened my eyes because it was time to get rid of this menace once and for all. But she obviously had other plans, as she was pulling her baggy sweatshirt up over her head to reveal the extremely low-cut t-shirt top she had on underneath it. Apparently, it was important for me to know she had impressive breasts. One of them had four Asian characters tattooed on it in a vertical line. Japanese? Chinese? Like I knew?

"What's that say?"

"Japanese for 'Samurai."

"Samurai. So you weren't kidding about the swords?"

"Oh no, I like swords. As a matter of fact, I wanna see yours. Wanna do something?" she said with a slightly satanic smile. We were back to that.

"You must have real daddy issues."

"Of course I do. And you have kid issues. Like I said at the restaurant, we're a perfect fit."

"I dumped my kids' mother and she poisoned them against me. That's all there is to it. It's not like I mistreated them or ignored them. They just decided I was a piece of shit."

"Well, my daddy thought I was a piece of shit. Your kids were wrong, my dear old daddy was wrong, so let's look for love in all the wrong places."

"There couldn't be any wronger place and I think you should go."

I got up -- apparently, too quickly. Because I was struck by an immediate dizziness so severe, I fell back in the chair.

"You don't look good, Super Dick."

I had a very bad feeling as everything swirled and twirled around my head. "How did you do it?" I finally whispered.

"It was easy, Super Dick," she laughed. "When I was pretending I couldn't find the bottle of Coke Zero in the kitchen, I was really stalling for time while I opened it up and put in the shit. Then I screwed the cap back on and brought it out to you."

"And you opened it in front of me, so I wouldn't know the seal was already broken."

I felt like I was going to fall out of the chair, that's how hard the vertigo was hitting me. I shut my eyes again and heard her approach.

"Now, I'm not going to hurt you, Super Dick. But I'm also not going to be denied." She helped me out of the chair and led me to the bedroom, and I was in no shape to resist.

"I don't think I'm going to be much good like this…" Eydie yelped as Veronica walked me past the closed office door. "And the dog…"

"Let's get you on the bed, Super Dick. You're going to need to be lying down…"

She had that right.

Soon, I was on the bed drifting in and out of consciousness. I heard phones ring, Eydie bark and I remember Veronica taking off her pants and her top. There were more Japanese characters tattooed here and there around her torso, and I quickly saw she could have used her own trip to the Bloomingdales lingerie department, because she was lacking underwear. It felt like I was either playing the lead in a bad porno or on a date with Bill Cosby -- whatever the case, I couldn't do much about it. I was unable to move and I could barely keep my eyes open without an enormous effort.

"Super Dick," I heard her whisper in my ear, "I'm going to take care of you and you're going to like the experience." Then she chewed on my neck and her hand went to my groin. She started rubbing and somehow, my Super Dick was responding.

"What all…was in…the Coke…" I asked as best as I could.

She put my hand on her breast, the one without the Japanese characters, and answered, "A few things. A little special cocktail…for your…"

"I get it," I said.

She pulled off my pants, she ripped apart my nice white shirt and I heard its buttons hitting the hardwood floor. Then she spread herself out on top of me and rubbed herself against me, all of her against all of me.

"Is this so bad, Max?" she asked as she kissed my limp lips. "Is it?" She laughed to herself. "How many guys your age get this kind of action?" More kissing. A tongue. "Too bad you didn't want to play, Super Dick. I know your kind. You have hidden reserves of passion, don't you?"

"Me…and your dad…" I said.

I could feel her anger rise and she grabbed my balls, and not in a nice way. I winced and groaned in pain and she thought that was pretty funny too.

"I forgive you, Super Dick." She rubbed my chest. "I forgive you…"

She started moaning. She was really getting into it. Her animal noises competed with the dog's. She kept grabbing parts of me and rubbing them against parts of her. Then she maneuvered herself to a sitting position on top of me and put her finger in my mouth, not deep enough for me to bite it, which I would've.

"It's time for us to bond, Max. It's part of the process…"

Process…?

"This could be the last time…the last time…so enjoy it."

The last time…?

Suddenly, I was inside her – not really by choice.

 "As a great man once wrote," she said, punctuated with various gasps and moans, "True beauty…is something that attacks…overpowers, robs, and finally…destroys…"

I'd have to look that one up.

Did she, in the words of the Rolling Stones, make a dead man come? I couldn't tell you. Somewhere in the middle, I either blacked out or lost all recall, because the next few hours went by in a kaleidoscopic blur, with more dog barks and phone rings and Veronica doing things to me that I couldn't make out. Then she was gone and I was left lying on the bed naked, still unable to move, wondering what had happened, what was now happening, if I was going to die from what she gave me -- and also what time it was, since the dog had to eat. But I couldn't get up to do anything about the desperate howls from behind my office door. The window darkened, then the window brightened up.

And then somebody was shaking me awake.

The Interview

It took a while for me to get to my feet.

PMA had showed up first thing in the morning, Friday morning, because he had been calling and texting without any response from me. Concerned for my welfare, he decided to skip his classes again and catch the first plane into La Guardia in the a.m. He arrived at my place, rang the bell and banged on the door, and then let himself in when nobody answered. Even though he had a key to the place, he didn't need it -- Veronica left the door unlocked whenever she finally finished with me.

He came down into the apartment to find me lying naked on the bed, except for my socks and whatever was left of my nice white shirt. He shook my shoulder, then my eyes half-opened and I saw in his eyes how much of a goddamn mess I looked like.

"Max? What the hell?"

I tried to focus.

"You okay? Max, are you okay, do I have to call somebody?"

I got my eyes the rest of the way open. "Is there a window open? There's a draft…" I croaked as I lifted my head off the pillow.

"No, it's because you don't have any pants on!"

"Yeah, that would explain why my balls are cold." My head went back down.

Meanwhile, the dog was barking up a storm. She had been stuck in my office all night without food or water or a bathroom break.

"Let the dog out…" I said to PMA as I tried to get under the covers.

I heard PMA walk down the hallway and open the door, then I heard Eydie's little claws click-clacking down the hallway until she was in the room and leaping right on top of my face. She licked it frantically and desperately, afraid of losing her keeper again.

"FUCK!" screamed PMA, still down the hall. "There's crap and pee all over the floor!"

He started to walk back towards the bedroom, but reconsidered when Eydie, standing up on the bed, threw a few unearthly growls at him.

"You gotta give her food and water," I said, getting up on one elbow, watching the world go in every direction at once. "Cans of food in the pantry. Open one, put it all in the food dish on the floor in the kitchen…and change the water in the other dish."

"Okay," he agreed unhappily and headed for the kitchen.

I stroked Eydie's head. "You okay, pup?" She licked me some more and I cracked, I started crying like a newborn. My emotions were totally out of whack, I could already tell, like I was a stroke victim who couldn't stop every emotion from leaking out when it hit. But a couple of minutes later, I got back my control, carefully got my feet down on the floor and sat up on the bed a minute.

I stood up and made my way to the bathroom, holding on to the walls as I struggled to walk that endless five feet. The dog followed me every inch of the way, acting like she was never going to let me out of her sight again. But, then again, that's how she always acted. I got in the bathroom and shut the door on her. When I came out, she was still there, so I struggled to get to the kitchen. PMA was standing there, shocked that I had made it that far.

"Max, what are you doing? Get back in bed, dude."

"Dog won't eat unless I'm in the kitchen."

PMA hurried to my bedroom to get my bathrobe, then ran right back, determined to get it on me. Apparently, he had seen enough of my ass for one morning. As he draped it around my shoulders, Eydie growled, jumped and nipped at his legs.

"Max, what the hell happened to you?"

I put my arms through the bathrobe sleeves and leaned against the kitchen wall. Eydie saw the food, saw I wasn't going anywhere and made a beeline to eat the dinner she should have had fifteen hours before.

"I was raped." I finally said.

"WHAT?"

"You heard me."

The landline rang.

"Can you get that?" I asked PMA. He ran to the office and ran back with the phone.

"Max, the office floor is disgusting," he said as he handed me the receiver.

"I hate to say this, but, clean it up, will you?"

"Yeah, sure," he said unhappily. He went for the bleach cleaner and the paper towels in the closet as I answered the phone.

"Max?"

It was Becky Parks.

"Max, where have you been? I've got you set up at CNN this afternoon for the interview, I've been trying to reach you since last night!" Her voice was urgent and borderline furious.

"I was…indisposed."

"Are you all right? You sound funny."

"I'm still a little indisposed…interview? This afternoon?"

She sighed as if she was dealing with an errant child. "At 3 at CNN. You know the studios at Columbus Circle?"

I paused. I knew I had to do this. I just had to figure out if I was capable of it.

"Yeah…yeah, I know them…who am I talking about?"

"Who are you talking about?"

"I mean who am I talking to…"

"I went for Blitzer and Anderson, but we would have had to wait too long for that to happen. It's more important to get you on TV ASAP…so you'll be on set with the afternoon anchorwoman. But they *assured* me the interview's going to play in heavy rotation all weekend…are you sure you're okay?"

"What time is it?"

"About 10:30. Max, I can cancel this…"

"No, no. I had a late night…is all. I'll be all right."

Pause.

"Okay. If anything changes, *please* let me know as quickly as you can. And definitely wear something nicer than you wore with Matt Lauer, I watched that interview this morning. Also, I wanted you to go through your story with me, talk it out with me, before the interview."

"Give me some time, Becky, give me some time."

"I'm only doing this to help you, Max."

I thanked her, hung up and slumped back against the kitchen wall. PMA returned, gingerly clutching some very nasty paper towels filled with pee and poo.

"I'm gonna take these out of here and throw them down the garbage chute."

"Not a bad idea."

After he left, I managed to get a Coke Zero out of the fridge. Before I took a drink, I checked the cap about forty times to make sure it hadn't already been unsealed.

I needed to keep moving, I felt like it was the best thing for me. So I got dressed and took Eydie down to do her business, in case it hadn't all been done already in the office. Turned out it hadn't been. The air in the courtyard felt cold and good and I took in a few deep breaths to continue clearing my head.

When I got back, I sat down in the living room with PMA and told him everything that had happened. He was speechless.

"What did she give you?" he finally said.

"I think what she gave me last time, along with something to keep me down and something to keep me up."

"Down and up?"

I nodded. "Down on the bed and up in the…"

"I got it," he quickly said. "You were raped. You were actually raped."

And then he started laughing. And laughing and laughing. I tried to tell him that wasn't very politically correct, but nobody takes woman-on-man rape seriously. God knows I wouldn't.

"I need to do an interview on CNN this afternoon," I said. "You need to come with me."

That made him stop laughing.

"Max, there's no way, look at you."

"And we have to stop at Bloomingdale's on the way. Because I need to look nice."

"Max, you're not listening to me."

"Non-negotiable. I have to get on top of this situation before it gets worse."

I got to my feet. I didn't fall over. That was an accomplishment.

"Wait, aren't you going to call the cops on her? You can't just let this psycho get away with this."

"Yeah. I'm going to call the cops. And then they're going to laugh even harder than you did." I hobbled out of the room with Eydie at my heels. "But I am calling somebody."

Mighty Mel answered his own phone.

"Hello?"

"Mel? Max. Your grandniece did some damage to me."

"Who?"

"Janine. Dark hair, Japanese characters on her right breast."

"Japanese what on her what what? Who the hell are you talking about? I don't know any girl like that, thank God."

"I was afraid you'd say that."

"Well, who told you I did?"

"Candy. Your other grandniece."

"Candy? Grandniece? Who's telling you this bullshit, Candy's not related to me."

"Yeah, I thought that was coming next. But she said you'd say that…"

"That she was my fucking niece? Max, you're not hearing me. She's not related to me. Look, I got rid of her after what happened to you, so why am I lying?"

"Well," I said feebly, "Somebody is."

"It ain't me, bubby. I hardly knew her. She came in here one day a few weeks ago wanting to be an unpaid intern to get some working experience. The salary was right, she was a college grad, so I said, okay, she could come in a couple times a week and cover for me if she wanted. That's how much I knew her. She did a good job, but if she can't control her weirdo friends…"

"They told me a completely different story, Mel."

"Fucking kids today, right? Anyway, forget about them. Find me Mikov. The producers are setting up a Blue Fire booth at the Jersey Comic Con in a few weeks and we need things settled by then. So I'm hoping you'll tell me you got somewhere on this."

"I've got some leads."

"Good. Keep on 'em, because I paid you a shitload of money to. Anything else?"

"Yeah, Candy said she told you to hire me. That true?"

"Yeah, that's true. I didn't know anything about you or what happened with that Black Cloud outfit…"

"Dark Sky."

"Whatever. Anyway, Candy knows I need to find Mikov, she comes in and shows me all the articles and clips and shit. I was blown away. See, I don't watch the news, I watch Turner Classical Movies, so how would I know about you?"

"How would you. Okay, thanks, Mel, I'll check in next week."

The comedy group Firesign Theatre put out an album in the seventies called *Everything You Know Is Wrong*. I was beginning to relate to that whole concept. I hung up, then went and stood under the shower for a half-hour.

I had the feeling this was going to be a long day.

They dressed me at Bloomingdale's and I paid about nine hundred bucks for the privilege.

I had nice new slacks that fit my new leaner waistline, a belt to go with it, and a handsome cashmere sweater, charcoal grey to complete my casually elegant ensemble. Since we had my sizes worked out for my new svelter frame, I got a few other things as well. My wardrobe really hadn't expanded since my trip of necessity to Banana Republic last year, so I thought I might as well upgrade my look, especially since I was running in the upper-crust circles these days. I even bought PMA a couple of shirts that I saw him admiring. I did, however, stay out of the lingerie department in case security recognized me from before.

While we were shopping, Becky kept calling my cell and I kept not answering. I would feel like a dope rehearsing for an interview and I wanted to conserve my energy for the cameras. To stop her from calling, I finally texted her and said I would be at the studio at 2:30 as requested. What I needed to do now, after all the clothes shopping was done, was sit down and regain my mojo -- I was still weak, still drained, still very on edge. PMA and I ate in the train car restaurant at Bloomingdale's, Le Train Bleu, and, with our new clothes on, we looked like we almost fit in with all the other old rich people. We had about an hour before we had to get to CNN.

"You look better, Max."

"Must be the clothes." I sipped on my iced tea. "I don't feel better."

"Well, your color's coming back. So what are you thinking? About the girls at Chesler's office?"

"I'm thinking I'm being targeted."

"The drug makes you paranoid, Max, remember that. Again, this could still only be about Candy having a friend who was weirdly obsessed with you. Could be that's all."

"When my rapist was raping me, she said that it could be the last for me."

"What, having sex? Maybe it was a joke, maybe because you're old?"

"I ain't Mel Chesler old, kid. That was a message. Besides, that was a pretty sophisticated designer drug she gave me, specially designed for me. So maybe she's not a freelance internet writer after all. Maybe her expertise is in chemicals."

"I don't know, Max."

"You know about Senator Marks, right?"

He looked down at the table. "Anything could have happened to him."

"But anything didn't. You know that…" I had to stop because the room was swirling again and the colors were back. I held on for dear life "I don't want to talk about this anymore now. I gotta think happy thoughts and focus on the interview."

My brain settled down and then our food came. We ate quietly. There were demons in the air that he didn't want to see and I didn't have the strength to talk about.

Speaking of demons, Becky Parks was anger personified. When I walked into the CNN studios at 2:35, her eyes were burning with such raw hatred that they could have shot laser beams at me and melted my face – but she still managed to keep her bullshit smile in place.

"You're a little late," she said in a sing-songy voice with a warehouse full of rage behind it.

"But I look good. This is Jeremy," I said, introducing PMA to her. "He's my assistant." I could tell he was pleased I acknowledged his position publicly as he shook Becky's hand.

"Well, I'm sorry you didn't have time to rehearse…" she said, eyeing the Bloomingdale's shopping bags that PMA was carrying.

"I'll be fine, Becky. Promise."

The first sign of trouble arrived when a production assistant came to get me from the green room, a few minutes before the interview was scheduled. He looked at me like we were in India fifty years ago and I was an Untouchable.

"We need to get you on set, Mr. Bowman."

Up until then, everybody had treated me like a king. Now the energy and the atmosphere had completely changed. People averted eye contact with me as the P.A. seated me on the set. Some were snickering after I passed them, like I had a "Kick Me" sign attached to the back of my new cashmere sweater. I felt my psyche reacting, I felt the panic building, but I worked hard to tamp down all the madness in my mind. I had to keep reminding myself that this might be all in my head, like the clones on the tram.

The Anchor was one of those cable news blondes, hot, professional and made of steel. After I sat down next to her at the news desk, she did not make small talk with me or attempt in any way to make me feel at home, the way Chuck Woolery used to do with *Love Connection* contestants. The commercial break was currently in play and, after getting some notes from a producer, she turned to me with a tight smile and said, "We're on in thirty."

"That's seconds, right?" I tried to joke. "If it's minutes, I'll go lay down."

She ignored me. The red light on the camera came on and we were on the air.

"We're back and with a guest you may know, Max Bowman," she said to camera. "Many of you will recall his heroics in taking down the Dark Sky secret military operation last year." She turned to me. "Hello, Mr. Bowman."

"Hi, America," I gave a little wave to the camera.

"Now, Mr. Bowman, this week you've been surging on social media for reasons that aren't so heroic. As a matter of fact, you scared a lot of people. Let's take a look at one of the videos shot on the tram that links Manhattan to Roosevelt Island here in New York City …a video that's gotten over a million hits…"

I didn't bother to look over at the monitor to watch the clip. I was trying to keep myself very, very calm and centered. After it was over, she turned back to me.

"So what can you tell us about that incident?"

"There's not much to tell. I was working on a case and somebody slipped something in my drink."

"A drug, you're saying."

"Yes, a drug is what I am saying, some kind of hallucinogenic that made me extremely disoriented and paranoid."

"And you're saying that drug caused you to attack innocent people, Mr. Bowman?"

"You can call me Max."

She nodded with a little smile. I went on.

"Yes, that's exactly what I'm saying. I thought the CIA had sent people to get me and, in my confused state, I thought the passengers were those people. I have to apologize to everybody who was on the tram that day, I was out of my head and literally didn't know what I was doing. Even more than usual."

I chuckled, but the Anchor didn't join in the merriment. She looked to me like a prosecutor waiting to pounce, but the drug was still in my system and I kept telling myself I was imagining all the hostility. Still, I was starting to sweat through my new cashmere sweater.

"Well, I'd like to ask you if you were also out of your head…when you allowed this picture to be taken…"

I blinked. What picture? I looked over at the monitor.

No.

No no no.

No no no no no.

Veronica's jihad on my junk wasn't over yet. As a matter of fact, her most damaging strike had just hit me. On the monitor was a picture showing me, naked on my bed and on my back, with my chemically-enhanced boner sticking straight up into the air like a flagpole without a flag. The boner was pixilated for home consumption.

"We just received this picture and a few others like it, Mr. Bowman, minutes before we started this interview. We can barely show this one on the air, the others we can't, because somebody else is…well…let's just say she's engaged in various intimate activities with you. We had a heated debate about whether to even show this one picture, but it was decided, since you were coming on CNN to clear the air with the help of a *paid publicist*…"

She hit those two words with a sledge hammer. I glanced over at the exit door to the side, where Becky was watching. She flinched.

"…it was in fact relevant to your overall behavior and fair game," continued the Anchor. "So where did these pictures come from? Why did you allow them to be taken?"

"I…I didn't!" I said with a trace of outrage.

"Then how did this happen?"

"I was raped!"

If there were three words in my life I could take back, those would be them.

There was a huge gasp from the crew in the studio and the Anchor recoiled as if she had been slapped. Becky Parks, standing to the side by the exit door, was now looking like she had just shit her pants and didn't want anybody to smell the result. Holy fuck, how did my life come down to this -- having to justify my pixilated boner on CNN live?

"Are women really that desperate to have sex with you?" the Anchor pressed on.

"No, it's not about…"

"Did you see that picture, Mr. Bowman, the one we just showed? It sure doesn't look like rape or I don't believe you would have been so…well, excited, I guess is the right word." She turned to the camera. "Ladies and gentlemen, I do have to apologize for the subject matter here, as I said, we were uncertain as to how to deal with this…"

"Wait, wait, I was set up…" I was sweating like a pig now, which was, ironically, in keeping with what the Anchor already thought of me. "I was dosed again, dosed with the same drug…"

"Mr. Bowman," she said interrupting. "You're blaming pictures of obviously consensual sex acts on drugs…you're saying a woman *raped* you…"

"They…they're trying to get me…"

"Mr. Bowman, it's pretty apparent you just might have some kind of problem that perhaps is best addressed in a rehab program. I'm very sorry your little publicity tour didn't work out…"

"MK-Ultra."

"What?"

"MK-ULTRA!" I screamed. "MK-ULTRA!"

And that's when the Bloomingdale's food, the salad that hadn't been in there for long, made its comeback.

I vomited all over the CNN news desk.

The Anchor screamed. I looked around desperately. Fight or flight? There was no fight left, so I flew. I jumped out of my seat, blew past Becky Parks and PMA and ran out the door like a madman.

Which is exactly what I was becoming.

The Nurse

Lugging our Bloomingdale's bags, PMA came running down Columbus after me and caught me without too much trouble. He grabbed me, pulled my new cashmere sweater all to hell and hailed us a cab. Rather than risk a subway or a tram incident, he had the cabbie drive all the way over to Queens via the RFK Bridge and then back over the Roosevelt Island Bridge to get us home. He held me down on the seat while I tried to keep my eyes from popping out of my skull and the cabbie tried to pretend nothing strange was happening. We all did our jobs.

When we got back to my place, I made my way past the jumping, yelping dog and barreled my way down the stairs and into the bathroom, where I threw up again. Then I sat on the tiled floor, afraid to move. Eydie ran in and jumped in my lap, where she started licking my face, even though it probably wasn't very tasty at the moment.

PMA appeared in the doorway, looking down at me with a grave expression.

"Max," he said. "That wasn't good."

"Really?" I answered. "Did you just get that bulletin off the CNN headline service?"

I managed to get the dog downstairs to do her business, then I went on my office computer, even though my head was bursting with pain. I just needed to know what was going on and I had that need met in spades. On Twitter, #BowmansBoner was trending. Elsewhere, all the photos that hellspawn Veronica had unleashed on the internet were showing up everywhere, with parts either blacked out or pixilated ala CNN. Pro that she was, Veronica managed to keep her face out of all of the pictures, but some other parts slipped in. A few Japanese characters made an appearance in one shot. Beyond the tribute to Toshiro Mifune, it was just a series of stills of Veronica playing all sorts of games with my Super Dick, which, I was starting to think, wouldn't feel super again for a very long time.

PMA came in. "What the hell is this about the Bloomingdale's lingerie department?"

As the late, great playwright Franz Liebkind once said, "Boy…ven things go wrong…"

I followed PMA back to the living room where, on the TV, a local news reporter was interviewing the woman at Bloomingdale's who had scoped me out looking at women's underwear a few days ago. She saw me on CNN, recognized me and came forward with her story. A model citizen.

The security guy was with her, backing her up and he said the store surveillance video was going to be tracked down and released. To me, the whole incident was a harmless joke. To her, I was a full-on pervert. It was another brick in the wall of my professional mausoleum.

My cell rang. I answered it.

"Hello?"

"WHAT THE FUCK IS WRONG WITH YOU YOU PIECE OF GARBAGE? YOU SCUMBAG, I SHOULD COME OVER THERE AND CASTRATE YOUR BALLS!"

"Todd, 'castrate your balls' is repetitive. The definition of 'castrate' *is* to cut off your balls."

"FUCK YOU, ENGLISH MAJOR! BECKY IS FURIOUS AT ME YOU MADE HER LOOK LIKE A COMPLETE LOSER CNN IS BARRING HER AND HER FUCKING CLIENTS ARE YOU HEARING ME FUCKHEAD?"

"Yes, Todd."

"FUCK THE BOOK DEAL, FUCK YOU, WE ARE DONE!"

"Have a nice life, Todd."

He was already gone before I got that last remark out.

"Who was that?" asked PMA. "I could hear him screaming every word from here."

"He was my bud," I said wistfully.

"Max, what the hell is going on?"

I turned to him, feeling the sweat pour down my back yet again. "It's pretty obvious, isn't it? Somebody is trying to destroy me."

I sat down. And then I passed out.

I woke up a couple hours later, still on the couch. PMA had put a blanket on me and was sitting next to me. He was watching the TV, where some slight, thin dark-skinned man wearing an expensive shirt was pacing onstage in front of a crowd. He was young, maybe in his late twenties, with short, carefully-cut hair, and he was wearing one of those headpiece-microphone deals, the kind that the TED talkers liked to wear to make them look impressive. That seemed to be his goal too, but, to me, he was falling a little short of the mark.

His words, delivered with a slight foreign accent that I couldn't identify, started to poke through the fog as my brain gradually woke up.

"Re-occurring cycles…we all fall prey to them. We engage in the same negative behaviors over and over. Well, my methodology will free you from these re-occurring cycles."

"Does this guy know that the word he wants is actually 'recurring?'" I finally asked.

PMA turned to me with a start. "You awake?"

I sort of nodded.

"This is the guy Andre Gibraltar invited me to meet with Saturday night," PMA answered, pointing to the TV.

This guy? He seemed a little low-octane for the steroid crowd. But I watched him a little longer to see what his deal was. He was getting fired up, but in his own bizarre little way, kind of like some quiet filing clerk you never noticed before who was suddenly excited about having a cheese sandwich for lunch.

"Everything comes to you when you relinquish the need to control everything and accept all as it is. When you deepen your commitment to your inner self and your health, you will naturally find your place in the world. You must accept and take ownership of *NOW* -- not the past or future but *NOW*. "

PMA was mesmerized. I looked at him the way I looked at my older cousin one day in church, when I realized in horror that he was actually buying all the crap the minister was saying.

"What's this guy's name?" I asked.

"Keenan Van Zola. He's starting a whole new movement."

"Good luck with that," I answered.

PMA let it drop. "Hey, you okay? You can sleep some more, I fed the damn dog."

"Thanks, but I'm up. Keenan Van Zola motivated me to take ownership of now."

"He's a quarter Cherokee."

"Great."

"You feel any better?"

"Hungry."

"When you're a little more awake, I'll get something for us. If your stomach's okay."

I sat up a little and rubbed my face with my open hands. PMA watched me.

"And Max, this time you need to see a doctor. That shit is still in your system, and now you got two doses in you."

"Don't think a doctor can do much. Have to wait it out."

A pause.

"Max, at some point, you have to listen to reason. This is really serious. Dick pics, the tram video, you throwing up on CNN…I mean, you own the internet right now and not in a good way."

"Got it, I'm a laughing stock in every possible way. Where's my phone?"

He picked it up off the coffee table and gave it to me. "It was in your hand when you went down. Who are you calling?"

I took it. "The bane of my existence."

"Pretty impressive for a guy your age," Howard said when he finally picked up. "But maybe don't go around yelling 'MK-Ultra' over and over. They're not very happy with you around here."

"MK-Ultra is in Wikipedia, for fuck's sake, it's not like it's top secret. Besides, I'm being targeted and it's someone with access to you."

"Max, that's the drugs talking."

"Howard, there's an old saying – just because you're paranoid doesn't mean they aren't after you. You were asked to investigate something called Blue Fire right before I got the job. And then you were asked not to investigate it. Reason? Maybe so you could tell me that and *make* me paranoid."

"Oh, here we go…"

"Some woman a third to a half of my age decides to dose me twice with some kind of drug that never quite gets out of my system -- and then she rapes me."

"Sticking with the rape story? Really? Send her over to my place, I'd like to get raped by that."

"She takes dick pics and releases them right before I go on CNN. Why? To make me melt down on national television."

"Max, I don't know what you're into these days, but you better get some help. I'm willing to do what I can, but you have to admit you need that help first."

"No, Howard, *you* need help. They used you and they'll do it again, just like they did last year. I'm sweating right now, I can't see straight, I can't trust half of what I'm thinking, but I know this much is true. There's some kind of blowback going on, that's why Senator Marks is missing and that's why I keep being set up. Every once in a while, you call yourself my friend. Well, I need one right fucking now, what do you say?"

"I say I can't help you, Max."

He hung up. That was his usual answer when it came to this juncture.

My phone was buzzing - I saw there was a text from Jules. When I opened the message, there was more profanity in it than there was in *Good Fellas*. Bottom line was she wasn't buying the rape either. How dare I do this while she was preparing to open Saturday night. I was to leave her alone. Like forever. Anyway, that was the gist of the message, I just tried to skip over all the very colorful adjectives and compound nouns, because they were just a swirl of "f's".

I slumped back against the couch, waiting for the ceiling to crash down around my head.

"Howard blew you off again?"

"Yeah," I answered, "and Jules never wants to see me again."

"Max…"

"Other than that…"

"Max…"

PMA was working his way up to something. Something I wouldn't like.

"…you should let all this go."

"Come again?"

"Look, Max, we got lucky last year, even you have to admit that. I mean, they never thought we were any threat and that's how we got away with taking them on. This time, if they really are after you, you don't stand a chance. You have one way out, and that's to let it all go. If you stop, maybe they'll stop. Besides, you've solved the Mikov case. The sister told you what happened to him, right?"

"All I saw was a pile of ashes."

"So this old woman just kept a bottle of ashes around in case you happened to show up?"

"Hey," I said to PMA, "what's with the attitude?"

"I don't have an attitude, I just want to save your life. You said you had some money in the bank. So why not…just take it and move?

Get out of the city. Move to some quiet place and have a life. You deserve it."

He was right. That's what made sense. The problem was, however, that I was at one of those points where you did one of two things and the choice you made would define the rest of your life.

Last year, I had accomplished something significant for the first time in my almost 60 years. Something important. Not many guys like me ever got to hit that kind of high note. I became somebody and should have enjoyed my new station in life. But I didn't. Instead, I let everything, including an emotionally-disturbed dog and a girlfriend going through medication hell, knock me back down to earth.

But the reality was, it wasn't about the dog, it wasn't about Jules, it was about *me*. I felt old, I felt lonely, I felt depressed and I was walking through my life, ignoring all the good things that had happened to me, letting temporary shit pull me down in the muck. Why? Because deep down, I felt like I didn't deserve happiness and so, as usual, I made it my mission to destroy whatever piece of it I had. As a result, I lost all the good things I worked so hard to get. I lost the woman I loved, my new elevated professional status, and now I was in the process of losing my sanity.

So I had a choice. I could either do what the kid was telling me to do, run away with my tail between my legs, become David Muhlfelder for good and go live in a crummy apartment in a no-account beach town somewhere, always looking over my shoulder…

…or I could do what I already knew I was going to do.

I looked PMA square in the eye and said, "Fuck you."

"What do you mean? What did I do?"

"Fuck you," I said, "and fuck them."

"Max…"

"No, seriously. What the hell kind of life have I had so far? Pathetic. You know how many women I've slept with? Five -- and that number includes the one who raped me."

"TMI, Max."

"My parents disowned me, my kids dropped me like a bad habit…"

"Max, I know your life story."

"So do I. And I know the one and only highlight from it is from the one and only time I actually found the balls to put everything on the line, when you and I took on Dark Sky. But now the fuckers want to take even that one thing away from me. They want to drag me through the mud and turn the world against me. Why? Maybe because if they discredit me, they can change the conversation in their favor."

"Max, I know what you're saying, I really do, but these drugs are doing things to you. I looked up that MK-Ultra program. The CIA did scary things to people, people who didn't even know what the hell was going on…"

"People like me."

"Yes, and you should just make yourself scarce before you end up like them!"

"Look, you should get back to school. I'm going to be okay and I'll sort shit out."

I got to my feet and it wasn't easy.

All I had, all I ever had really, was my mind. It worked pretty good. Even when I got drunk I was still always able to focus. I could beat this. I just had to keep my brain working. I had to mentally fight whatever was in my bloodstream, whatever wouldn't die, whatever wanted to keep me down and keep me crazy, and I had to fight that fight every minute of the day from here on out.

That was the only way this would work. Then I'd find out what was really going on.

The kid looked me up and down. He saw the fire in my eyes. So he doused the flames in his. Instead, he took a deep breath and steeled himself for whatever we were in for.

"I'm not going back to school, Max. Not yet. We're not having that argument again. But I just don't see where we have a move. Do you?"

"Somehow, Mikov is the key to this," I said. "I don't know why, I don't know how. But his sister freaked out when I asked about the CIA and that means there's more to this that I don't understand and more that I need to know."

"Okay, but how do we find out? What do we do now?"

"Tonight, nothing. Tomorrow, we go visit a nurse."

That night, I spent a little time trying to track down Candy and Janine, aka Betty and Veronica, to no avail. They were two more additions to Mighty Mel's suddenly growing gallery of ghosts, two more that came in and out of his sphere and left no trail to follow, just like Mikov.

I also brought the kid up to date on what else I learned about Mikov. I shared the super-gay comic and he was properly speechless. But he also noticed how the Dr. K villain from Blue Fire was similar to Dr. Kanuskey in the underground artwork. He agreed there had to be a connection -- and he was intrigued that I had tracked down Kanuskey's nurse, Sandra Bennett, the person we would be visiting the next day. If Kanuskey was our guy, she had to know something.

The next morning, Saturday morning, I was sore, but okay. I had slept moderately well with only a few nightmares that jolted me awake. I couldn't remember what they had been about or who had been involved; either my subconscious was sparing me or it was being eaten away by the drugs.

PMA and I had a little breakfast and got ourselves together. Eydie was left to howl on her own in the apartment and we walked down to the island's garage to retrieve my Nissan Rogue. Once again, I had taken along my David Muhlfelder fake identity kit and left my iPhone at home as a precaution, in case I was being tracked. I also tried to disguise my appearance as much as possible, as I didn't want people spotting me and then asking to see my now-world-famous boner. So I wore my reading glasses, a retro Sinatra hat Jules had given me for my birthday and I slicked my hair back so it resembled the top of a hedge fund manager's head. I didn't know if all that would be enough, but I did know that today would be the first day of my not shaving for a while. I needed to hide as much of my face as possible.

As PMA and I approached the parking garage, I noticed there had been a recent call to my super-secret CIA cellphone. From a number I didn't recognize. Well…what the hell. I called it back.

"Took you long enough."

"Howard?"

"I had a hunch you'd hang on to this phone. Luckily nobody ever noticed it was gone. The beauty of bureaucracy."

"What number are you calling from?"

"Beats the hell out of me, I bought another burner. Thanks to you, I get a new one every year now. Now, let's catch up. A few days ago when we spoke, you told me you quit the Blue Fire case, is that true?"

"Not anymore. I reconsidered."

"Ah ha. Okay, then, congratulations on attempting suicide yet again. Because everything you yelled my way yesterday? All I can say is, you may not be wrong. Maybe you are being targeted. Most of D.C. thinks Marks' disappearance was some kind of political payback too.

But just because you may be right doesn't mean you should push on with this. If you're dumb enough to keep yourself in the line of fire…"

"It doesn't matter what I do, Howard," I explained. "If it's blowback for Dark Sky, they're going to keep coming for me no matter what I do. But maybe now you can tell me who asked you to investigate Blue Fire, and what you were supposed to investigate. Maybe give me something to work with for a change."

"You know, I got problems too, you know I was mixed up in that Dark Sky fuckfest too, so don't give me your self-righteous act."

"It's the only act I got. I don't juggle and I don't spin plates."

"Seems to me all you do is both of those things."

"Howard…"

"Okay, look, I got the request from some brownnosing mid-level flunky who works for bigger people than me and would never in a million years admit to me who the order came from. But this was the original assignment -- Blue Fire was a new drug the Agency had developed and somehow, it had gotten out of one of our labs. And suddenly it was on the street and frying brains left and right."

"So maybe that's why mine is currently on the griddle."

"Yeah. So, again, I'd make myself scarce if I were you. Anyway, like I told you, after they told me all that, the flunky called back later and said, forget it, the situation was under control, so, again, I don't know what it was all about."

"Blue Fire."

"Blue Fire, just like the name of your comic book hero."

"What the fuck."

"That's why I reacted to the name. I don't know what I can do if anything, but if you want to call me, use this number, because if you try me at the office again, I'm not going to take the call. I don't want anyone knowing we're talking, got it?"

"I'll be the soul of discretion, Howard."

"Bite me. So, what have you found out about Mikov?"

"Not enough to talk about it yet."

"You don't trust me."

"Howard, I don't trust anybody except my dog. And even she shits on my rug every other day."

"All right, fine, I hope you and your shitty rug are very happy together. Again, call me at this number when you're ready to talk."

"Storing it now."

In order to drive through Queens, you needed to have a black belt in street driving. Queens was worse than driving through Manhattan, where the nonstop gridlock meant you couldn't really build up enough of a head of steam to get into any serious trouble. In Queens, traffic moved well enough most of the time, but you never knew when you'd make a turn into a closed road, get jammed by a double-parked vehicle, or encounter a lethal pothole. Complicating matters was the fact that any painted lines on the streets that defined which lanes were which had been worn away long ago, leaving you to decide on your own where your car should be.

And you had better guess right.

Fortunately, Astoria wasn't very far at all. When you came over the bridge from the island, you were basically deposited at the southern edge of the town. And that was good, because I didn't know how many miles I could do in my state of mind. PMA had offered to drive, but I felt more comfortable handling the wheel myself. I knew the territory and I wanted to make my brain work as hard as possible on simple tasks to keep it out of the hands of the drug.

It only took about fifteen minutes -- and thirty traffic lights, twenty double-parked delivery trucks and ten one-way streets -- to reach the Astoria Home for Long-Term Care. I was lucky enough to find street parking nearby and the kid and I headed for the entrance. According to their website, visiting hours had just begun.

The Home was a nice one, not one of those horror shows some low-rent newscast might end up doing an exposé on. I asked to see Sandra Bennett at the front desk and a nurse came to fetch us.

"Sandra doesn't get many visitors," she said in a way that indicated Sandra really didn't get *any* visitors. "How do you know her?"

"I don't," I said. "We're actually investigating a former employer of hers and we wanted to ask her a couple of questions." I flashed my P.I. license that was in my wallet, holding my thumb over the name. I was clever like that.

"She's not in any trouble, is she?"

"No, of course not." I put away my wallet and pushed my reading glasses up on my nose to look more dignified. "It's just she's the only one left who worked with him."

"I will have to ask her permission."

"I understand."

We waited outside the doorway to her room for a minute or two, and then the nurse came out and nodded to us. We were clear to go in.

Sandra Bennett was close to ninety and could have passed for a hundred -- she was clearly not in the best of shape. She was in a hospital bed in a nightgown with an oxygen tank close by, as well as a host of medications on her bedside table. Her grey hair was thin and sparse, her skin was blotchy and mottled and her eyes seemed foggy, either because of all the pills or because she had been laying in a bed in an anonymous room for years feeling like she was in the waiting room for the grave.

"Who are you?" she demanded as she turned off the TV with a remote. Her voice was hoarse, harsh and filled with suspicion.

"My name's David Muhlfelder," I said, "and this is my associate, Jeremy Davidson."

Associate. I could tell the kid liked that. After all, yesterday he had only been my assistant. You could advance quickly in the ranks when you worked for Max Bowman Inc.

"Davidson?" she said.

"He's General Donald Davidson's grandson, if you remember him."

PMA smiled uncomfortably. She stared at him a moment and brightened a bit.

"Why, yes, I can see the resemblance. I admired your grandfather very much. Very masculine."

The kid nodded, even while his discomfort level rose. She turned back to me. "Nurse Schmidt said you had questions…"

"You worked for a long time for a Dr. Frederick Kanuskey, correct? He had a practice here in Queens, I believe."

Her face misted over, presumably with glorious memories. "He was a very great, great man. A very brilliant man."

"He was a psychologist?"

"One of the best!"

"Wonderful. Well, I was wondering if you remember someone named Ben Mikov, if he was a patient. He would've been very young at the time."

She looked at me blankly.

"His name might have been Ben Michaels at the time," I added.

"Oh, Benny! Of course! He was Dr. Kanuskey's son."

Son?

I looked at the kid. He returned my WTF glance.

"Yes, Dr. Kanuskey adopted him as an adolescent. He felt it was the best way to really help the boy."

"But his parents were alive and well. And they were okay with this?"

"Yes. They knew of the boy's problem and wanted it solved by any means necessary."

I gave the kid another look. This was getting increasingly freaky.

"His problem. What was his problem?"

She looked away. "Well, it's all the rage now, isn't it? Morality is only a quaint old custom to be left in the attic with our hats and our gloves and our manners. And Dr. Kanuskey's work…all for nothing now. His genius and his systems…they will all be lost…like all of our decency and ethical standards." Her face grew red as she continued in a loud voice. "Let the piggies roll around in the mud! Let them get covered with the filth and let the filth get deeper and deeper until we all DROWN in it!"

"I'm not following," I said gently, even though I was all too aware of where this was going.

She turned back to me and fixed her now-clear eyes on me. "The boy liked other boys," she said bitterly. "Do you understand?"

Out of the corner of my eye, I saw PMA fall back a step as if he had been punched in the gut.

"You mean homosexual," I said.

"I mean pervert! Dr. Kanuskey dedicated his life to curing these poor children of their disease, and, now, where are we without him?"

"To be clear, we're talking about conversion therapy."

"Yes."

I sat down in a chair next to the bed. This was getting heavy and so was I, so I needed to get off my feet.

"If you don't mind, can you tell me what was involved in Dr. Kanuskey's methods?" I asked, now wanting nothing more than to leave the room and leave this evil old witch to die.

"The tragedy is they would put him in jail today for what he did then to save these boys. Political correctness…ridiculous. Because it all worked! Every single time!"

"Mrs. Bennett…"

"Miss. He used a combination of treatments -- electroshock, experimental medications, confrontation therapy…"

"Confrontation therapy?"

"Yes, the doctor would sit down with the boy for a frank conversation. He would tell him exactly what his future would hold if his deviant behavior continued. How, if it did, it would destroy his life. He would share details of the kind of life the young man could expect to live, as well as the pain and shame this would bring to the parents and family who loved him. He would then ask the boy, do you want to be a piggy in the mud? Is that what you want for your parents, your grandparents, to be a filth monger? Who wants a piggy for a child???"

The Sandra Bennett in front of me was now a much different woman than the one who was lying in bed when we entered. She was alive and she was on fire. Apparently, all she needed to revive her spirit was just a little spark of hate. Behind me, I heard the kid leave the room. I would've gone after him, but I didn't want to stop her while she was in a talkative mood. I was finally getting somewhere.

"What is wrong with him?" she asked innocently, watching PMA depart.

"He's got a weak stomach, don't worry about him. I'd like to ask about the medication involved in the treatment. What kind of drugs did Dr. Kanuskey use? You said they were experimental."

"Oh yes, Dr. Kanuskey worked closely with the government on some very effective treatments, not in wide usage at the time. This was when LSD was used for therapeutic reasons, before the dirty hippies began getting high as the sky with it. You heard what happened to Art Linkletter's daughter? Jumped right off a building! The sad part was that it was such a promising program, but unfortunately, it was shut down. You know, Cary Grant used LSD."

"He also shacked up with Randolph Scott."

She looked at me as if I had just said the Pope drank goat's blood.

"Let me ask you something, "I went on. "Have you ever heard of MK-Ultra?"

She began fiddling with the front of her nightgown nervously. "I heard Dr. Kanuskey speak of it, some sort of government initiative. But he never would explain more about it. It had to do with how he got the LSD."

There it was. The direct connection.

"And Ben Mikov…Ben Michaels…he went through all the forms of treatment you're talking about. The LSD, the electroshock treatments, the confrontation…"

"Yes. All of Dr. Kanuskey's patients did -- and thank God! They came in homosexual and they left healed and healthy! Of course, Ben and the other boy had more treatments than the others, over a much longer period of time. After all, they were a part of the family."

Other boy?

"Wait. What other boy?"

"Oh, Dr. Kanuskey adopted another boy who required that kind of special attention. His parents also reached the determination that there was nothing they could do and he needed to be left in the doctor's hands."

"Another homosexual."

"The boys were never allowed to share a room, of course."

"Can't be too careful. What was this other boy's name?"

Suspicion crept back into her expression.

"Why do you want to know?"

"It could be very important. Especially if he has some knowledge of Ben. Were the two boys close?"

"They were like brothers. That was the situation, absolutely, yes. Again, why do you need to know this?"

"I've been hired to find out what happened to Ben. You realize he was a comic book artist for a year or so?"

"I had no idea," she shook her head. "When the boy turned eighteen, he went elsewhere. He was of age, no one could stop him."

"Where did he go?"

She shrugged. "I don't know."

"Can we go back to the other boy? His name? I don't mean to push, but…"

She looked away.

"Ma'am, at this point, I don't think it will hurt anything to answer my questions. I'm not trying to hurt anyone, including you and including these two boys."

She still refused to look at me. "I have told you too much already. That's what comes of having no one to talk to for too long, you get thirsty for talk like a man crawling across the desert." She shook her head in self-recrimination. "Dr. Kanuskey told me not to speak of these things and I have betrayed him."

"He's been dead for thirty years, ma'am."

"Some things do not die."

I was going to ask her if she could be a little more ominous, but that's when she threatened to call the nurse and get me kicked out. She said she was tired and didn't have the energy to talk anymore. She was, of course, lying.

PMA was waiting in the lobby.

"I don't know how you could stay in the same room as that woman," he whispered in a hiss. "She's a monster."

"I was doing my job," I replied. "Sometimes I have to be nice to people I don't particularly like. Unfortunately, that's part of being a professional. Ask a lawyer or a doctor how many people they deal with that they hate and they'll still be telling you horror stories a week from Tuesday."

"Let's get out of here." He hurried out the door to the street and I followed him.

After a few steps down the sidewalk, I turned to him. "Kid, it's okay."

"What's okay? That shit she was spewing?"

"I mean, *you're* okay."

He looked at me. "What's that supposed to mean?"

"I mean you've never been gender-specific about anybody you've been "seeing," and I don't give a shit, which is why I've never brought it up. You're still my unofficial son…but feel free to resign from the position if that's too much for you."

I walked over to unlock the car. He stood there staring at me.

"Wouldn't have been good, being the grandson of General Davidson and being gay, I imagine. It sure didn't do your uncle any good to be in that position. Would make somebody pretty mixed-up about the whole thing," I said over the roof of the car. "But, shit, kid, it's 2016. He's dead, you're not. We all need to move on."

He said nothing and got in on the passenger side. I got in the driver's seat and drove us back in the direction of the island. He still wasn't talking, so I didn't open my mouth either.

Walking back from the garage to my apartment building, we passed by the Farmer's Market, held every Saturday beneath the underpass that came down from the bridge to the island. You could buy a mean strawberry rhubarb pie there. All the produce was top-rate too, brought in by Mennonites who lived in central Pennsylvania. How they found their way to selling lettuce and tomatoes on Roosevelt Island on a weekly basis was something I never figured out.

As I walked past a long table filled with fruit, one of the little Mennonite kids ran up to me and asked me if I wanted a tract. A tract? That was a new one. To me, the right question would be who the hell *does* want one? But the boy was sweet and innocent, so I decided to humor him. I took his little slip of paper and glanced at the bold heading on top of the block of religious text, a heading that read…

PREPARE TO MEET THY GOD!

Everything was feeling a little too ominous today.

Little Latin Lupe Lu

I was chomping at the bit to follow up on what I had gotten out of Sandra Bennett. But when we got back to the apartment, a huge wave of fatigue crashed over me. After Eydie delivered her usual assault/greeting, I told the still-silent PMA I was going to lie down and have a little nap after I took the dog down to do her business.

The little nap turned out to be four hours long. I woke up and saw it was 4:30 in the afternoon and the sun was low in the sky. This time, I remembered my primary nightmare -- it was the villainous Dr. K, rendered in menacing Mikov-drawn strokes and shadows, administering electroshock treatment while demanding I drop this case. Not pleasant.

When I came out to the kitchen, PMA was there eating an apple. He informed me I had been screaming for real while I slept. I wasn't surprised. I saw he had put on one of his new Bloomingdale's shirts and I asked what was up.

"That event's tonight. The one Andre Gibraltar invited me to -- with Keenan Van Zola."

"Still think you need that kind of self-help shit?" I poured myself a little glass of Jack.

"Like I said, you could use it too. They said it was okay if I brought you, so you're welcome to come."

"Sorry, I got plans."

"Plans?"

"Jules' opening is tonight."

"Wait, she invited you to go? I thought you weren't talking."

"No. I'm just going to hang in the back of the club and hopefully she won't know I'm there. But I want to see how she's doing."

"For you, that's almost sweet."

"Yeah. I'm sweet." I threw back the drink. "I needed that."

PMA continued to work on his apple as I poured myself another drink and thought a moment. For a second, I was afraid of losing him too.

"Tell you what," I said. "There's a good Greek place right off the tram across the river. You and me can get some dinner there, then we can go our separate ways. Deal?"

"Deal."

A couple hours later, we were munching on some pita bread at the Greek place on 3rd and 60th. I had asked for a table in a dark corner and the maître d' had been kind enough to comply. I really didn't want to be recognized as Crazy-Dick-Pic-CNN-Vomiting-Man, so, again, I wore the reading glasses, slicked back my hair, kept my stubble and wore the Sinatra hat. We both looked resplendent in our new Bloomingdale's duds as I explained to the kid what I had learned from Sandra Bennett after PMA had left the room.

"So Dr. Kanuskey adopted *two* kids, Mikov and this other one. And then for years, the asshole put them through hell." I could see the kid didn't like to think about it. Come to think of it, neither did I. "Electroshock, LSD…the whole nine yards, I guess. Wasn't all that unusual back then."

"Yeah," he said bitterly. "I'm aware."

"And that's just what Mikov drew in the gay porn comic -- the doctor zapping the shit out of him."

"Jesus. How did he and the other kid have any brains left between them?"

"Well, Mikov had enough left to draw his masterpiece. I'm talking about *Blue Fire*, not the comic with all the cocks."

"I *know*, Max."

"The next step is to try and track down the other kid he adopted. See if he'll tell us what became of Mikov. They must've been close -- since they were both in the same hostage situation."

"You ever find any record of Mikov's death?"

"Nothing anywhere. And I looked under Mikov and Michaels."

The kid thought a moment. "Did you try Kanuskey?"

I nodded. "I was going to do that, but then I fell asleep for four hours. Both the boys could have ended up with his last name. Tomorrow, we'll check that out."

Our dinners arrived. I got fish, the kid had chicken. We started eating. Finally, he stopped and looked at me.

"You're not getting rid of that dog, are you?" PMA finally said out of nowhere.

I chewed and didn't say anything.

"You love that dog, Max. Admit it."

I looked down at my food sheepishly. "I'm getting used to her."

"You – fucking -- *love* that dog."

"Hey, I've never had anyone around who loved me no matter how badly I fucked up. Besides," I reminded him, "You're not admitting a few things yourself."

He gave me a hard look. "I'm gay. Is that what you want me to say? I said it."

He dug back into his food.

I nodded. "Good. Next time you're in the bathtub, I'll throw in a plugged-in toaster and try to cure you."

"That's very funny, Max. Maybe you should be the opening act for Jules. You can do thirty minutes of homophobic jokes, that'll go over big in New York."

"All I ask is that you don't rape me. I'm still getting over the one from the other day."

He dropped his fork on his plate and glared at me.

"This is exactly why I didn't tell you. Every day now, it's just gonna be an endless stream of crappy homo jokes. And trust me, you don't have to worry about me coming on to you, you're not my type."

"Why not? I'm attractive for my age."

"I think I'll join the CIA after all. Maybe they'll assign me to kill you."

"I'll put in a word for you with Howard."

"You're the best, Max."

"Hey, I got my shit together. It's been over a day since I threw up on national television."

He blew me a kiss and life actually felt good for a moment.

After dinner, he headed for his power meeting with Keenan Van Zola and I headed for the club at 78th and Madison where Jules would be making her niterie debut with Cuban Pete. I had it all figured out in my head. I would hover in the background where she couldn't see me, she would have a spectacular set, and then I would swoop in out of nowhere to congratulate her. She'd be so relieved that she had done well, not to mention thrilled beyond belief that I was there, she'd hug and kiss me and we'd get back together.

At least, that was the plan. The only thing that might go wrong was if she stunk up the joint.

I carefully waited until 8:05, five minutes after the show was supposed to start, before I entered the club, which was called "The Song Is You," after the name of a song Sinatra recorded about five hundred times. As usual for one of these cabarets, there was a lot of faux art deco décor, as well as pictures of the legendary old guard, Ella, Frank, Tony, Duke, Billie, and so forth, lining the walls.

I walked through the small lobby, past the bar and towards the actual stage area, where you had to pass by a hostess at a podium to seat you. On the podium was a sign reading, "8 PM The Havana Hot 5 with Julie Nelson." The Havana Hot 5. Must've taken Cuban Pete all of two seconds to come up with that scintillating name. At the moment, the Hot 5, all by themselves, were playing an instrumental of *Brazil* on the small stage, indicating all of Latin America was up for grabs this evening. Jules had yet to make her entrance.

I asked the lovely brunette hostess, who was in some kind of black spandexy evening gown outfit that hugged her tighter than a lonely python, if there were any tables available. I was being polite, because I could plainly see that at least half of them were empty. I also asked for one in the back corner, closest to the door. Again, I wanted anonymity, but I also wanted to be able to make an unseen exit in case this whole performance went down in flames.

But I didn't tell the hostess that and she didn't ask why I wanted to stay out of the way. She just smiled, handed me a drink menu and showed me where to sit, happy to add at least one more head to what was a far from successful turnout, especially for a Saturday night.

I ordered a Jack from the waiter and slid my reading glasses down my nose so I could look over the Hot 5 a little more closely. They were definitely Cuban, although I wasn't sure they were all that hot. They were all dressed in white, as Cubans are wont to do, and one was on the conga drums, another guy was on the timbales, there were two horn players and someone I believed to be Cuban Pete himself on piano. He seemed to be in charge, yelling instructions in Spanish to the other band members and mostly standing as he banged on the keyboard. He looked to be in his fifties and about three feet tall, but that was probably my resentment talking. He also had a small moustache on his squat round face, as if he was Hitler after too much cake. They finished *Brazil* with a big conga drum flourish and bowed to the scattered applause, which I contributed to, because, again, I was nothing if not polite.

My drink came as they started to play -- hand to God -- *Babalú*, the theme song of Ricky Ricardo aficionados all across the world. By then, it was obvious that these guys came not to praise Cuban music, but to bury it. That, in turn, made it necessary for me to order my second Jack halfway through their second tune. In the meantime, I was glad to see a few more tables had filled up, bringing us up to about a two-thirds occupancy rate.

After the end of *Babalú,* screeched by Cuban Pete himself, the bandleader grabbed the microphone sitting on top of his piano and waited for the applause to die down.

"I thank you very much. I appreciate your kindness, ladies and chentlemen," he said into the microphone with his Cuban accent, which made the ends of sentences go up even when they weren't questions. "And now, I would like to eeentroduce our very talented 'girl singer'…"

From the sidelines came Jules' response: "I haven't been a girl singer since the Clinton administration!"

Titters from the crowd. Pete looked slightly amazed anybody had laughed, but quickly rectified that situation. "Eeesent she funnneeeee?" Crickets. "Heeeere she eeees…Miss Juuuulie Nel-sohn!"

Jules came out in a new and dazzling dress that hit her newly-slim body in all the right places, as the almost-crowd applauded. She took the mike from Pete.

"Thank you!" she shouted out to the tables. "That was Pete Quintana and his Havana Hot 5, give 'em a hand! Hey, they don't cost nothin' - - so give 'em a few hands!"

More applause. My second drink arrived. I took care of it. I was happy, but wanted to be even happier.

"Folks, on a more serious note," Julie continued, "I am so excited about tonight. I know a few of my friends are here…"

Some clapping and hooting from random tables.

"…and they know what I've been through. A year ago, my singing voice was gone. I never thought I'd be up in front of a crowd again, unless it was to announce fucking bingo numbers or something…" Some pretty good laughs. "But last year, I had an operation…a very important operation…"

The audience waited expectantly.

"…AND LOOK HOW BIG MY TITS ARE NOW!"

Shocked surprised waves of laughter and a lot more applause, that turned into a standing O. I stayed in my seat, because the waiter was stopping by my table and handing me back my credit card. I looked at him curiously.

"No good?"

The waiter shook his head. "No, it's not that."

"Seriously," Jules went on from the stage, "the operation brought my voice back. I think it's better than ever, but now, it's your turn to vote." She turned to the band. "Hit it, Pete!"

As the drums started beating, I strained to hear what the waiter was saying. It seemed to be about me not having to pay for the drinks. I asked why. He said some people at the bar were taking care of it.

The drums kept going as I thought about what it might mean if somebody was taking care of my drinks. I didn't have to think long. The walls were melting already.

Boom BA Boom boom boom boom Boom BA Boom boom boom boom…

I stood up quickly and knocked over a chair. Then I moved and knocked over the whole damn table.

Boom BA Boom boom boom boom Boom BA Boom boom boom boom…

That goddamn song. He was making her sing that goddamn song.

Boom BA Boom boom boom boom Boom BA Boom boom boom boom…

People were staring at me. I lurched towards the bar. I moved through the colors. I stepped over the dissolving floor.

Boom BA Boom boom boom boom Boom BA Boom boom boom boom…

"Talkin' 'bout my baby…" Jules was singing. "A little Latin Lupe Lu…"

Da Da Da DAAAA.

I held onto the little podium to stay upright and the lovely brunette, startled, jumped back. I felt more eyes on me.

"She's a hot footin' baaaabbbeeee…" Jules sang more loudly than she should. She knew something was going on in the back of the room and she didn't want to lose the crowd. "There ain't no dance she couldn't do…"

Da Da Da DAAAA.

I turned to the bar and it was going this way and that. But I saw enough to recognize Veronica, toasting me with a glass of something. There was a guy sitting on a stool next to her, blocked by her sitting figure, but with his hand on hers.

"She's a groovy little baby…"

Da Da Da DAAAA.

I moved on. Somebody who was probably the manager approached me. I pushed him out of the way and moved to the right so I could see who was sitting with Veronica.

"A BOPA BOPA LUPELU…"

Da Da Da DAAAA.

As the manager fell against the wall, I saw who it was.

It was Mr. Barry Filer. It was Mr. Barry Fucking Filer, second in command to Andrew Wright at Dark Sky.

"A SHAKE IT SHAKE IT SHAKE IT LUPE!"

Da Da Da DAAAA.

He was smiling his creepy little smile as he looked in two directions, neither of which seemed to be mine, but I knew they both were. I knew his fucked up eyes were loving every minute of this.

"WATUSI PRETTY BABY…"

Da Da Da DAAAA

I lunged towards him. He picked up his drink and stepped back and left me to fly into the bar, where I whacked my head and got knocked back towards the opposite wall.

"C'MON AND DO THE WHO-CHEE-COO…"

"There goes the Super Dick," laughed Veronica.

I had to make my brain work the way it should. I had to get out of there. I had to get out of there now. I ran for the door, which seemed to be eighty miles away, but Mr. Barry Filer suddenly grabbed me by my jacket and pushed me backwards, once, then twice, then three times, until I was flying by the podium and back into the tables, one of which had people sitting at it.

There was crashing. There was screaming. The band stopped playing. And I looked up and into Jules' startled, shocked, freaked-out, and ultimately, disappointed eyes.

"MAX?"

I heard Mr. Barry Filer telling a couple of big guys how he had just been defending himself and I heard a few other people saying they saw me attack him and I felt the big guys grabbing me and pulling me towards the door and I felt myself fly out into the cold, cold night and onto the cold, cold sidewalk.

My reading glasses flew off my face. I stared at them lying next to me on the concrete. One of the lenses was broken.

A car pulled up to the curb, a big black car, and a big man got out of the car and picked me up and got me on the feet. But he had to keep holding onto me or I would've been right back down with my nose on the sidewalk.

"MAX?"

I turned and saw Jules in the doorway. Then I saw a giggling Veronica push her way past her, then run and grab onto the other side of me, the side of me that the big man wasn't holding on to. They put me in the car, the big man got in the driver's seat and Veronica got in the backseat with me.

As we drove off, Veronica licked the side of my face.

Zombie Apocalypse

I couldn't get my mind right. And I couldn't get my body to do what I wanted it to do either.

Veronica had dosed me again -- and now I was down and out again. They counted on me going to Jules' opening and they counted on getting more of their designer drug in me.

They counted pretty good.

I had my eyes closed for most of the car ride because I couldn't bear to have them open. Too much came flying at them when I tried to see straight and it felt like it would break my head in two. I focused on staying awake and staying lucid. I focused on keeping me separate from what the drug was doing to me. Whether I could be successful, I didn't know.

"Barry Filer…" I finally managed to say.

Veronica giggled again. "Crazy dude, right? Can never see what he's looking at. And ugly enough to take paint off a wall."

And that was all I was going to find out about that connection, about the guy who had brought me into the whole shadowy Dark Sky network in the first place.

We drove through the entranceway to a renovated pre-war residential building, and, from what I could tell, it was one of those posh places where you could drive up and park right near your apartment. In other words, a very pricey building, the kind where you could buy a unit for a cool twenty million and then have the privilege of paying ten grand a month just for maintenance costs.

The big guy helped me out of the car and to my feet again. Then he put my arm around his neck and walked me into a condo. When we got inside, Veronica, still giddy with delight at her capture, told him to drag me into the bathroom to take a piss.

"God, I hate this fucking part of the job," the big guy said, but he supported me until he got me semi-standing in front of the toilet. Then he pulled down my pants and undies and actually guided my Super Dick so my stream made it somewhere inside the bowl.

Neither of us got an erotic thrill out of the experience nor did we initiate any eye contact, which meant he probably wouldn't ask me out for a second date. After he was done draining me, he put me back together and Veronica told him to dump me on her bed. He let me fall there, on my back, and I heard him leave through the front door, which slammed loudly behind him.

I opened my eyes and looked around. If I squinted, I could make it work without getting a visual overload.

That's when I saw the giant framed black-and-white photo of a muscular Japanese man holding a sword like he knew what he was doing. I knew who it was, only because Veronica had left him a big fat juicy clue. She had said, as she climbed on top of my Super Dick, "True beauty is something that attacks, overpowers, robs, and finally destroys." Those words were written by Yukio Mishima, a Japanese author who, in 1970, decided to end it all by committing *Seppuku* right in a public square. Seppuku was a Japanese suicide ritual in which someone actually disembowels himself by shoving a short blade into his abdomen and slicing it open. To paraphrase Daffy Duck, it was a great trick, but you could only do it once.

Next to the Mishima photo was the more concerning item; a massive case of swords and knives mounted on the wall. They looked like the real deal, genuine razor-sharp weapons of death. What did Veronica use these things on? Well, over in the corner of the room was one of those dressmaker dummies -- a padded female torso on a stand that seamstresses would use to measure clothes. This particular one was pretty cut up, like a life-size Barbie body that fell into a blender.

Veronica entered the room, barefoot and wearing some sort of silky multi-colored Asian robe. She slinked across the room, then crawled over my helpless body and looked me in the eyes.

"Hi, Super Dick."

"Mishima…?" I managed to say, aiming my eyes at the wall photo.

"Yes, that's Yukio Mishima. Very good, Super Dick, you win today's trivia challenge," she said with a gleam in her eye.

"Why…are you doing this to me?" I asked.

"Mishima wrote, 'Anything can become excusable when seen from the standpoint of the result.' And I have to produce a result with you, Max Bowman. This is all part of the *process*." She started moving her fingers over my lips.

"What…process…"

"The process of making you a *warrior*, Super Dick, a warrior for greatness. Right now, your brain is clogged, filthy, corrupted by the world, the culture, all the fuckheads around you. The good news? Me and the drugs are going to clean you out and make you *pure*."

"…pure?"

"Yeah, it's simple. When you're the most defenseless, I work your deepest emotions. Your *passions*…your *anger*…you do have some anger in there, don't you, Super Dick?"

Anger. I never felt a lot of anger in my life -- until now. But she was digging deep into my soul, her and the drugs, accessing parts of me I didn't want to acknowledge. I had successfully kept a lid on all that, but now the strain was showing. I had to concentrate as hard as I could to fight the shit that was raging inside me, because if she broke all that open, she would win. So I pushed back as hard as I could. I distracted myself by trying to figure out who was behind all this, while I also focused on trying to determine whether or not I could move any part of my body.

"Who…do you work for?" I managed to ask.

"I'm self-employed. Independent contractor. I get 1099ed."

She reached into my pants pocket and pulled out my iPhone, then she put it in the drawer of the bedside table.

"Barry Filer…" I said again in a distant mumble.

"Super Dick, stop saying that name like I'm going to tell you anything awesome. That would make me oh so dumb."

I kept trying to move a finger. A toe. Anything that would give me some hope of making a move.

"But here's the good news," she went on as she walked over to the case of swords and opened it up. "No viral videos this time. Too dark inside that nightclub. Besides, we're never going to top you blowing chunks all over CNN. That was epic. But there's bad news too. I won't be riding your Super Dick this time around. This session ain't about pleasure."

She pulled out a medium-sized blade and started spinning it around at a blinding speed.

"It's about *pain*."

Then she threw it at the dressmaker dummy where it landed right in its cold dead dummy heart.

Apparently, she practiced a lot.

As she walked over to the dummy and pulled out the blade, I tried my fingers and toes again. I discovered I could move my fingers -- a little. The effort was exhausting. But…I could.

She walked back over to me and gently drew the tip of the blade across my throat. I could feel it cutting the surface of the skin of my neck, nothing too deep, but still very unsettling. And she began murmuring, "Other people must be destroyed. In order that I might truly face the sun, the world itself must be destroyed…"

"Mishima…?" I asked. I was starting to really hate that guy.

She abruptly threw the blade at the dummy again, punctuated by some kind of Japanese exclamation. Another perfect hit. Then she sat down next to me, bent over and licked the long cut on my neck. A tear trickled down my cheek.

"Let's get down to the facts, Max," she whispered in my ear, "My daddy left my mommy when I was seven. I never got over it. You left your little girls too, didn't you?"

"They weren't…little…"

"Oh, I know, but they felt little inside, didn't they?" she said in a little girl voice. "Sad and alone. We all think if daddy leaves mommy, he doesn't love me either, and then we go Booooo hooooo."

She got up off of the bed, which I was more than okay with, and started stroking the upright lamp on the bedside table.

"Maybe you wonder…" She removed the lampshade from the lamp. "…how do I know so much about Max Bowman? Well, they told me things. Like about the divorce. And the girls…Grace and Lorie, I believe are the names in question…"

She wet her finger and touched the bare light bulb. She flinched with pain and quickly withdrew it. She looked at me.

"Beauty is something that burns the hand when you touch it," she said with a thoughtful expression. Fucking Mishima.

She came back towards me, holding the lamp, leading with the bare bulb. There apparently was more than enough cord to keep the lamp plugged in while she had her fun.

"Grace and Lorie decided not to talk to daddy anymore, didn't they? And then Lorie…killing her baby like that. Tragedy. Probably wouldn't have happened if Daddy had stuck around."

Oh, Jesus.

She slowly brought the bare bulb of the lamp closer and closer to my face.

"I wonder if this will hurt. Should we see if it hurts?"

"No," I replied from the back of my throat.

"I think we should." She brought the bulb to within a hair of my cheek. I closed my eyes. I felt the burning of the bulb on my flesh -- and then I felt it stop.

I opened my eyes. She was pulling the bulb back away from my face with a satisfied smile.

"Not too bad, cowboy. But I may have ruined your beautiful complexion."

She put the lamp back on the bedside table and replaced the lampshade with exaggerated elegant movements like she was one of those *Price is Right* models, the ones Bob Barker used to creep out. I noticed next to the lamp that there was a box of Kleenex. I had to hope it wasn't there to mop up any accidental blood spillage.

"How did it feel to be a grandfather for just a couple of minutes, by the way? To know your only grandchild died such a horrible, horrible death."

Oh, Jesus God, get me out of here.

"You put up a good front, Max Bowman. Pretending the bulb didn't hurt. Pretending the dead baby didn't hurt."

She half sat on the bed and pulled my head towards her until my face was squashing her Japanese characters. What was next on the agenda? I was about to find out, because she slowly undid my pants with her free hand, then she stuck it inside and started playing with my goods.

"Super Dick, you can't be *that* impervious to pain. And I need to hear you scream. Now…what's going to make that happen? Maybe…this?"

She squeezed my balls. Hard. This time, there was more than one tear coming from my eyes.

"You know, I heard your mommy and daddy weren't so nice to you either. As a matter of fact, they threw you out of your own fucking family, just like your kids did."

She held on to my boys for dear life. I strained not to scream. I didn't want to give her that.

"Then there was the CIA. They threw you out the door because you were a drunken loser. Great hopping Christ, you are some kind of a fuck-up, Max. We haven't even gotten to what you did to your girlfriend tonight. Julie Nelson makes her big debut, and you bring all your shit into her club and turn it into a whole new kind of disaster. You know what, Super Dick? I think I was right about our little tryst being your last one ever. Because I really think that *my* pussy is the last one you're ever going to get into. Which is an honor, really. Maybe I'll put a plaque on top of it…"

She squeezed even harder. I winced. I couldn't imagine how much this would hurt if the drugs in my system weren't numbing part of the pain.

"The plaque would read, "Here Is Where Max Bowman Had His Last Fuck. Rest in Peace, Super Dick."

More squeezing, more pressure. Finally, I couldn't hold it anymore. A little strangled gasp of pain escaped from my mouth.

Satisfied, she relaxed her Kung Fu grip. She pulled out her hand and started licking the ball sweat off it. I wished the drug would do me a favor and erase that image from my mind forever.

"You're perfect to be my substitute dad. You're even more pathetic than my real one." She laid down beside me and stroked my cheek, the one on my face fortunately.

Then came a new wave of weirdness.

She was now chewing on my nose. And she chewed with energy. I hoped the skin was staying on.

And then she clamped down on it with her teeth. That time I yelled.

"YEAH!" she screamed with delight in her voice. "That's what I want to hear!

I pushed a couple more words out of my mouth. "Mel Chesler." Focus on the case.

She shook her head in disbelief. "You're never off the clock, that's what I like about you. My goshers, I never got to meet Mel Chesler. Only my gal pal Candy did. She worked that angle for us. And Mel didn't even know who Candy really was either. Jesus St. Croix, men are so stupid."

"Mikov," I said. "Blue Fire."

"I don't give a shit about old broken down comic book dweebs, Super Dick. Besides, working hours are OVER." She was angry and getting frustrated with me. I was interfering with the process. "And how the fuck are you still awake? That shit should've put out your lights by now."

She slapped me. Hard. I blinked. And then I let my eyelids flutter…and close.

I could feel her staring at me for a few moments, wondering if I was really out. She grabbed my cheeks and shook my head like it was a baby toy. I kept my eyes closed. She let go and I let my head fall to the side.

"Well, it was a start, Super Dick. Don't worry. We'll get there." She patted my cheek again, the one she had hit with all of her might. "While you drift off, I'm going to go have a little nosh. I need some nutrition for our next session. That's when we get serious. But right now, I'm hungry, Super Dick. Hungry enough to eat a DEAD BABY."

She shouted those last two words as loudly as she could, right in my face. But I kept my eyes shut and tried not to react in any way. I must have done my job, because I heard her get up and leave the room.

I was alone, but I could feel the emotions churning away inside of me, threatening to break down the walls I had carefully built over the years to contain them. She wanted them to spill out and consume me, she wanted to use what was inside me against me. And those bad feelings, mixed with the overwhelming panic about what she had in store for me next, could easily paralyze me if I let them.

But I couldn't let that happen.

I had a feeling our next "session," as she called it, would place my psyche permanently in her hands. I had to find a way out and it had to be now. My balls were aching more and more, but that was a good sign. It meant at least some of the medication was wearing off. I tried to see if I could still move my fingers. I could and it was easier than it was before. Just then, I heard her rummaging through the refrigerator looking for something to eat, so I knew I had time to see what I was capable of beyond playing the piano.

I opened my eyes and looked around the empty room. Shit, this was hard, the drug was overpowering and so was my emotional abyss. My heart felt too heavy to pick up, my will felt too ripped up to rally. All I wanted to do was shut my eyes again and block everything out.

But I couldn't surrender. I had to pick myself up and get to work.

I strained to determine if the paralyzing part of the drug was maybe wearing off, like I suspected. Last time, I had just passed out during the raping portion of the program, so I had no idea how long that component had really lasted. But I had a hunch the chemists involved assumed the victim would pass out sooner rather than later, so maybe those immobilizing ingredients weren't designed to be so long-lasting.

Still, fighting what remained was going to be hard. My mind and body didn't feel like they had that kind of fight in them.

That's when the verse popped into my head, the verse that little Billy Gerger said to himself to become the hero he needed to be. It wasn't Mishima, but it would do.

I started moving my lips, saying quietly to myself, *"Blue Fire must be pure…Blue Fire must be sure…"*

I tried the arm. I was able to pick it up. There was some numbness, but it was fading.

I tried my leg. The same. It was difficult, but I could move it.

I managed to button my pants and zip them up over my aching balls.

"For Good to be purged of Evil," I continued, "Blue Fire must…endure."

With that, I slowly and quietly tried to get my feet down on the floor and I made it. The next step was to stand up. I was afraid I'd immediately collapse to the floor and bring Veronica running back in, but I went for it. I heard the freak-woman in the kitchen, singing some sort of Japanese fight song and pushing buttons on the microwave, so that would mean another couple of minutes, maybe.

I swayed back and forth. As usual, there was some room-spinning involved. But I did it. I was on my feet.

And then I felt that was all I could do. I was groggy as fuck and sad as fuck. I could feel the tears welling up again in my eyes. But…Blue Fire, motherfucker. If that's the drug they put in me, then that's the hero I would have to become. Burn through the depression and the numbness.

Burn through it and endure.

I started moving, but so slowly I might as well have had bricks taped to my legs. If she did come back, she could knock me down by blowing on me.

I needed a plan.

I grabbed my iPhone carefully out of the bedside table drawer, put it back in my pants pocket and then looked again at the box of Kleenex by the lamp.

Maybe…?

I pulled out a bunch of the tissues and jammed them in the space between the lampshade and the hot bulb. Then I moved as quickly as I could behind the bedroom door, which was open and against the wall just across the space of the open doorway from the bedside table.

I didn't know if this was going to work, but it was all I had.

Blue Fire must endure.

I leaned against the wall behind the door, conserving my energy. I knew I couldn't close my eyes or I would lose it all together, so, to motivate me, I imagined all the horrible things Veronica might do to me if she got me back down on the bed. Stuff a dozen hardboiled eggs up my ass. Play tic-tac-toe with a soldering iron on my forehead. Cut off my nipples and sew them to my eyelids.

Then, after I don't even know how long because time and space weren't defining themselves very well for me, I smelled the burning. I saw the smoke. Then I heard the smoke alarm, which I had spotted on the wall not far above the lamp.

And I heard Veronica running towards the bedroom.

"What the fuck…" she muttered as she entered.

I imagined her standing there in the open doorway, seeing the flames from the tissues that had now caught on fire. I imagined she then saw that I was no longer on the bed and looked around the room trying to figure out where the hell I was hiding.

Then I heard the bulb explode with a horrendous POP.

That was what I was hoping for. That and the sound that followed – the sound of Veronica screaming in pain. That was my cue.

I let my body fall against the door with all my weight, so it would swing around and slam into her frame.

BOOM.

She fell back on the bed, shrieking obscenities, while I moved like fast-drying cement around the door and out of the room.

I saw the front door at the end of a long hallway. I continued lumbering towards it, occasionally stopping and holding onto one of the walls to stay upright.

Then I heard her coming after me.

"You're too fucked up to get far, Super Dick! And now I'm REALLY GOING TO FUCK UP YOUR SHIT!" The delight was gone from her voice. Now, it was filled with pain, anger, despair and hatred. Which meant if she caught me, the party really was over.

And, Jesus, she was close. I heard her footsteps coming closer as she continued moaning with pain.

"Nobody does this shit to me! Nobody!" she yelled, half-crying. She was the victim here. "I WILL NOT FAIL! I WILL NOT LOSE HONOR!"

I didn't turn my head to see how close she was. Instead, like a dedicated sprinter, I kept my focus on the finish line -- which was the door out of this perverse palace. But I also knew that, at the rate I was going, there was no way I was going to beat her to that door. I needed a game-changer.

Up ahead, I spotted a side table with some kind of metal vase resting on it.

When I reached the table I grabbed the vase, turned and spun around, smashing it across Veronica's face, which I now saw, for the first time, had pieces of singed light bulb sticking out of it. She staggered back from the hit. Blood spurted from her nose. But I wasn't taking chances. I brought the vase back down on top of her head and she collapsed in a heap.

She was a mess.

But somebody else with more time in their schedule could stop and feel sorry for her. Me, I opened the door with what strength I had left and staggered out into the hallway.

I found the door to the car ramp off the hallway, then went down it as fast as I was able, almost falling down a few times in the process. I finally made it to the bottom, where a garage gate was the only remaining thing standing between me and the street. I spotted a button on the wall you could use to open the gate from the inside and punched it. The gate went up and I went out.

From there, I kept moving -- just not too well.

I didn't know how long it would be until Veronica got to her feet and alerted the troops in the area, so I pushed myself onward, not even taking the time to fish the phone out of my pants pocket and call for some kind of help. That kind of delay could be fatal. I just kept moving forward down the street. I might have looked drunk, or homeless, but, hey, this was New York City and at this hour of the night, I just looked normal. Anyway, the streets were pretty deserted. It must have been after midnight, because I didn't even see a cab I could try to hail.

Wherever I was, I was close to the water, because I could see my island, the northern tip of it, in the moonlit distance over the East River, which seemed as if it was just a block or two away. That meant they had taken me to the Upper East Side. I spotted a massive park overlooking the river, a park that had tennis and basketball courts, a playground, and acres of grass and trees. This was where the well-to-do Upper East Siders came out and played during the day and, as usual, the city had provided them with the best of everything. For me, it would serve as a hiding place until morning.

I knew I didn't have much more in me. The drugs were still pushing me to collapse and my resistance was running on empty. I was shivering from the late February cold and sweating buckets at the same time, because my system was completely screwed up, so screwed up I wouldn't have been surprised to see piss come out of my nose. But my body didn't care about hot or cold or comfortable or hard cement. It just wanted to crash and it wanted to crash now.

I stumbled my way through the park's idea of a forest and found an out-of-the-way corner, where I put myself between the back of a big oak tree and a small cement wall that held back a slightly elevated playground area.

Then and only then did I pull my phone out of my pants pocket.

I messaged PMA, told him I wasn't sure where I was but I was in deep trouble. A big park, Upper East Side, near the water was all I knew about my location. I pressed the "Send" button and let myself go under. It was a relief, but, at the same time, it was terrifying to fall back into the blackness.

A few hours went by, along with a lot of demonic dreams, until suddenly, some noises woke me up. I wondered if maybe PMA had tracked me down, so I made myself open my eyes to find out. It was still the middle of the night, the moon was glaring down at me and I felt like I was freezing to death.

But then I heard more noises. It wasn't just one person roaming around nearby. It was a big group.

I could make out footsteps, a shitload of them. But they were unevenly spaced, off somehow, like a marching band made up of three-legged musicians. I turned towards the small wall behind me and got up to a sitting position. That was enough to enable me to see over to the other side. And that's when I saw them for myself.

The zombies.

Maybe it was the drugs talking, but they sure as hell *looked* like zombies. They were moving slowly, like the old-style George Romero kind, the ones that walked slowly and spastically, but relentlessly at the same time.

Except it seemed as if these zombies were on some sort of group outing, as opposed to a brain-eating competition.

They were all walking in a line, about fifteen yards from me. It was too dark to see them very clearly, but there were about a dozen lurching through the park, arms extended as if they were trying to hold on to the air around them.

And also -- they seemed to have chaperones.

Yes, there were two guys, one on either side of the zombie line, dressed in solid black uniforms and holding what looked like modified hi-tech cattle prods. They used the prods to zap errant zombies that tried to stray from the pack. Wait, was "pack" the right word? Just what did you call a group of zombies? A herd? A troop? A congregation? A swarm? Was I witnessing a gaggle of zombies?

My mind reeled as one of the keepers yelled, "Move it, deadhead!" at a zombie who had stopped to smell a tree trunk. The zombie kept sniffing. The keeper poked him in the back with the prod -- *ZZZZzzzap!* -- and the zombie moaned and shuffled along.

This had to be a fucking dream. This couldn't really be happening.

But just in case it was, I got to my feet to get a better look, just as the living dead entered the park's large playground area, which was filled with climbing structures, slides and other kid-friendly recreational equipment. I crawled up over the wall to higher ground and leaned on a tree to get closer to the action.

Most of the zombies were male, only two or three were female, and some of them were quite a bit older than you'd expect, maybe old enough to be on zombie Medicare. They all wore the same institutional white pants and shirt, as if they were inmates at some zombie asylum, as they marched onward to the playground equipment.

Then things got even weirder – because it was zombie playtime!

The keepers directed their charges to different activities -- apparently, they wanted to make sure the zombies got a good workout -- prodding them when they were reluctant. So now, suddenly, there were zombies climbing rope ladders, swinging on swings, sliding down slides and hanging from overhead rings.

This had to be the drugs. Had to be.

I inched closer to get an even better look at this madness. Just then, I noticed one of the bigger male zombies was turning on a keeper who seemed distracted. Distracted by what? I followed his line of sight --

and saw the keeper was checking out the ass of the youngest female zombie.

And for his sins, he got a pair of powerful zombie hands around his throat.

The trainer let out a strangled yelp as the deadhead choked him. The other trainer heard him, ran over and jolted the big male zombie over and over again to make him let go.

In all the confusion, one of the other zombies on the perimeter of the playground, the one closest to me, seemed to sense I was there. He turned in my direction. I stood still by the tree, trying to remain undetected in the darkness, but he kept shuffling closer to my position until he was only a few feet away.

I took a step back behind the tree, but then I stopped, because I was close enough to see his face in detail. He was one of the elder zombies, my age and more, with crazy grey hair sticking out every which way from the top of his head. There was something familiar about him, something very, very familiar.

Suddenly, he saw my face peeking around the tree at him.

I stopped breathing as he hurried his slow shuffle and stuck out his hand towards me, like Frankenstein's Monster as played by Karloff when he would reach out with a single stitched-together hand for some simple human understanding and empathy -- and invariably get villagers' torches in return.

"Ahhh," the zombie elder said. "Ahhh..."

Holy fuck.

As he stepped into the moonlight, I finally got a good look at his face.

Holy, holy fuck.

This zombie was what was left of Senator Abe Marks.

Spooked, I struggled to get back over the small wall and, when I got there, I let myself drop back between it and the giant oak tree. I hit a little hard and the breath was knocked out of me. Panting, I looked back over the top of the wall and saw Zombie Senator Marks still heading in my direction, reaching out. There was something overwhelmingly sad about his face, like he'd been robbed of whoever he had been and only wanted to get himself back.

The keepers, who had finally subdued the renegade, spotted Zombie Senator Marks coming my way, and one of them rushed over to jolt the old man back towards the playground. Luckily, the keeper didn't see me. Zombie Senator Marks let out a loud whine when the shock hit him, a whine that was as much about disappointment as it was about pain, and, a few moments later, the keeper and the Senator were back with the rest of the group.

I exhaled in relief.

Just then, there was a buzzing in my pants pocket -- coming from my phone. I pulled it out and saw that PMA had answered my text. He messaged me to activate my "Find Friend" iPhone app and send a request to share my location with him. That took me a few minutes to figure out, but I did.

And then I leaned my head against the tree and closed my eyes, still seeing in my mind the haunted expression of what I thought was Senator Marks, an expression that was pleading for someone to give him sanctuary.

It was something we both needed.

Intervention

Somebody shook me awake.

I gasped, thinking either the zombies were back or their keepers were about to recruit me into their living dead posse. But when I opened my eyes, all I saw was PMA staring into my face with a whole lot of worry.

"Max? You okay?"

"I'm not sure 'okay' is the right word," I said. "Are the zombies gone?"

"Zombies? You saw zombies?"

"I saw something. What time is it?"

"Around 6:30, 7."

Over his shoulder, I saw the sun was coming up. It was Sunday. Sunday in the Park with Max. I turned back to PMA, who was staring at my face.

"Somebody work you over?"

"Huh? What do you mean?" I asked.

"Well…there's like some kind of burn on your cheek, a big cut on your neck…and on your nose…are those teeth marks???"

"Yeah, the rapist bit me."

He shook his head, trying to will this new information away.

"You gotta be freezing," he said, taking off his coat and draping it over me. "Can you walk? If you can, I'll get an Uber to pick us up out at the park entrance."

"I can make it that far."

He helped me to my feet. We headed out as he made the Uber arrangements on his phone. When he was done, he looked at me again, still freaked that I had been sleeping in the park all night.

"Jesus, Max, what the hell happened to you? How did you end up here?"

"I'll tell you later. It'll take a couple of hours."

It would actually be a couple of days.

I lost the rest of Sunday and all of Monday. Since Monday was Leap Day, that was a bonus 24 hours anyway, so no harm no foul. Through those forty-eight hours or so, I only woke up when I had to hit the toilet and I immediately fell back asleep when I got back to the bed.

And, of course, the dog wouldn't leave my side.

But when it was time for *her* to hit the toilet, PMA would patiently put on her leash and drag her out to the elevator and downstairs to the courtyard, even though, the entire time, she would whine, growl, shake with fear and generally be a complete asshole to him. But when we were both on the bed together, I held onto her for dear life. I needed some warmth and contact from a living being, even if her breath smelled like Milk-Bone.

Tuesday morning, I woke up and almost felt normal. I knew I needed to eat something, I just hoped it would stay in my stomach. The dizzies had started to subside a bit, so I made it out to the dining room table. PMA made me some eggs and I wolfed them down. The dog was happy to see me up and about. PMA seemed guarded and distant.

"I almost called an ambulance," he said as he sat down with his own breakfast.

"Probably wouldn't have done any good. That shit was in my system too long by the time you got there."

"Jules told me what happened at the club Saturday night," PMA said--a little coldly, I thought.

"So what--she's done with me, right?" I felt the bad emotions welling up, pouring over me, pulling me down.

He shrugged. "We didn't get into it." He was being too quiet--not just about Jules, but about everything.

"Where's my phone? I want to call her."

"Max, don't."

I bit my lip and I held back tears while my insides shook.

My world was continuing to crash down and as usual, all I had done to cause the catastrophe was show up somewhere. But I had to put the brakes on myself. I was beginning to realize stress was the big trigger for this drug's continual comebacks and I had to keep myself calm. The kid was right. I shouldn't call her for my own emotional health right now. I took some deep breaths, then finally turned back to him.

"Here's one part she didn't know about. Mr. Barry Filer was there that night."

PMA stared at me in disbelief.

"The Dark Sky dude?"

I nodded, then got up to move over to the couch. I needed to get my head down again.

"He was with the rapist. And they got to my drink before I did."

I told him everything--about getting thrown out of the club, about the car pulling up and taking me away. I told him about Veronica's swordplay, her bulb-torturing and her ball-squeezing, not to mention the fact that she knew everything about me and my personal history. And then I told him about the zombies in detail, and that's when I said I thought one of the undead was, in fact, Senator Marks.

And that's when I really lost him. He started staring down at the floor.

"What?" I asked.

"This is too much." He looked up at me. "This is too much."

"You already said that."

He shut down. He kept staring at the floor. I figured maybe I'd change the subject.

"By the way, how was your power event Saturday night?"

That took him away from the floor. Suddenly, his eyes were lit up like a Christmas tree.

"It was…kind of amazing."

And then he looked off into the distance, even though there wasn't much of it in the apartment.

"Amazing?"

"This was an opportunity, Max, a real opportunity. It was a small group of about thirty people. There were political leaders in the room…along with doctors, lawyers…"

"Indian chiefs?"

He looked at me quizzically.

"Well, you told me this guy was a quarter Cherokee. Go on."

"Keenan Van Zola is looking to motivate a whole new level of thinking in this country. Raise the bar. Take us out of the quagmire."

"Quagmire? What the fuck are you talking about?"

"Re-occurring cycles, Max."

"Re-occurring?"

"Yeah, re-occurring cycles."

"We already talked about this. The word is *recurring*, not re-*o*ccurring," I said impatiently, not liking where this was going. The only part of PMA I ever had a problem with was the earnest part. And this was getting super-earnest.

"Whatever. The problem is we all get into them." He looked at me with judgment in his eyes. "We obsess over shit and never rise above it. And we abandon our potential."

"I repeat--what the fuck are you talking about?"

He frowned and got up. "Forget it. I'm going to take the devil dog for a walk."

Eydie, who was now on the couch with me, snarled at him--now that I was up and out of bed, she wasn't going to leave me willingly. I petted her reassuringly. "C'mon, be a good girl, go with him."

PMA gave me a withering look as he went over to get her leash. I continued petting her and realized that, whatever happened to the kid the other night, maybe it suddenly made him feel too good for the likes of me. There was definitely a wedge between us--but what had put it there, I didn't exactly know.

Maybe my surrogate son was just rebelling against his surrogate father.

After PMA dragged the snarling, whining, yelping dog out the door, I grabbed a Coke Zero out of the fridge and went to sit down at the computer in my office. I had some work to do. I had to ignore the rats running around in my brain and focus on facts and clues as to what the hell this was all about.

I started by getting my most unpleasant task out of the way-- returning a call from Mighty Mel--and, yeah, it was definitely unpleasant. He screamed at me, saying the Blue Fire movie was going to be unveiled at the Jersey Comic Con this weekend and he needed some answers before then, all the shit I already knew. And, oh yeah, he had paid me a lot of money and he didn't want to have to fucking sue me to fucking get it back.

So there was that.

Luckily, I already had a plan to get closer to the truth, and that was to try and track down Mikov's foster brother, the one that Dr. Kanuskey's former nurse told us about. Whoever he was, he had to have some answers. So I went online in search of some more Kanuskeys, not only to see if the brother showed up anywhere, but also to see if Ben Mikov showed up with that last name, since Dr. Kanuskey had officially adopted both of them. Again, since it was not a common name in these United States, it wouldn't take long to see if this trail led anywhere.

And it didn't--just a couple of seconds, as a matter of fact. The Kanuskey search results were nonexistent. A complete dead end.

Maybe I just needed to go back to bed, since I was still recovering from my two-day nap. Waking up to Mighty Mel's threats, PMA's weirdness and Jules' ongoing rejection was tearing my already-fragile outlook apart at the seams. Besides, I could feel that this time around, the drugs had gone deeper and done more damage. Some more rest would probably help.

I was about to get up from the office chair when…

Bing.

Facebook private message.

I clicked on the FB tab and saw I had actually received a few of those messages over the last couple of days, all from my new friend, Bruce Canun, the head of the Mikov group.

On Sunday, he wrote:

Get anywhere yet? Did that underground comic help?

On Monday, he wrote:

You around?

And just now…

You didn't disappear like Mikov, did you? LOL

LOL, the internet's version of the laugh track and just as obnoxious. I answered him.

Been laid up for the last few days. Back on the case now.

Bing.

Glad to hear it.

I was about to get up and leave again, when something hit me. Call it my spider-sense again, but all of a sudden, I wondered, why was this strange internet guy suddenly messaging me every day about Mikov? What was he after? Was he really that obsessed with comics--or something else?

I typed another response.

You seem awfully anxious about this.

A long pause. And then…

Bing.

I have to admit, I have some skin in this game.

What kind of skin? I thought a moment. And then, even through my drug-addled haze, the answer seemed obvious. Maybe too obvious.

I messaged him back.

Is Canun your real name?

It seemed like a hundred years…but finally, I heard the *Bing* I was waiting for.

Yes.

So much for that idea. I had thought that "Canun" seemed awfully close to some bastardized version of "Kanuskey," so maybe…

But then…

Bing.

Well, my father changed it actually.

Steady, Max. Don't get carried away.

From Kanuskey, maybe?

Bing.

How did you know that?

I sat up straight in my chair. Holy shit, he was a part of this. I typed carefully with trembling fingers…

Wild guess. Are you related to Dr. Frederick Kanuskey?

Bing.

He was my grandfather. Not proud to admit it.

Jackpot.

Still, I had to be cautious. Sure, Bruce Canun seemed like the real deal, but considering the events of the past few days, who knew? Maybe he was stalking me to find out what I was up to. I typed again.

> *Who's your dad?*

Another century-long pause. Then finally…

Bing.

> *Somebody I don't want anything to do with. BTW, are you THE Max Bowman?*

Busted.

> *Yeah--have you seen my penis on social media?*

Bing.

> *LOL. What's going on with you?*

Good question, but one I wasn't going to answer until I knew more.

> *Hard to explain here. Can we talk? You must know more about Mikov than I ever will.*

Bing.

> *OK, full disclosure. I actually knew Mikov when I was a kid – he and my dad were raised together in kind of a weird set-up…*

"Weird set-up." I guess that's what you'd call your grandfather taking your dad and Mikov away from their biological parents and trying to brainwash them.

> *… so I was hoping you could find out what happened to him. There are a lot of mysteries in my life I don't have answers to.*

I leaned back again. My paranoia was rearing its ugly head and I decided it was time to pull back until I found out more.

OK, well, like I said I'm back on the case now. I'll let you know if anything pops up.

Bing.

Coming down for the Comic Con this weekend if you want to meet up and compare notes.

The Comic Con. The one Mighty Mel was freaking out about, where they were supposedly going to announce the Blue Fire movie.

That might work out. Gotta go, will be back in touch.

Bing.

Thanks! And remember..." For Good to be rid of Bad…Blue Fire must endure!"

I sighed for my own benefit.

I'll keep that in mind.

Now, I had a new name to do a search on. "Canun." That was his father's name and that was the guy I needed to find, Mikov's foster brother. I typed it in the search box, but Google kept trying to sidetrack me by showing me bargain trips to Cancun instead of anyone with the last name of Canun. While I had no doubt that kind of vacation would do me a world of good, the timing wasn't quite right. I insisted to Google that it show me results on *Canun*, not *Cancun*, and it finally deferred.

First off, I spotted Bruce's name; turned out he was an IT guy who lived in Connecticut. Then I saw another Canun had come up; one who lived right across the river in Manhattan by the name of Dr. Reginald Canun.

Yes, Dr. Canun was a psychiatrist just like his father. He worked at a combination clinic and laboratory, all under the umbrella name of Rosenbaum Research. Turned out the clinic/laboratory was on the Upper East Side. On Gracie Square, near Carl Shurz Park.

The park where I saw the zombies.

Coincidence? Or conspiracy? Who knew? To a drugged-up freaked-out mental case like me, anything was possible.

My obsessive musings were interrupted by the sounds of the front door opening, and PMA and the dog coming in. I was ready to rush out and tell PMA everything I had discovered--when I heard another set of footsteps coming in behind him.

I suddenly felt paralyzed. Sweat began running down my forehead.

I was having a full-on panic attack.

Nobody said anything, so I had no idea who was coming in with the kid. Without even thinking about it, I took the gun, the one gun I owned, the one that had put a hole in my raincoat and into the leg of that maniac Herman last year, out of my desk drawer. I quickly checked to make sure it was loaded. Yeah. It was.

Still no words from the intruder. I slowly and quietly got up and made my way out into the hallway, holding the gun in front of me with both of my shaky hands and with my finger on the trigger, more than ready to use it to save myself from whoever was after me this time.

Then I saw who was standing behind PMA.

And, boy, did she see me.

"HOLY FUCK, MAX, YOU PSYCHO FREAK!"

It was Jules.

She was staring at the gun, pointed in her and PMA's general direction, with shock and horror.

"What the hell are you doing here?" I asked in an almost-whisper as I lowered the gun. "You're supposed to be at work!"

"Yeah, I know," she said softly, taking the gun away from me and handing it over to PMA, who quickly unloaded it. "Let's just say, fucking push has come to fucking shove."

Jules was in one of her buttoned-down business outfits, which was appropriate, because the expressions on her and PMA's faces indicated this interaction was going to be *all* business. While my eyes darted back and forth between them, they had a hard time returning my anxious glances. This wasn't going to be pleasant. The sweat continued to roll down my face and my back. Was the rubber wagon outside waiting for me?

PMA put Eydie in the office, leaving me bereft of any emotional comfort, and gently pushed me towards the living room. I sat on the couch and hoped I didn't look as bad as I felt. I tried to compose myself, tried to look as normal as possible, tried to will this trial away. From the way they continued to avoid my eyes, I knew none of it was working. They each grabbed a chair from the dining room table and turned them to face me.

"Let me guess. We're having an intervention," I finally said.

"Yes, Max," Jules quickly agreed, "We are. And considering you almost just shot me in the head, maybe you should acknowledge it's FUCKING OVERDUE. I mean, was me getting a tomahawk to the head in this living room last year not enough for you?"

I looked at the two of them. "You're serious about this?"

"Yeah, we are," answered Jules. "And you know what? *You* better take it seriously because I took the rest of the day off for this shit, and I'm already getting death threats from the boss because of all the time I've missed rehearsing the act."

"How is Cuban Pete?" I tried to change the subject.

"Well, he was much better after you left Saturday night and nobody else was there to completely fuck up our set."

Oh, Christ. Here we go.

"But it's okay, we went back and guess what? Your whole fucking fiasco ended up putting the crowd on our side, even though I was a complete emotional wreck after all that shit went down. I mean, Jesus, I felt like Judy Garland without her pep pills, being held up for the camera by Gene fucking Kelly on the set of *Summer Stock*. But, hey, we ended up getting a standing O, so I guess you did us a favor."

PMA's turn. "Max, now you have to do yourself a favor."

"Quit the case," I said, guessing where this was going.

Jules and PMA both nodded vigorously.

"You realize it's not just the case that's the problem," I continued. "It's what Jules was just talking about. Last year. Dark Sky."

"Max, you can't say that," insisted PMA. "You don't know what's going on and you're paranoid from the drugs.

"It's not just the drugs," I said to them. "Howard's acting weird again. The nurse linked Kanuskey directly to MK-Ultra. I showed up at the club where Jules was playing, and Veronica and Mr. Barry Filer, Mr. Barry Fucking Filer, were in the audience. Then somewhere in the wee small hours of the morning, I saw a zombie that used to be a U.S. Senator…"

Jules interrupted me. "Of course you did, Max. And let's not forget when you saw CIA clones on the tram."

I looked down at the carpet. It needed a good cleaning. Just like my head.

"Oh yeah," she added. "And of course--you were *raped*." She did air quotes on the "raped," which I thought was more than a little unfair.

"Max," PMA said, "You can't take much more of this shit. You just slept through Monday. And look at you, pale, sweaty, out of your mind…"

"I have to see this through…"

"See what through? Your FUCKING DEATH??" Jules was losing what little patience she ever had. "You know what, I got enough on my plate! I'm a little old to be couch-surfing at my age, but that's how I'm living, in a two-bedroom apartment with three Cubans who don't know how to pick up! Talk about the fucking Bay of Pigs!"

"Then come back here."

"You get it together and we'll talk, I'm not going to sit here and watch you turn into Corky from *Life Goes On*!"

"I don't even know what that means!" I said holding my head in pain.

"Okay, c'mon!" As usual, PMA was the mature person in the room. "Let's not argue, I want Max to see something." He got up and turned on the TV. While it warmed up, I looked at Jules.

"You think I'm losing it?"

She looked at me sadly. "Honey, you've already lost it. Now it's just a matter of *containment*."

"I recorded this the other day, in the middle of a cable news show," PMA continued as he hit the PLAY button on the DVR remote.

A hot blonde anchor, not the one I threw up on, was interviewing a Congressional representative from our very own great state of New York, Eddie di Pineda. I had seen this dipwad before--he was hard to miss, since he was attracted to cameras like a fly to horseshit. A handsome, boyish second-generation Puerto Rican, Eddie, rumor had it, was being fast-tracked for bigger things. So far, the only talent I saw he had was wearing a caring and empathetic expression while selling whatever horrible fascist line of thinking his Super Pac overlords needed him to peddle.

"…but Max Bowman, the man who supposedly exposed Dark Sky, he's had some recent and very public meltdowns…" said the anchor.

Representative Eddie took a moment as if to gather his thoughts, but, to me, it seemed like they had all been gathered for him way before the interview.

"…and that's my concern," he began in a well-rehearsed monotone. "I don't like to judge. But I will say this was a man who was praised for his integrity, who was seen as some kind of heroic everyman, someone who all by himself managed to bring down this company…"

 "All by himself," I repeated for PMA's benefit. "Kid, you never get your due."

He shushed me.

"…and yet, we suddenly seem him doing all sorts of questionable things in public. So we have to ask, can he be trusted? Were last year's events as clear-cut as he presented them?" Representative Eddie quickly answered his own question. "Dark Sky was a wonderful patriotic company in my opinion, as well as an excellent resource for our military overseas and our brave men and women in the service. Their funding cuts off in just two months and I think that should be a matter of grave concern for all Americans."

"Oh, shut the fuck up," I said.

PMA shushed me again.

"Now, this Max Bowman…" Representative Eddie continued, "…seems to be some kind of attention-seeking maniac or perhaps even a drug addict. Which leads me and many, many others I've spoken to who know much more about this situation than I do to again wonder, how much of what happened last year was some kind of stunt on his part? How much of it was smoke and mirrors designed to unfairly impugn Dark Sky?"

"There's no evidence of that, Representative di Pineda," interrupted the anchor, to her credit.

"No, not yet," parried Representative Eddie. "All I'm saying is Max Bowman does not appear to be the hero we all believed he was. And, as you know, the world is just as dangerous today as it was when we were putting Dark Sky to work over in the Middle East. As a matter of fact, it's a lot more dangerous. There was no ISIS then, Syria was more stable…frankly, today we need all the help we can get. And the help we need is no longer going to be available, because Congress, over my objections, ended the Dark Sky government contract and…well, we're the weaker for it. And a lot more vulnerable even here at home."

"Turn it off," I said with a lot more hostility than I realized I had in me. PMA did as I asked. I fumed silently a moment.

"Max," PMA said softly, "whatever you think is going on, whatever I think is going on, the point is, you can't win now, okay? They've discredited you and now what's going to happen is going to happen. It's out of your hands."

"Barfing on CNN is never a good career move," added Jules helpfully.

"Then what was Saturday night all about? If they already discredited me, why did they dose me again?"

"I don't know, maybe to keep you on your back so you can't rebut this guy? Or maybe this psycho woman is just a freak who wants to keep messing with your head for her own reasons. All I know is, you need to lay low for a while and concentrate on getting better, before something else happens."

"Look, both of you, I appreciate that you're worried about me…" I tried to rally, but I was fading. I felt the bottom falling out from under me. I felt myself falling through space. "But…I took the money…from Mel…and I…I…the Comic Con is next week…and…"

I was sweating again. They were looking at me like I was a sick child that didn't know any better.

"Then just get a death certificate on Mikov." PMA jumped in. "That's all you need to do. That's all you need to do. Let everything else alone, Max."

"But…"

"Go back to the sister in Pennsylvania and ask her what name it's under. This shouldn't be hard."

I shook my head, wanting to make them understand, wanting to die. "You…you guys are missing the big picture here. If I don't do anything…they're going to keep coming after me…they want to…to destroy me…"

I felt myself leaving my body, watching this sad, pathetic, aging man completely losing his shit. I was no longer in control of him. He was a shell of a human being who couldn't hold it together, couldn't stop the tears anymore.

"…and there's shit all…I can do about it…"

"Max…?" Jules said uncertainly, too worried to even use a four-letter word.

I watched as Max Bowman began sobbing uncontrollably again. He cried. He cried and cried. Sweat and tears were both forming rivulets that poured down over his cheeks. I understood his pain. I understood it was hopeless. If I made any moves, the dark forces would get me. If I didn't do a goddam thing, they would get me. It was hopeless. I was painted into a corner and nothing would save me.

I felt myself fall to the floor. Jules rushed over to my side. I started sobbing again. She hugged me.

"I love you even when you cry like a girl," she said.

"That's so…heteronormative," I said as I sniffed loudly so snot didn't run all over my face.

I looked up, through the tears, and saw her and PMA looking at me with concern and pity. I hated seeing that in their faces, I hated being helpless, I hated this whole fucking thing, but I couldn't get my mind right. I couldn't.

And I really hated that, for a flash of a second, I thought I saw Mr. Barry Filer, laughing his ass off in the corner.

Augustine Bravino

My condition wasn't improving. As a matter of fact, it was getting a whole lot worse.

I had started losing chunks of time.

Because the next thing I knew, I was on the I-95, a little south of Philly, riding shotgun in my own car. PMA was driving. I had no memory of going to get the car or getting into it. And I had no idea where I was going.

"Where are you taking me?" I asked with a sleepy voice.

"You don't remember?"

I shook my head.

"Jules insisted I had to get you out of the city. So I'm taking you back to D.C. with me. You can crash in one of the bedrooms at my mom's house."

"Your mom's house? Is this okay with her...?"

"I'll make it okay with her. You should be safe there until you shake the drugs. You know you saw Barry Filer in your living room, right?"

I turned with a start to the back seat. Eydie was sleeping there safe and sound.

"Yes, I brought the dog too," said PMA. "Another thing for my mother to yell at me about."

"You didn't bring my iPhone, right?" I suddenly asked with a whole lot of urgency.

"You already asked me that five times," the kid replied. "I brought your whole David Muhlfelder fake identity kit, including the CIA phone. Everything's in your pockets. There's nothing we have that can be traced to you."

He glanced at me and saw that I looked more lost than ever. And, for some reason, that made him angry.

"I'm not messing around this time, Max. This time, when we get to my house, I'm getting you to a psychiatrist, we're getting you some tests, we have to find out what those drugs did to you. It's not getting better on its own and you know it."

"You're right. I know it." I answered. It was all I knew. What I didn't know was what to feel, how to feel, who I was or what to do with myself. I was numb.

"And then, I want you to think about going to this group with me."

"Re-occurring cycles?"

"Yes, Max, re-occurring cycles, and yes, you already told me twice that 're-occurring' isn't a word, but it's the term Keenan uses, so…"

"Tell me more about what Keenan says. It helps me to focus on other things."

"Well…Keenan is all about getting you past your everyday mindset, going beyond your self-imposed limits and finding your happiness through directed action--tapping into what *you* want, instead of what the world wants from you. You can make your own reality and make it work for you."

This was starting to sound familiar. I looked at the kid. His eyes were weird.

"So let me ask you something," I said, trying to dig deeper. "What does Keenan say about when other people…need things?"

"Other people's needs get in the way. I mean, I love Jules, but when she went off her meds, her problems dragged you down to the point where you weren't functioning, right? I think that's what you told me."

"So…Keenan would say I didn't need to be there for Jules when she went through that. So I could function."

"No, I don't know if he…I mean…I'm just saying, other people can drag you down if you don't…"

"…ignore them?"

He didn't know what to say about that. I did.

"Kid, that's some Ayn Rand shit right there. Which makes me wonder…"

"It has nothing to do with Ayn Rand, her name was never mentioned, you're making this into something it's not. Look, just come to the next meeting. This one was an introductory one, just me and a bunch of other newbies. The next one will have some of the members that have been in this thing for a while and they can all explain it a lot better than…"

"Wait, there are members? What are they members of?"

"I'm going to find out more next time."

"Sounds a little creepy."

He sighed. "Another conspiracy, Max?"

Whatever. The time for talking was over.

A couple minutes later, we were at a gas station off an exit. The kid was filling the tank while I sat in the car and played with the satellite radio. I came upon *Wuda Cuda Shuda* by 2 Chainz featuring Lil Boosie. Okay.

After the kid was done, he replaced the pump and came over and knocked on the window. I rolled it down.

"I'm gonna get a bottle of water, you want anything?" he asked.

I looked at him. He should have had this. Or, to put it in 2 Chainz talk, he shuda had this.

"Coke Zero," he nodded to himself, finally remembering who he was dealing with, and headed toward the minimart.

After he was inside, I got out of the car, causing Eydie to momentarily panic. I motioned to her to calm down. It didn't work, but when she saw I was merely walking around to the driver's side to get back in, she jumped up and happily licked my hand. I petted her gently and started up the car.

"Don't sweat it, pups," I told her. "We're getting out of here."

Then, as I saw the kid coming out of the minimart with our beverages, I drove off.

Without him.

I didn't feel good about leaving PMA stranded at the gas station. But I didn't have much of a choice. If I didn't follow through on the case, if I didn't fight back against the shit in my system, I knew in my gut I was a dead man. PMA was too scared to fight--too scared of what might happen to me and maybe what might happen to him. Last year had been traumatic for both of us and I certainly didn't blame him if he was mentally retreating to the safety of Keenan Van Zola and re-occurring cycles. I just knew I wasn't strong enough to argue with him and, at the same time, do what I needed to do.

So maybe I was taking Keenan's advice after all. I was ignoring the kid so I could function. Of course, in this case, the kid would be okay without me for now--I wasn't leaving him in a bad situation, just at a random Stop and Shop. I was the one running headfirst into trouble, I was the one going back to face whatever I had to face. As I told PMA, they were going to keep coming at me no matter what I did. Instead of waiting for that happen, I had to take control of my own fate. So that was what I was going to do.

Sorry, kid.

I lost another chunk of time.

I don't know when I decided to go back to Freemansburg on my way home to New York, but somewhere on the road, I must have made that choice and turned off to take the I-78 west. The kid was right about one thing--I did need to get a death certificate on Mikov to placate Mighty Mel and justify my fee. So it was back to the sister for more fun and games.

And now here I was, back in the parking lot of the same decrepit bar where I parked before. As I gazed aimlessly out through the windshield, I was more than a little amazed that I made it there in one piece. I supposed it was like when you took the same route home from work every damn day of your life and put your brain on autopilot while you made the trip. Didn't mean you were in danger of running over somebody, just meant you were operating on reflex alone.

At least that's what I told myself while I got out and inspected the car to see if I had actually run over anybody.

There was no damage as far as I could see, so apparently I was able to drive while unconscious. It was fun to add new skills at my age. Somewhat relieved, I let Eydie out and walked her over to the grass to shit and piss her. Her soft eyes were looking up at me the whole time as she took care of her business, because she knew something about me was still way, way off.

"Don't worry, Eydie," I told her. "I'm okay, pups. Daddy just has snakes in his head."

That's when Augustine approached me.

I had spotted him hanging back in the corner of the parking lot that backed up against some trees. He was skinny, about 5'10", in his early thirties maybe, with a small moustache, goatee and short brown hair, and he was wearing a thick brown corduroy jacket, brown jeans, and sneakers. He was very brown and, I thought, vaguely European, maybe because he was holding the cigarette he was smoking in a slightly affected way.

He came a few steps toward me and said something I couldn't understand.

"What?" I said.

"That your dog?" he mumbled a little louder with a slight accent. Again, vaguely European.

"Yeah." I didn't like this guy and I didn't like his vibe.

"What are you doing here?" he asked next, tapping the ashes off the end of his cig.

"Just visiting," I said. What the fuck?

He looked around, then brought his head back around to me as Eydie finished shitting.

"What do you do?" he asked.

"What do I do?"

"For a living, boss. What do you do?"

"I'm a baseball stadium inspector," I replied as I gathered the dogshit in the poop bag. He looked at me with a little smile and mumbled something else.

"What?" I said.

"I used to play for the Cardinals," he said.

"The ones in St. Louis?" I asked, walking over to the dumpster to get rid of the poop bag. He shrugged. He had the build of a check-out clerk, not a second baseman. But then again, we were both being ridiculous. The undertow, however, was definitely not amusing.

"What are you doing here?" he asked again.

"Why are you talking to me?" I asked back, this time in a rough way.

"I like your dog," he answered. "What's your name?"

"Ralph Kramden. And you are?"

"Augustine," he said. "Augustine Bravino. This is a pretty town."

I looked over at the bar. It was mid to late afternoon and there was actually a light on inside.

"Hate to break up this party," I said, "But I have to go. Have a nice day."

He mumbled something and threw what was left of his cigarette onto the gravel.

"What?"

"I don't like nice days." And then Augustine Bravino walked off.

I entered the bar with the dog, as I had before, and found my old friend the bartender wiping down the place.

He saw me and immediately started hollering at me.

"You!"

I pointed to myself questioningly.

"Yeah, you. What the hell did you say to old lady Michaels? After you left town last time, she called and ripped me a new one for telling you her address, Jesus, man, don't do that to me again."

I sat on a stool and put forty bucks on the bar.

"That ease the pain?"

He eyed the bills and nodded casually as one might at the successful conclusion of a maybe not-so-wonderful transaction.

"Jack?" he asked me.

"Jack," I answered.

He poured and I watched.

"You know a guy named Augustine Bravino?"

He gave me a look that indicated he had never met anyone or anything close to an Augustine Bravino. I took care of the drink.

"You going back to see the old lady?" he asked.

"Yep."

"Glutton for punishment, ain'tcha?"

"You have no idea, pal."

After I sucked down two Jacks, Eydie and I trudged back up the hill behind the bar to pay a return visit to Debra Michaels. I was still disturbed by Augustine Bravino. I didn't know what that was all about and it set me back on edge, but the booze calmed me down a little. I had to be calm if I was going to deal with Debra Michaels again.

"Eydie," I said to the dog as I banged on her door, "We're going to try and make this quick. Provided the old bitch actually answers the door." I looked back up and saw that the door had already been answered and I was looking straight into the semi-angry but semi-amused eyes of old lady Michaels. It was like she couldn't be mad at me. It was like she was happy to see me again.

"I meant a different bitch, not you," I said.

"I've been thinking about you," she said.

"I'm memorable," I replied.

"What do you want? I told you I didn't want to talk anymore."

"Can I come in and not talk some more? It's still cold out here."

She was already done pretending she didn't want me around, so she opened the door and I walked in. That's when I saw she had a bunch of Mikov pencil sketches spread out all over the floor. They were impressive as always in their own dark and demented way.

"Wow. More Mikov. How much of your brother's work do you have?" I asked as I picked up the dog and walked gingerly around the artwork, looking it all over. There had to be about twenty to thirty of them, all on papers torn out of a sketch pad.

"All of it," she said glumly. "Such a waste."

"Doesn't have to be. And shouldn't be," I said, sitting down with the dog in my lap.

"You think they're good?" She seemed surprised. "These are things he didn't even finish."

"Between this stuff and what you have hanging in the other room, you could put together a coffee table book of his art. Get it out there in the public eye. Nobody even knows any other Mikov art exists, comic book nerds would pay a fortune to have it."

"Comic book nerds." She rolled her eyes. "Oh, to be worshipped by comic book nerds."

"Don't knock it. I was one."

"Yes. But you grew up."

"Some would argue with that assessment."

She sat down across from me, but she kept her eyes on the artwork.

"I've had all this in storage for years, ever since he…" She stopped and looked up at me. "I just couldn't bear to go through it all. Your visit made me get it out. I forgot how other people responded to his work. It made me *need* to look at it all again."

"Well, I need something too. That's why I came back."

"What?" she asked, freezing up.

"Something that proves your brother passed away. I need it to close out this case."

"Well, I don't have anything like that," she snapped. "Just his ashes."

"Okay, well, what name was he using when he…" I trailed off.

"…when he killed himself. Say it. We're adults here."

"That's right, you assumed I was a grown-up. Look, I can track down the paperwork, I just need you to tell me what name he was using at the time, where it happened maybe…"

She crossed her slim legs and considered me. She was wearing a relatively new track suit of some kind that showed that she was still in pretty good shape for being in her early seventies. Our eyes met and connected in some other dimension. There was some kind of spark between us. She knew it and I knew it. And we both knew it was too weird to mention.

"This is for Mel Chesler?" she finally asked.

I nodded, pretty much knowing what was coming next.

"I wouldn't spit on the floor for Mel Chesler."

"I'm aware," I said. "But would you spit on the floor for me? Because if I don't get this, I'm pretty well screwed."

"I think about you because you interest me. You seem like the creative type, yet you wander around knocking on people's doors for a living. You don't add up."

"Neither do you."

That caused her to lean back a little. "How so?"

"I don't know exactly. How you look, how you move…something different. Were you a dancer?"

She burst out laughing. "Oh, good Lord, you're insane."

"Speaking of insane, tell me about Dr. Frederick Kanuskey."

The laughter stopped.

"Your parents let him take your brother away. I have the feeling that was the start of his troubles."

"Kanuskey wasn't a doctor, he was a butcher. He just carved up minds instead of meat."

"I've heard. Electroshock, drugs, other atrocities…all to try and make Ben Mikov what he wasn't."

"Well, my father the rugged manly steelworker couldn't deal with my brother being…" She let it drop off. "He saw an article about Kanuskey in a magazine or something. He wrote to him, Kanuskey answered, they had a few phone calls…and the next thing I knew…" She paused. "Well, I didn't have a brother anymore."

"What about Reginald?"

Her eyes flashed. "You *have* done your homework," she said with a little piss and vinegar, heavy on the piss. "Ben's foster brother. Yes, he was a willing patient for Dr. Kanuskey, from what Ben told me. But Ben had more fight. More spirit."

"You got a little yourself."

"There's nothing left to fight for."

I nodded towards the artwork on the floor. "His legacy."

She considered it again, studying it, looking for some relief from her ongoing pain.

Meanwhile, Eydie started licking my hand. I petted her again and something went a little warpy in my mind. I had learned to recognize that feeling as a signal that I would be sinking again relatively soon. I didn't want that to happen in front of the sister. I got up, still holding the dog who was still licking my hand.

"Look, Debra, I'm sorry, but I have to go…can you help me out or not?"

She looked disappointed. "I thought maybe we could look through the artwork together. It would help if there was someone here that understood and appreciated his work…"

"I'll take a rain check, I have to get back to the city. But I need to know what name your brother was using when…"

She stood up. "And I already told you. As long as I live, I will never do anything that would benefit Mel Chesler in any way." She wasn't angry. She was just stating a fact.

More warpy feelings. I had to get out of there. I got to the door when I heard her get up. I turned to see her walking carefully around the sketches on the floor and approaching me. She saw I was growing unsteady.

"Are you all right?" she asked.

"What drugs did they use on your brother?" I asked back, with my words coming out in a rush. "This is for me, nobody else. What did the CIA give Kanuskey to feed those kids? If you know, you gotta tell me."

"What are they doing to you?" she asked, almost in a whisper.

"Fuck if I know. That's the scariest part."

Her eyes widened. "I don't know if I can trust you."

"You got a computer?"

She shook her head.

"If you can get on one, look me up. Max Bowman. You'll see what I did and maybe you'll understand why they want to get me."

She put a hand on my arm.

"Stay here. You'll be safe."

"I can't. I can't."

Eydie barked. I put the pooch down on the carpet and as I straightened back up, before I knew what was going on or could process it, she gently took my face and kissed me. It wasn't a peck, it was a long loving kiss and it was on the lips.

And as it happened, that's when I saw it.

And that's when I knew I had to go.

"Goodbye, Debra."

I opened the door and left.

The last thing I remembered was walking back to the bar parking lot towards my car and seeing Augustine Bravino standing next to it, smoking another cigarette, asking me, "Did the baseball stadium pass your inspection?"

Then I woke up.

I was lying across the back seat of my car and it was dark outside. There were other cars in the lot now, customers of the bar I assumed, because it was night. What time, I didn't know. I checked my pockets. I still had my wallet, my CIA phone, my keys, everything.

But not everything.

It was just hanging there limply, over the back of the front seat, with nothing on the other end.

Eydie's leash.

She was gone.

I ran through the parking lot and threw open the door to the bar with such force, the glass in it rattled and threatened to break. I pushed my way through the minor mob of small town drunks whose purpose in life had been shut down two decades earlier with the steel mill and went right to the bar, where the bartender was filling a glass from the tap.

I hurled myself across the bar, put my hands around his neck and started screaming, "WHO IS AUGUSTINE BRAVINO? WHO IS AUGUSTINE BRAVINO?" over and over again, until a few of those small town drunks pulled me back off the bar and onto the floor and kicked me over and over again. Only one of them was really serious about it, and he was the one wearing the fucking boots of course, and I felt some serious hurt in my rib section.

And then suddenly, I was being thrown out of the bar, through the open doorway, just like in an old southern-fried 70's Burt Reynolds movie, hitting the gravel, looking up at the neon Budweiser sign in the window, feeling all the hurt that had just been inflicted on me, as I heard the bartender yelling at me, "NEVER COME IN HERE AGAIN YOU FREAK, NEVER!"

I got to my feet and stumbled my way to the car. The back door was still open from when I rushed out of it, so I shut it and opened the front one, got in and drove a couple of miles until I was nowhere in particular. Then I pulled over and fell asleep and had nightmares about Mr. Barry Filer and Veronica and Dr. Frank Olson, and when I woke up, it was morning. Wednesday morning.

Dr. Reginald

Okay, where the hell was I?

I ended up parking the car in a field of dead weeds, off to the side of a dirt road leading into the woods, so I could crash and burn. I wasn't sure how far I had gotten from Freemansburg, but I knew I made a point of not driving too long, because I was very conscious of the fact that I would soon be unconscious.

I got out of the car and stretched--and immediately knew that was a mistake, because there was a sharp pain coming from my left side, where the drunk with the boots had gone for blood. I had either a cracked or a bruised rib, that I was sure of, but there wasn't much I could do about it, I knew ribs and broken toes were beyond medical solutions. I groaned and walked around the car a couple of times, wondering why it wasn't warmer. We were two days into March, for God's sake.

I tried not to think of Eydie, who couldn't bear to be separated from me by a door. Now she could be in another state for all I knew. Then there was PMA and Jules, both of them either worried sick about me--or maybe finally just giving up on any chance of my salvation.

I leaned against the car and sucked in some clean morning air, something in short supply back in the city. Then I thought, how the hell did Augustine Bravino find me in Freemansburg? Especially when I did everything I could not to get tracked this time around? It didn't make sense. And that's when I realized just what an incredible mind-blowingly Guinness-World-Record-setting fucking moron I was.

I knelt down and instantly saw it under the car.

A GPS tracking device. Maybe fifty bucks from your neighborhood Radio Shack, back when there used to be Radio Shacks. I pulled it off and considered throwing it into the woods, but then I remembered how James Bond handled this sort of thing back in the day when Sean Connery ruled supreme. So I got back in the car with the device and drove to the nearest town that had a minimart--a town appropriately named Hellertown--and went in to buy a Coke Zero to wake myself up. When I came back out, I spotted an old battered pick-up truck in the parking lot and attached the GPS device to the bottom. That would keep Augustine and company occupied for a few minutes.

And all that reminded me of something else I should have already thought of. Eydie had a microchip implanted in her shoulder, most dogs did for ID purposes. Did the chip have a GPS component? Could I track her location with it?

There was hope.

I drove back to the city, repeating the mantra over and over in my head.

Blue Fire must be pure...

Blue Fire must be sure...

For Good to be purged of Evil...

Blue Fire must endure!

No, it wasn't as catchy as the Green Lantern oath, but it was all I had. And I needed something. I didn't want to cry hopelessly about my missing dog, the way I had on my seventeenth birthday when I backed over the family dachshund, and I definitely didn't want to lose another chunk of time. I wanted to be stronger and better than that, so I repeated the Blue Fire incantation over and over, keeping my mind tight, alert, working, focused and just this side of sane. But only just.

I made it back to the island and, when I got back inside my apartment, I immediately used my CIA smartphone to put in a call to the vet's office about Eydie's microchip. A recording told me they wouldn't be in for another hour, they were off Wednesday mornings. So I showered and did a little grooming. Trimmed my ear hair, my nose hairs, flossed, and, in general, did what I needed to do so I could feel like an acceptable member of the human race again. I stopped and looked at my unshaven face in the mirror. I had almost a week's growth now. My facial hair would give me some measure of anonymity--it was further along than a fashionable stubble, but still very, very far from a lumberjack beard.

Still in my bathrobe, I made myself a bagel and then sat down in front of the TV to get my bearings. I wanted to find out what was happening on my favorite network to throw up on, CNN. After a few minutes, I picked up a pretty big piece of news. Late yesterday, the governor of New York had appointed Representative Eddie di Pineda, the guy advocating for Dark Sky getting its funding back, to the still-missing Senator Marks' seat. The fix was in. I had no doubts in my mind that the creeps would have their contract renewed before their final 60 days was up.

The phone in the office kept ringing. Was it PMA trying to figure out where I was? Mighty Mel demanding to know if I had done my job? Satan letting me know my reservation on the next ferry to Hell was confirmed? That last one might have been the only call I would have taken.

But death wasn't the plan for me. Obviously, if they wanted to kill me, I would already be dead. Instead, they seemed to be systematically destroying every aspect of my life--while being careful not to actually take that life away. Or maybe they were trying to make me kill myself so they didn't have to bother, but that wasn't a move I was about to make. Not that I thought suicide was immoral or any of that shit. I just never saw the point for some reason. Now I was beginning to, and maybe that change in attitude was part of their agenda. Who the hell knew.

The doorbell rang and snapped me out of my morbid musings.

Did they know I was here? I was lucid enough to double-lock the door after I came in an hour or two ago, and the thing was about six inches thick, so I knew nobody was getting in unless I wanted them to, but I still carefully and quietly walked up the stairs to see what was up. I didn't want anybody to know I was on the other side of the door.

Nobody tried to find out.

After a moment, an envelope was shoved under the door. Outside, I heard whoever it was walk away, so I climbed up the rest of the steps and picked up the envelope. I turned it over, but there was nothing written on it anywhere, not even my name. I ripped it open and found a small Ziploc bag inside. And inside that bag, I saw a little blood and hair of some kind, wrapped around something small and metallic. I manipulated the contents with my fingers through the plastic, moving things around so I could make some sense of it.

Then I realized the color of the hair was familiar. Then I realized it wasn't hair, it was fur.

Then my heart stopped.

Apparently, they had dug out Eydie's microchip from between her shoulder blades and immediately stuck the whole mess, blood, fur and all, in the Ziploc. Another message. There would be no way to track where she was, if she was even still alive. If she wasn't, that would mean I had two dead dogs on my lifetime resume. But I couldn't go there, not yet. I had to keep it together. I had to have some kind of hope in place. And I had to stop visualizing those assholes cutting her up to rip that thing out of her.

I fell back on the landing, groaned because of my aching side and sat there for a few minutes, repeating my new mantra...

Blue Fire must endure, Blue Fire must endure, Blue Fire must endure...

After a while, I managed to get up and go to my bedroom, where I packed up some shit in my rolling carry-on, locked up the apartment and walked down to the subway station.

Nobody was going to know where I was for a while.

I checked into a boutique hotel on the Upper East Side, just a few blocks away from the building that housed Rosenbaum Research, Dr. Reginald Canun's place of employment. It was a hotel where a room for a couple of nights cost more than a month's rent in some places. But this was New York.

I crashed on the bed for a while, trying to sleep, but I couldn't stop the visions of Eydie howling and desperate with fear, not knowing where I was--or where she was, for that matter. The really sad part was this was the best case scenario. The worst? Her little dead body was in a dumpster somewhere. That thought caused my stomach to cramp up and, again, I had to try to block it out.

Still, sleep finally came. My exhaustion and poisoned system combined to take me down for a few hours. When I woke up, it was close to five in the afternoon. I had to make a call and hoped it wasn't too late, otherwise I might waste another day or two. To wake me up a little, I got a Diet Coke out of the minibar fridge--hotel fuckers never stocked Coke Zero. After checking the seal, I took a couple of swigs, then I opened up my CIA phone and punched in a number.

"Dr. Canun's office," said a young woman's voice.

"I need to see Dr. Canun for a few minutes tomorrow," I said.

A pause. "He doesn't really take appointments, he's not that kind of doctor."

"I know, this is personal. I have some important news about his brother that we should talk about."

"Oh." That shook her out of official demeanor. "Please hold."

A few minutes went by.

"Hello?" It was a man's voice, but extremely…well, there was no other word for it, the voice was prissy. "Who is this? What brother are you talking about?"

"Benjamin Mikov."

A pause.

"You didn't answer my other question. Who is this?"

"My name is David Muhlfelder. I've just returned from Mikov's sister's house. I really think we should talk. And tomorrow, I'm only in town for another day."

Another pause.

"He's not really my brother."

"And Kanuskey wasn't really your father. I know the deal, Reginald."

Another pause, and then a sigh of surrender.

"Look, if you want to come in tomorrow, I can give you a few minutes around three. But that's about it. I really don't have much to say about all this, truth to tell. I mean, how are you involved in any of this?"

"I'll tell you tomorrow at three." And then I hung up.

Yeah, I had lied a few times. But as a fortune cookie had once told me, "For a good cause, wrongdoing may be virtuous."

Thursday afternoon. I had spent as much time as possible sleeping, eating room service and getting as much rest as I could. I knew I was once again about to sail into uncharted waters and I wanted to be as strong as I could be for the next round of strangeness.

It was a little difficult getting ready, due to my rib and other assorted bruises left by the assorted shoes of Freemansburg, but I moved slowly and got myself together. I put on another one of my new Bloomingdale's shirts and a sport coat on top of it. The mirror told me I looked a little pale, but not unusually so for the tail end of a New York winter. Besides, the fledgling beard covered most of it, not to mention the burn on my cheek. I looked good enough. I threw on my winter coat and left the room.

I took the elevator down to the small lobby and headed for the exit. That's when I heard a familiar voice.

"Good morning…"

I turned and saw PMA, who headed across the lobby towards me like a heat-seeking missile.

"How could you just leave me in the middle of nowhere like that?"

"How'd you find me?" I responded.

"Well, first of all, I knew you'd come back to New York because you're a dumb stubborn son of a bitch. So I went to your apartment, let myself in and looked around. You were gone and so was your suitcase. Then, because I remembered you kept talking about the Upper East Side, I just started calling all the hotels up here and asking for my good friend David Muhlfelder."

"Your phone on?" I asked with concern.

"It's off and I left it in my car. And I'm paying twenty-two bucks an hour parking so you're going to pay me back for that."

"How'd you get home?"

"Do you really care?"

I shrugged. "No." I checked my silver watch. "I gotta go, I'm late for an appointment."

"You mean *we're* late for an appointment." He followed me out the hotel door.

"Kid, I don't blame you for being pissed, but it's been a rocky couple of days." I dug out the Ziploc from the pocket of my sport coat and showed it to him. He looked at it questioningly. "That's Eydie's microchip. They took her from me in Freemansburg. They had a tracking device on my car."

His face darkened as he stared at the Ziploc a moment, then handed it back to me without a word.

"Don't tell Jules about this," I cautioned.

"Where are we going?" he asked.

"To see Dr. Frederick Kanuskey's son."

If PMA had been drinking a beverage, he would have done what was known in dramatic circles as a spit take. "How the hell did you find him?"

"Through Dr. Frederick Kanuskey's grandson."

"Max, sometimes you amaze me."

I nodded. "Sometimes I amaze myself. So we're friends again?"

"As long as I'm not abandoned at any more gas stations in the future," he answered.

It was only a few blocks to the building that housed Rosenbaum Research. As we got closer, I recognized it immediately, because every day as I walked Eydie on the island, I stared at it from across the river. Its design fascinated me. Fourteen floors tall, it had an elaborate asymmetrical open-air rooftop design that featured a series of square columns and chimneys that resembled a sort of small, stacked Acropolis.

And there it was--a large park, across the street from the building to the north. The same park where I spent the night with the zombies a few days ago.

"It's in here?" asked PMA. "Isn't this the building you always point out from the island? The one with the freaky roof?"

"Yeah. I actually looked up the place once. It was built in the late 1920's. Almost went under after the market crash in '29. Now it's probably worth more than all of Wall Street was back then."

As we approached the building, we saw a few of the floors went down below street level, but those levels were walled in, creating a tall and very narrow walk space accessible only by a stairway to the side. I peered downwards. Seemed as though it was mostly used for maintenance, there were a few trash cans and not much else. The windows down there had metal bars installed on the inside, probably to keep out intruders.

"That's weird," said PMA looking down with me. "What's on the other side of the wall? The one opposite the building?"

"The FDR."

"The expressway?"

"Yeah, FDR Drive, it goes up along the side of Manhattan along the East River--you can get to the Bronx from there. It was built in the thirties."

"But it's so quiet. You can't hear a peep."

"That's how strong and thick that wall is. They made it that strong and thick so people on the Upper East Side don't have to hear traffic at night."

I then pointed to the bike and pedestrian path overlooking the river that crossed in front of the building. "The FDR goes right underneath that walkway. This building used to actually be right on the waterfront for a few years before Robert Moses decided to put in an eastside expressway and screw everything up."

"Robert Moses?"

"Really? Geez, kid, look him up. This is why you need to get back to college."

"I think that ship has sailed for this semester."

We turned back to the building and walked towards it, just as the vehicle exit door opened and a familiar-looking gate lifted to allow a blue Mercedes to exit. I recognized it all, except for the Mercedes, because I now was positive that this was the building where Veronica had tried to imprison me before I escaped into the night. I couldn't believe the park was right across the street. I must have been wandering around in circles before I finally found it.

"This is where she lives," I said out loud, not meaning to.

"Where who lives?"

"Veronica. This is where she took me after they drugged me at the club."

"In here?" PMA still didn't quite know whether to believe me on these things. "Are you sure?"

"Pretty much."

"Then maybe we shouldn't go back in here."

I thought a moment, then shrugged. "I got nowhere else to go."

I headed for the entrance. PMA followed me. "Max," he said nervously, "Seriously, maybe we should get out of here."

I kept walking.

"This is like when we drove to Montana to pay a casual call on a secret paramilitary camp. We should try to get some help or something, why would you do this by yourself?"

"Just want to make sure God still likes me," I muttered as we approached the doorman, who lived up to his job title and opened the door for us.

We entered and walked up to the Concierge, whose station was set up only a few steps into the lobby. The message of that placement was, if you didn't have legitimate business in this building, you weren't going far.

"Can I help you gentlemen?" he asked in a tone that combined a minimum of civility with a maximum of indifference.

"We have an appointment with Dr. Canun at Rosenbaum Research," I responded. "My name is David Muhlfelder."

He turned and made a call, repeating the information. He nodded to the phone, hung up and turned back to us.

"Fourteenth floor. The elevator porter will take you up to Dr. Canun's area."

Elevator porter?

The kid and I looked at each other, then headed to the elevator not far away, where, yes indeed, an old uniformed man stood inside. As we entered, he gave us as small a smile as he could manage and hit the button for 14, the very top of the building. I noticed that he smelled like the cedar chest my mother used to keep in the basement.

"Is this building entirely occupied by Rosenbaum Research?" I asked politely.

"No, sir. They have the top two and bottom two levels. In between are co-op apartments."

"Kind of unusual set-up in this kind of neighborhood, isn't it?"

"Yes sir," he said, dropping the microscopic smile and replacing it with a thin frown.

With that, the elevator doors opened up to a reception area, where a handsome young man-boy in a crisply-pressed white shirt sat at an expensive wooden desk.

"Mr. Schmidt will help you from here," said the porter and just like that, our budding friendship was over. We approached Mr. Schmidt, who looked up at the two of us with some consternation.

"Are you Mr. Muhlfelder?" he asked. I nodded as he eyed PMA. "I don't have a Mr…"

"Davidson," PMA volunteered.

"…on my list."

"He's my associate. If he causes any trouble, I'll spank him and you can watch."

Mr. Schmidt frowned as he got up. Of the many amenities this building offered, apparently humor was not one of them.

"Follow me, please," he said, turning his back to us.

He led us through a large open area where technicians in lab coats did things that technicians in lab coats did. Scattered about the various workstations were computers and fluids and beakers and so forth. Apparently, they weren't kidding about the research part of the name. The question was, what kind of research? Everyone looked perfectly normal. It didn't seem like the lair of a mad, evil genius--the light was too good.

I was almost disappointed.

The kid nudged me and motioned to the big open window on the eastern wall. I turned and saw the breathtaking view it offered--the East River, my island and, more specifically, the site of the demolished lighthouse where the kid and I had made our final stand last year. I flinched a little.

Finally, we made our way through the research area, an area which took up most of the floor, and arrived at the open door of a large spacious office with its own spectacular view of the river and the island. Inside was a man I assumed was Dr. Reginald Canun, sitting behind an elegant modern desk.

Dr. Reginald was typing furiously on his keyboard. To the side of the desk was a sitting area, made up of some severe modern design-porn furniture--two chairs and a loveseat, separated by a triangular glass coffee table. It all looked beautiful, but not comfortable. This was a guy who shopped for what looked right, not for what felt good for watching a game and having a few beers.

Noticing us, he finally looked up from his computer screen, then got up with a face full of fear and suspicion. He was in his seventies, thin as a weed, with a small grey goatee and glasses, wearing a baby blue cashmere sweater. If he was ever cast as a lead in *The Odd Couple*, he would definitely be playing Felix.

"This is Mr. Muhlfelder," announced Mr. Schmidt, indicating me with his hand.

 "Who's the other one?" Dr. Reginald asked, looking at PMA with a puzzled look.

"He's my associate," I answered before Mr. Schmidt could jump in. Schmidt for his part gave Dr. Reginald a look indicating he would get rid of us if he was given the word.

"It's okay, Archibald," said Dr. Reginald. *Archibald?* "It'll be fine."

Mr. Schmidt left, giving us one final dismissive look. Dr. Reginald stepped out and shook our hands. His palm was sweaty.

"I assumed this would be a private conversation…" he said, once again eyeing PMA.

"He knows everything I do," I said as if I didn't give a shit. I didn't. I had a hunch this guy was connected to all the stink I had been encountering and, if that were true, once I got going, I wasn't going to let him off the floor. Veronica was right. There was some anger in me and I felt it bubbling to the surface.

We entered the office ahead of him. He shut the door behind him and motioned for us to sit down on the loveseat. We did, but it was a little cramped. He sat down across from us on one of the chairs.

"So, as I said on the phone," he began, "I'm a little confused as to what…"

"Do the zoning laws allow for this kind of set-up?" I interrupted. "I've never seen this kind of operation in a residential area."

"The Foundation took care of it," he said matter-of-factly.

"The Foundation?" I asked.

"Yes, we're funded by a private foundation."

"What foundation?"

He was already getting agitated by the stream of questions. "The Rosenbaum Foundation, we're Rosenbaum Research, get it?"

"Who's Rosenbaum?"

"I've had enough of this line of questioning, thank you very much."

"What happens on the bottom levels?" I asked, totally ignoring him.

He blinked in surprise. How did I know about the bottom levels? Elevator porters. You can't trust 'em.

"That's where the clinic is, where the patients are treated. I don't oversee that component. Just up here, the research division, okay?" he answered. "Now then…"

"The very bottom levels? Below street level?"

He nodded impatiently.

"So you keep the zombies down there?"

That was the first thing I said that triggered what was apparently a pretty severe tic on Dr. Reginald's part. The whole right side of his face seemed to close up and reopen with such a violent quick action that I thought it might crack his cheekbone or pop out his eyeball.

"You okay?"

"*Zombies?* Where did you hear…"

"There are rumors going around," I went on. "I was just curious."

"What will they think of next? Vampires?" he fumed. Then he looked at me a little more closely. "*Now* I know who you are," he finally said in his bitchiest tone. "The facial hair threw me off. Aren't you the man who…"

"I tossed my cookies on CNN is what happened. My real name is Max Bowman." I could feel PMA rolling his eyes next to me. "I was afraid if I used that name to make this appointment, you might not see me."

Dr. Reginald sat back in his chair as if he was a preacher and I was a stripper.

"So, you lied. Lovely. Why would I care who you were? You said this was about my *brother*. Or was that a lie too? Because it is certainly beginning to seem like that's the case."

That's when somebody opened the door and announced there was a problem with the Shapiro trials. Whatever that meant. Dr. Reginald looked at us, looked at the woman who had barged in with bad news, then quickly got up, frustrated that he had to go attend to whatever the hell was going on.

"Give me a minute," he said to us with a modicum of snip, and bolted out the door behind the woman, pointedly leaving the door open behind him.

I turned to PMA, who said to me in a tone that somehow combined awe, wonder and derision, "That guy is a real faggot!"

I looked at him with wide eyes. "And what the hell are you?"

"I'm not like that. I bet he has a life-size poster of Lady Gaga up at his house."

I laughed. "You're a credit to your race."

"What does that mean?"

"I mean, what are you so angry about?"

PMA shook his head to make the conversation go away. I got up and went over to Dr. Reginald's desk, on top of which sat several framed pictures. "Looks like he's hetero to me," I said, picking up and showing him an intended-to-be-romantic photo of Dr. Reginald and what I assumed was his pinched and long-suffering wife.

"No way."

"Okay, we'll move on," I said as I put it down and picked up another framed picture. It was of Representative, soon-to-be Senator, Eddie di Pineda. I showed the kid that one too.

"Look," I said. "Autographed and everything. Maybe that's why zoning laws weren't a problem."

"Max," the kid said nervously, "just please come sit back down."

"Why?"

"I don't know, you seem really angry and you're being really aggressive with this guy. We're going to get thrown out before you find out anything. Or worse."

"I'm just getting warmed up, kid."

Just then, the good doctor came back in. He saw me standing and holding the picture of di Pineda and didn't like it.

"I just noticed this guy's picture," I said to him. "Senator Eddie now, right? How do you know him?"

Dr. Reginald shut the door behind him with a stern schoolmaster's expression, walked over and took the photo out of my hand.

"You call me and say you want to discuss a brother I haven't seen in thirty years. And now you want to cross-examine me about the pictures on my desk? I don't think so, Mr. Bowman."

I walked up to him, ready to go toe-to-toe.

"Thirty years, huh. And how long's it been since you saw your son, Dr. Canun? His name's Bruce, right? Seems like a nice guy."

His massive tic struck again.

"He's quite the comic book fan," I continued. "Well…of your brother's work anyway."

"My son and I are estranged, Mr. Bowman, which you obviously already knew or you wouldn't be asking. You seem to want to make me angry."

"Only because a lot of people have been making me angry. You ever hear of a drug called Blue Fire?"

That stopped his mini-fit in its tracks and reignited his epic tic.

"I have a feeling maybe you have," I went on. "I have a feeling maybe it was developed here at this facility. I have a feeling maybe you named it for your long-lost brother Ben's work. Because how the hell else did it get that name?"

He spluttered a little.

"His sister says he killed himself," I finally said to see where that hit him. "You know anything about that?"

If boxing matches were fought with emotions instead of fists, you could say I just knocked Dr. Reginald Canun down to the mat with a flurry of punches to the gut. He turned away from me, walked over to one of the chairs in the sitting area and dropped down in it as if his bones had suddenly disappeared.

"No," he said softly. He looked out the window. His eyes grew wet. Finally, someone was crying besides me.

"Sorry to deliver the bad news," I said to his back. "But apparently your adopted father did a number on him and he never quite recovered. But you…you survived Dr. Kanuskey's program …"

"Ben…Ben fought Dr. K tooth and nail. He just didn't understand…Father was trying to *help* us. But Ben wouldn't *trust* him."

"But you did. You went with the program."

"Yes!" he exclaimed. "I had a wife and children the way you're supposed to!" He was exasperated.

PMA couldn't hold it in any more. "The way you're *supposed* to?"

Suddenly recovering from his brief moment of grief, as if a switch had been flipped, Dr. Reginald shot PMA a look of sheer contempt. "Let me guess…" he said in his most condescending way.

"Go ahead," said PMA. "Guess."

"I don't care how many marches you people throw," Dr. Reginald said angrily, "It still doesn't make your lifestyle *natural*. You can't make electricity by shoving a plug into another plug, now can you?"

"What?" replied PMA, somewhat confused.

Dr. Reginald turned to me. I was still standing behind his desk.

"Why would I believe anything you say? You walked in here a liar and leopards don't change spots on the spot." Clever. "So I need to see some proof to back this up."

"Proof is also what I'm looking for, Dr. Reginald. And so far, all I have to show for my efforts is this."

I walked over with determined steps, took the Ziploc out of my sport coat pocket and threw it on the coffee table. Dr. Reginald stared at it in horror.

"What in GOD'S NAME is THAT?"

"It's from my dog. A dog that was stolen from me yesterday. A dog I want back."

The tic crushed his face again as a freaked Dr. Reginald jumped out of his chair and onto his feet.

"WHAT the HELL is going on here? WHO the HELL are you people?"

"Let's get back to Blue Fire, Dr. Reginald."

"If you don't get out, I'm going to call security. And believe me, you'll wish I hadn't." He walked back behind his desk and reached for the phone.

"Don't touch that fucking thing!" I barked. I was through screwing around. "Not until you tell me more about Blue Fire. I understand some went missing a few weeks ago…"

"How did you know about that?" he asked in a hushed whisper.

"I have friends in high places."

That flummoxed him a little. "Well…yes, we lost a small amount, but got most of it back. So no harm."

"No harm. What if somebody got three doses of it? Would that maybe do some harm?"

He laughed. "Three doses? That doesn't happen. And if it did, that individual would need to be in our care, no one else understands how to handle the effects. I mean, the individual would NOT be functioning very well."

I sat back down on the loveseat next to PMA.

"Yeah," I answered. "Maybe that person might throw up on CNN."

"Oh, now you're going to tell me…"

"He got dosed with it three times, doctor," PMA weighed in with appropriate authority. "I saw it for myself."

We suddenly had Dr. Reginald's undivided attention.

"It makes you think the walls are melting," I continued. "That everybody's out to get you. If you're under stress, it triggers the effects all over again, even when you think it's out of your system. If you take too much of it, you start blacking out, losing chunks of short-term memory. Stop me if I'm getting anything wrong."

"It…it depends. You have to be prepared for it and, and, and kept *away* from stress…"

"Whoever's behind your foundation, doctor, is out to get me. And if you have a few hours, I'll explain it all," I said a little more quietly. It was time to back off. I had dumped about eight hundred pounds of shit on his head in little more than five minutes and it was going to take him some time to dig out from under it.

The door opened again. It was the same woman who had interrupted us before. And she repeated what she had said before. Something was still wrong with the Shapiro trials.

"Okay, OKAY, Elaine, give me a minute. And CLOSE THE DOOR!"

She did so. He looked at me. "How long ago was your last dose?"

"A few days ago."

"You're staying near here?"

I nodded.

"Give me your number."

"You give me yours, Doctor. That's the way this has to go right now."

He sighed again and read it out to me. I programmed it into the CIA phone.

"Are you available after work?" I asked.

He sighed with a profound weariness. "Call me around seven. Look, I don't know what's happened to you, but I want you to know we run a very, very tight ship, a very ethical ship as well, and…"

"I'll call you around seven, Doctor."

"Fine. And please--take *that* with you!" He pointed at the Ziploc bag. I picked it up and put it back in my pocket.

As we walked through the research area on our way out, I looked back and saw Dr. Reginald still standing there in the doorway to his office. His shoulders were slumped and he was staring at the ceiling, as if he was hoping for divine intervention, the kind of divine intervention that would make it as if we had never showed up that afternoon.

I turned back towards the exit from the research area and caught a glimpse of a female worker, an assistant type, not a lab coat type, talking to one of the researchers and taking notes on what she was being told.

It was Candy…aka Betty.

SaveMaxBowman.com

Walking back to the hotel, someone recognized me.

I saw the look in this hipster's eye as we walked by, a look I had already learned to identify from my brief period as a celebrity. It was a look that said, despite my beard and new hairstyle, he knew who I was and was about to tell me so.

I sped up my walk so I didn't have to hear any dick jokes, but behind me, I heard the hipster boy yell, "Fight the f-in' power, Max!"

I turned and the hipster boy gave me two big thumbs up, a practice I didn't think hipsters engaged in, then he went on his way. It was my first indication that something else was in the air. I turned to PMA to see if he understood what had just happened.

"Maybe he hates CNN?" he said.

When we got back to the hotel, I fired up my Chromebook and, on a hunch, did a search on my name, something that was always hard to do if you didn't want to feel like a self-absorbed prick. That's when I discovered that when I yelled "MK-Ultra" live on the air, I unwittingly sparked a whole new conspiracy theory.

My outburst was becoming a rallying cry for a whole lot of people distrustful of anything the government ever did--not that they didn't have good reason for that attitude. Several new websites loudly proclaimed that the CIA had doped me up in an effort to shut me up, and that CNN was complicit in my downfall. They maybe had it half right.

After a little more web surfing, I discovered that MaxBowmanTruth.org and SaveMaxBowman.com were the two websites about me that were getting the most traffic. I was on my way to becoming this generation's Dr. Frank Olson--all I had to do in order to finish the process was…well, die.

I called Dr. Reginald at seven and asked him to meet us in the park near the playground. It would be a little chilly, sure, but there was no sense in going to a bar with him, I wasn't about to drink any beverage served to me by someone I didn't know and, in any event, it was better to be outdoors in public.

He showed on the dot, wearing an expensive and fashionable winter coat, but looking tense as fuck. It was dark, of course, but Dr. Reginald and I sat down on a bench underneath a streetlight, near where I had seen the zombies climbing and sliding just a few days before. PMA stayed standing and prowled around as I had asked him to, acting as a lookout. He was fine with the job because the good doctor pissed him off to no end.

Poor PMA was obviously not yet comfortable with his sexuality. Growing up with a celebrity general for a grandfather had to make him hypersensitive about his masculinity. So he sought out motivational "thought leaders" like Keenan Van Zola and Andre Gibraltar, gurus who might have the keys to becoming a strong and focused guy-man that would triumph over his inner gay man. But he was fighting a battle he didn't need to wage. He was just fine as is. Hopefully, he would figure that out for himself, because, for the time being, he wasn't about to believe anybody else who delivered that judgment.

"Okay," Dr. Reginald led with, "I came out here to meet you because, if you've really had three doses of Blue Fire, you should most definitely be under our care. You must get treatment at our clinic downstairs, I'm afraid of what will happen to you otherwise."

I gave him a hard look. "I'm afraid of what'll happen to me if I listen to you. I think if I go in there, I ain't comin' out."

"Mr. Bowman, please stop with the dramatics, I don't know why you think this is some kind of cheap spy movie, but I'm just trying to help you…"

"You worry me, Dr. Reginald. You worry me because I have the feeling you'll do just about anything anybody in charge will tell you to do, won't you?"

"I sleep well at night, Mr. Bowman. And yes, I do trust those in a leadership role, I…I…I find they're usually there for a reason."

"Yeah. And that reason is usually because they're relentless and ruthless pricks. Most decent, honest people don't think they have any business ordering other people around. Those in power live for that kind of authority. They love the control and they love to play God. Me, I love a cheeseburger."

"I don't know what that means."

"It means I'll probably have a heart attack in the next five years. Anyway, I still want to know who's funding you. In other words…who's Rosenbaum?"

"There is no Rosenbaum as far as I know. It's a private foundation, I don't really interact…"

"You're in charge of the research and you don't interact with the people who fund you?"

"There are go-betweens, they…"

"Who are these go-betweens?"

"Stop! Stop!" The tic again. He held his hand up to his forehead. "I don't handle interrogation well."

I took a deep breath. I couldn't lose him, so I changed gears and softened my voice.

"Then let's go back to your brother Ben. I wasn't lying when I told you I had heard he killed himself, but I need proof. Do you have any idea what name he was using in his last few years?"

"I told you, I haven't seen him in thirty years. Last I knew, he was Ben Mikov. But that was a long time ago." He paused. "And if he really killed himself…I just can't believe…" He almost teared up again. "He had so much talent…such a *horrible* waste…"

"Dr. K broke him, didn't he?"

Dr. Reginald took a deep breath. "Father's methods were misunderstood. There weren't any sophisticated tools available then, just primitive, brutal…" He stopped. The tic again. "I *appreciated* what he did for me, even if Ben couldn't…wouldn't."

"So you liked getting your gayness zapped out of you?"

He looked off into the distance. "No…no, of course, I didn't. Well, I should say, I didn't care about me. The hard part was listening to Benny scream…over and over…so much pain…so much."

He kept looking. I let him. I wanted to see where he would take this.

Finally, he turned back to me. "That's why I decided to carry on Father's work. His objectives were admirable, all he wanted was to help us live normal lives, there just needed to be…a better way to get there. That's why I devoted myself to creating Blue Fire."

"Blue Fire. A kinder, gentler way of mindfucking?"

"You make everything into something dirty, don't you? It's a tool, *that's* all, and it certainly beats running four hundred volts through someone's helpless body!"

"Well, getting your mind twisted in knots isn't so great either. So tell me - what's in this fucking shit and how do I get rid of it?"

"It's a complex blend of psychoactive drugs…dissociatives, deliriants…well, you wouldn't know what I'm talking about."

"You're right."

"We're…we're still in the process of perfecting it. And, if we get it to where we want it, we will be able to cure people of everything from drug addiction to violent impulses to…to…"

"It's mind-fucking."

"Jesus, Bowman! This is groundbreaking! Imagine the endless opportunities for people to rid themselves quickly and easily of self-destructive habits and attitudes…"

"Okay, fine, whatever, just tell me, how long does it take to get this shit out of your system?"

That's when he gave me the really spooky news.

"You…you don't."

"What does that mean?"

"I…I mean…it's designed to replicate itself in your bloodstream…" he said carefully.

"What?" I said in disbelief. "What kind of…"

"With most drugs, the beneficial effects are temporary. After the initial doses, Blue Fire remains inside the patient to support the transformation throughout their lifetime." He saw the horror building on my face and seized on it. "This is why we need to get you into the clinic, you don't know what you're dealing with," he said in an urgent whisper.

Oh, Jesus.

"Blue Fire does things no other drug has ever done before. It's very powerful drug and it only becomes more powerful, and the patient's state of mind during treatment is crucial to its success. We have professional trainers come in to work with our patients *before* Blue Fire is administered…to make sure their mindset is in the right place, so the drug can target the right behaviors, the behaviors we want it to destroy…"

"For Good to be purged of Evil…Blue Fire must endure…" I said, finally getting it. "That's why you named it Blue Fire. You named it for your brother's creation…"

"My God, that was a beautiful piece of work for a cartoon."

"But how does it find the behaviors you want to target? How does it know what part of you to destroy?"

"Well…that's the part we're trying to get down…"

Oh, Jesus Jesus Jesus.

A lot of thoughts were flying through my head again and none of them were good. This drug didn't go away--if he was telling the truth, it would just keep making more of itself inside me, never leaving my system, becoming even more invasive and working to destroy parts of my personality.

My stress levels were rising. I couldn't stop that and I couldn't stop the next attack that I felt coming on. I could tell this was going to be a bad one. It suddenly looked like everything around me kept skipping a half second every so often, like a series of jump cuts in an experimental movie. My head felt hollow, all the sounds around me felt like they were one dimension removed from me.

I was starting to fall apart again.

Not even realizing I was doing it, I got up and started scanning the park around me, looking for PMA. Meanwhile, Dr. Reginald was eyeing me closely, because he could obviously tell my condition was quickly deteriorating.

"Bowman, let me take you into the clinic," he said with urgency. "I promise you no harm will come to you…"

"No, I'm not anxious to get locked up in your zombie basement…"

Things were swirling. I didn't have much time.

"You're talking nonsense again, Mr. Bowman," he said as he got to his feet and gently put his hand on my shoulder. "You need help…"

"KID!" I yelled.

I searched the park area around me, looking for him, but it was pitch black and I couldn't see anyone. Finally, across the way, I saw somebody standing under a streetlight. Somebody familiar. He was waving.

It was Mr. Barry Filer.

He had the same weird smile on his face as he did before in Freemansburg. And he was looking straight at me--well, as straight as Mr. Barry Filer could look at anyone.

"KID!" I yelled again in another direction. Where the hell was he?

"Look, you can't be out on your own," implored Dr. Reginald. "You have to come back with me, believe me, it's for the best." He pulled out his cell phone. "I'm going to get some help over here to take care of you."

Bullshit.

I pulled away and limped off as fast as I could. The limp came from the pain in my side, my rib was aching to beat the band all of a sudden and it hurt to move, but I had to keep going. I turned, but nobody was following me. All I saw was Dr. Reginald standing back by the bench, shaking his head sadly. For me--or for him? Or for both of us?

I thought to myself that I didn't really have to run away. Nobody was going to try and stop me. They were letting me get away on purpose.

Why? I knew the answer.

They weren't going to stop until I lost everything.

The next thing I knew, I was back in my hotel room, panting violently. I lost another small chunk of time, because I didn't remember getting back to the room at all. I was sitting on the bed and *Family Feud* was on the TV. They were about to play Fast Money, where the winner would get twenty thousand dollars. *That* I remembered.

Then I remembered something else. The kid. That's right, PMA. They got him. Just like they got the dog.

I grabbed my CIA phone and furiously scrolled for Jules' number. I hit the button and waited while it rang on the other side. I prayed she was going to answer.

"Hello?"

She did.

"YOU HAVE TO LEAVE TOWN – NOW!" Was that me shouting? Yes, it was.

"Max? What the hell? I'm rehearsing!"

"How the fuck good can you sing *Little Latin Lupe Lu* anyway? Listen to me–they're after everyone connected to me! They just got PMA! You have to GO!"

"What? What the fuck's going on?"

"You have to fucking leave is what's going on!"

"AND WHERE THE FUCK AM I GOING TO GO? I'M FUCKING BROKE!"

And just then the door to the room opened and in walked PMA.

"WHERE THE HELL DID YOU GO?" he yelled at me. Okay, wonderful, I try to save people's lives and suddenly everyone is screaming at me.

"Is that PMA?" demanded Jules.

"Yes…" I said quietly.

"You're an idiot. Let me talk to him."

I gave PMA the phone. He went off into the bathroom with it so they could talk about me behind my back. A lot of whispering, then he came back out and gave me back the phone. I took it. But there was nothing on the other end. Jules had already ended the call.

"Why did you run off like that?" PMA asked.

"I saw Mr. Barry Filer under the streetlight…I thought…I thought they got you…"

"Max, that was me under the streetlight…I was waving to you to let you know I was there."

Still sitting on the bed, I lowered my head and massaged the sides of it with my hands. "Oh Jesus. Oh Jesus. He was trying to get me into the clinic…I thought it was a set-up…"

"He was only trying to take you back to the clinic to *help* you. I talked to him after you disappeared, before I went looking for you…"

"I can't trust them. I can't trust any of them. I saw Candy in the research lab…she's working there…"

"The friend of the rapist? Max, c'mon. You already thought you saw Barry Filer at the nightclub, and Senator Marks playing with a bunch of zombies. You're seeing a lot of things…"

"The building…it's the same one where Veronica took me…"

"Max, you said yourself you couldn't tell what building she took you to, it was dark…"

"It's the same garage…I'm positive…"

"Max, I'm sorry, I can't trust *you* right now. No offense, I don't know if you can separate what's real and what's not."

I pulled out the Ziploc and held it up. "This is real."

"Max, I'm sorry about the dog, obviously, there *is* something going on, but you can't trust yourself right now, you can't trust your own *mind*...."

"Eddie di Pineda...the guy who took Marks' place, the guy who's trying to get Dark Sky's funding back...he's real...his picture was on Dr. Reginald's desk..." I laid back on the bed, because I knew I was going under.

"Shit, Max, shit, you should've gone to that clinic for help..."

PMA's voice was far away, but I could still hear it.

"Don't call him, kid, don't do it," I said as the black came up to meet me again. "You can't trust him..."

I started drifting in and out of consciousness and at one point, I heard the door open and some voices talking. I felt someone kiss me on the forehead. I opened my eyes and saw an angel.

A foul-mouthed angel.

"Get some fucking sleep, you fucking idiot," Jules said in her own inimitable warm and loving way. And then she was gone.

The next morning, Friday morning, I woke up earlier than the kid, who was snoring loudly on the small couch in the room. He was half laying, half sitting on it with a blanket over him.

Then I saw the bottle on the desk. A prescription pill bottle. That meant I hadn't dreamt it--Jules had actually been here last night. I went over and looked at the label. Jesus, she must have been worried about me.

She gave me all her Xanax. That was like Kim Kardashian giving away her giant ass.

"Jules brought those over…she thought maybe they'd do you some good," said the kid sleepily, as he sat all the way up.

I stared at the bottle. "I don't know. I'm a little afraid to add anything else to whatever is going on inside of me. To tell you the truth, I'm a little afraid to do anything."

"You're not the only one. I almost called that doctor about three hundred times last night. Max, if what he said was true…"

"*If.* He doesn't trust me and I don't trust him."

"Max, you know you're not getting better. You're getting a whole lot worse."

PMA was right. The new wrinkle of losing recent blocks of memory had me scared shitless, as did the news that Blue Fire might actually be replenishing itself in my bloodstream. I kept thinking about the zombie play group I had stumbled upon. And I had to wonder, was that the ultimate endgame with Blue Fire? Did it completely melt your mind until you were stumbling around in the dark on a playground in the middle of the night, getting electrically prodded by a couple of keepers? Was I the next deadhead going down the slide at 4 a.m.?

I kept all that to myself, because I didn't want to freak out the kid. Of course, I couldn't freak myself out either or it might trigger another episode. This bastard drug had me painted in a corner and the worst part was I had nowhere to turn to get the answers I needed.

Well…maybe there was one place.

I called Howard's burner phone number. No answer. That was to be expected, as he was probably in his office by this time in the morning and wouldn't want to actually talk until he got to a safe place.

"Who were you trying to call?" asked the kid.

"Howard."

"Speaking of people you can't trust…"

"I can trust him halfway. That's more than I got anywhere else."

"I'm gonna go shower."

"Have a lovely time."

I turned on my Chromebook as the kid shut the bathroom door behind him. I checked my email and there was one message from none other than Mighty Mel. And being the ninety-year-old that he was, he had written it in all capital letters and less-than-readable grammar:

VERY DISSAPPOINTED NOT TO HERE FROM YOU. COMIC CON IN SECAUCAS TOMORROW EXPECT YOU TO BE THEIR WITH UPPDATE – WE ARE UNVEALING BLUE FIRE MOVIE AT 3 – TICKET WILL BE AT DOOR WITH YOUR NAME ON IT. THEIR WILL BE CONSUQUENCES IF YOU DO NOT SHOW

REGARDS MEL CHESLER

I had never seen anything "unvealed" before. Maybe it involved bringing a calf back to life. The whole thing was written like an illiterate telegram, except there was no "STOP" between the sentences.

My CIA phone rang. I picked it up, knowing it had to be Howard.

"Let's make this quick, I'm in the stairwell," came his pleasant greeting.

"What do you know about Rosenbaum Research? Or the Rosenbaum Foundation for that matter?"

There was a pause. A long pause. Oh, boy.

"How are they involved?" Howard finally asked.

"I'm not sure how they're *not* involved."

 Another long pause.

"You might remember the Agency has a few shell nonprofits we run money through. To bankroll things we don't want other people to know about."

"Like drugs that turn people into zombies."

"Get me a photo of the zombies, preferably one where they're posing with Bigfoot, and you can make them a part of this conversation, I promise you. Anyway, I'm pretty sure the Rosenbaum name is on a couple of those shell organizations."

"So this is the Agency's operation."

Howard sighed. "Max, you know how it is. I only get to know what they want me to know. And if I poke at it, they'll trace it back to you and we're both fucked."

"Instead of just me."

"We've had this conversation."

"You're right, Howard."

"I am right, Max, and I'm the guy that told you to not take the Mikov case, remember?"

"I remember too much. So who's Rosenbaum anyway?"

"I have no idea if there even is one."

"So they just came up with the name out of nowhere?"

"I have no idea." He was losing patience and so was I. "They just slap random names on things..."

"Few things are actually random there, Howard, we both know that. They took my dog, by the way. And cut the microchip out of her with a Boy Scout knife from the looks of it."

"Max, your stories keep getting crazier and crazier, I can't follow."

"You can't follow? Let me review for you. I've been dosed three times with some drug called Blue Fire that apparently not only doesn't leave your bloodstream, it continually multiplies itself inside it. Blue Fire was developed by Dr. Reginald Canun, foster brother of Ben Mikov, two men who were adopted as teenagers by an insane gay conversion psychiatrist named Dr. Frederick Kanuskey--and I think the drug's just the latest attempt by the CIA to find a fast and convenient way to create spooks."

"In other words, we're back to MK-Ultra. You going to go on CNN and scream that again? You know, you've got a whole tribe of MK-Ultra truthers putting up websites in your honor. Keep the craziness alive, Max."

"Howard, this shit is in me and it's scaring the fuck out of me."

"Then go see a fucking doctor!"

"For an experimental drug they've never heard of? What fucking good is that going to do me?"

"Then come down here and see me, Max, I'll do what I can for you. That's all I can do."

"So you're going to guarantee my safety."

"I..." That's as far as he got before his voice trailed off--"I."

I got up from the hotel desk chair and started pacing. The words started pouring out of me as if I had no control over them.

"I just realized this is a toxic relationship, Howard. And I'm through with you. You're as bad as the phony doctor I talked to yesterday, the one who follows orders just because that's who he is, because both of you walk through your lives thinking you have no other choice. Well, you do have a choice, but it's a hard fucking choice. If you want to play it safe at the same time your employer wants to fuck up the world, that's your business, but it's a rotten business and it turns you into a rotten guy. You can sit there and say you're not doing anything wrong, that I got myself into this fucking mess all by myself and you can pretend to wash your hands of it, but you're as dirty as any of them, Howard, because you walk in there every day and do their bidding, never knowing what the fucking consequences are because you never bother to care, no, you just put your blinders on, you put your hands over your ears and you cash your check every week. But I'm the fuck-up, Howard, because I didn't buy into all of it, the bad marriage, the toxic job, the going along to get along, I couldn't make that deal and, instead, I drank too much and blew it all up on purpose. Maybe that just makes me weak and sad, but I'd rather be that than you, because you're completely insignificant by design. Goodbye, Howard. Let me know if you hear from Rosenbaum."

I hung up and sat back down. I was shaking. I was crying again. But I had to keep it together. *Blue Fire must endure, Blue Fire must endure…*

Bing.

I turned to the Chromebook. My browser was open to Facebook. Bruce Canun was messaging me again. I clicked on his message.

> *I'll be at Comic Con tomorrow afternoon…meet up?*

Sure. I wanted to at least meet the whole Kanuskey clan before my mind turned to cabbage.

> *Meet me at the Blue Fire booth around 3 or so. You know what I look like. You even know what my penis looks like.*

Bing.

> *Yes, unfortunately, but please wear pants anyway.*

A joke. A simple stupid joke, a small display of normalcy. Somehow it made me feel better. But not much.

Then that brief moment of normalcy went up in a puff of smoke, because I noticed weirdness was swarming my Facebook page. I had about a thousand "friend" requests on Facebook. People were posting on my wall, asking if I was "that" Max Bowman, wanting me to tell the truth about the government and what it was trying to do to me. Yes, shouting MK-Ultra on CNN had definitely been a good career move--I was now the lucky bastard at the center of a lot of crackpot conspiracy theories, some of which, sadly, were all too true.

Well, it couldn't hurt.

So I started accepting all the random Facebook requests, until my finger started hurting from hitting the "Confirm" button so many times. And then I decided I should let my new legion of fans know what was going on.

I posted the following:

> *Thank you for your support. My outburst on CNN was indeed a product of a mind-altering drug administered to me without my knowledge. I currently fear for my life because, as a result of my efforts battling Dark Sky, I have been targeted by unknown powerful forces. They have kidnapped and mutilated my dog and also attempted to sexually assault me after drugging me. I continue to fight for freedom and the dream of America our forefathers began this country with. Please tell everyone you know that the threat to all of us is real and to watch this page, where I will attempt to update you all on a daily basis. If I fail to post during a 24-hour period, know that I have probably been taken prisoner by the fascist forces trying to bring me down. A clue: Watch for zombies in Carl Shurz Park in NYC in the wee small hours of the morning.*

Okay, so I gilded the lily a bit. Okay, so maybe I wasn't walking around focused on restoring the American Dream all that much. So maybe I was just trying to stay alive and sane. But why not do what I could to fire up my base of support? The Donald Trump model for creating a massive angry mob of support by acting batshit crazy had proven to be an extremely durable one so far in 2016, so why not learn from the best?

Feeling empowered, I went back to my email and replied to Mighty Mel that he would see me there at the Comic Con tomorrow afternoon. Then I shut the lid on the Chromebook. As the laptop powered down, so did I. I sat there, staring into space, suddenly feeling empty and scared.

And then I started shaking again, because I was thinking about Eydie again, thanks to my mention of her plight in my post. The poor mutt. I still had no idea where she was or if she was okay. I thought about myself again and how I wasn't any better off than the dog. I wondered how long it would be before they came after PMA and Jules. There wouldn't be any of my new Facebook friends in the vicinity to rescue me, I was pretty sure about that.

I eyed the prescription bottle on the desk. Jules' Xanax supply.

What the hell?

I opened it up and took a couple.

Keenan

It was a miracle. A minor one, but still a miracle.

I was better.

Amazingly, the Xanax turned everything around in my head within a few minutes. Considering the mess I was in, considering Eydie was still MIA, I probably ended up feeling *too* good, but that was the kind of problem I could deal with.

After some online investigation, I found out that Xanax is known as a "trip killer" --something that can stop an LSD experience in its tracks. I suspected the Blue Fire potion must have had that kind of psychedelic component and apparently I was right, surprisingly, since I wasn't the most experienced druggie. Now, here the kid and I were, riding an elevator to the top of a posh midtown hotel, on our way to a whole new evening of strangeness, because PMA was finally going to have his grand and glorious induction into Keenan Van Zola's elite inner circle.

It was an induction that almost didn't happen, because the kid didn't want to tell me it was scheduled for that night. Even after the Xanax had gotten my head out of the dumpster, PMA still didn't want to spill the beans about the event. He was so concerned for my welfare that he was willing to pass up the thing in life he was most looking forward to.

After we had some room service breakfast, we decided to take a break and go see a movie. There wasn't much else to do at the moment and we both knew we needed a mental time-out, so we went to see some Will Ferrell comedy where everybody yelled a lot and a few of them got pushed down into wet cement. About an hour into it, I took a nice nap and woke up just in time to hear everyone explain, to the tune of some treacly piano music, how much they cared about each other and how maybe they shouldn't go around pushing each other into wet cement. Words to live by.

But as the day moved into late afternoon, I could tell something was eating at PMA and I asked him what was up. That's when he told me the meeting was set for that night--the meeting where Keenan would introduce PMA to the Platinum Circle members and he would learn about the Bigger Picture. He told me he didn't care about going and would stick with me for the night, but I knew that was bullshit. If there had been wet cement around, I would have pushed him in it. I told him not only was he going, but I was going with him.

The Xanax had me thinking a little more clearly and I realized what was really bothering me about the whole Keenan Van Zola phenomenon. I wasn't jealous of his influence over PMA--I was petty, but not that petty. No, there were three things that smelled about this whole thing:

1. Keenan popped up out of nowhere at just about the same time as all this other shit started up. And PMA didn't seek him out, he was *invited* to meet up with him.

2. The kid was being accorded an awful fast ascension to the upper echelons of the Keenan cult. Not one re-occurring cycle was involved in this particular process, just a straight shot to the top for a college kid whose biggest claim to fame was his grandfather. Granted, that grandfather was a big name, but it still seemed odd.

3. The Keenan philosophy seemed to be just warmed-over Ayn Rand clichés, which wouldn't be worth mentioning except for the fact that Ayn Rand's bullshit also somehow factored into all this madness, it being one of Mikov's obsessions as well as some higher-ups at the CIA.

So it all made me suspicious. Which I'm sure the kid knew, which I'm sure made him doubly nervous about taking me along for the ride. But I promised to be good. And to spare him any embarrassment, I disguised myself once again as much as possible, by wearing new reading glasses I purchased from a nearby Duane Reade and slicking my hair back again Gordon Gekko-style. And of course, there was still my burgeoning beard to be reckoned with.

Now, here we were, in our new Bloomingdales duds, looking down about 50 stories through the floor of this glass elevator still rising to the top. My first thought was, who the hell was paying the freight for this extravaganza? Once the kid told me the meeting was taking place in this super-luxury hotel's no doubt super-luxurious penthouse suite, I looked up the room online (thanks, Trivago dude) and found out it goes for about 40k a night.

What does that buy you?

1400 square feet of luxe leather furniture, floor-to-ceiling windows, a wood-burning fireplace with a custom slate mantle, and a private balcony. Also, the master bath sinks are carved from blocks of crystal and the walls of the dressing room--because of course it has a dressing room--are lined in calfskin. All that's missing is a talking bidet that addresses you in the voice of James Earl Jones.

Even if this was just a one-night affair, it was costing somebody a pretty penny. And yet, Keenan told PMA membership in his organization was 100% free since he was all about creating a "global consciousness-raising" and therefore filthy lucre wasn't welcome. I was pretty sure they had a different idea about that last part down at the front desk.

The elevator opened on a small, empty foyer area with a door that I assumed led into the penthouse suite. The kid, nervous as can be, stepped out and I followed suit. We both looked around questioningly, wondering if we should just go ahead and open that door.

Then, out of the shadows to the side, some Asian guru-type appeared to greet us, so suddenly that we both blinked with surprise. He was bald, wore one dangling gold earring, was dressed in flowing multi-colored robes, had glowing perfect skin and was anywhere from thirty to seventy years old, it was impossible for me to tell.

"I am Chandu," he said in a vague and soothing tone.

I bowed just for the hell of it.

Chandu responded by eying me warily as he turned to the kid and asked for his name, for Chandu was carrying a clipboard that contained the evening's guest list.

"Jeremy Davidson," the kid answered. I often forgot his real name and it often surprised me when he gave it.

Chandu found PMA's name on the list and was mightily pleased, and then he asked me my name. I told him I was there as the kid's guest, I wouldn't be on his list, and suddenly he was mightily displeased. He asked us to stay put and disappeared behind the main door to the suite.

"If it's a problem, I'll go," I said to ease the kid's worries.

"If it's a problem, we'll both go," he answered. "I can't leave you alone. We'll make this work."

Chandu returned and said we would need to speak to Keenan personally and, with that, he opened the door to paradise. Well, technically, it was only the door to the penthouse suite, but Chandu's beaming mystical smile made you feel otherwise. Still, I couldn't help thinking this guy's day job was managing a Chipotle's on 2nd Avenue.

We walked in and experienced maybe not paradise, but at the very least, some very high-class surroundings.

True, the long low living room area was cluttered with extra chairs and sofas for this gathering, but you couldn't help but be overpowered by the lavishness of the furnishings and the jaw-dropping views of what looked like all of New York City. Roughly fifteen to twenty people were seated around the room in various configurations, and in the center of it all stood Keenan Van Zola himself.

He wasn't that much more impressive in person than he was when I saw him on TV. He was around 5'9", 5'10", slender, dark-skinned, dressed in neatly pressed ivory linen slacks, sandals, and an honest-to-God white Nehru jacket that seemed to glow.

Keenan was chatting up another guest and Chandu returned to the foyer area to welcome/scare other arrivals. That gave me a little time to look around. I noticed an attractive female version of Chandu flitting about the room, going from guest to guest, taking drink orders. I watched as she took the order slips over to the suite's wet bar, which was overseen by two bartenders, two Jersey boys who wouldn't have looked out of place as extras in *Goodfellas*. Both of them wore the standard New York bartender garb of white shirt and black vest, but beyond that and the Jersey vibe, that was where the similarity ended. The smaller of the duo was doing most of the drink mixing and preparation. The big guy looked to be heavily muscled and seemed to be paying more attention to what was going on in the room than the drink orders. Which led me to believe he wasn't there to drop olives in martinis.

I stopped watching the bar and turned to the main attraction, Keenan, who was now approaching us. He offered his hand to PMA with a pleasant smile and, when PMA put his hand out in return, Keenan shook it with such a gentle touch that it was almost sensual.

"And who is this gentleman, Jeremy?" he asked PMA while staring at me. "Chandu said you brought a guest..."

"David Muhlfelder," I quickly interjected. I offered my hand and got the same tender half-a-shake back.

"I'm staying with him here in New York," PMA added. "He's interested in seeing what this is all about. Remember, I asked the last time about bringing a guest and you told me it was okay…"

"Yes, I should have been clearer. That was an introductory meeting with me alone. This is something else entirely." He was still staring at me intently.

"I'm sorry," PMA went on, "I didn't know. But he's having some medical issues and I really can't leave him alone. So, I'm sorry, but if he has to leave, I have to go with him."

The kid was doing good.

Keenan looked around the room, as if looking for someone to help him make a decision on this earthshaking matter. He was nervous about me, but too anxious to please to just go ahead and toss me out on my ass. He didn't strike me as a natural-born leader--more like the kid in the back of the class who didn't want the teacher to call on him.

"It will be all right," he finally said unhappily. "But, Mr. Muhlfelder, I'm asking for your discretion about what you see here tonight. Both of you, please find a seat, there are still a few guests that have yet to arrive."

He was letting me stay. That meant PMA was too big a catch for Keenan Van Zola, or whoever he was representing, to let the kid get away. Even the likes of me was not going to stand in the way of that.

PMA and I headed for a couple of chairs in a dark back corner, to make sure I didn't get recognized. I looked around to check out the other "members" of whatever this club was. It was difficult, since the lights were dimmed low, but, from what I could see, these were mostly white, mostly wealthy folks who were mostly in their forties to sixties. In other words, they were well-fed well-to-doers, part of the casual New York City ruling class that knew how to work their specific white collar rackets to pay the rent on their high-floor condos so they could reign supreme above the unwashed masses.

The funny thing was, I recognized more than a few of them. I spotted a handful of clients who had hired me in recent months, clients who paid me too much money for too little work. Luckily, they didn't notice me. Yet.

As music played softly in the background, ersatz sitar crap even George Harrison wouldn't have been able to stomach, the drink hostess approached us. "Hello," she said with a vaguely Indian accent, "I am Kanhopatra and I am pleased to take your drink order. All beverages are complimentary, including a full bar, beer and wine. What can I bring you two gentlemen?"

I had a feeling if you woke her up in the middle of the night, she would repeat that entire paragraph word-for-word as a reflex action.

The kid turned to me and asked me what I was going to have.

What I was going to have. A drink. A fucking drink. Hold the phone and stop the presses.

Fuck, NO.

I waved off Kanhopatra. "We're fine for now."

She left, and didn't seem happy about it. Once she was out of earshot, I turned to the kid. "Did Keenan serve drinks at the other meeting?" I asked.

The kid nodded. "Yeah, why? What's the matter?" Then he realized what I was getting at--that maybe everyone here was literally drinking the Kool-Aid. He rolled his eyes.

"Max, don't start…"

"I won't start if you do me a favor. Don't get a fucking drink while we're here."

"Fine," he said, pissed. I was already defiling this holy temple.

I turned back to the entrance to the living room, where Keenan was receiving more newly-arrived guests. A last-minute clump of them was causing a minor traffic jam as he tried to give everyone their proper share of his undivided attention before they took their seats.

That's when, to my shock and surprise, I spotted a few more familiar faces--specifically, Todd, my recently-resigned entertainment lawyer and Becky Parks, my also-recently-resigned publicist, arriving together arm-in-arm.

"Isn't that the woman we met at CNN?" asked PMA, a little confused.

"Yeah. Matter of fact, I know a few people here."

"You do?"

I didn't answer. I didn't have to. Because, just then, Chandu opened the door and ushered in the final mystery guest--Senator Eddie di Pineda.

There were some excited murmurs around the room as people recognized the newly-crowned political star of the moment. Senator Eddie embraced Keenan warmly and Keenan returned the affection. There was even some light applause from the guests looking on.

The kid watched for a moment, mouth open, then turned to me. I saw surrender in his eyes. He knew now. He goddamn well knew.

"What the hell?" he said.

"What the hell," I repeated. It was pretty obvious. This wasn't just about raising global consciousness.

Senator Eddie took a seat near the front, in an executive chair that had obviously been reserved for him. Then Keenan raised his hands as if he was going to levitate something, which caused the crap sitar music to stop in mid-strum.

"Greetings and salutations, good friends," Keenan said to the group, which now numbered in the forties. "I welcome you all to our monthly gathering of the Rosenbaum Initiative."

The *Rosenbaum* Initiative?

The kid and I looked at each other again.

"Our work here grows more important by the day, which is why I am so pleased and honored to see you all here tonight. Together, with your help, we will continue to lead the world out of the darkness of self-destruction and forge a path to a much, much brighter tomorrow."

Senator Eddie stood up and applauded. So everybody else felt obliged to stand up and applaud, even me and the kid.

As I stood there and pretended to clap, I watched as Kanhopatra crossed the room, took a tray of drinks from the smaller of the Jersey Boys bartenders, and disappeared into a back room. A few moments later, she came back out with those self-same beverages, which she began passing out to guests.

Why would a hostess take a tray of drinks into a back room?

Probably so that someone could add the proper pharmaceuticals without anyone noticing.

It was all falling into place. That was why PMA had seemed so off after meeting with Keenan. They probably doped him with a much milder dose of Blue Fire, the drug made him more receptive to Keenan's ideas, and then it shut the door behind them so they couldn't get out.

Now imagine the same thing happening to a whole group of people-- prominent, successful movers and shakers--over a series of monthly meetings. You wind up with an army of brainwashed bigwigs primed to do somebody's bidding.

But whose bidding?

Certainly not Keenan's. He clearly lacked the power and presence to be anything more than another puppet whose strings were being pulled from a few levels above. Obviously, he was no mastermind. He was a packaged commodity and, to me, not a particularly well-chosen one. Why him? Where did this guy come from?

Why any of this? What was the end game?

Then I thought about all the faces I had recognized in the room. All those former clients of mine, they had called *me,* right after I got my P.I. license, before I was even out there promoting my services. Even Todd had reached out to me on his own, hiring me for a job before I asked him to sell my book. And Todd had referred me to Becky. This was a network that did what it was told--because, obviously, it was told to engage with me so they could keep track of my whereabouts.

And the kid! They knew he worshipped Andre Gibraltar, so they used him to recruit PMA, which separated him from me, and--win win! --they got to use him as well. The Davidson name was gold in this country, so having the kid on their side would pay a lot of dividends in terms of influence.

And all of this under an umbrella with that magical Rosenbaum name on it.

My skin was tingling. The enormity of this seemed absurd and at the same time self-evident. As we all sat down, the kid turned to me again. I saw the same emotions at work in his eyes.

"What the hell is this all about?"

Then Chandu opened the door one last time to let in one last guest.

Dr. Reginald Canun entered.

Keenan's face erupted with a spasm of joy. He rushed over to Dr. Reginald and heartily embraced him with even more love than he had for Senator Eddie.

"I thought you couldn't make it!" he exclaimed.

Dr. Reginald smiled tightly. "Busy times at the lab."

Keenan turned to the crowd. "This is the man who found me when I was nothing. Who mentored me and molded me and shaped me into the leader I am today. This is the man I am proud to call…my father!"

Father?

Senator Eddie stood and applauded once more, so, once more, everyone else stood and applauded, including us.

"*He's* his son? I thought you were hooking up with his son tomorrow at the Comic Con?" PMA whispered-asked.

"I think this must be a very different son," I answered. "Maybe the same kind of son Dr. Reginald was to Dr. K." I gave PMA a knowing look and saw he knew exactly what I was driving at.

Dr. Reginald took another seat of honor near the front as Keenan once again addressed the crowd.

"Before we begin, I'm proud to introduce some new members we are welcoming to our Elite Circle this evening. I would like you all to welcome them to this incredible group. Please raise the lights a bit?"

Kanhopatra pushed up the dimmer switches by the wet bar. Uh-oh. Suddenly there was way too much light in the room and nowhere for me to hide. I had to hope my pathetic disguise would work. After all, Lois Lane never noticed Clark Kent was Superman with glasses on. And comic books were always based in sound logic, right?

"First, Deborah Kilgore Ford, here from Chicago," Keenan said, pointing to a woman to his left. "Deborah is a noted entrepreneur who will bring much value to our discussions."

Across the room, Deborah, who seemed nice, stood up and everyone politely applauded. Me, I began to sweat.

"I would also like to welcome Ray Jacobs, one of the top design minds in the advertising business…"

Ray, a white-haired handsome man, stood up, nodded and waved.

"…and Mr. Shawn Shepheard, all the way from Canada…a motivational speaker and thought leader. He has great, great energy!"

Shawn, a few chairs away, stood up and pumped his fist in the air, yelling "Go Canada!" He was probably expecting a laugh, but didn't get one. I wasn't laughing because I had suddenly remembered, it had been about twelve hours since the Xanax and it was probably wearing off. Which might have been one reason the sweat was suddenly pouring out of me.

The other reason was the next introduction.

"…and finally, Jeremy Davidson, grandson of the late great American general, Donald Davidson."

Much applause. PMA quickly stood, gave a wave and quickly sat down.

Maybe nobody spotted me sitting next to him. Maybe we were in the clear. I stared at Kanhopatra, forty feet away, still standing by the dimmer switches, mentally willing her to turn the lights back down. If this was all over in a few seconds, I could get away with this whole thing.

But I hadn't accounted for Senator Eddie's laser-sharp political instincts. He rose to his feet again and waved for PMA to keep standing.

"This man's grandfather was a great American hero, and I believe all of us in this room here today should honor his memory!" boomed Senator Eddie.

Even though the kid had helped me torpedo his pet cause, Dark Sky, Senator Eddie most likely was seeing an opportunity--an opportunity to possibly sweet talk the kid into coming over to the Dark side and help the Senator's quest to restore its funding. Whatever his motivation, Senator Eddie left PMA no choice but to stand up again as waves of applause filled the room.

Which meant it was only a matter of time.

My bestie Todd, of course, was the first one to spot me. And point at me. And then yell...

"That's FUCKIN' MAX BOWMAN!"

I slumped down in my seat. Like that was really going to do me any good. I glanced over at Dr. Reginald, whose tic was suddenly back with a vengeance. He knew me being there wasn't going to add up to a fun night for him.

"Max Bowman?" asked Keenan.

"Sitting next to the Davidson kid!" yelled Todd.

Keenan laughed. "No, no, no. That man's name is David Muhlfelder." Oh, Keenan, you trusting soul, you.

"He LIED to you, Keenan! That lowlife LIED TO YOU!" Todd pointed at me again. "Get the fuck up, Bowman! So the whole goddamn room can see you!"

I got up and gave everyone a little friendly wave.

"Todd!" said Keenan a bit desperately. "You are bringing a great deal of bad energy into the room!"

"Bad energy?" Todd shrieked. "BAD ENERGY? This guy has bad energy ingrained in his FUCKING DNA!" Becky Parks nodded vigorously to show her approval.

I raised my hand.

"Yes, Mr. Muhlfelder," said Keenan. He wasn't quite getting what was going on.

"Your drink person. Kemahatrapo?"

"Kanhopatra, good try," said Keenan reassuringly.

"Whatever. I'd like to see what she's doing in that back room with the drinks. If you wouldn't mind."

A moment of tense silence.

Suddenly, Senator Eddie jumped into the breach. He turned to face me. "He *would* mind, Max Bowman. Keenan may be too spiritually pure to be affected by the discord you came here to sow, but the rest of us are not."

"Okay, fine." I said. And then I began walking over to the door to the back room. "Then no one should mind if I open that door, since I'm the problem, not what's being put in the drinks."

As I passed Keenan, he put his hand on my arm in the nicest possible way.

"Please, Mr. Muhlfelder," Keenan said, still not getting it, "I must ask you to leave if you are not who you say you are."

"He's FUCKING NOT!" screamed Todd.

I patted Keenan on the head and continued heading for the door. When I was a few feet away, it opened of its own accord, and Kanhopatra emerged with a tray of drinks. She saw me, she saw everyone else staring at her and she froze like a statue, like she was an escaped inmate caught in a spotlight against a brick wall in some old

1940's cartoon. She looked to Keenan. Keenan looked back at her blankly. Guilt was in the air.

I couldn't see what was behind Kanhopatra and she quickly closed the door behind her to make sure I couldn't. So I went for the doorknob.

Then a hand came down hard on my shoulder.

I turned and, for my trouble, got knocked down to the floor by the fist of the bigger of the two Jersey Boys bartenders, who had rushed out from behind his post to take me apart. Now he was standing over me with a rather threatening glower.

"The door you want is over there," he said, jerking his head towards to the suite's exit.

I had fallen on my bad rib and I lay there moaning. The kid rushed over to make sure I was okay. As he knelt down next to me, I could feel an air of uncertainty in the room, as if the tide could turn with a few well-chosen words.

Senator Eddie stood up to make sure that would not happen.

"Ladies and gentlemen," he bellowed in his most authoritative stentorian tones, "Listen to me. Max Bowman lied about Dark Sky…"

"DAMN STRAIGHT!" yelled Todd.

Senator Eddie gave Todd a stern look, then continued, "…and he's lying to you now!" He turned to where I was lying on the floor. "Leave, Max Bowman! You're an enemy of this great country, and frankly, an enemy of everyone in this room!"

Some angry murmuring as the kid helped me to my feet and the big Jersey Boys bartender watched me warily. I motioned to the kid that we should get the hell out of there. But before we could take a few steps in that direction, a voice rang out.

"Wait! If he's lying, it should be easy to prove. So show us what's in the room, let's clear the air. I mean, why IS she taking the drinks back in there?"

I could've kissed whoever it was. I turned my head in the direction of the voice and saw the face of Shawn Shepheard, the Canadian motivational speaker. Maybe he was a fan of SaveMaxBowman.com.

I pulled away from the kid and once again went for the door to the back room. Big Jersey Boys bartender came after me, but forgot to keep an eye on PMA, who kicked him in the nuts. Big Jersey went down like a sack of potatoes, Keenan screamed and I threw open the door.

Standing there, inside the back room, was my least favorite date, Veronica, wearing a snappy little cocktail dress. She was standing at a sink with a large glass container of a blue liquid--and an eyedropper to measure dosages.

"Hi, Super Dick," she said brightly, smirk firmly in place. "How's the dog?"

Oh no you didn't.

"YOU FUCKING BITCH!" I screamed. "WHERE IS SHE?"

I forgot about my rib, I forgot about my sweat, I forgot about the room full of movers and shakers and went for her fucking throat and after I got it, a whole lot of frustration, anger and just plain old Clint Eastwood-style vengeance that had had no outlet for too long was suddenly erupting out of me and all of it was completely focused on Veronica's throat.

Sometimes you don't know how much hate you can actually carry around inside your soul until you get the opportunity to unload it all at once. That moment is exhilarating. All limits are gone. You feel completely free, completely justified in doing everything you can to destroy a fellow human being. That was me. And I was having way too good of a time with it.

She was gagging. Clawing at me. Making Linda Blair noises from the back of her throat, like she was trying to access her evil to find a way to somehow defeat me. But she didn't have enough to keep me from my final objective, which was to stop any chance of any breath ever getting to her lungs again.

"Max!" screamed the kid, "You're going to kill her!"

He didn't understand that was the point, nor was he paying attention to the big Jersey Boys bartender, who, after getting back on his feet, plucked the kid off the floor and deposited him on another part of it ten feet away. He then yanked me off Veronica and threw me on top of the kid and pulled a gun out from the back of his pants. He cocked it and aimed it directly at my head.

"Get the fuck out of here," he growled.

From inside the back room, I could hear Veronica wheezing, gasping, trying to get her bearings. I had failed. Goddammit, I had failed.

"Please!" said Keenan holding up his hands. "Violence is forbidden here!"

"And that's why Max Bowman must leave!" said Senator Eddie. Why always my whole name? Why? Senator Eddie turned to me with his best morally indignant face. "Sir, your lies aren't welcome here and neither are your savage ways! I'm going to undo the harm you've done to this country, you can bet on that, Max Bowman!"

PMA and I got to our feet. We were shaken, bruised and battered as we headed towards the exit. I was also rattled to my core. I had never felt so strong a murderous impulse in my life, and I knew it had to have been the Blue Fire roaring back to life in my system. The Xanax kept it at bay for a few hours, but it was only a temporary solution, a

Band-Aid over a growing psychic cancer, and once its effectiveness was gone, the Blue Fire seemed stronger than ever.

My right hand was aching from the effort I had put into strangling Veronica as I reached for the doorknob. But it began turning on its own, before my hand could get there.

Because there would be one more surprise guest attending the evening's festivities. When the door opened, Andre Gibraltar was on the other side of it.

Wearing an expensive black silk shirt unbuttoned halfway down and cut to show off his muscular torso, the Ultimate Fighting Champion stared at us, even as we stared back at him. His many tattoos were mesmerizing, his figure imposing, his presence intimidating…

"Shit, it's over already?" he slurred at us. "I knew I was late, but fuuuuuuuuck…"

…his breath, whiskey-soaked.

Andre collapsed to the floor in front of us. He was completely and utterly wasted and I had a hunch vomit was the only move he had left.

"Andre's here," the kid wearily announced to the room as we stepped around his hulkish frame to take our leave.

Comic Con

So. I had just tried to kill a woman with my bare hands. I could cross that off my bucket list.

What the hell was happening to me? Of course, I knew the answer; Blue Fire was happening to me--again and again and again. I didn't really plan on ever trying to choke the life out of anybody, let alone a girl thirty years younger than me, so God only knew what I was going to surprise myself with next. Maybe I'd throw acid in the Pope's face, maybe I'd cook and eat a Boy Scout. The sky was the limit.

I popped two more Xanax in my mouth when we got back to the room and waited impatiently for their effects to kick in. I wanted to be a civilized human being again, not an out-of-control maniac. In the meantime, I just shook and shook with raw emotion.

The kid went in to shower and when he came out in the hotel bathrobe, drying his hair with the hotel towel, I was better, but he wasn't. He looked as deflated as a basketball that had been sitting in the corner of a garage for too many years.

And who could blame him?

In one night, he had seen both of his role models, Andre Gibraltar and Keenan Van Zola, unmasked, respectively, as a drunk and an ineffectual fraud. And he had seen me try to choke the life out of another human being. What happened when the people you trusted to show you how to act didn't know how to act themselves? Nothing good.

When I felt okay enough to function, I went to the room desk, opened my Chromebook and discovered another thousand or so friend requests that had popped up on my Facebook page. Once again, I was a sensation with a whole lot of strangers. Many of them seemed like angry wackos, but it wasn't a time to be choosy about who my friends were. So I clicked away, confirming one after another, without bothering to find out the slightest shred of information about who these people really were.

Meanwhile, PMA finished drying his hair, threw the towel back in the bathroom, grabbed the TV remote and collapsed on the couch. He turned on some random movie and sighed. He sighed a lot. His sighing was starting to make me want to sigh, so I thought it was time to speak up.

"You okay?" I asked.

"Yeah," he said in that unconvincing way that people use when they know they really aren't okay, but aren't quite ready to admit it.

"Look, nobody's pure, kid. Gandhi slept with his grandnieces, Mother Theresa's clinics were filthy hellholes, and Martin Luther King Jr. banged whores. He had a dream and an erection, like most guys. You learn what you can from everybody and you move on, because nobody's perfect, you included."

The kid nodded and kept watching. On the plasma TV screen, there was a movie explosion and the resulting fireball threw the hero into some bushes. Not enough to keep PMA's attention. He started flipping channels.

"Besides," I went on, being the pain in the ass I was, "You don't need some freak to tell you what to do. You can figure it out on your own."

"No, I can't. I don't know how to be me," he replied without an ounce of happiness. "People think because of my last name, I'm supposed to be some kind of hero. And I'm certainly not supposed to be a homo. Everybody expects me to be something I'm not, but I keep trying to be that thing so I don't disappoint anyone. You're like the only person who doesn't expect something out of me."

"Yeah, I do. I expect you to be you. And, it turns out, you are."

"It's not that simple, Max."

"Except it actually is. It took me long enough to figure it out for myself and there's no point in you stumbling around that long. Listen to the wise words of Ricky Nelson in his late-career hit song, *Garden Party*. 'If you can't please everyone, you got to please yourself."

No answer. Not even the obvious question I expected from him, "Who the *hell* is Ricky Nelson?" No, the kid just kept watching the TV until even he couldn't pretend he was actually paying attention to anything on the screen. He turned to me.

"Why does it even matter what I think I am? It's just an illusion anyway. It doesn't matter what I think or what you think. If some drug can change your brain that easily, it just means all we are is a bunch of cells in search of a clue."

"Don't make this into an existential crisis, okay?"

"But it is an existential crisis, Max. Doesn't it freak you out? I mean, we're just like…like talking animals or something -- like Pavlov's dogs. Ring the bell and we get hungry. Shock our brains and we're not gay anymore. Give us Blue Fire drinks and we'll help you take over the world. I mean, what's the point? We're not deep or spiritual. We're idiots."

"Kid, I know you may still not believe me, but when I saw Senator Marks in the zombie party, it was pretty clear his brain had been emptied out, but when he saw me, he still recognized me. He still reached out to me, because something inside him was still there and desperately wanted to connect. I know I'm not the most optimistic person in the world, nor the most enlightened, but even I believe in something bigger than us. I don't believe in trying to slap a label on it or building a church around it, but I know there's something in me that goes beyond eating, drinking and shitting. And I know I have to trust it, even if it sends me in the most fucked-up direction imaginable."

PMA looked everywhere but at me. Finally, he turned off the TV and sat up on the couch. "Well, at the moment, all I want to do is survive. So how do we do that? I mean, here we are again, Max. We're in over our heads and it seems like the whole world is lined up against us."

"Not the whole world," I said, turning back to the laptop to confirm some more Facebook friends. "I got a couple thousand internet pals ready to burn Washington D.C. to the ground on my behalf."

"Those are just trolls."

"I prefer to think of them as like-minded colleagues."

"MAX!"

The kid's tone was serious--and loud. I turned back to him. He was in no mood for fucking around.

"What are we going to do? There's some weird drug in you that's melting your brains, Dark Sky is coming back, some guy named Rosenbaum is brainwashing people...I mean, what do we do? Maybe we should just *Thelma and Louise* the whole thing and drive off a cliff."

"*Thelma and Louise?* Boy, you are gay."

"Max--*what are we going to do?*"

He was right to push. I had been trying to regain my emotional equilibrium, so I was avoiding thinking about the mess we were in. It was too fucking overwhelming. Plus, I was afraid of too much stress reawakening the Blue Fire in me.

"Get me some Jack out of the minibar and we'll talk."

The kid got up to fulfill my request.

"Tomorrow," I said, "we're taking your car to Jersey, to the Comic Con in Secaucus. I gotta talk to Mighty Mel and maybe we'll find out who's behind the Blue Fire movie."

"We already know. It's some guy named Rosenbaum. Rosenbaum is in charge of everything," the kid said bitterly as he poured drinks for both of us. "And his mission is to name everything Blue Fire. Blue Fire the comic book hero, Blue Fire the drug, Blue Fire the movie… It's all about Rosenbaum and Blue Fire."

He handed me my glass. I clinked mine with his and we both took a good belt. Then the kid looked at me straight in the eye.

"After tonight, they're not going to screw around, Max. They're just going to take us out. There's no reason not to."

"Then why am I not dead already?" I asked. "Why are they going to the trouble of repeatedly drugging me?"

"That last time you weren't supposed to get away. And now that I'm not going to play along, they have no reason to go easy on me. So what do we do?"

The kid was right. There wasn't much we *could* do. I had to go see Mighty Mel tomorrow and wrap up the Mikov case, or face the wrath of whatever shyster lawyer he had on retainer. But other than that, I just needed some time alone with the Xanax. I couldn't go from Jekyll to Hyde again. I couldn't let that happen.

"We go to the Comic Con tomorrow…then we take off. You're right, we need to disappear for a while, maybe a long while."

"Good. Thank you." He sounded relieved.

I picked up the bottle of Xanax and threw it to him. "Take a couple of these. We both need some sleep tonight."

He looked at it. "Ordinarily, I'd say no. But tonight…"

"Exactly," I replied. "Tonight bites my ass."

The next morning, Saturday morning, the kid went out for a run. Me, I went down to the hotel's overpriced sundries store and bought a roll of scotch tape for eight dollars. I came back up to the room and carefully ripped off the top of one of the sugar packets that the hotel left next to the coffeemaker. I emptied out the sugar in the waste can and put a few of the Xanax pills back into the empty packet. As the kid returned to the room, he saw me scotch-taping the packet with the pills to my armpit.

"You're taping sugar to your armpit?" he asked.

"There's Xanax in the packet. If they grab me and drug me again, maybe I can use it to fight the shit off."

He shrugged, which meant I had a good idea for once. "When do we need to get going?"

"Soon as you get showered and dressed and I put my shirt back on," I said. "We have to make a stop before we head out to Jersey."

Maybe a half hour later, I was rapping on the door of a third floor apartment in Morningside Heights. It was around ten a.m.

The door opened and there stood Jules in her bathrobe, the one with the smiling clouds on it. There were many days where I didn't understand how the clouds kept smiling, but, hell, the robe was cute. Jules looked at me like she never expected to see me again, like I was already a ghost and she wasn't sure whether or not she wanted to be haunted by me.

"Max…? How did you find me, I never told you…"

"Remember what I do for a living?"

"Do I fucking ever. Come in."

I walked in. The place was a disaster. Her shit was all over the living room and her couch-bed was still unmade. I couldn't believe her bandmates wouldn't even give her a bed. Some kind of gentlemen.

"I like what you've done with the place. Where are the Cubans?"

"They had some fucking family brunch thing down in the Village. There are about forty thousand relatives for every Cuban, did you know that? Rabbits got nothin' on them."

"I only have a minute or two," I said maybe a little too impatiently. "The kid's double-parked behind a Fresh Direct truck. But I wanted to thank you for the happy pills. They're currently saving my life."

She nodded and started folding up the bedding on the couch, as if in a trance. There was a distance between us and I knew what it was all about. I had taken two more Xanax that morning, but no amount of pills could dispel the aura of tragedy that was clinging to me today. Since Jules was part-witch, she had no trouble picking up on it. She sensed why I was really there.

"You could have sent me an email," she finally said as she stuffed the blankets violently to make them fit into an already-overcrowded closet. New York apartment living was all about shoving shit into spaces where that shit didn't really fit.

"True," I said. "But I also hit the ATM and I wanted you to have this." I passed her a few hundred dollars from my pocket. "And I want you to do something I asked you to do a few days ago, but this time I won't shout it out like a paranoid-schizophrenic. If there's any way you can get out of town for a few days…"

She gave me a look.

"…well," I concluded weakly, "it might be smart."

"Max, you and me, we don't do fucking smart. Otherwise, I'd be a lawyer instead of working for one and you'd be head of the CIA, scary as that idea is to me. We don't do what we're fucking supposed to do. Which is why we're both doomed."

She hit that last word a little too hard. How did everybody get more depressed than me?

"Speak for yourself," I said with my hands back in my pockets. "I've got a dental appointment next Tuesday and I intend to show up for that cleaning."

Out of nowhere, she suddenly grabbed me like she had no control over her body and kissed me like there was no tomorrow, because a large part of us thought there wasn't. Me, I took my hands out of my pockets and did what I could with them. We both needed what happened next, we just didn't really know how to ask for it.

When I finally made my way back down to the street, PMA was sitting behind the wheel looking plenty pissed.

"That was a lot longer than five minutes, Max. I thought you were just dropping off the money," he fumed.

"If we get through this," I said, "I'm going to marry that girl."

He gave me a look.

"Oh. *That's* what took so long."

"We'll come back after the Comic Con. I want to see if she'll come and disappear with us. That okay?"

"Okay by me."

And then we continued driving across the island of Manhattan.

"How many of these things have you been to?" the kid asked as we made our way through the Lincoln Tunnel traffic.

"What things? You mean Comic Cons? Never."

He looked at me in surprise. "I thought you were a big comic book fan."

"Yeah…but that kind of stopped around 1972, when I started high school. Or more accurately, when I first got to touch a girl's breast."

"But you still read them now."

"Just the old ones from back then. And just because they started reprinting them all in books."

We drove on another minute. The kid turned to me. "So how much do you think Mel Chesler knows about what's going on?"

"Mighty Mel? I think all he knows is somebody is going to pay him a million bucks for the rights to *Blue Fire*. And that's all he cares about."

"So maybe nothing's going to happen at this thing. Maybe nobody will even know you're going to be there. And then we can drive away."

"Just like *Thelma and Louise*," I said.

I knew he wanted today to be easy. So did I.

Once we finally got out of the tunnel, it was only a few minutes to get to the site of the New Jersey Comic Convocation, the Meadowlands Exposition Center in beautiful Secaucus, New Jersey, where you held events you couldn't afford to pull off in New York. Not that the city didn't have its own Comic Con, that was a huge deal, but that also happened in November. This was March and this was Jersey, but this one was still apparently a big deal. We were lucky to find a parking spot.

As we joined the throng of fanboys and girls heading toward the main entrance, we received our first big surprise of the day. Blue Fire signage was everywhere outside the main hall, including large banners on the poles leading up to the doors and a huge sign hanging over the main entrance. All of them featured artwork, lifted from Mikov of course, of Blue Fire himself, shooting blue flames out of his arms. On top of his heroic pose was a giant headline reading, "FEEL THE BURN OF BLUE FIRE--COMING 2018."

The kid and I looked at each other. We knew they were going to announce the movie here, but we didn't know they were going to actually take over the place. Now I knew why Mighty Mel was so nervous about having Mikov's paperwork. Whatever production company was launching this movie wasn't messing around. They wanted it to be THE big deal of this Comic Con and it wouldn't look too good if all of a sudden they couldn't nail down the creator rights.

As we got closer to the main doors, we got another shock.

There were about twenty guys, all around the same size, running around in Blue Fire costumes. Since the neon-blue costumes covered them from head to toe, they looked like some kind of mutant Blue Man Group from the future--you couldn't tell one from the other. The only thing that detracted from the whole effect was the fact that they were all rocking oversized fanny packs, which held the piles of laminated promotional cards they were handing out to everyone entering the hall.

I grabbed one for myself from the nearest Blue Fire and read it out loud to PMA.

"*Blue Fire--The Movie* coming in 2018. Come to booth 676 for free comic book and don't miss our special *Blue Fire* Panel in Room C at 2 pm."

Then I saw the logo of the production company underneath. I showed it to the kid.

Rosenbaum Productions.

Yeah. Rosenbaum Productions. The kid had called it. We were now officially in the middle of a bad joke where the punchline was always the same. Rosenbaum.

We went to the Will Call window where I got the ticket that Mighty Mel said he would leave for me. But then when we went to buy the kid one of his own, we got another rude surprise.

The damn thing was sold out.

"Turn your phone on," I told the kid. "When I find Mighty Mel, I'll see if he has an extra ticket for you. I'll text you, you'll meet me at the door, I'll get you in."

He wasn't happy about it, but there wasn't much else we could do. Security was tight and nobody around was willing to give up or sell a ticket to us. So once again I was on my own.

Or was I?

Because I noticed that I suddenly had a new friend trailing after me. One of the costumed Blue Fires had followed me into the convention hall and out onto the exhibition floor.

Sure, there were countless other attendees wearing superhero, supervillain and anime costumes, not to mention armor, outfits from movies like *Star Wars* and *Lord of the Rings* and every other geek sensation that you could think of. And there were a few fat guys around my age wearing tight tucked-in Batman t-shirts. Even Adam West would have told them to go home and work out a little before trying to pull off that look.

But this particular Blue Fire seemed unwilling to let me out of his sight.

I tried to ignore him and, instead, took in the booths and all the wild and wacky shit they had out on the floor. There were giant robots, moving monster and dinosaur models and towering cartoon figures from the latest upcoming CGI animated monstrosities. I was glad I had the Xanax in me or I was sure the overwhelming visual assault of this event would have had my hallucinogenically-haunted mind turning cartwheels.

When I finally turned around to check, I saw the one Blue Fire impersonator was still following me.

I finally stopped at a booth where a shirtless muscle man dressed as an ancient barbarian was picking up a platform that three fanboys were standing on as casually as somebody else might pick up a glass of water. I wasn't so much interested in the demonstration as I was in what the Blue Fire impersonator would do. What he *didn't* do was continue walking past me--no, he just stopped a little further back in the middle of the aisle and began handing out the promotional cards to passers-by as if that was his plan all along.

So it was official. He was stalking me.

I decided to be proactive. I walked back over to him and took a card. Then I just stood there, a couple feet away from him, staring at him.

"Blue Fire," I finally said. "What's up?"

He gave me a perfunctory thumbs-up, as if I was just another random fan, and then turned away. I walked around to the other side of him and took another card.

"Blue Fire," I said again. "How's it hanging?"

He slowly walked away in the direction that we had come from to avoid further contact. That's when I noticed there was something about the odd way he moved that seemed familiar. He was slow, deliberate and focused, as if he weren't quite right. But since he was leaving, I was satisfied I had done my job, so I moved on to try and find the Rosenbaum Productions booth. It wasn't hard. You just had to look for the giant inflatable Blue Fire figure, of course.

When I got to the booth it was mobbed with nerds, and I soon found out why. The booth workers were giving away free reprints of that rarity among comic book rarities--the very first issue of *Blue Fire*. Even though it was only a reproduction, everybody wanted to get their hands on the freebee for their collections. I muscled my way through the crowd to get closer.

Working the counter was a team of freshly-scrubbed kids in their late-teens-to-early-twenties wearing *Blue Fire* polo shirts. They were relentlessly sunny and upbeat to even the most overbearing fan. To me, they resembled Mormon missionaries trying to convert heathens to the wonders of Ben Mikov's defining work. They stood out mightily from the help at the other booths, nerdy kids who looked more at home in the Comic Con crowd.

Then I finally spotted Mighty Mel.

He was sitting behind the counter at the end of the booth in one of his ancient frayed suits, grumpily autographing the comic book reprints with a thin black Sharpie for a long line of excited geeks of all ages desperate to meet a real-life comic book pioneer in the flesh. I pushed my way to the front, ignoring the weak protestations of the waiting fans who thought I was line-jumping.

"Mel?" I said loudly, interrupting a young guy whose face was covered with green paint and was gushing to an indifferent Mighty Mel about what an honor it was to meet him. Mel looked up at the sound of my voice, threw the signed comic book back at the green-faced geek like he was tossing a fish to a dolphin, stood up and grabbed my arm with his gnarled old hand.

"We gotta talk. Now."

He put up a pre printed sign that read "Back in 20 Minutes," eliciting a cascading wave of disappointed moans that traveled down the autograph line like a moving echo. Meanwhile, one of the Blue Fire team members lifted up a section of the front of the booth to let me in. As I entered, I gave a glance backwards and saw my Blue Fire stalker was back, watching me closely from the middle of the aisle.

"Before we talk," I said to Mighty Mel, "I have an associate outside who needs a ticket in. You got one?"

"You get no more fucking favors from me, Bowman," he snarled, just as a handsome Ronald-Reagan-in-training approached me from the other side of the booth. This guy was tall, well-built, and generically handsome with brown hair and greying sideburns and he projected the same kind of bland pleasantness the Great Communicator once did. He was wearing one of the *Blue Fire* polo shirts, khakis and a name tag that read, "Hi, My Name is Brad." He offered me a hand to shake.

"I'm Brad Palmer, head of operations for Rosenbaum Productions. You're Max Bowman, correct?"

"I'm Max Bowman, correct. So, Rosenbaum around? That's the guy I really want to meet."

Brad laughed politely. "Oh, no one gets to meet Rosenbaum, not even me!"

"Shame. I just wanted to see if he had my dog."

Brad gave me a look and then laughed as if I had made a joke he hadn't gotten. But I was as far from making a joke as you could imagine.

"Brad," Mighty Mel jumped in anxiously, "Can I have a minute with Bowman before you talk to him? I need to…"

"Mel, let's keep everything out in the open here, okay? I want to know what's really going on with the Mikov situation." Then to me, "Mr. Bowman, Mel says you've been able to secure the rights from his family? Is that true?"

I looked from Brad to Mel and back to Brad again.

"Well…not so much."

Brad's face fell as I told him how I had tracked down Mikov's sister and how she claimed that Mikov had killed himself. I added that I hadn't been able to find any kind of official confirmation of his death.

"But if the sister says it happened," answered Brad quickly, "then we can just have her sign off on the rights. We can assure her that she'll receive a generous…"

"Here's the problem with that," I interrupted so he didn't get his hopes too far up. "The sister is not very fond of Mr. Chesler. As a matter of fact, she made the statement she wouldn't spit on the floor for him."

"The hell. I don't even know the bitch!" exclaimed Mighty Mel.

"To be fair, it's not even about Mel," I explained. "She just doesn't want anything to do with a movie of her brother's work. She says Hollywood will ruin it."

"We have nothing but the highest intent to represent the purity of Ben Mikov's vision," declared Brad in appropriately earnest tones. "Perhaps if I could communicate that to her personally…"

"She's not too open to a dialogue, I have to say."

"We have a very gifted screenwriter already working on this. He wrote one of the *Iron Man*s. I'm not sure which one."

"I thought you said he wrote one of the *Thor*s?" asked Mighty Mel in confusion.

"Do you really need her okay?" I asked.

"Technically, no," Brad answered. "I've reviewed Mel's paperwork and he has full control over the rights. But, as you may have read, the original creators of these superhero characters have successfully filed claims against movie producers, saying they have rights to compensation…and in some instances, they've won."

"All I can tell you is that she's the only other surviving family member," I replied. "And I doubt she'll make any kind of fuss. She claims she doesn't need any money, she has enough to live on and doesn't want to hear about any movie based on Blue Fire."

He took that all in.

"Well…I would have to consult with our lawyers about this situation. Do you have a card, Mr. Bowman? I'd like to work with you directly on this if need be."

I fished one out of my wallet and handed it over to him. As he stared at it intently, I decided to keep on fishing. "I was wondering. What other movies has your company made?" I asked.

He looked up with a start. "Oh. This will be our first."

"But *you* have experience…?"

He smiled confidently. "My first film as well, Mr. Bowman. But management trusts me to get the job done."

"And management is Rosenbaum?"

He laughed again and clapped me on the shoulder. "You're a character, Mr. Bowman. You just need to stay off the internet, am I right?" Another laugh. This one had a little more bite to it and seemed to be encouraging me to stop asking questions, or questions might be asked about me.

"Well," I said, wrapping things up, "give me a call if you need any more information. I've discovered a lot about Mikov's background and I'll help any way I can. By the way…you wouldn't happen to have an extra ticket to this thing, would you?"

"To the Comic Con? Why, actually, yes, I do. My son Dylan was going to come with me, but…"

He dug into his pocket, found the ticket and gave it to me.

"Here you are. Now, if you'll excuse me, I want to give our legal team a call. We'll be in touch."

He shook my hand and walked away as he pulled out his cell phone. I turned to Mighty Mel, who seemed to be cooling down.

"Maybe this whole deal won't get fucked up after all," he muttered to me.

"Maybe you shouldn't have overpromised Brad about the rights," I answered. "Why the hell would you tell him this was all taken care of?"

"Listen, you fuck, don't you talk to me after all the shenanigans you've been involved with. You got your money. Now beat it."

Another satisfied customer.

Blue Fires

I left the Rosenbaum booth no wiser than I was when I entered it and texted the kid to meet me at the entrance. Then I looked up from my phone, and saw my old friend the faux Blue Fire still staring at me from across the aisle. I decided that was enough. I wasn't going to fuck around anymore, I just wanted to hook up with the kid and get out of here as quickly as possible. The Blue Fire stalker could get a new hobby.

And then, as I hurried to the main doors, I heard a voice call from behind me.

"Max Bowman!"

I turned to see what I was in for now. And I saw Bruce Canun.

I had forgotten I was supposed to meet him here at the Comic Con because, mentally, I had checked out of the whole Mikov case. And again, I didn't even know if this guy was on the up and up. I looked him over. Bruce looked just like his Facebook photo, a guy around my age, maybe a little younger, with brownish-grey hair. Fortunately, he wasn't wearing a Batman shirt, but a plain button-down shirt and jacket. He sure didn't look deadly.

"Bruce. Sorry…I…look, I have to go meet somebody at the entrance…so this is kind of a 'Hello, I must be going, kind of thing, I guess," I said apologetically.

"You like Groucho? The Marx Brothers?" he asked excitedly.

"Yeah," I said, even though I hadn't watched any of their stuff in years

He exclaimed happily, "Swordfish!"

"*Horsefeathers?*" I asked.

"Yeah, the password." He started singing, "Whatever it is, I'm against it! And I've been saying since I first commenced it…I'm against it!"

Part of me relaxed. I had a feeling Bruce was exactly who he said he was--an IT guy from Connecticut. But still, I had to interrupt his singing and go find PMA.

"How about you walk with me? I just have to find my partner."

"Sure, sure."

"Thanks."

"Your excellency!"

I looked at him blankly.

"You're excellency! You're not so bad yourself! *Duck Soup*! C'mon, Max. Hey, you should join my Marx Brothers group on Facebook."

"Yeah, I'll check it out. Let's walk. So I've had the pleasure of meeting up with your father, Reginald…"

"I'm so sorry."

"He seems…"

"He's a closet case, Max, just go ahead and say it. It's why I don't talk to him."

"Because he's gay?"

"No, because he tries to do to other kids what my grandfather did to him."

"He's still doing gay conversion?"

"I think he finally stopped, just because it's probably going to be outlawed. And you know, when gay conversion is outlawed, only outlaws will be gay converted."

"What about your mom?"

"She's as much in denial as he is. I had to stop talking to both of them, I was losing my mind. But you know what they say…time wounds all heels."

"Groucho."

"Don't mind if I do."

I thought I made too many bad jokes on a daily basis, but this guy took the cake.

I exited the hall with Bruce and looked around. No sign of PMA yet. But the many Blue Fires were still out on the front steps working the incoming crowd.

"So," I turned to Bruce. "You really knew Mikov?"

"If you knew Mikov, like I knew Mikov…" he sang. Then he decided to actually talk like a person. "Yes, yes, I knew Mikov. He was kind of my uncle when I was young, since he grew up with my father. He even wrote to me a few times after he disappeared."

"Do you remember why he disappeared?" I asked.

"I was hoping you could tell me. My parents wouldn't talk to me about him. What have you found out?"

"I found his sister. She says he killed himself."

"Wow," Bruce said quietly. "Wow. Either that man is dead or my watch has stopped, huh?"

Ladies and gentlemen, Bruce Canun, winner of the "Most Inappropriate Usage of a Groucho Joke" award. Still, he was obviously saddened by the news.

"Look, maybe we could go somewhere to talk," Bruce finally said, "Rather than stand out here getting assaulted by men in Blue Fire suits. I mean…everything you've been telling me is huge to me. I've been looking for some closure for so long, I'd love to hear whatever you know, even if it's not that much. And maybe I can even help."

"Well," I said, "We can't go anywhere until my partner shows up."

"Okay, okay. It's just hard because I don't have anybody to talk to about this, nobody else understands. I mean, I was an only child…"

"Only child?" That reminded me. Keenan Van Zola. Dr. Reginald had said *he* was his son. Which meant… "Don't you have a brother named Keenan?"

Bruce grimaced.

"Keenan was the last straw," he muttered angrily, too perturbed to even throw in a Groucho joke.

We were interrupted by loud giggling. There was a group of girls engaged in some anime cosplay, wearing weird little Japanese outfits and brightly colored wigs. They looked like one of the posters on Veronica's bedroom wall come to life. I gently maneuvered Bruce and myself a few feet away from them.

"Why was Keenan the last straw?" I asked. "He's a lot younger, right?"

"A lot younger. My father 'adopted' him after I had already moved out."

"Adopted him."

"Yeah, the story I got was my father was at a medical conference in South Africa. He found out from the hotel staff that this boy who was hanging out in the lobby, asking to do odd jobs, was basically living on the streets. His family threw him out…because he was…"

"Gay?"

"Exactly. Well, my father became obsessed with this kid, and finally pulled all sorts of government strings to adopt him and bring him back to the States. And then…he went to work on him."

"Went to work on him?"

"Tried to turn him straight. My grandfather adopted my dad and messed with his head, my father repeated the whole sick cycle all over again."

"So that was a re-occurring cycle."

"Isn't the word 'recurring?'" asked Bruce.

"Just testing you."

"Anyway, I found out about all this one night when I came over for dinner and my father introduces this poor spaced out kid to me as my brother. He starts going on and on about how he's going to mold Keenan into this extra-special being and how he's going to prove my grandfather's methods were valid." Bruce paused and then looked at me. "Frankly, I think my dad just fucked him in the ass when nobody else was looking."

"That's the most ridiculous thing I ever heard," I said in spite of myself.

"I thank God every day I wasn't born gay," Bruce said, almost to himself. "Not that there's anything wrong with it…but that's the only reason I escaped my father's craziness. He really didn't care about me at all. And after a while, I really didn't want to be a part of that family anymore. Maybe I just didn't want join any club that would have me for a member…"

"Groucho," I said.

He nodded, but the joy was gone. He looked at me like a lost puppy. "So your friend's not showing, can we go talk somewhere? Just a Starbucks or something?"

I looked around and saw no sign of PMA. Maybe *he* went to a Starbucks. I got out my phone. Still no response to my text. This wasn't good. I texted again.

Call me when you get this. Need to know you are okay.

"I want to go back in," I said to Bruce. "Just to make sure he didn't get in somehow on his own."

We walked in, and I noticed the Blue Fires were coming in after us, all of them in a clump. They were hurrying and, as they passed by us, one of them shoved a card at Bruce, who took it. As we walked out onto the exhibition floor, Bruce stopped to read the card. I kept my eye on the Blue Fires to see what they were up to. They were getting into some kind of formation in the middle of a large, open space where two aisles intersected. People started to gather around to see whatever show they were planning on putting on.

And then Bruce chuckled loudly.

"What's so funny?" I asked, noticing he was laughing at something he read on the card.

"Well, Mikov sure would have appreciated this. Rosenbaum Productions. Who better to make this movie…"

"Rosenbaum?" I said as if somebody had electroshocked me. "You know who Rosenbaum is?"

Bruce looked up from the card. "Well, I don't know who *this* Rosenbaum is…I'm talking about the Rosenbaum that Mikov worshipped."

I looked at him as though he knew the location of the Holy Grail but didn't think it was any big deal.

"Max, you don't get this?" he finally said in disbelief. "Ayn Rand's birth name was Rosenbaum, Alisa Rosenbaum. You know how crazy Mikov was about her. He was always going on about her when I was a kid, I know her entire life story. I thought she had to be brilliant. Then I grew up and found out she was a nut."

Ayn Rand was Rosenbaum?

Suddenly, there was shouting…

"BLUE FIRE MUST BE PURE! BLUE FIRE MUST BE SURE!"

All the costumed Blue Fires were doing some kind of war dance that I didn't understand as they chanted the Blue Fire incantation.

"FOR GOOD TO BE PURGED OF EVIL…"

I thought I heard a shot. A shot?

"…BLUE FIRE MUST ENDURE."

And then I saw Bruce slump to the ground. He dropped his card. It now had a bullet hole in it.

I knelt down next to him--and that's when I saw my Blue Fire stalker standing a few feet away. He was putting a smoking gun back in his fanny pack.

There were screams as the people around me caught on to what was happening. But the Blue Fires were yelling so loudly, they didn't hear. My Blue Fire joined the other Blue Fires as they continued their goofy superhero dancing. They were moving around in circles and switching places, so I lost track of which one was which. It was like one of those animated games they showed on the Jumbotron at the ballpark, where they hid a baseball under one of three batting helmets and you had to pick with one it ended up under. I always lost track. Not a good omen.

A couple of security guys rushed over.

"Call 911!" I yelled at them. "Somebody shot him!"

One security guy got out his phone, the other knelt down on the other side of Bruce, who was bleeding badly from his chest.

"Don't worry, we'll take care of you…"

"Somebody already took care of me…that's the problem…" he mumbled. A jokester to the end.

I left him with the security guy and said, "I'll be back." But just as I got up, the Blue Fire party broke up, and all the neon blue costumed figures scattered in every direction, running manically at people and throwing promotional cards at them.

There were too many of them. And they all looked alike.

I ran through the crowded aisles, trying to get close enough to each one to see if I could identify my stalker, trying to figure out which Blue Fire was moving differently than the others. I shoved my way through many disgruntled geeks, my sweaty panting face undoubtedly discouraging them from any kind of interaction. I was sure I looked like an insane person, running up to each Blue Fire one by one, spinning him around, trying to figure out if he was the right Blue Fire. But I didn't have a choice.

An announcement came over the P.A. telling everyone to be a calm, that there had been an incident and that there might be an "active shooter" on the premises. That had the opposite effect of making everyone calm, and there was much screaming and running for the exits. Suddenly, I was fighting my way against the tide of fanboy humanity, their panicked faces rushing at me from every which way. I got shoved to the side by the rush of costumed geeks and then some idiot dressed as a *Star Wars* Stormtrooper who was running for dear life pushed me even further away from the aisle, propelling me into a twelve-foot tall model robot sporting a giant illuminated head. I yelled, "FUCK!" because my bad rib figured prominently in the crash. The giant robot made some random electronic squawking sound as it fell to the ground, nearly taking out some guy in a Galactus costume. Destroyer of worlds, my ass.

The place was emptying out quickly and the Blue Fires had joined the rush to the exits. Then, behind an empty booth in a back corner, I saw a flash of neon blue go past the group of anime cosplay girls, the same ones who had been giggling near me outside, who for some reason didn't seem all that concerned with that whole active shooter thing. I ran right through the middle of the cosplay cuties without giving them a second look, because I didn't want to lose that flash of blue.

And I didn't. Because he didn't want to lose me.

I saw him, calmly standing in an empty back corner, staring back in my direction, waiting for me.

I stopped and caught my breath. What the hell was he up to?

He was silent. He did not move. I wasn't even sure if this was my guy. But I slowly walked towards him as if he was.

"Why did you shoot him?" I asked.

When I got to a few feet away from him, he mumbled something low in my direction, so low I couldn't make out what he was saying.

That's what made me realize who he was.

He reached up and pulled off his mask and gave me his full creepy toothy grin.

"Augustine Bravino," I whispered.

"I was trying to shoot you. Somebody bumped me."

Then he pulled a phone out of his fanny pack, hit a button and held the screen in front of him for me to see.

"Look at this, stadium inspector."

On the screen was a video of Eydie--yelping and howling in a cage of some kind.

"You goddamn piece of shit…WHERE THE FUCK IS SHE?"

Homicide was back in my heart. Once again, I knew I wouldn't stop until the person in front of me was dead. I started to rush him and then I screamed, because something suddenly pierced the back of my neck.

The pain was overwhelming. Whoever was stabbing me was jamming the weapon into me as hard as they could.

I gasped for air and turned to see who was behind me. It was one of the anime cosplay girls.

I looked a little more closely at her.

"You're going down, Super Dick."

It was Veronica, wearing an orange wig and a black and white schoolgirl outfit and looking mightily pleased at what she had just accomplished. Then I saw what was sticking in my neck. It wasn't a weapon at all, but an empty syringe. Empty, because its contents were already in me.

A couple of big guys emerged from an emergency exit door. Augustine squeezed past them and left the building as they started heading for me. They were clearly going to carry me out because I already realized I wasn't going to be making it under my own power.

My last thought, as I collapsed to the floor and lost consciousness, was *What the fuck happened to PMA?*

The Clinic

Okay. This wasn't what I wanted for Christmas. And as far as I knew, it could be Christmas.

I woke up in a small empty room, maybe ten feet by ten feet, that had padded walls and a floor to match. It was the kind of place where you'd put a mental patient. I had no idea how long I'd been out.

As I managed to focus my vision, I saw there was a door in the middle of the wall to the right of me. I turned to the left – another door in the middle of *that* wall. Neither of them had doorknobs or any kind of mechanism that would allow someone to open them. Other than that, there was nothing else in the room but me and a small surveillance camera I spotted in one of the corners of the ceiling. No windows. No way out.

I was lying on my chest, flat on the warm, soft floor, still wearing my shirt and pants, but my shoes, socks and coat were gone. So was everything in my pockets and my nice silver Banana Republic watch. Oh, and they had taken my belt. The wound in my neck still ached, my rib still ached, as a matter of fact, my entire fucking body ached. This wasn't really what the doctor ordered for a fifty-nine-year-old guy whose idea of exercise was walking the dog every other day.

The dog.

They had Eydie. And they probably had PMA. The way these guys worked, they probably took my mom out of the assisted living hellhole she was in down in D.C. too--unless they figured out I cared more about the dog than her.

Oh, Christ. My head.

I stayed still a moment, trying to figure out just how fucked up I was from Veronica's unexpected shot to my neck. The answer? Pretty fucked up.

Then I remembered the packet of Xanax I had taped to my armpit. I had a feeling they hadn't strip-searched me, otherwise they would have put me in some sort of institutional uniform or at the very least, some *Minions* pajamas. That meant there was a chance those pills were still there. That would be good.

I let a few more minutes go by. I needed my head to clear a little before I did anything, but I also didn't know how much time I had to make any kind of move. And if I didn't manage to get those pills in my system to douse the Blue Fire that was undoubtedly beginning to rage inside of me, I might never get another move to make. Probably the only thing saving me at the moment was the Xanax I had already had in my system. But that dose of Max's little helper was either already gone or wearing off, depending on how long I had been out here on the floor, because I was feeling the crazy bigtime.

I glanced at the camera up in the corner of the ceiling without moving my head or opening my eyes very far, hoping whoever was watching the feed on the other end wouldn't notice. I wanted to ballpark the angle of the camera's view so I could try to get myself out of range--and, of course, do it in a way that looked natural. No one watching could suspect I was anywhere near my right mind. So I gave a little groan for the benefit of anyone listening in and slowly lifted my head. It wasn't pleasant. It felt like my neck was trying to yank a train car loaded with steel off the ground.

I continued to avoid looking up and began crawling slowly towards the corner of the room directly below the camera. If I made it, the most it would be able to pick up would be my legs. Getting there was hard work, like swimming through half-frozen mud, but I inched my way slowly and surely ahead until my head was butted up directly into the corner.

I waited there for a few moments. I was exhausted from the effort and now I was nauseous too, so I had to wait until my stomach calmed down. It wouldn't be good to immediately throw up the medication I was desperate to get into my system. Finally, I propped myself up a little bit on my elbows, keeping my legs in place as much as possible. Then I leaned slightly on my left elbow and reached under my shirt into my left armpit with my right hand.

Thank you, Jesus, or whoever was taking his shift. The packet was there, still taped in place.

I lowered my head. Things were spinning. Fucking Blue Fire. It was pushing me to stop, to give up, to surrender, darkening every thought and feeling inside me. But I stayed up on my left elbow and managed to quietly rip off the tape holding the packet to my skin. I pulled out the packet, took out three Xanax and popped them in my mouth. I've always been good at swallowing pills dry, so they went down quickly and easily.

There were two more pills left in the packet I was holding in my right hand. There was no way to reattach the packet back to my armpit, the scotch tape was off and too much of a mess to get back on. I didn't really have a chance to pull off anything super clever, so I just shoved the packet into my shirt pocket. Since they had already searched my clothes, maybe they wouldn't bother to look. Maybe.

I put my head back down on the floor and closed my eyes. I knew the Xanax couldn't undo everything Veronica injected in me. I just had to hope it could take care of enough of it.

More time passed. I can't say how much because I went under again. But when I woke up this second time, I could tell the Xanax had cleared away some of the murkiness inside my brain. I wasn't ready to do any cartwheels--I didn't know how to do one anyway--but I felt like I could cope. And I also knew I had to play like I couldn't for the time being. Wherever they were keeping me most likely had heavy security and my only chance was convincing them that I was incapable of anything.

I crawled back towards the center of the room. This time around, it was easier, but I still made it look as difficult as before. Then I allowed myself to collapse back on the floor as if I was completely spent and waited to see what would happen next.

A few minutes passed before I heard a high-pitched electronic beep, then one of the doors without doorknobs swung open. My head was already turned that way, so I half-opened my eyes and saw a big guy dressed all in black entering. It didn't take me long to recognize him-- he was the guy who had helped me take a piss at Veronica's place. He bent down and rolled me over on my back to look me over. I kept my eyes half-open and tried to look confused and out of it. It wasn't hard.

"Awake?" he asked.

I blinked a couple of times. He frowned and worked hard to get me to my feet. I kept my body limp, forcing him to do all the heavy lifting. He had some kind of ID card hanging around his neck on a lanyard, which he grabbed and passed in front of the other door in the room, which also opened with a high-pitched electronic beep. Inside was a small utilitarian bathroom, with only a metal toilet and matching sink, along with a roll of toilet paper on the floor. Since my bladder was close to bursting, I felt relieved, but not as relieved as I did after he walked me into the room, undid my pants and once again helped me guide my urine stream into the toilet.

This guy had an interesting specialty. I wonder how he described it on his résumé.

When I was done, he zipped me up and rebuttoned my pants, then gently lowered me back down to the floor, where he left me on my chest again. Then he stared at me a moment, like he was wondering who I was and why this had happened to me. But guys like him couldn't afford to think too much about what they were doing, so he turned to the door he had entered through, waved his ID card at it, and then walked out after it opened with another high-pitched beep.

A couple more moments passed. Then the door opened again…and in came our first special guest star.

It was Dr. Reginald. Time to get this party started.

He wasn't alone. Coming in after him was Keenan, carrying two canvas folding chairs, the kind parents sit in on the sidelines while watching their kids run around attempting to play soccer on a Saturday morning. Keenan unfolded the two chairs and placed them side-by-side in front of the door, facing the top of my head. Then they both sat down in them.

"Max?" Dr. Reginald asked quietly, even gently.

I slowly rolled onto my side and looked over at him. He was wearing a white lab jacket and he seemed sad, upset, even guilty. Keenan, wearing casual wear, had his hand on the good doctor's arm as if he were reassuring him. Or something.

"Where…am I?" I made it sound like I was a lot more fucked up than I was. The truth was my head was continuing to clear.

"You're in our clinic, Max."

The clinic. Pretty much what I already suspected. I was down in the depths of the building, on one of the floors beneath street level. Probably adjacent to their zombie ward.

"Why…?" I asked.

"Sh, sh, sh," he said. "Do *not* try to talk too much, you've gotten a very heavy dose and you need a lot of rest."

"Put your mind at ease," added Keenan in soothing tones. "Try to bring light into it. Visualize beautiful things."

Oh, brother.

"What day…?"

"It's Sunday, Max, maybe one or two in the morning. Frankly, I'm quite surprised you're actually conscious. When they told me you were moving around, I thought they were mistaken…but…here you are."

I wasn't supposed to be capable of moving at this point? That meant the Xanax I already had had in my system really did help me out. But Dr. Reginald gave me the cue I needed. I had to act as helpless as a baby. I let my head fall back to the floor, to a place where I couldn't even see him or Keenan the boy wonder. Then, to really seal my Oscar nomination, I even let myself drool a little.

"Max?"

I said nothing.

"Max, if you can, move your head if you can still hear me. What I am about to say to you is very important and I want to make sure you understand…as well as you can in your condition."

I moved my head a little.

"Okay, good. I just want you to *appreciate* your circumstances. Nobody here wishes to harm you, nobody here wishes to harm anyone, it's not what we're all about. But we *are* doing important work here, very important work with many important things involved, things…" He stopped a moment. "Well…it's very involved and it will be very hard for someone in your position to understand. I get that. You see us as the bad guys, and you, you think you're fighting for truth, justice…the American way."

Gee. And I thought I was just fighting to keep you from turning my brain into a kumquat.

"But here's the reality and here's the part you don't really see. We're the ones fighting for this country. We're fighting for real freedom, personal freedom, the kind of freedom that America was founded on. Once you understand the mission here…you will realize we're on the same side. Yes, it's true, some may get overly aggressive about safeguarding what we're doing here…but that's just to protect our vision. It's enormously difficult to keep anything pure in this filthy world…and sometimes…"

He stopped. He was getting emotional. I could hear it in his voice.

"Father, please," I heard Keenan weigh in. "You don't have to apologize…"

Dr. Reginald made some kind of choked sob. Wonderful. He somehow thought he was the victim here, instead of the poor slobbering fool doped to the gills lying on the floor in front of him. He was more fucked in the head than I was.

Time to break the news to him.

"Your son…" I said with a gasping croak.

"My son?" Dr. Reginald replied sharply. "Keenan?"

"No…Bruce…" I whispered.

"Bruce?" asked Keenan with some confusion. "What about him?"

"Shot…shot at Comic Con…" It was getting hard talking like this. I felt like I was performing some kind of pseudo-Shakespearean death scene and I didn't exactly have the dramatic chops for it. Then again, if Mel Gibson could play *Hamlet*…

"He was *shot?*" Dr. Reginald's voice went up an octave. "Is he *dead?*"

I slumped my body so they would think I passed out. I wanted what I had just told them to sink in and besides, I didn't have the patience to hear any more of their bullshit. They were just going to talk in circles.

The only way I might learn anything interesting was if they thought I couldn't hear them.

"Max?" Dr. Reginald almost shouted at me. "Max, are you awake?"

"I think he's out, Father," added Keenan helpfully.

"Did you hear anything about this? About your brother getting shot?" Dr. Reginald hissed in a whisper at Keenan.

"Father, I have been with you the whole time we've been here, they only told us they brought Mr. Bowman in."

Only me? What about the kid?

"But they're going too far, who knows what else they're doing that they haven't told us about. It's getting more and more out of control!"

"I know, Father, I know," Keenan said sadly.

"I mean, what are they going to do with him if he doesn't cooperate?"

I assumed he meant me.

"He will most likely join the others, Father. It is for the greater good."

The others. That didn't sound good. That sounded like me ending up climbing on the jungle gym in the park at 3 a.m.

"Keenan, you are such a…such a rock."

"As you are for me."

It was quiet for a moment. I squinted my eye open a bit. They were hugging it out with some special father-son bonding time. When they finally separated, I closed my eye and played dead again. I heard them get up and start to fold up their chairs.

"Look, there's nothing more we can do. He's made his own bed," Dr. Reginald muttered and I again assumed he meant me. "He's been poking his nose into all our business. I don't like him, he's rude and nasty and maybe…maybe this is what needed to happen."

"Karma," Keenan offered.

"Your grandfather can deal with him now," Dr. Reginald said with an accepting finality.

The door beeped open and I heard the two of them leave. For the sake of the camera, I stayed on the floor. But I had heard a word I didn't like. A word that made me want to get up and pound down that door and run out of here screaming.

That word was "grandfather."

One of the clichés you hear constantly is the hardest thing you can do is nothing. Me, I always thought the hardest thing you can do is hammer a railroad spike into your own forehead, but I was beginning to reconsider my answer, because it felt impossible to keep still. I knew I had to continue to lie on the floor and make them believe I was out of it, but inside I was churning. I kept worrying about the kid and my dog. Were they both dead? Was I going to join them?

Eventually, I let it all go, because there was nothing else to do. And I fell back asleep.

I was awakened again by the high-pitched beep of the door mechanism unlocking. It swung open and in came the big guy again, aka He Who Helps Others Pee, accompanied by another big guy, one I hadn't seen before. One held the door open while the other wheeled in a gurney - and then they both bent down and struggled to pick me up off the floor.

"I still don't get it," He Who Helps Others Pee finally said, grunting with the effort of carrying my future cadaver. "If he needs another injection, why not just do it in here? Why do we have to move the piece of shit?"

"Don't know," said Other Big Guy, also grunting. "The wheelchair warrior wants him on the main floor for some reason."

The wheelchair warrior?

They carefully put me on top of the gurney, and then turned me over on my back. Just for fun, I let my head fall to the side and drooled again.

"Gross," said Other Big Guy.

As they rolled me out of the room and down a narrow hallway, I opened my eyes again to see what I could learn about this facility. At the moment, all I could see was the white wall across from my head.

As we moved down the hall, we passed a couple of the barred windows that I had seen from outside when I first checked out the building, the barred windows that were below street level. At the time, I thought the bars were there to keep people out; now I realized they were probably there to keep them in.

The gurney turned a corner and suddenly I was facing a huge glass wall that housed a much larger version of the room I had been imprisoned in, a room that was padded head to foot. It was about as big as the inside of a typical 7-11.

This unusual room had a few unusual accessories; a padded picnic table of sorts and some other padded furniture. It also had shit and piss all over the floor along with some uneaten food--because the room was filled with zombies.

Yes, a dozen or so zombies, the same ones I had seen frolicking in the park, were all quietly spread out on the furniture or on the floor. One was actually lying on top of a pile of crap. I looked more closely at that one, because I recognized him.

Turned out it hadn't been a dream, a hallucination or a mirage that I had experienced a few nights ago. No, the Senator from the great state of New York, Abe Marks, a personal hero to me for pursuing the Dark Sky investigation, was now literally rolling around in his own shit, because his brain was no longer sophisticated enough to understand how to use a toilet.

And yet, I couldn't help thinking he was still more qualified to hold office in his current condition than his replacement, Senator Eddie di Pineda.

We made a right at the glass wall of the zombie ward and went down another hallway, where I spotted a long, rolled-up hose and some other heavy-duty cleaning equipment in the hallway. I imagined the help hosed down and mopped up the room while the zombies enjoyed their outdoor time in the middle of the night. That was what they got for their turndown service. And this was the life I could look forward to if I didn't find my way out of here.

My insides shivered.

The two big guys continued to wheel me forward into a large open area with a few vacant hospital beds and some other scattered medical stations. I could tell from the darkness outside the windows that it was still the middle of the night, so nobody was up to much of anything. As a matter of fact, I saw only one anonymous technician in a white coat puttering around.

They left my gurney next to one of the long medical counters that had a variety of testing gizmos and equipment as well as an IV drip stand next to it. After the big guys had parked me there, they stopped and looked at each other with unhappy expressions.

"Okay, we're done here. We might as well go and get it over with," said He Who Helps Others Pee.

Other Big Guy sighed. "I'll get the cattle prods."

Cattle prods. They must have meant the electronic zappers I saw being used on the zombies in the park to keep them in line. These two were probably the designated chaperones for zombie duty that night. Which meant they were about to take the patients outside.

They left me there, unrestrained, just lying on the gurney--that's how confident they were that I wasn't in any condition to do anything. My head was beginning to fog up again, which meant the Xanax I had swallowed just a few hours ago was already getting worn away by the massive amount of Blue Fire in my system. A shudder of panic ran through me, until I remembered I still had two pills in my shirt pocket that the big guys hadn't spotted.

I just had to get to them without anybody else on the floor spotting me.

As my head was still on its side, I could only see a portion of the area around me. The one technician I had seen in the room was in the far corner looking at some shit on a computer screen. But I had no idea what was going on the other side of my gurney. Spooked by the thought of rolling around in my own turds, I decided to take a chance. I slowly turned my head over to the other side, taking care to make my movements slow and jerky, almost as if I was in the middle of a bad dream, something I could only wish was really the case.

The other side of the room was deserted. Okay. I would go for it.

I slowly moved my hand to my chest and let it rest there. I stopped and waited. Nothing happened.

I started to hear a whirring noise in the distance on the other side of me, but that was probably just another technician doing some kind of technician-type thing. Anyway, I was committed now. I decided to try to reach into my shirt pocket to see if I could at least palm the Xanax pills.

The whirring got louder.

I ignored it and slowly extended my fingers inside the pocket, while, at the same time, keeping my head still so I wouldn't draw a lot of attention. I felt the pills with the tips of my fingers and used them to slide them into my palm. It took a bit of doing, but I succeeded. I then withdrew my fingers from the pocket as the whirring's volume increased to an annoying level.

What the hell was it? An automated floor waxer? An indoor drone? Whatever it was, it seemed to be coming closer.

I stopped moving again and waited. But nothing happened. Should I turn my head and check? That would only draw more attention to me. Besides, I heard no footsteps. So I slowly finished the final phase of my covert pill drop.

I pulled my hand up towards my mouth, ready to release the pills into it.

And that's when another hand grabbed my wrist. A hand that felt dry, leathery and boney.

"Shtop, Mister Bowman."

It was a phlegmy voice with a heavy German accent that sounded about a thousand years old. But the goose pimples on my body were telling me it was, in reality, only about a hundred.

I turned my head. And found myself face-to-face with the face I didn't want to be seeing.

Dr. K himself.

The fucker was still alive.

Rosenbaum

You don't meet the inspiration for a master comic book villain every day.

But there, right in front of me, sitting in a brand new gleaming motorized wheelchair, was Dr. Frederick Kanuskey, Dr. K himself. He was neatly-dressed in a brown three-piece suit. He wore thick glasses and had a bushy brown and grey walrus moustache that completely obscured his upper lip. A short squat man, his old gnarled face emanated hatred, anger and a fierce energy that time had barely dimmed. He was smiling at me, the kind of fuck-you smile you never want to see in your lifetime, because it was the grin of a man who had been waiting to get his hands on you for very unpleasant reasons.

"OPEN ZEE HAND!" he shouted at me.

I did and the pills fell out. He broke into another satisfied smile as he picked the pills off the gurney's surface and examined them.

"Xanax. Ah! Zat explainz it. Zat is vy you are avake!" He nodded to himself, then abruptly threw the pills over his back, where they clattered on the floor behind him. The lone technician still in the room immediately ran like a frightened hall monitor to where they landed. He scooped them up and took them over to a nearby sink, where he washed the pills down the drain, along with my hopes of survival.

Dr. K then pressed a button on the arm of his wheelchair and yelled into a little microphone dangling on the end of it.

"ROBERT! NICK!" His words echoed out through the facility's P.A. system. "I haff someone I need restrained NOW!"

The two big guys came rushing back into the room as I turned back to the old man.

"How the fuck old are you?" I asked.

"Ninety-eight, Mr. Bowman. But…I don't look a day over ninety-zeven, do I?"

He cackled at his stupid joke as the big guys ran up to my gurney and pulled out a couple of restraining straps. With practiced, efficient moves, they pulled the straps tightly over my body, one across my chest and one across my legs, and fastened them down on the other side of the gurney. They were snug, so snug, my arms were pinned down.

"Comfortable?" asked Dr. K with a twinkle in his eye. I smiled painfully and nodded. I struggled a little, but it was pretty clear I wasn't going anywhere.

"We were getting ready to take the deadheads out, that okay, Dr. K?" asked He Who Helps Others Pee. Dr. K nodded impatiently, and the big guys left.

"The deadheads," I said. "Senator Marks and the gang."

"Ja, Mr. Bowman. Zat iz the tragedy of our clinic. Most of zee people vee brink in here end up vorking viz us. Those zat don't…"

"…end up rolling around in their own shit."

He shrugged with a "What can you do?" kind of face.

"Vee drug and vee drug, to try and make zem cooperative…but zometimez…"

"So…you didn't really die a couple of decades ago. The CIA just made it look like you did."

"Ja…it vas necessary. Zere vere many lawsuits…disgruntled parents. Zey didn't understand my methods."

"You and Mengele. Misunderstood."

He laughed heartily and then he started coughing as though his lungs were going to come shooting out of his mouth.

"Excuze me…" He hacked a few more times. A few drops of his spit landed on me. Nice. "Zis fuckink cough."

"You were a part of the MK-Ultra program…?"

"Ja, of course. Zat iz vy zey brought me over here."

"Just another sicko Nazi doctor we imported from Germany after the war."

"Prussian to be precise. I vas a teenager when the Nazis took away our state's independence. But it verked out to the good. Zey saw I was shmart and let me work with their scientists and learn. Zey had some good ideas." He looked over at the technician, who was back at his computer screen on the other side of the room. "Valter! Come!"

"And gay conversion was a great way to practice brainwashing people?"

"Two birds wiz one shtone, Mr. Bowman--vee fix zee perverts and vee also get to learn zom valuable zinks about zee human mind."

He started coughing violently again as "Valter" the technician approached.

"Yes, Dr. K?" asked Valter.

"Vake Janine up, she vill vant to zee zis, I am sure."

Janine. My precious Veronica. My mind was reeling.

Dr. K saw my look of revulsion and laughed again. "You know Janine, no? Vonderful chemist. And Blue Fire made her a great warrior! Haff you zeen her wiz a shvord?"

Yeah. I had zeen her wiz a shvord.

Then I heard more whirring coming from the other side of my gurney. And I saw Dr. K staring in that direction with a suddenly nervous expression.

I turned. And I saw the face of Mr. Barry Filer.

Except it wasn't *exactly* Mr. Barry...

A bizarre sort of robot-on-wheels--really a video-monitor-on-a-metal-rod-on-wheels--had rolled up next to my gurney. And filling the screen was the monstrous pockmarked face of Mr. Barry Filer in glorious HD quality.

It reminded me of the robot with J. Jonah Jameson's face that Spider-Man fought on a regular basis. This thing wouldn't do in a fight, however. It looked like a good swift wind would blow it over.

"Herr Filer," said Dr. K.

"Y-y-you finally got him," said Mr. Barry Filer, after he silently belched into his hand. "C-c-congratulations," he added, sarcastically.

"How are things, Barry?" I asked.

"V-v-very good, M-M-Max," he replied with a smile. "Expecting to g-g-get Dark Sky back on track soon."

"Great news. Now, *where* are you?"

"G-g-getting ready for our reboot. We're having a k-k-kind of 'think tank' out west. Beautiful c-c-country out here." He stopped and turned to Dr. K. "D-d-doctor, make sure Max Bowman never leaves our sight ag-g-gain."

Valter had returned to the clinic area, so Dr. K yelled over to him, "Prepare a syringe, Valter!"

"I'm getting another dose of Blue Fire, I take it?" I said with a chill.

"Ja. You VILL take it. And many, many more."

Just then, down the nearby hallway, I heard the zombies being herded out of the building, as well as the constant "zzzzap!" of the cattle prods keeping them in line. How did this twisted piece of madness end up smack in the middle of the Upper East Side without anyone catching on? How much longer could they get away with this? Didn't matter, it would be long enough for them to completely fry my brains, especially if they were about to dose me again.

"I would advise you to stop f-f-f-fighting, Max," said the virtual Mr. Barry Filer, as if he was reading my mind. "Y-y-you fight too hard and you lose your mind. Like the n-n-nearly late Senator M-M-Marks."

"What's this all about?" I asked weakly.

He smiled and said nothing.

Dr. K whirred over towards Valter to check on the syringe. Now that the big boss was watching over him, he wasn't going to take any chances. I don't know who souped up his wheelchair for him, but that thing could move. Abruptly, the virtual Mr. Barry Filer revved up his own set of wheels, turned and followed after him in a slower and clunkier fashion.

I was all by myself for the moment.

Hopelessness was creeping over me again. My restraints were too strong and too tight to escape from, so I wasn't going to get out of this mess easy. As a matter of fact, it was beginning to look like I wasn't getting out at all.

Then someone started stroking the top of my head. Somebody had walked up behind me, and, unfortunately, I recognized both the touch and the resulting goose pimples of dread it raised on my skin.

"Super Dick. Here at last."

Veronica was in back of me.

"Where's my dog?" I asked, straining to look up over my own head. But I couldn't see her.

"My place. Fourth floor. I torture it on a daily basis and pretend it's you." She yanked a hair out of the top of my head. Ouch. The anger rose up in me again and so did the urge to rip her head off her neck.

Veronica, trailing her hand from my head down to my chest, walked over to where I could see her. Evidently she had been sleeping, since she was wearing what looked like Japanese silk pajamas, unbuttoned to show a little cleavage as usual. She pointed to a few small marks on her face.

"That's where the light bulb pieces hit me, Super Dick. It's better now…but for a while there…*I didn't like to look at myself in the mirror.*"

She delivered that last part with such a frightening ferocity that I turned away in revulsion.

"My neck hurts a little too, Super Dick. Hurts a lot. You've done a lot of bad things to a girl who's just trying to help you along. And now, you get me out of a deep sleep for this. How am I supposed to get my beauty sleep, Max Bowman? How?"

Suddenly, more whirring.

Veronica looked up in awe as if God Almighty himself was approaching. And maybe he was. Maybe this was Rosenbaum in the flesh. Or the person I had to believe was actually Rosenbaum.

"Hello, Mr. Bowman. Long time no see," came the voice on the other side of me. A voice I never wanted to hear again. I turned my head to see for myself.

There, in the video monitor at the top of another robot-on-wheels like Mr. Barry Filer's, was the visage of the King of the Spooks himself, Andrew "Uncle Andy" Wright.

Wright was the former CIA bigwig turned mysterious Pentagon higher-up who was capable of pulling so many top-secret strings that nobody knew exactly how much power he had, only that it was a lot and you shouldn't fuck with him. Uncle Andy had willed Dark Sky into existence and then, under its umbrella, put his psycho son Herman and PMA's tragic uncle Robert out into the wilds of Afghanistan to ruthlessly slaughter their way across the countryside.

When the kid and I exposed the organization's cutthroat ways, ways which had resulted in the deaths of several respected American officers and almost eliminated the two of us, Andy crept back into the darkness and disappeared. After Dark Sky's misdeeds had been exposed, after his son died violently in the process of trying to kill me, I didn't think he would ever have the will, the guts or the means to make this kind of trouble again, even though he was never charged with any crimes.

But I always underestimated the professional assholes who really ran the world. And evidently, he'd been running this particular operation for quite a few years.

"Hi, Uncle Andy. Or should I say…Rosenbaum?" I asked.

Uncle Andy's virtual face almost smiled.

"Are you out west with your good friend, Mr. Barry Filer?"

"I am, Mr. Bowman, I am. In beautiful Sedona Arizona. Have you ever been here? The red rock canyons are magnificent."

Imagine that. Uncle Andy and Mr. Barry Filer, out in Arizona and at the same time, rolling around here in the basement of hell. God bless technology.

"Haven't had the opportunity."

"And you won't get it either, sorry to say. You've taken up far too much of our time, Mr. Bowman. Now I'm glad we can move on to other things. Janine, can you please give us a few minutes?"

Veronica nodded and walked away. Her leaving was how I spelled relief. I turned back to Wright.

"So, what's shaking in Arizona?"

"Quite invigorating and refreshing. The mystics say there are energy vortexes here, some with magnetic energy, some with electric. For someone of my advanced years, it really is stimulating."

I glanced over towards where Valter, Dr. K and the virtual Mr. Barry Filer were gathered. I saw Valter turn and show Dr. K a syringe filled with blue liquid. Dr. K held up a hand, indicating he should wait. He saw that Uncle Andy and I were having a heart-to-heart.

"You guys planning Dark Sky's return? I hear congratulations might be in order," I said, turning back to Wright, stalling for time.

"Let's just say we're cautiously optimistic."

"Thanks to your new wonder drug."

"Let's just say we're cautiously optimistic," he said again.

"And you're making movies now, very exciting. Who's this Brad Palmer, your movie producer?"

"Former Director of Communications at Dark Sky, Mr. Bowman. There were quite a few stellar employees I had to find new opportunities for because of you, however I'm confident they'll be able to remain in their current positions. But enough about us, Mr. Bowman, let's talk about you. I'd like to know who *you* work for. Are you some kind of Russian mole? In the pocket of the Chinese? I thought last year must be a fluke--but this time, I must say, it's been equally frustrating dealing with you. Whoever trained you must have been superb. So superb that I'm taking this time out of my day for this conversation simply to learn more about your employer."

"I'm flattered you think so highly of me, Andy, but I'm not working for any foreign powers. I'm just a guy trying to get by."

Andy suddenly let his smile drop, along with his mask of civility.

"Well, you're not going to be' getting by' any more. You took my son away from me, Mr. Bowman," he said in an icy tone.

"I didn't kill him. Robert Davidson finished that job."

"You bear the responsibility, Mr. Bowman. You're going to pay the price. You don't get to where I am by allowing your enemies to escape punishment."

"So you are going to kill me."

"Kill you? Oh no, no, no. Did you kill *me*, Mr. Bowman? No, instead, you caused the death of someone very close to me, my own blood. My only son, Mr. Bowman. I will carry that pain around till the day I die. Fathers aren't supposed to bury their children. I had to. And I will never forgive you for bringing that to pass. You are going to feel the pain I felt--and I will not rest until you do."

His virtual face was shaking with rage. And I was beginning to wake up to what he was planning.

"You have the kid, don't you? You've got Jeremy, along with my dog." I said quietly.

He smiled and said nothing.

Furious, panicked, my emotions racing beyond reason, I suddenly and uselessly started struggling to break out of my restraints. There was no chance of success, but I couldn't control myself. Blue Fire wanted me to lose my shit.

"As I said, Mr. Bowman, you're going to feel my pain. That gives me no pleasure." Andrew Wright paused and set his ancient jaw. "It's just…*business.*"

CRASH.

Wait…what?

Loud, violent noises were coming from somewhere else on the clinic floor. A smash and another crash and voices yelling and big heavy footsteps running. And then some panicked screams I can only describe as "zombie-like." And more screaming and yelling and running.

And then gunshots.

Virtual Andrew Wright turned and rolled towards Dr. K, Virtual Mr. Barry Filer, Veronica and Valter, who were all staring towards the hallway where the noises seemed to be coming from, the same hallway that led to the zombie ward and the outside door.

I heard Dr. K say something about the back elevator. He turned and whirred his way back across the length of the conference room at about 120 mph, followed by Valter and Veronica. Dr. K bellowed over his shoulder at them, "BRINK BOWMAN!" Valter quickly stopped and ran to the back of my gurney to wheel me out as Dr. K and Veronica ran down a different hallway leading out of the main clinic floor.

Left behind in the general flight were the virtual Mr. Barry Filer and Andrew Wright, whose rolling monitors weren't nearly as fast as Dr. K's chairs. They were slowly rolling towards Valter and me.

"MAX?" someone yelled from the hallway where all the commotion seemed to be happening. It was another familiar voice.

It was PMA's.

What the hell?

It was true, it was PMA and he had a lot of company. He ran in leading a group of about fifteen burly working class guys that looked like they were from Queens or Jersey, or maybe both, wielding baseball bats and other instruments of destruction. Most of them were wearing stocking or baseball caps, a few had neck tattoos and they acted like they meant business. A couple had handguns and one guy was holding a shotgun--and its barrel was smoking, because he had just blasted a hole into the ceiling.

"Wait…!" I yelled as a couple of the goons bashed the backs of Wright and Filer's video monitors, sending them crashing to the floor. Guess that was the end of those conversations.

Valter was so freaked out he ran for the back hallway too, leaving me behind.

PMA ran over to my gurney.

"What the hell…?" I asked him as I watched the goons start picking up every piece of computer equipment that looked like it had value and stacking it up on one counter.

"YO, FUCK THOSE DOUCHEBAGS UP!" one of the burly guys with a Yankees cap yelled back down the hall in his best New Yawk accent.

"What's going on?" I asked with some alarm.

PMA grimaced. "The zombies…they're ripping apart their keepers. I made the mistake of taking these away from them." He held up two of the cattle prods.

"HEY, LOOKIN' GOOD THERE, LIVING DEAD, KICK SOME GOVERNMENT ASS!" yelled another goon at whatever atrocities were going on, fortunately out of my sight.

PMA found the release buttons for my restraints and freed me. Aching, I got off the gurney.

"What happened to you at the Comic Con?" I asked, sorely confused. "I texted you and…"

"I got jumped in the parking lot," he interrupted. "They took my phone, my keys, everything, then gave me a knock on the head and left me behind the dumpster."

"They didn't try to bring you in?"

He shook his head.

"And who are your new friends?" I said, eyeing the goons who had redoubled their efforts to gather everything in the clinic they could sell on EBay.

PMA shuddered. "After I came to, I looked everywhere for you. Couldn't find you, so I thought they probably brought you back here. I called the cops, they weren't much help, so I went back to the hotel room and when you weren't there, I knew you were probably in deep shit. So I turned on your laptop, went on your Facebook page and posted that you needed help, and whoever was close and available should meet me in the park at midnight. These are the guys that showed up."

"Yo! Jerry!" one of the goons yelled to PMA. "Max okay?"

"He's good!" yelled PMA.

"Hey, all right then!" he yelled back. The rest of them cheered. "FIGHT THE POWER, MAX!" yelled one. "TAKE BACK AMERICA," yelled another one. The guy with the shotgun blew another hole in the ceiling. "TAKE THAT, ZIONIST CONSPIRACY!"

"Interesting group," I said to PMA. "You did good, kid, thanks. Now you gotta call the cops, get them over here. And get the Jerky Boys to help you get the zombies back in their playroom."

That's when I saw one of the zombies had made his way onto the clinic's main floor. I nudged PMA and pointed in his direction.

It was the Zombie Senator Marks, and he was shuffling towards me with something resembling recognition again. He wanted to connect, but had no idea how.

PMA and I stared at him--and we waved at the goons so they would know to leave him alone.

"Jeez. That is Senator Marks, isn't it?" PMA finally said.

Marks turned to PMA at the sound of his name. There *was* something left.

"See what you can do for him," I said. "I gotta go."

"Go? Where?"

"Fourth floor. I think that's where they have my dog."

"Max--you're not going anywhere in here, especially alone."

"I'm going. Call the cops and wait for them here." I eyed the goons warily. "Besides, I don't know what the Justice League of America here is going to do if we leave them alone. Try to keep control."

"Max, no, seriously, you can't go up there by yourself!"

I pointed to Marks, who was still standing, not moving, staring at me in wonder.

"Stay here for him. He's been through enough. I'll be okay."

"Okay, but, Max..."

I turned and hurried away down the same hallway that Dr. K, Veronica and Valter had gone down.

"MAX!" he yelled after me, "WAIT! I HAVE SOMETHING FOR YOU!"

I kept going.

As I made it to the hallway, I realized the floor seemed very cold and that's when I remembered I wasn't wearing shoes, or socks for that matter. I started down the hallway, huffing and puffing, and noticed the walls were starting to melt. I had forgotten that the Blue Fire was still in my system and the Xanax was almost used up.

I kept focused. I ignored the colors and the streaks and the hallucinations. I kept going.

I passed by some kind of equipment room and I saw a few more of the cattle prods hanging on the wall, inserted into what looked like charging bases, as if they were Dust Busters in a kitchen. They were as close to weapons as I was going to get at the moment, so I ran in and pulled out two of them to take with me. I looked them over to figure out how they worked and that's when I saw, on their backs, a small dial you could use to control how much power they shot out of their tips. At the moment, they were set to low.

I cranked the fuckers all the way up.

Then I continued down the hallway for what seemed like ten miles, but that was only because I was convinced I was turning into a zombie and it was getting harder and harder to move. The Blue Fire was back with a vengeance, manufacturing nightmares in my head. I knew it and I had to fight it.

I had to endure.

Inferno

I was going to get my fucking dog. I didn't know how I would do it, but I was going to get my fucking dog.

I continued down the hallway until I found the elevator. I got in and punched the "4" button and let myself fall back against the wall.

My hands were sweaty. My paranoia was increasing. I became convinced the moisture in my palms would cause the cattle prods I was holding to electrocute me. Since they were only the length of a Coke Bottle and the width of a thick pole, I stuck the zappers in the back pockets of my pants. They fit easily. I just had to remember not to sit down.

The creaky old elevator was slow going up, so I closed my eyes to rest. But that quickly backfired, because I immediately saw thousands of costumed Blue Fire figures running through the veins in my body, incinerating everything in sight. My body shook and my eyes shot open again, just as the elevator stopped. I was sweaty, dizzy, nauseous. The usual symptoms of being fucked in the head.

The elevator doors opened and I lurched out into a hallway I immediately recognized from when Veronica held me captive here. I knew which door was hers. I carefully and slowly walked towards it, and saw that it was open a crack.

I gently pushed it the rest of the way open.

Inside was the long interior hallway and the small table where the vase I had conked Veronica on the head with used to be.

As I tiptoed down the hallway, I saw her bedroom door was also open a crack. From inside, I heard some anthemic pop music loudly playing, featuring a sonic wall of female voices singing in Japanese. An anime soundtrack? A tribute to Mishima? You had me. I knew as much about Japanese music as I did about needlepoint, Finland and rodeo events.

But I had to assume Veronica was in there. So I had to proceed carefully. I edged my way towards the bedroom door and peeked inside.

Veronica was shooting up.

There she was, sitting on the bed, looking like a desperate heroin junkie, only what she was shooting into her track-marked arm was a familiar blue liquid. She had changed out of her pajamas and was now wearing shorts and some kind of long white short-sleeved coat, a coat that looked like it was made of vinyl or some other similarly slick shiny material. It had a few Japanese characters running down the middle of the front where it buttoned up.

She wasn't looking at me, so I had no idea how she knew I was there. But she did. Because she said, in a lovely melodic tone…

"I seeeeee you…."

I pushed the door open the rest of the way and stood there like a lamppost.

"I just want the dog," I said, trying to control the fury building up in me. I hoped this would be a simple matter but knew of course that it wouldn't be. I had too much anger and she had too much of that cobalt shit in her.

She turned to me with a powerful, gleeful smile and big crazy glowing eyes as she finished getting her Blue Fire fix.

"Blue Fire, Super Dick. When you work with it…it works with you." She took in a big breath as she felt the ecstasy and the rush of the demon drug. "It makes you *strong*."

I gritted my teeth and said again, "I just want the dog."

She yanked the now-empty syringe out of her arm with a quick sharp motion and put it down on her bedside table, never taking her shining eyes off me the whole time.

"You just want your dog."

She got to her feet.

"Well…I just want to hurt you."

That's when she opened her coat to reveal its very lethal lining. Inside were small swords, ninja stars and knives, long and short, inserted into specially-made pockets. I had a feeling she had been waiting for the right opportunity to use it, and that it was her gift that kept on giving.

"Maybe we should try a healthier approach to our relationship," I said, backing up a few steps, suddenly freaked out of my mind, my mental seesaw reversing positions.

"I'm making an executive decision, Super Dick. And that decision is you need to die."

She pulled out one of the swords and waved it around.

"How did this happen to you?" I asked, not sure that I wanted the answer.

"I became my true self, Max Bowman. When I started working for Dr. K, I was a mild-mannered science nerd just out of Cornell, afraid of the world, someone who wished she had the courage of a warrior princess…someone who wanted to be as brilliant and dangerous as Yukio Mishima."

She pointed her sword at me.

"Now…*I am.*"

She licked her lips. I continued backing up, my soul filling up with fear. She continued stepping forward, smirking with fury, eyes narrowed with hatred.

"You could have been like me, Super Dick. You just needed to allow yourself to be indoctrinated into the ideology. Blue Fire is going to help create a new warrior class. A new *ruling* class. A new era of transformation, powered by *people who get things done.*"

People who get things done. Okay. Got it.

I had backed up halfway down the hallway towards the door that would take me out of the apartment. I was starting to feel like Eydie wasn't even here, because, God knows, she would have made some noise by now. Maybe Veronica never had the dog. Maybe she killed her.

"Blue Fire unlocks all the magic, Super Dick. You probably don't even know that's why you had such a hard time with Herman and Robert Davidson last year. I treated them, honey baby. Me and this clinic *made* them what they were."

Holy shit, so *that* was why those two had been so unhinged. And that was why Robert was so conflicted. He was trying to fight the Blue Fire. He was trying to fight what they had turned him into.

Herman, however, was different. Herman was like Veronica, he loved how Blue Fire made him feel and he loved how it empowered his darkness. Evidently, Blue Fire worked the best if you had a big juicy seed of rot at the core of your being, because it watered that seed and allowed it to bloom into the kind of pure aggressive action that would fulfill all of your darkest dreams.

The good news was that I apparently didn't have that seed of rot in me. The bad news was that, as a result, the Blue Fire in me was going to break me.

"Look…I just want my dog. Is the dog here?" I pleaded with a tone of desperation, not wanting to become a Benihana entrée.

She pulled out another sword and then spun and flipped the two weapons in her hands like they were batons and she was leading the neighborhood marching band. As she demonstrated her ability to juggle sharp objects, she laughed and laughed and laughed. Me, I was sweating. Sweating and sweating and sweating. And I was still backing up, one step at a time.

That's when I heard Eydie.

Suddenly, I could hear her directly behind me, howling in a way I never heard her before, yelping with desperate abandon. I turned and saw someone else I didn't want to see, holding my beloved mutt.

It was my old friend, Augustine Bravino, still wearing his Blue Fire costume--well, except for the part that went over his head. He was standing in the open doorway, holding Eydie in his hands, clutching her tight against his chest, trying with all his might to keep her from jumping out of his grasp and coming to me, because that was all she wanted to do. I saw where they had dug the microchip out of her back. The area was shaved and bandaged.

She was okay. They had actually taken care of her.

The tear came back to my eye.

I couldn't believe she was still alive, I couldn't believe she still looked healthy and I couldn't believe she still remembered who I was.

I had to keep it together. I couldn't melt into a crying little kid who just got back the dog he thought he'd never see again.

"Okay, just let her go," I said as coldly as I could manage. "Just give the dog back to me."

Augustine mumbled something.

"What?" I exclaimed harshly. Why wouldn't he let me have her?

Finally, he smiled pleasantly and spoke up a little. "She's my dog now. I like her."

From behind me, I heard Veronica let out with her laugh a few more times. I turned. She was still approaching, still leading with her swords--while Augustine and my dog were on the other side of me, blocking my escape.

"So you're not torturing the dog," I said to her.

"I'm a card-carrying member of PETA, Super Dick. Why would I hurt an innocent animal? Especially when I can shred your goddam face?"

The perspiration was flowing down my forehead and into my eyes. I leaned back against the wall, putting my hands against it for support. And also to get those hands on the cattle prods in my back pocket. I turned back to Augustine, who was still petting the yelping dog, still smiling serenely even though Eydie was yelping and desperate and completely crazed to get to me.

Then I turned back to Veronica. "What the fuck is wrong with him?" I asked.

"Augustine? Oh, he's a half and half. He made it through the Blue Fire trials, but…you know, he lost a few brain chunks along the way," she explained. "But he's *very* dependable."

"Where'd you dig him up?"

"Just another Dark Sky soldier, Super Dick. It just kind of didn't work out with him is all. But don't worry, he takes good care of your fucking mutt," said Veronica. "Which is good…because *you* won't be able to take care of her. Because…"

She raised her swords over her head.

"…you're going to die."

As she rushed me, I pushed myself off the wall and, at the same time, pulled the cattle prods out of my back pockets. As I flew forward, she missed me with her blades while I turned and lunged with the prods and got her right in the neck with both of them. I left them there for a few seconds on her skin to do as much damage as I could. Maybe it was the Blue Fire, but again, I felt good about that damage, too good, even when I started smelling the burning flesh. After all, I had turned the fuckers all the way up to the max.

I was going too far again and I caught myself. I pulled the prods back from her neck. She let out a little gasp of pain, passed out and collapsed to the floor.

I turned around to confront Augustine.

He was no longer there.

As I put the prods back in my pockets, I heard the bell of the elevator door closing outside the apartment and ran out to see which direction it was going in.

Up.

I turned back towards the apartment and to where Veronica was on the floor. She was motionless, but I had no idea when she would be up and back after me again--a couple of neck burns weren't going to stop her for long. That meant I couldn't afford to wait for the elevator to come back down. But I paused long enough to see where it stopped.

The 14th floor. That's where the lab was.

I opened the stairway door and hurried inside. I would have to climb ten floors and hope I wasn't going to be pursued by anybody faster than me. At this point, that category would have included paraplegics and one-legged dwarves.

As I went up the stairs, stopping at each landing to try and catch my breath, mopping the sweat off my forehead, I started running through everything in my mind--everything that had happened, everything that I knew, now that I had confirmation that Andrew Wright was overseeing everything. The more I kept my mind focused on a task, the more it would be distracted from the effects of the Blue Fire.

At the core, this whole operation was about ideology; Uncle Andy wanted to impose an Ayn Randian viewpoint on America to justify his own power-hungry plans--plans he used Dark Sky to try and implement. He kept Dr. K set up in his Queens practice to secretly pursue the goals of the MK-Ultra program, even after it was officially shut down. And he had Keenan groomed as a "thought leader" who could seduce rich and powerful influencers across the country – and secretly dose them with Blue Fire cocktails to seal the deal.

Mikov? He was part of Uncle Andy's early propagandizing plans.

Dr. K might not have been able to turn Mikov heterosexual, but he did succeed in brainwashing him with Rand's extreme views, because those views formed the storytelling template for the *Blue Fire* comic book; "justice" at any cost and no mercy for those who violated his idea of black-and-white "morality." Whoever stepped out of line faced incineration--Blue Fire the hero would see to that. And, now, so would Blue Fire the drug.

So why was I brought into this whole mess? Why did they connive to get Mighty Mel to hire me? Most likely because they *did* want to find Mikov--after all, they still needed him to sign off on their new propaganda project, the *Blue Fire* movie. And maybe they also wanted to make sure he wasn't going to suddenly pop up out of nowhere and sound off about his childhood tormentors. Mikov was a loose end that had been dangling out there for too long.

But, of course, Wright didn't just want me around to find Mikov, he also wanted to get me close enough to poison me with Blue Fire. That way he could, in the words of Dr. K, "kill two birds wiz one shtone."

So maybe I hadn't delivered Mikov, but they did manage to get four, five, maybe even six doses in my system, doses that were replicating themselves, according to Dr. Reginald. Did that mean that the damage already done was irreversible? I had no idea, I just knew that one way or the other, I was fucked.

But I still kept climbing the stairs. Why? Maybe I just wanted to choose the way I was fucked.

I was a sweaty mess who could barely breathe when I finally reached the 14th floor, so overheated that the cold of the concrete floor actually felt good on my filthy bare feet. I rested a few moments, then slowly opened the stairway door, which thankfully wasn't locked, and saw that I was in a dark and empty corner of the lab.

I also saw smoke. A lot of it.

Somebody had started a huge bonfire at the back of the lab where Dr. Reginald's office was. And it was easy to spot the firebug in question, because at that moment, in the middle of the lab area, Dr. Reginald himself was pouring a huge gallon container of some chemical all over the floor, presumably to start another blaze.

Coming to stop him was Dr. K, whirring towards him at supersonic speed, screaming, "NO, Reginald! SHTOP! YOU VILL DESTROY EVERYZING!"

"We HAVE to destroy everything!" a hysterical Dr. Reginald screamed back. "You want them to find evidence of what we've done?? You saw the security cameras! They're taking apart the downstairs clinic and the cops will be up here soon to arrest us!" He turned back to the blaze in his office. "Walter--GO LOCK DOWN THE ELEVATOR!"

"I already did!" he yelled back.

"The BACK elevator!" Dr. Reginald shrieked in response.

Valter emerged from the smoke around the office and ran over to the elevator, not far from me, and punched the button. When the door opened, he ran inside with key in hand and presumably brought the thing to a stop. Which also brought to a stop the possibility of anybody coming up to help me.

I ducked behind a nearby desk so Valter wouldn't spot me. It was a good plan, but completely unnecessary. When Valter came out of the elevator, he didn't go back to help Dr. Reginald or Dr. K, no, he simply quietly and quickly slipped into the stairway I had just come up from and left. I was beginning to think that what Valter really excelled at was running away. Which was sensible. Maybe he wasn't going to be Employee of the Month, but he also wasn't going to get burnt to death or thrown in jail.

And that last item was a distinct possibility for Dr. Reginald and Dr. K. Outside the window, the one on the street side of the building, I saw the lights of a few cop cars approaching.

And so did Dr. Reginald.

"They're coming! It's over! It's over!" shrieked Dr. Reginald as he threw a match on his new chemical spill. The flames erupted from the floor and singed his lab coat, throwing him back against a nearby desk.

"NEIN! Ve haff nozzing to fear!" shouted Dr. K. "Zee men downshtairs--ZEY are the trespassers! ZEY vill be arrested!"

Dr. Reginald got back on his feet and shook his head violently. "And if they recognize the missing United States senator that happens to be down there? Or the missing U.S. attorney? Or one of the others whose brains we ripped apart…? NO, Father! You've taken my work, you've corrupted it and you've doomed us!"

Dr. K looked around the lab area, desperately searching for help. "VALTER! VALTER! GET THE FIRE EXTINGVISHER!"

There was, of course, no Valter to be found. Dr. K whirred himself across the room at top speed to a wall where a fire extinguisher was mounted. But then came Problem Number Two: it was too high for him to grab from his hi-tech wheelchair, which apparently didn't have the jet power necessary to launch up from the floor. Dr. K reached and reached and reached with all his nonagenarian might to no avail. He stopped and searched through the smoky lab for help.

"KEENAN! VERE ARE YOU?"

Good question. I looked around from my vantage point, and saw Keenan sitting at another desk across the room. His head was in his hands down on the desktop and he seemed to be heaving convulsively, as if he was weeping with all his might.

Not a good moment for the Kanuskey fam.

I turned back to Dr. K, who was still trying to reach the fire extinguisher. Now, he was actually trying to push himself up and out of the wheelchair to gain the few inches of height he needed, like a midget trying to play basketball. He fell back in his chair exhausted with the effort. Meanwhile, Dr. Reginald had moved on to a new area to set on fire. He once again was pouring whatever flammable fluid he had in the gallon container all over the floor.

I didn't care about all this drama. I cared about the guy I had come up here after. And I finally spotted him lurking behind Dr. K. Augustine Bravino was still holding Eydie, but in a manner where he had a hand free to close around her snout so she couldn't make much noise. That's why I hadn't heard her. I got up, pulled out one of the zappers and started to make my way over to him through the smoke.

And that's when my brain rebelled.

Something had exploded in my skull and I instantly fell to the tiled floor in excruciating pain. It hurt so bad I couldn't see straight. I began coughing from the smoke, flames were burning up to the ceiling in the three spots Dr. Reginald had set on fire and he was now in another section of the lab starting on a fourth--with a whole new, full gallon container of fire-friendly juice.

The good news was nobody had seen me collapse, everyone was too preoccupied with their own crap, especially Dr. K, who finally had seen Augustine coming up behind him.

"Augustine! Zank Gott! Take zee fire extinguisher! Vee must put out zee firez!"

Augustine slowly shook his head. "That won't be enough. Have to stop fires at the source."

And then, clutching Eydie, he pivoted and headed towards Dr. Reginald, who had just ignited another minor inferno. He stood there, clutching the gallon container and watching the flames rise.

I tried to lift my head off the floor. The pain was starting to fade, but it still hurt too badly to move. But I had to make myself. I got up on my knees, just in time to see Augustine remove his hand from Eydie's snout, reach into his Blue Fire fanny pack, pull out his pistol, the same one he had presumably shot Bruce Canun with, and aim it at Dr. Reginald.

Uh oh.

Augustine then reverted his low monotone muttering. I couldn't understand him. Neither could Dr. Reginald. Neither could anyone in the history of mankind. "Augustine, what are you saying?" he demanded to know. "Put the gun away!"

"You shouldn't do this, you are going to burn my dog. You really need to stop," Augustine said, bringing the mutter up a few positions on the dial.

I got to my feet because I knew what was coming next. But I was helpless to stop it.

Augustine shot Dr. Reginald in the shoulder.

Dr. Reginald screamed in pain and fell back against a nearby lab counter, knocking off glass beakers, jars and bottles, all of which landed on the hard floor and broke into a million pieces. As he fell, he let go of the gallon container, which dropped into his newborn fire. The container began rapidly melting. Which wasn't a good development, considering what was still inside of it.

I got back down on the floor and covered my head as best I could to shield myself from what was coming next.

An explosion as the fires ate through the gallon container. A giant fireball as all that liquid ignited at once. More glassware flying across the room, breaking all over the floor, along with bits of burning odds and ends. Pretty cool to watch on YouTube, not in real life.

"NEIN!" shouted Dr. K, reverting to his native Nazi language as he began whirring his way over to the scene of the shooting as fast as his mechanical wheels would take him.

Augustine's answer? He casually turned and shot Dr. K twice in the chest.

Dr. K's head slumped as his wheelchair continued to whir forward at a dangerously high speed. The chair began to accelerate even faster, as if Dr. K's hand was still on top of whatever controlled it. Augustine stepped out of the way as the chair zoomed past him and crashed through one of the giant top-to-bottom picture windows in the side wall. I watched in disbelief as Dr. K and wheelchair flew out into the night, separated in mid-air and both chair and man plunged downwards towards the street twelve stories below.

Again…would've been a YouTube winner.

I got back up on my knees, fighting the pain, just as I heard Keenan let out a plaintive wail from his desk. Meanwhile, his foster father, Dr. Reginald, singed from the explosion, moaned from the lab counter he had been blown back against.

"I've been shot…" he said over and over to no one in particular. "I've been shot."

Augustine put his gun back in his fanny pack, looked around the room and saw the various blazes growing out of control, including the huge one that had been ignited by the melted gallon container. It was now all too much for one fire extinguisher--the fresh air rushing in through the broken window added more life-giving oxygen to the infernos. But at least it was clearing out some of the smoke out too. Thanks for that, Dr. K, or whatever was left of you down on the pavement.

"We have to get out of here, little baby," Augustine said to Eydie as he gently petted her. He coughed from the smoke and started walking past me towards the stairway door, not even realizing I was there.

Which was good, because otherwise I don't think I would have been able to get away with what I was about to try.

I got up and zapped him from behind with both prods. It was his turn to be on his knees, which instantly buckled from the voltage and took him down to the floor in a kneeling position. He didn't scream, he didn't let out any kind of noise at all. Instead, as I circled around to the front of him, he looked up at me uncomprehendingly.

"Give me my dog," I said.

He didn't argue. He submissively handed up Eydie to me. I put one of the prods in my back pocket and took her.

And that's when Eydie went crazy.

She lunged at my nose and began licking it as if it were a piece of steak. She was all over me--because we were reunited and it felt so good. For a few moments, I couldn't see, because she was so all over my face and, because I only had her in my one hand, it was hard to control her.

Finally, she calmed down a little and I could finally see. And what I saw was Augustine, still kneeling, slowly reaching for the gun in his fanny pack.

I dropped Eydie like she was radioactive and quickly zapped him full force on the side of the head with the prod that remained in my free hand. He fell over with a pained look. Then I traded up. I took his gun and threw the prod to a place where it couldn't come back to zap me on the ass--I aimed for a nearby blaze of fire and hit the mark.

Eydie jumped on me, anxious for me to pick her up again. I grabbed her and hugged her tightly as I tucked Augustine's gun in the back of my pants' waistband. Yeah, I cried a little more. But my head was still throbbing and my feet were still bare and I still had to get my dog and myself out of this building of the damned.

I started moving towards the elevator. Luckily, there wasn't much debris on the ground around me, but I still trod gingerly around whatever shit I could spot. I made it to the elevator without any major damage.

I entered the elevator and checked the control panel. No dice. Valter had taken the key with him, so I wasn't going to be riding this baby back down to the bottom. It would have to be the stairway--if I could keep myself from fainting and rolling down all fourteen flights.

So I opened the stairway door and started climbing down, but I didn't get very far. I heard somebody coming up from a few flights below. There was no way to tell if it was friend or foe. Eydie had the usual reaction--she suddenly started viciously barking and snarling at the as-yet unseen intruder.

"Augustine, is that you?" Veronica yelled from below in enraged and quavering tones. "Is Bowman up there?"

I just wanted to pull out the gun right there, pull it out, run down and shoot her with as many bullets as there were left in the gun. But I had to keep control. Besides, I couldn't take any chances of having another seizure in front of her or she'd turn me into human sushi.

So I started going back up.

But then I realized, as I saw all the smoke flowing out from the bottom of the door of the 14th floor, the door I had just come through, that going back into the lab wasn't really an option either.

So I kept going up. There was only one more flight.

"AUGUSTINE!" Veronica shrieked impatiently, climbing higher, coming closer. "SPEAK UP! IF YOU'RE FUCKING MUMBLING, I SWEAR TO CHRIST I'LL SLIT YOUR GODDAM THROAT!"

I kept moving up the stairs while Eydie kept on barking. Much as I loved her, she never really did what I wanted her to when I wanted her to. But then again, who did?

I got to the top of the stairs, to the final door, which had stenciled painted letters on it that read "ROOF ACCESS." That wasn't an ideal place for me either, so I stopped on the small dark landing in front of the door and listened. From the footsteps I was hearing below, it seemed as though Veronica was now only a flight or so under me. She moved a lot faster than I could in my condition and she'd be up here attacking me in another minute or two if I stayed where I was. Again, I was out of options.

I opened the door and went out onto the roof.

The Edge

It was damn cold up there.

There was a stiff wind blowing across the roof and I was still only wearing my Bloomingdales shirt and jeans. I shivered, held a confused Eydie close and looked around this wild, weird rooftop that was almost as old as the formerly-living Dr. K.

This was the same rooftop I saw from across the river every day on my walk with Eydie--the one with the Acropolis-looking-structure on top. Now that I was on it, I could see that the roof was not flat, but had several levels. The columns that created the mini-Acropolis didn't look so mini in person, they towered about 30 feet above me and supported a four-sided structure with three smaller square stone columns going from the top to the bottom of the structure's front opening.

It looked a lot like the rooftop temple from the climax of the original *Ghostbusters,* where Sigourney Weaver summoned Gozer the Gozerian. Maybe I was walking in Bill Murray's footsteps. They would've been a lot more fun than mine at the moment.

From down below, I heard the blare of fire engines. The smoke pouring out of the 14th floor's broken window must have alarmed any neighbors who had insomnia, so I guess somebody made a call. Between the FDNY and the NYPD, not to mention PMA and the Jerky Boys, maybe everything would be okay. Maybe I just had to wait it out up here until the coast was clear and Veronica was locked up, or preferably, killed by the authorities in a violent, painful manner.

I tried to relax and thought about what it might be like if I made it through this, how Jules could move back in with me and we could make things work again. Maybe after all this, both of us had wised up enough where we could stop acting like insane children. At the very least, I now understood just how the wrong medication could make you think the wrong thoughts. I just had to hope the magical powers of Xanax could keep the Blue Fire under control long-term. I wished I had those last two pills right now. And I wished I had a phone, so I could call Jules, let her know I was okay and just get to hear her voice.

Then I looked up at the sky and wondered what time it was, because I had lost track of everything governing normal human life. There was no sign of sunrise yet and there wasn't much of a moon in the sky. It was dark, it was cold, it was windy and I still didn't have any shoes on, which made walking around on the roof particularly unpleasant, since it had a thick layer of dirt mixed in with years of pigeon shit coating its surface.

Then I heard the door to the roof open.

I had to assume it was Veronica, so I had to get moving. I climbed up the stone stairs and into the *Ghostbusters* temple. Once I got up there, I switched Eydie over to my left hand and pulled out the gun, then hid in the far back corner, in the deep dark shadows.

From my vantage point, I could barely make out Veronica, sword in hand, coming through the doorway. I saw her head snap around, searching for me. And I saw her pull a second sword from her coat lining, so now both of her hands had the means to kill.

Fear and hate overwhelmed me. Something about that woman unnerved me, even though I had bullets and she only had blades, but I guessed that was a result of the "treatment" she had given me. She was the one who messed with my mind after my Blue Fire doses to make sure the drug fucked me up as much as humanly possible. She was the one who made sure it reached deep down into the far corners of my psyche. Whenever she was around, I felt a black cloud darken my mind.

My heart was beating hard. I leaned against the back wall of the structure and looked out at the sky, where I spotted some flying demons. Undoubtedly something manufactured by my own sick mind.

Except there actually *were* things flying through the sky.

I rubbed my eyes and the demons vanished, replaced by a couple of police helicopters shining spotlights on the building. Spotlights that danced across the roof.

Spotlights that exposed me to Veronica's line of sight.

"You piece of fuck," she hissed, spotting me from the lower level.

I raised the gun and aimed it at her shadowy figure. "Don't move," I said. My hand was shaking. I didn't know if I could hit the side of the Chrysler Building in my condition. Eydie, restless, was moving around under my left arm. I tightened my grip on her.

"Fuck you," she said moving forward, beginning to climb the stone steps up to the structure. "You can put as many shots in me as you want, Super Dick. I'm not stopping until you're a dead man." Her voice was still quavering with emotion and raw unfiltered pain.

As she stepped up into the structure, one of the chopper spotlights illuminated her as well and I finally got a good look at what I had done to her with the prods. The nasty burns on her neck were so severe, so discolored, so deep, that pieces of mangled, charred skin were dangling from the seared areas.

She caught me looking.

"Do you see what you did to me *this* time, Super Dick? You see how you ripped apart my fucking neck?"

She came closer.

"But I don't mind the pain," she seethed. "It just drives me on."

She was about twenty-five feet away from me. I wasn't going to fuck around, so I fired the gun.

I missed.

Then and only then did I stop to question how many bullets I had left.

Augustine had shot Dr. Reginald once and Dr. K twice. But had he reloaded since he shot Bruce Canun at the Comic Con?

I didn't have time to check--because Veronica, who had paused for a moment after my shot had gone astray, was now slowly and purposefully walking towards me, swords in hand.

I held on to Eydie as I cocked the gun again, trying to steady my hand and focus my vision. Veronica suddenly crossed the swords in front of her chest, making a protective "X" that blocked her torso, some kind of Wonder Woman shit.

I fired.

I heard the bullet strike metal as one of the swords flew out of her hands. Her defense had done the job. She laughed at me.

"Can you get any more fucking pathetic?" she cackled.

Turned out the answer was yes. I fired again, but I was out of ammo. All I heard was a quiet little "click."

She came at me.

Furious at her, furious at myself for not checking the load, I threw the goddamn gun at her with all my might. She laughed again and stepped out of the way, easily avoiding it. It flew off the structure and I heard it land with a clatter on the level below.

"Okay, Super Dick…if you want your fucking dog to live, put her down," she snarled. "Right now. I don't give a shit if she comes between you and me. If she does, I'll rip you both apart. This is Judgment Day…AND I AM THE MOTHERFUCKING LAWGIVER!"

I nodded slowly and carefully bent down to put Eydie down on the roof, just as the chopper spotlight swung back our way and lit up Veronica again. Now I could fully appreciate the joyful murder in her eyes. Eydie jumped on my leg, wanting me to pick her back up. I gently pushed her away with my foot.

"So what are you going to do?" I asked Veronica. "Just slice and dice me in cold blood?"

She was now about the length of the sword away from me, if she pointed it straight out towards me. In other words, she was a couple of steps away from being able to cut my head off.

She took those couple of steps and stopped.

"Sounds about right," she said and, fast as fucking lightning, she slashed at my chest with her sword. My Bloomingdales shirt was cut in two across the front. There was a long gash on my bare chest underneath it, shallow but scary.

Her big mistake was not just killing me with that first swoop, because Eydie, as I knew she would, ran at Veronica, growling angrily and lunging at her, snapping at her chest. Veronica, being one of those human haters who were animal lovers, couldn't bring herself to just kill the dog, so she shoved Eydie aside with the side of her arm.

"GET AWAY, DOG! GET AWAY!"

And that gave me time to pull out my remaining prod, still in my back pocket.

She saw me move and turned back to me, but it was too late. I got her in the neck again. She screamed in agony, brought her sword around and got me in the arm, but only grazed it. My sleeve was slashed, there was some blood, but it wasn't enough to stop me. I shoved the prod back against her neck one last time, and this time, I left it there like I had back in her apartment.

Right on one of the painful open wounds I had already made.

She shrieked an octave higher than I thought a human voice could go. She dropped the sword and I kicked it off the side of the structure and onto the lower level.

She backed up. This time it was my turn to move forward. This time, I shoved the prod at the t-shirt she was wearing under her open jacket, zapping her in the stomach. She screamed again and suddenly, I felt myself surging with energy, black energy, and I reached forward with my free hand and went to rip her jacket off. The pocketed arsenal made it heavy but I managed to pull it off her and throw it down over the side.

Weaponless and vulnerable, she stared at me with wide, terrified eyes, eyes that couldn't believe this was happening to her, eyes that couldn't believe she suddenly had nothing left to kill me with and it was just her and me.

I wanted to make it just me.

"Remember the hotel?" I said menacingly. "Remember what I did there?"

"Please," she said, backing up some more, half-crying, "I'm really hurt…"

I could give a shit. I held up the prod to go at her again, but it was about out of juice. I tossed it away. And then I half-whispered like I was the devil himself, "Well, you ain't seen nuthin' yet."

And then my hands went for her throat.

I was going to be the LawGiver, not her.

I began choking her with all my might, which was suddenly off the charts strong. My hands gripped her throat directly over her third-degree burns, causing her inconceivable pain just as she desperately tried to gasp for air.

Where was I in all this? I didn't know, because I was having an out-of-body experience. I didn't know who was strangling Veronica, but I didn't seem to be involved, I was just watching as some unstoppable murderous psychopath attempted to inflict as much pain as possible before he killed his prey.

Yeah, I turned into Veronica. The Blue Fire finally found my darkness and fed it, gave it light and power and made it my whole being.

I saw she was about to pass out from the pain of the burns and the lack of air. Maybe pass out permanently. And I felt Eydie jumping on me, whimpering, wanting me to hold her. Something I unconditionally loved was trying to stop me from killing someone I unconditionally hated.

And I hesitated.

Until that moment, I had been holding myself morally superior to every other Blue Fire victim. I assumed I was better than they were, stronger than they were, because I hadn't gone completely off the deep end yet. But I wasn't better than they were. My seed of rot was alive and well, and it wanted to see Veronica not just dead, but humiliated, brutalized and destroyed.

Oh, God.

I pulled my hands off her throat and staggered backwards. At that moment, my body went limp and I sunk to the ground in a sitting position. Eydie jumped into my lap.

Veronica, somehow still standing, made some kind of unintelligible, almost inhuman sounds as she put her hands over the wounds on her neck. In an extreme state of shock, she stumbled around in no particular direction, finally heading towards the back edge of the structure.

That back edge didn't have a lower level behind it. It went straight down to the street.

I heard her whisper, "La beauté c'est la mort," as she let herself fall over the side.

I wept for her. I wept for my own humanity. I wept for my pup.

PMA found me a few minutes later, still sitting on the rooftop structure, still absently petting Eydie. He approached me and pulled the prescription bottle containing the rest of the Xanax out of his pocket. He told me that was why he wanted me to wait before I left the clinic, when I rushed out without listening to him. I nodded and he fed me a couple of pills. Eydie growled at him, PMA threatened to throw the dog off the roof, so things were back to normal.

Yeah, things were. I wasn't.

As we both waited for the Xanax to kick in, PMA told me that he and his goon army managed to lock the zombies back up in their deluxe suite, but when PMA told them he had called the police, they took all the stuff they had collected, everything that might be worth anything, and ran back to wherever they had parked their pick-ups. When the cops finally arrived, PMA was left to try and explain everything as best he could. They, in turn, let him know there was some kind of fire on the 14th floor and that they had spotted a couple of people on the roof.

"You're okay?" he asked.

I sort of shrugged.

"So who else was up here with you? The cops said they thought they saw two people."

I told him what had happened, all of it, including what I had done to Veronica. He told me it wasn't my fault, it was the drugs. I told him I considered it a draw.

He helped me and the dog get back downstairs to the clinic, past the all the firefighters running up the stairs. Once we got there, we talked to the cops for a while longer, explaining what had been going on in this building for so long and asking why nobody had done anything about it. The cops explained there had been a lot of orders from above to ignore the weird reports coming in about this address. Rumor was those orders came as a result of political pressure from former Congressman and new freshman Senator, Eddie di Pineda.

The cops couldn't ignore my weakened condition, so PMA finally talked them into letting him take me back to the hotel where we were staying. This was one of those times when PMA's pedigree and last name gave him much-needed leverage, so they took all our contact information and said they'd be in touch. I could tell one of the boys in blue knew who I was--he kind of smiled when he wrote down my name. But, thankfully, he left it at that.

Even though the hotel was only a few blocks away, PMA got us an Uber and, as it took us through the nearly-deserted streets, the sun started to finally appear on the horizon. It was a relief to get back to the room and feel safe for the first time in quite a few days. PMA bandaged my wounds and I crawled into bed and fell asleep with Eydie by my side. The whole time I slept, I kept feeling my hands on the burns on Veronica's neck.

And once in a while, I let out a scream.

I woke up in the late afternoon, Sunday afternoon. I lay there a few minutes, trying to get my thoughts together, trying to ignore the pain in my rib, my wounds, my whole body. I looked out the window and saw the sun was already low in the sky. I went down when it was coming up, now I was waking up when it was going down.

Nothing felt right.

The room door suddenly opened. PMA came in with Eydie, who was wearing a new leash he must have bought for her. When she saw me, she ran so hard towards me that she yanked the leash out of the kid's hand. She leapt on top of the bed and onto my belly, knocking the wind out of me.

"I took her out to do her business," he said. "I also got her some food before, so she's okay. I think she's finally used to me." As she power-licked my face, PMA looked me over. "How are you feeling?"

"I've been better. Any Coke Zero in the minibar?"

He opened the fridge and pulled out a Diet Coke. He walked it over to me, along with a couple Xanax. I sat up, took the Xanax and washed them down with the Diet Coke. He sat down by the desk.

"So about an hour ago, I called one of the cops from last night, the one who gave me his card. He told me the firemen managed to put out the fires in the lab pretty easily. Dr. Reginald's okay, he's in the hospital getting treated for some burns and the gunshot wound and Keenan's getting treated for smoke inhalation. That Augustine guy's being booked. Turns out his description matches up with a lot of unsolved assaults in the city."

"And the old Nazi's dead too."

"Yeah. Of course, I didn't know he was still alive, so…a lot of surprises." He took out a can of Coke for himself and popped it open.

"And Veronica?" I finally asked.

"Also dead," he said simply.

I let out a heavy sigh.

"Max, you know it was the drugs that made you go crazy. And her falling off the roof, that was just an accident, right? I mean, you stopped yourself from killing her."

"I don't know, kid. It's gonna take a while to look at myself in the mirror again."

"Well, it probably wasn't a very pleasant experience before, either."

I smiled even though I didn't want to.

"Oh," he remembered, "they took all the zombies over to Gracie Square Psychiatric. I guess Senator Marks' family is flying in to take care of him. You know, they ID'd a lot of important people in that group besides him."

"Important people that must have been in Andrew Wright's way."

The kid blinked.

"Andrew Wright?"

"Yeah, remember good ol' Uncle Andy? Well, I had a teleconference with him right before you came into the clinic. This whole thing was his doing."

"No shit."

"No shit. Did you know your uncle Robert was getting juiced with Blue Fire? And Herman too? And that's the real reason they were so psychotic?"

"Wow. Wow." He shook his head and let it all sink in.

"Yeah, pretty fucked up. And I bet that, once again, they won't be able to tie anything back to Uncle Andy and Mr. Barry Filer."

"It'll be hard, there's not much evidence left in there. All of the computers in the lab got burnt up in the fire, and the ones in the clinic were all stolen by your Facebook fans."

I sipped the Diet Coke again. The kid looked at me.

"So what did Wright say to you?"

"He mostly talked about how he wasn't very fond of me. How I took his son away. How he was going to make me feel his pain."

"Make you feel his pain…?"

"Yeah, I thought he meant kill somebody close to me, like what happened to him. I kept thinking he was talking about doing you in, but they didn't even bother to bring you into the clinic. Guess he was too afraid of your family connections to do anything but try to make you a member of Keenan's special club. So what the hell." I shrugged.

The kid had an uneasy look on his face.

"So…you think he was just talking about the dog…? That doesn't sound…"

He stopped himself.

I picked up his wavelength.

"Did you get another phone?" I asked carefully.

"Yeah, a cheapie from a store around here."

"Did you try calling Jules?" I asked even more carefully.

He didn't want to answer, but he did. "Yeah, a couple of times. But no answer."

"No answer," I said.

The kid shook his head.

I ran into the bathroom and threw up.

Then, as fast as I could, I got dressed and PMA drove us over to Jules' place, leaving Eydie in the room. On the way over, I kept calling her number on PMA's new phone, but there kept being no answer.

When we arrived at her apartment, the expression on the face of the Cuban who answered the door told me everything I needed to know.

He let me in, then he and his other Cuban bandmates told us Jules was found dead that morning in the street downstairs, on her way back from the place where she bought her morning latte. The Cubans heard the shots and went down to the street to see what happened. They saw Jules lying there in her own blood, which was mixing together with her spilled latte in a small stream that flowed over the edge of the sidewalk and into the street.

There was only one witness.

He told them, as well as the cops when they finally got there, that a car had pulled up, shots were fired and the car drove away. Nobody even got the license number.

The Cubans were devastated. I was beyond that.

After a while, after we sat around with the Cubans crying for an hour or so, the kid and I went back and checked out of the hotel, then, together with Eydie, we drove back to the island. And then we were all back in my apartment for the first time in days and all I could think was that nothing had changed inside. It seemed like, after everything that had just happened, that everything should be different. But it wasn't.

Andrew Wright did the job, all right. He made me feel his pain. But this score wasn't even. The math didn't add up. His drugged-up psychotic murderous son died attempting to kill me, PMA and PMA's uncle. My Jules died trying to get a latte.

So if Uncle Andy thought everything was now square…he was very, very wrong.

Last Call

"La beauté c'est la mort."

That's what Veronica said before she let herself drop off the top of the building.

The words stuck with me, so I managed to look them up, even though French wasn't exactly my specialty. Turned out it was another quote from Mishima, who, I guess, was bilingual. It meant, "Beauty is death."

Those were three words I didn't feel belonged in the same sentence.

I wasn't finding any beauty in the events of the past few days. Jules' death alone would have been enough to send me into hiding for a year. Add the whole Blue Fire ordeal I'd just barely survived and there wasn't enough left of my spirit left to fill a shot glass. Luckily there was enough Jack in my freezer to fill about a thousand of them.

The kid stuck around, as I knew he would, to make sure I didn't go completely to hell while I put myself back together. He found out from the Cubans that Jules' parents back in Kansas were having her body flown home for the funeral. I wasn't invited. I met them once and it hadn't gone well, because they didn't approve of their daughter, who was in her late forties, shacking up with a guy. They called it "fornicating." Horrors. No wonder Jules fled the state as soon as she had a driver's license.

So I was left to mourn on my own. But I couldn't just sit shiva because first of all, I wasn't Jewish and second of all, there were still a few lingering issues to deal with.

On the petty and inconsequential level, Mighty Mel called one last time to tell me that the *Blue Fire* movie had been cancelled and that I should refund at least half his money, if not all of it. I asked him how many millions he had in the bank at that moment. He asked me what fucking difference that made. I answered that I had done my fucking job, I would send him a complete report in a fucking week or so, and if he didn't like it, fuck him. He was screaming as I hung up on him. Hopefully he would die before he could sue me.

On the more significant and potentially dangerous level, I realized I was almost out of Xanax, which was the only thing between me and whatever Blue Fire was still in me. So I once again figured out a way to kill "two birds wiz one shtone." The kid and I went to visit Dr. Reginald in the hospital. He told us he was mending nicely and explained that, short-term, the Blue Fire would stay in my system for another six months or so. Even though it did replicate itself to an extent, it still weakened over time, then finally dissipated, unless another dose or two was administered. And he didn't see how that would happen since he had destroyed all of it in the lab.

He also wrote me a prescription for more Xanax. That was nice of him.

And finally, on the decidedly ironic and idiotic level…I was the guy again.

Yeah, my professional status was back up at the top of the seesaw. Once the cops got all the details from the survivors of the Rosenbaum Research debacle--basically, me, PMA, Dr. Reginald, Keenan and Valter--they held a press conference. Once again, I came out the big hero, and once again, Matt Lauer wanted me on *The Today Show*. Not only that, but suddenly Todd was calling, all apologetic, wanting to go back after that book deal. Suddenly, clients of all shapes and sizes wanted to hire me. And now Bloomingdales was offering me a giant gift certificate just so I could continue wearing their clothes in public.

I even heard from Candy, aka Betty, who was soooo sorry for everything, but she was just working for the Foundation and had noooo idea of everything that was going on. I didn't believe her and I didn't care that I didn't believe her.

And after that, I let PMA answer the phone, because I'd had enough of all of it.

Instead, I just sat and drank and sulked and thought about Jules. And how I wanted more than anything to have her yell at me to hop off her tits and then call me a cocksucking son-of-a-whore fuckface asshole. It was the little things.

Finally, after a few weeks of not eating, not showering and not giving a shit, I decided it was time to take care of one final piece of business.

It was the first day of Spring when I was ready to go. Somehow, that felt appropriate. I still felt a little shaky, so the kid volunteered to drive me and the dog to my destination. He wanted to know what I was up to, but I only told him I had one last loose end to tie up.

When we arrived in Freemansburg, I had PMA park in the bar parking lot, the same one where Augustine Bravino had stolen my dog. I asked him to take Eydie for a walk, because I had to attend to this task by myself. He and the dog grudgingly agreed, and I headed back up the hill behind the bar, back to Debra Michaels' house.

I knocked on the door. She opened it and seemed happy to see me.

"I didn't expect you back here."

"Can I come in?" I asked.

She opened the door the rest of the way and I entered. I took a seat in the same chair I had sat in before. Debra, dressed in jeans and a bright, spring-like sweater, because, after all, it was now spring, sat down across from me.

"You seem sad," was the first thing she said to me.

"Yeah. A lot has happened and I wanted you to know about it. Because of this case, I found out a lot more than I bargained for. Like Dr. Kanuskey. He was still alive."

She sat back and blinked in disbelief. Then she realized how I had worded that news.

"*Was?*"

"He flew out of a fourteenth floor window in his super-fast wheelchair."

"I don't know if you're joking or not."

"Unfortunately, I'm not. He was running a lab and clinic on the Upper East Side, brainwashing innocents with a new drug developed by Mikov's foster brother Reginald."

"*What?*"

"It was a powerful hallucinogenic. Reginald named it 'Blue Fire.'"

She was speechless.

"Not only that, Reginald also adopted a gay kid who was rejected by his folks and raised him to be straight."

"Oh, Jesus. Oh Christ." She was silent again. "Do you want some tea or something?"

"Thanks, but no. Anyway, if you go online and check out the *New York Times* from about two weeks ago, I believe the date was March 6th, you can read all about what happened to Dr. K and Reginald's lab. Well, you'll get the who, what, when and where, but nothing about the why. There's nothing in the article about the whole thing being run by an ex-CIA guy who was attempting to rule the world, or some stupid shit like that. But if you skip around in that same issue, you'll also read about a cabaret singer named Julie Nelson who was gunned down in the street after buying her morning latte.

That was the woman I was going to marry."

"Oh."

I was silent.

"So that's why you're sad," she finally said.

"The guy who was backing Dr. K and his facility had her killed. Not that I can prove it. Or much of anything else."

"Is Reginald all right?"

"Yeah, he'll be okay. Might go up on arson charges, though."

A pause.

"I don't even know what to say, Mr. Bowman." Some tears appeared on her face. "I mean, I don't understand. I thought this was just about making a *Blue Fire* movie. How are Reginald and this drug involved?"

"The people behind Reginald and his drug were the ones that wanted the movie made. But you'll be happy to know that movie is no longer happening. And now Mel Chesler wants to sue *me*."

That made her laugh. Then she thought a moment.

"So why did you come all the way here?" she asked. "Just to tell me all that? I appreciate it, but it wasn't necessary, especially with your…loss…"

She looked down at the floor. She was sad for me--and sad about me.

"Well, I also came here just to satisfy my curiosity. Because I still don't really know what happened to your brother. And that's what I was originally hired to find out."

She raised her head and looked at me again. "I told you," she said with a defensive tone, "I told you he killed himself a few years ago."

"But I still wonder why he fled the comics business so abruptly…"

"This is ancient history. Mel Chesler was cheating him…"

"I get that. But why didn't Ben just go to another publisher?"

"And get cheated by somebody else? The business was totally corrupt…"

"But that's how he made a living. And why would he decide to completely disappear from the face of the earth like that? That takes a lot of effort. And how the hell did he support himself all those years if he wasn't selling his art?"

"I wish I had answers, Mr. Bowman, but as I've already told you…"

"I had a few theories. I just wanted to share them with you."

She said nothing. I went on.

"I think that, okay, maybe Dr. K didn't succeed in making Mikov straight, but he did succeed in drumming all that Ayn Rand garbage that he and his CIA cohorts swore by into his skull. And I think that once Dr. K saw how talented Mikov was, he pushed him to create the *Blue Fire* comic, to sell those ideas in a shiny superhero package that kids would love. Propaganda at an early age can be pretty effective, don't you think?"

"I suppose," she said.

"But maybe Mikov got to the point where he realized he had been trained to believe in things he shouldn't believe in…and now he was perverting his art to sell a morality that was actually amoral. Maybe it made him have kind of a nervous breakdown. And maybe he ran away into the night, scared of his foster parents and his government coming after him for betraying his 'mission'…"

"What's the point of this, Mr. Bowman? I really don't…"

"This won't take long. So first, I thought about how Mikov could have supported himself all those years." I reached into my coat pocket. "He probably couldn't live with himself for very long by sinking to this kind of desperation…"

I pulled out the underground and graphic gay comics Mikov had drawn--the comics Bruce Canun, who I was happy to learn had recovered from his gunshot wound, had given me. I handed the scanned copies to Debra.

"Where did you get these?" she asked as she quickly folded the papers back up, unable to look at the artwork for more than a second.

"From Reginald's son, Bruce. Anyway, I thought about how Mikov could survive despite not working for a living, and the only thing that made sense was that his foster brother took care of him--that maybe Reginald, once he got his own practice going, supported him on the sly. That would take care of his money issues and help Reginald ease some of his guilt over his part in Dr. K's master plans."

She looked away.

"Do you think that might have happened, Debra?"

She turned back. "I suppose. I don't know."

There was another lingering silence. I broke it this time.

"You know, it's not so easy to change people. Dr. K thought you could. He was wrong. His kid Reginald did. He was wrong. My parents, my ex-wife and even my kids thought I could be a different person if I wanted to. They were wrong. You can't change somebody's fundamental nature. They can improve themselves a little…or they can let themselves fall apart…but they can't really change who they are."

"I disagree, Mr. Bowman," she said quietly but firmly.

"What's interesting,' I went on, "is that even men who want to change their gender…they can't do it all the way, no matter how much work they have done. You know why? Because there's one part of them they can't fully get rid of. Turns out you can surgically make an Adam's Apple smaller…but no operation can make it go away completely. Did you know that? I looked it up."

Her hand reflexively shot up to cover her throat as she stumbled through a few words. "What…why would you…"

I stood up. We were almost done here.

"I got confused after our last visit, because I did some research and discovered someone named Debra Michaels had died in a car crash about ten years ago…and it seemed to be the same Debra Michaels as…well, the same Debra Michaels you say you are. But I knew that couldn't be right. Because you're sitting right here in front of me, Debra. Safe and sound."

She looked up at me. "Yes. Yes, I am," she said softly.

"I'm glad you are. And I thank you for your time. I won't be bothering you again. And neither will anyone else, I think."

"I appreciate that," she whispered to the floor

"I'm sorry for everything, Debra. Very sorry. But enjoy some peace. You've earned it."

"Well…I hope you find your share too, Mr. Bowman."

I wasn't counting on it. But I nodded. And then I turned and let myself out.

Maybe Blue Fire wouldn't endure.

But maybe Ben Mikov would.

MAX BOWMAN

will return in

RED EARTH

Max Bowman has female problems. Specifically, three beautiful, rich daughters of three powerful and influential men—all of them with their own secret agendas. Unfortunately, Max doesn't know which one to trust or which way to turn, because a vicious killer is hot on his heels. And the most perplexing thing about this psychopath is that he isn't after Max himself—but everyone he knows and loves.

From New York City to Miami, from Washington D.C. to Sedona, Arizona, Max is on the run. And that's not easy when you have two broken toes.

"Top Pick! 5 Stars out of 5. Freaking amazing."

-   **Underground Book Reviews**

Want to help forgotten comic creators in need?

Visit www.heroinitiative.org and donate.

DARK SKY, the first volume in the Max Bowman series, is available at Amazon.com and other online book retailers.

Become a Max Bowman fan. Visit his Facebook page at
www.facebook.com/MaxBowmanBooks

<u>About the Author</u>

A novelist, screenwriter and ghostwriter, Canfield has lived in New York City, Chicago, Detroit, Miami Beach, Auckland, New Zealand, and his own personal Pennsylvania trifecta, Pittsburgh, Wilkes-Barre and his hometown of Bethlehem. He now resides in Long Beach, California with his favorite blondes, writer-editor wife Lisa and dog Betsy, but he will undoubtedly move again, because that's just what he does.

Canfield's books include the novels *Dark Sky* and *Blue Fire* (the first two books in the Max Bowman series); *What's Driving You???: How I Overcame Abuse and Learned to Lead in the NBA* (co-authored with Keyon Dooling and Lisa Canfield); *Pill Mill: My Years of Money, Madness, Sex and Drugs* (co-authored with Christian Valdes and Lisa Canfield); and *226: How I Became the First Blind Person to Kayak the Grand Canyon* (co-authored with Lonnie Bedwell. *Blue Fire* was a 2016 Silver Honoree in the Benjamin Franklin Digital Awards as well as a semi-finalist in the Book Life Prize in Fiction competition. *Red Earth* is a 2017 Gold Honoree in the Benjamin Franklin Digital Awards. He has also, believe it or not, co-written two Hallmark movies, *Eat, Play, Love* and *Yes, I Do* with Lisa Canfield.